Fairytales and FIREWALLS

Five Cyber Retellings

Hansel and Gretel | Cinderella | Little Miss Muffet
Sleeping Beauty | Goose Girl

K.M. Robinson

COPYRIGHT

FAIRYTALES AND FIREWALLS
Copyright © 2019 by K.M. Robinson.

CINDRILL

Cinderella Is An Assassin…But The Prince Is Hunting Her, Too

SUGARCOATED

Hansel And Gretel's Witch Was On Their Side

VIRTUALLY SLEEPING BEAUTY

Sleeping Beauty Is Trapped In A Virtual Reality World And Can't Wake Up

ALONG CAME A SPIDER

Cyberpunk Little Miss Muffet and Spider Are Hackers Saving The World And Tormenting Each Other

THE GOOSE GIRL AND THE ARTIFICIAL

The Princess' Artificially Intelligent Robot Steals Her Identity

To you tech queens and kings...

It's time for our stories to be heard.

PREFACE

Thank you so much for joining me for Fairytales and Firewalls. This is a collection of several of my technology/cyber-based retelling novellas, novelettes, and short stories.

I hope you enjoy Cindrill, Annika, Rora, Fet, and Goselyn's stories as much as I enjoyed writing them.

All of these stories are currently available as stand-alone books as well.

Happy reading!

-K.M. Robinson

CINDRILL

A Cinderella Retelling

CINDRILL

A CINDERELLA RETELLING NOVELL

K.M. ROBINSON

CHAPTER 1
CINDRILL

IT'S ENTIRELY POSSIBLE THAT I MADE THE WRONG CHOICE coming here tonight. He's gorgeous in his tuxedo, smiling at the crowd, waving to his subjects. His son isn't half bad either—his smile is radiant as I look at him through my master's scope, the target falling directly on the prince's chest.

A group of people surrounds him, congratulating him on his impending nuptials. His betrothed stands next to him, now obscured by the group of well-wishers.

"Change of plans," Master murmurs. He pulls the weapon back, returning it to its hiding place. "We're going down there."

This wasn't the plan—we were supposed to kill them from the balcony and escape. My job was to be the distraction so Master wouldn't get caught. Mixing with the people was never supposed to be a part of this.

He wheels around on his heels, stalking across the walkway to the stairs. I descend first, taking my place among the partygoers. I mix with the ladies in their incredible gowns—my own matches theirs tonight.

"A dance, mistress?" A gentleman of the court holds his hand out to me—no one else is dancing.

"Oh, uh, no," I sputter. "Thank you. I haven't congratulated the prince yet. Excuse me."

"Ridiculous, petty woman," he mumbles as I flee. "She wears a green gown, and suddenly she thinks she's the Summer Queen."

I ignore him as I brush through the crowd, batting my eyelashes whenever I bump into a man. I intentionally avoid the women—they'd look too closely at me.

My new job is to clear a path for Master—I'm the distraction. He will follow behind, and while I have the attention of the crowd, he will murder the king and his son.

I tuck one of my chestnut curls behind me and breeze through the people until I'm only a few feet from the prince's bride-to-be. She's a tiny thing—she may even be younger than I am. Her hair is piled on her head in blonde ringlets that are so fair that they're nearly white. The girl is attached to the prince's arm, looking nervous.

"Vila runs a charity for orphans," Prince Davian

informs his guests. He glances at her with a forced smile —I've only been in his presence for the last hour, but even *I* can tell this arranged marriage isn't doing anything for either of them. "She's very charitable on her father's behalf."

"Won't you miss working with the children, Princess?" A woman shoves a microphone at her.

"I'm sure I'll have responsibilities here that will keep me busy, but, of course, I'll miss the children." She tries to smile, but it's clear she's upset about leaving her charity. I can't say I blame her—I'd be mad if I didn't have a choice in my life too. Or, rather, I *am* mad that I don't have a choice in my life either.

Prince Davian rattles off a list of the foreign princess' virtues. The more he talks, the higher the princess stands. Perhaps she's coming to terms with the arrangement and she's stopping the wilted flower act... or maybe she's just proud of her many accomplishments.

I'm proud of mine as well, though I can hardly imagine how the prince would spin my achievements— how *would* one describe the actions of an assistant to an assassin?

Princess Vila catches my eye and smiles, appraising my dress. While hers is full on the bottom and sleek on top, mine isn't nearly as poofy. Hers is restricted to a bell-shape at the bottom, while mine flows loose enough to run in without tripping me as I move in these ridiculous shoes.

Master's apprentice, Claude, designed the outfit for me. He has a flair for the eye-catching. The top of my dress drapes in the front and plummets in the back, revealing a good portion of my spine. My shoes are tall but solid. I couldn't roll my ankle in them if I tried—and I *had* tried just to prove a point to him. The sides of them wrap around the top of my foot in a pattern that looks like waves on the seas or arching mountains that curl over on themselves—they look as fierce and vicious as I'm supposed to be. Vila almost looks jealous of them.

"I like your shoes," she murmurs.

"Thank you, Princess. I like your gown." She smiles at me, moving her hand to smooth her already perfectly-in-place dress. Now is as good a time as any—I have to get her out of the way for Master. "Would you tell me about your charity?"

She lights up, prepared to gush. The princess tells me all about the children there and the big fundraising event she's helping them plan. It appears I'm doing the world a favor by ending her marriage before it begins—she'll go back to her orphanage and the world will be better for it.

The screams are my first indication that something is wrong. A woman sobs as the crowd shuffles. Another scream fills the air.

"Shooter!"

The prince is pulled back by a guard, leaving the princess standing alone next to me. A man nearby falls, bleeding out on the ground. The king screams as a bullet rips through his upper leg—his guards pull the king back as Master approaches.

He's clothed from head to toe in black. A hood covers his head while a cape billows out behind him just enough to look impressive, but not enough for anyone to grab onto—Claude designed it that way.

Master moves toward me, but he doesn't make eye contact. Instead, he raises his weapon toward Vila.

She wasn't part of the deal. We're not supposed to be hurting foreign dignitaries, just the king and prince. Her kingdom is a friend of Master's—they've used him on occasion to fix some of their more discrete problems. If Master kills this girl, he's bringing a war down on our heads that we likely won't survive, but he doesn't seem to care.

"No!" I shout, stepping in front of her.

My job is to protect Master, and tonight, that means I must protect him from himself, even if that means my own death.

I pull out the weapon Claude embedded in the side of my dress, hidden by the folds of my skirt. Aiming it at Master, I threaten to shoot his arm to stop him. He seethes at me as I push the princess backward.

One of the guards takes aim at Master, releasing

several bullets in our direction—one whizzes past me, nearly striking Vila around my arm stretched across her. She screams, realizing how close she came to being hit.

Master reels back, a bullet burying itself in his upper arm. As he staggers backward, I turn, forcing the princess to run. She trips over her own feet, but I drag her along, carefully pointing my weapon away from her.

The palace is a flurry of screams accompanied by pounding feet as the court runs in different directions, trying to avoid Master's assault. The hallway is my best option, and I flee with my charge in tow. She gasps behind me but manages to keep up until I push her to run in front of me, using my hands to push her faster.

"Stop!" someone screams behind me. "Unhand the princess!"

Ordinarily, they might assume I was helping her, but the majority of the palace guards saw me pull my weapon on Master and it's only logical to assume that the people with weapons are working together. In truth, we are.

More fire sounds behind me, but I don't stop. My gaze darts around the hallway, looking for an escape. I can hear Master approaching, his telltale footfall rings in my ears above all of the other noise—I've been trained far too well to miss him.

"Kill her!" Master yells to me, his voice altered by one of Claude's devices.

I round the corner and see a doorway—a closet. I fling the door open and shove the princess inside.

"Stay quiet," I hiss, shutting the door as quietly as possible before running.

The guards rush around the corner, Master suddenly quiet. He escapes somewhere in the palace and deactivates his nanobot mask to change his appearance so no one recognizes him as the shooter, leaving me to take the blame.

Before I can reach the next corner, one of the guards reaches me—I shouldn't have stopped to save the princess—and he pulls on my shoulder. Thank goodness my dress is off-the-shoulder or he would have ripped it with the way he grabs at me.

I dip down, throwing him off balance and he slips to the floor as I try to speed up.

Searing pain rips through my right foot, and I cry out. As I turn to see what happened, I lose my shoe—I've been cut. The man who attacked me must have pulled a knife as he was falling and sliced the top of my foot around the shoe's intricate design. The green heel bounces away from him.

The man on the ground looks up at me, shouting something. The knife glints in his hand, but I don't stop, even as the prince's tirade continues from his place on the marble floor.

The nanobots peel off my face, racing down my body

to my leg to form a new shoe so that I can continue to run at the same pace. I turn as quickly as possible to conceal my identity—I can't let him see my face.

The hall sounds hollow as I pound across the marble in one green heel and one silver one—or silver until the nanobots have time to change color. For now, I'll have to tolerate the mismatched colors as the nanobots do a more important job—keeping me from sliding on the slippery floor.

I dart out into the night air. The sky is black as ink, but the stars twinkle in the crisp autumn evening. Master is waiting at the end of the palace drive, and I rush down the stairs.

CHAPTER 2
DAVIAN

"Are you all right, Vila?" I hold my hand out to the princess, helping her out of the closet.

"I'd like to go to my room now, please," Vila replies. She allows me to move her into the hallway and promptly turns on her heels. Her blue dress barely swishes around her feet as she moves—I wonder if her stylists did the same thing to the skirt that they did to her hair to make it stay in place despite running.

"Of course." I bow slightly to her. "My apologies for the intrusion. You must have been terrified to have that gun held to you—I'm sure you want to rest."

She looks a little bewildered at my statement, eyes wide and brow furrowed, but she doesn't challenge me. The princess nods and her people escort her back to her room.

"You're going to do something about this, Davian." My father's suggestions always come out as commands. "Her father will not be pleased when he hears about tonight. You need to take action *now* before he finds out and cancels the wedding."

When I turn, several guards are carrying my father through the hallway. His leg is dripping blood, but it blends in with his black pants so I can only see it when it hits the floor, leaving a trail of red from the ballroom.

"Of course, Father," I reply. "We'll hunt the girl down tonight."

"You've already let her escape—just how do you plan on finding her?" he questions.

"Everyone saw her, Father. We'll send the entire Guard out to find her."

"You can't be sure it is the right girl. We can't execute her without proof," he challenges.

I swallow, looking around as I try to figure out a quick answer. Silently, I lecture myself for tripping—I could have killed the murderess on the spot if she hadn't ducked and thrown me off balance.

"Her shoe!" I exclaim, eyes landing on the strangest shoe I've ever seen. Pieces of it curl around the sides, a hideous mark stretching across the fabric between two of the curls. "I managed to cut her foot while she was fleeing and she lost the shoe. All we have to do is match her scar to the pattern on the edge of the shoe, and we'll have our proof."

My father grunts in pain as the guards nearly drop him. He glares at me as if this was *my* fault.

"Find her—tonight. If the girl is not in our custody by tomorrow evening, we might as well send that girl home ourselves." My father isn't a fan of Vila's father, but we need a merger, and a wedding is the ultimate form of an alliance. "Once you get the murderess, torture her until she tells you the name of the hooded man, and then kill them both."

With arms resting across two of the guards' shoulders to stabilize himself, he tips his head back. They carry him down the hall toward his room, bypassing the exit to the infirmary—the royal doctors will be sent for immediately, if they haven't been already.

Alone, I glance around the hallway. I quickly turn and walk toward the security office—I'm going to need all the help I can get.

The office is dark, the overhead lights off. Filip leans forward in his chair, typing notes on his tablet as he stares at the bank of glowing screens in front of him. Leaning over, he says something into one of the microphones, releasing his hold on the button once he finishes speaking.

"Figured you'd show," he mumbles, knowing I had arrived before I announced myself.

"What happened?" I ask, taking a seat next to him. I cross my arms over each other and lean forward onto my knees, jaw tight.

"Looks like there was a team. They were pretty amazing about avoiding the cameras," he responds, still flipping switches and hitting buttons as he assesses the playback of the attack. "You can't even see them until they're right next to you. It looks like the girl came from the stairs, but I have no idea where the hooded man came from."

"She threw Vila in a closet."

Filip pauses to turn to me.

"She what?" He shakes his head. "No, never mind. As long as she's not dead, I don't care."

"It doesn't make sense that an assassin would choose *not* to murder someone, does it?"

"Maybe her orders were only to kill you and your father." He shrugs, turning away from me to work.

"She went out of her way to save Vila, Filip. And the other guy specifically told her to kill the princess." None of this makes any sense.

"I don't understand how these cameras went out. Look, " he mumbles, changing the conversation as he points at one of the monitors. "All of these cameras went out at the same time—they must have taken them down somehow or else I'd have footage of everything. I saw you talking to your father in the hallway after, but nothing before that—aside from you chivalrously pulling Vila out of the closet."

He shoots me a look to indicate my *chivalry* had been a little lacking. It's not my fault—I've tried to talk to the princess before, it's just not working well.

"So, you don't have *anything* for me?" I sigh.

"Not unless you can give me any information."

I quickly recount the scene in the ballroom, giving him as much detail as possible. He takes notes on everything, inputting it into his tablet so he can give assignments to his men when we're done.

"I've never seen anything like it, Filip." I run my hands through my hair. "Her face just…peeled off."

"Peeled off?" He looks at me as though I've lost my mind. Maybe I have.

"It was like her entire face shattered. I don't know how to explain it."

The girl's deep brown hair bounced with each step she took as she ran down the hall—she looked like she was straight out of a movie the way she moved. The green of her dress offset her pale skin, and if I hadn't wanted to kill her, I might have wanted to pursue her for other reasons. Not that I can do that anymore—I'm getting married.

Filip's face twitches like he wants to say something. Eventually, he turns back.

"I don't know how to explain that, but I think the

most important thing right now is to figure out where she went." He nods, reaching for his control panel. One of the monitors switches as I stare at an image of the outside of the palace. "They escaped—we know that much for sure."

"Father wants me to find her before tomorrow."

His eyebrows shoot up as he turns to me again.

"Before tomorrow?" His face grows cold. "Why?"

"Vila's father will pull out of the deal once he finds out his daughter was almost shot," I explain. "If we can't show him we handled the situation swiftly, we could have a serious problem on our hands."

"What do you need me to do?" Filip asks. He waits patiently as I explain about the shoe and how we'll conduct a search for the girl with the matching injury at first light.

"Okay, I'm in. We can leave Sturges in charge for a few days while I'm helping you hunt down the huntress."

"Huntress?"

"Murderess?" He shrugs, getting up to lead the way down the hall to find his second-in-command. "I don't know, pick a name, but I'm not traipsing around this kingdom with you without having something interesting to call her."

He pauses, straightening his shoulders.

"If you make *one* shoe joke while we're out there..." he pretends to threaten me. He knows me too well.

"Fine, no shoe jokes. You had to go and shoo away all my fun before we could even get started, didn't you?"

He grumbles beside me.

One way or another, we'll find that girl, and when we do, we'll get everything we need from her.

CHAPTER 3
CINDRILL

THE AIR IS DAMP WITH EARLY MORNING DEW AS I PULL MY hood over my head. My curls peek out annoyingly, and I attempt to tuck them back in the fabric.

I slink around the building, tugging on the pack Master sent with me until it sits more comfortably on my back. The weight over the small of my back is comforting.

A bird chirps somewhere in the distance, but the sound is crisp. I accidentally step in a patch of grass and have to pause to shake my boot off—I don't want to be covered in dew.

The sun is barely slipping over the horizon, and I shiver as the breeze brushes across my cheek. Master's friend won't wait long for me, so I don't have time to dawdle. I round the corner...and slam into the wall.

Pushing, I fight my attacker off behind me. He doubles over when I stomp on his foot. Yelling erupts as I throw my elbow into his nose, breaking it with a loud crack.

"Enough! Stop her!" a familiar voice shouts as several sets of hands grab hold of me. Struggling against them does nothing to help me. I jolt to a stop, torso moving forward while the men hold my shoulders in place painfully.

I look up into the eyes of the Prince Davian. He stares back at me, scrutinizing me with narrowed, hazel eyes as he tries to place me. I glare at him from under my long, swooping bangs.

He can't recognize me—he didn't see me without the nanobot mask last night. If I keep my mouth shut, I might be able to escape.

"What are you doing out here?" His voice is lower than it was last night. It's dark and gravely—just as I'd expect this early in the morning.

"Running errands, Your Majesty," I reply quietly, bowing my head.

"What errands?" His nose wrinkles as he speaks, lip curling up slightly.

"I'm picking up some parts for my father," I lie.

"For?" The prince sounds aggravated. His hands clench at his sides.

"He's a clockmaker, Your Majesty," I repeat the lines I've rehearsed with Master so many times before.

"And have you retrieved these items yet?" The prince frowns at me, not believing my story.

"Yes, sire." I turn to adjust the bag on my back where I've stored enough clock pieces to back my lie up. Opening my hand, I reveal several cogs.

"Very well," he replies tersely. "Check her."

The men lunge at me again, digging their hands into my arms. I cry out in pain—not because I can't tolerate it, but because it's part of my escape plan.

One of the men yanks the hem of my skirt away from my feet, and I scream in surprise, kicking at him. My foot slams into his face, cracking his nose. He reels back and bares his teeth at me.

"Unhand me," I protest angrily. *No one* gets to mess with my wardrobe and live.

Knowing I can't escape—*nor should I try*—I restrict myself to throwing one elbow back, crashing into a second guard who stumbles behind me.

"Touch me again and I'll break all of your noses," I threaten. Turning to the prince, I stare him down, challenging him. His eyebrow ticks up slightly, and he smirks as if he's amused at my antics.

"I suggest you cooperate miss, or else this won't end pleasantly for you."

"Why—you'll kill me?" I snap. I shouldn't try to take on Prince Davian, but my tongue can't help itself.

"Hmm, perhaps prison *would* do you some good."

"Doubtful," I mutter. If he tries to lock me up, I'll poison the guards and escape—it wouldn't be hard. The nanobots would form a pick, and I'd be out before he had any idea what was going on.

"Excuse me?" he yelps, surprised at how outspoken I am.

"May I go home now?"

"No. We have to check your foot first."

I blink at him.

I shouldn't do it…but I do it anyway.

"Why, do you have some sort of foot fetish, Your Highness?" I bite back my smile as he gapes at me, shocked at my words. "Relax, I won't tell anyone."

"No…I…no," he stumbles. Davian throws his shoulders back and turns to his guards. "Check her."

One of the men strings his arms through mine, pinning them behind me as he pulls me against his chest. I slam my foot into his, forcing him to release me when he instinctually curls over to protect himself. I lift my skirt and hold the wrong foot out to the prince.

"They will not touch me," I inform him before eyeing the shoe one of the men is holding—*my* shoe. "If you're so bold as to demand to see my foot, *you* will do the honors."

"He will do no such thing—" one of the men growls. I pull my hand back to hit the one approaching me.

"All right!" Davian shouts, stepping forward. "But you know if you even *look* like you're going to try to hurt me, you'll be put to death."

"I wouldn't *dare* hurt the prince of Davengreen," I say innocently. I add in my sweetest voice, "And you'll be sparing your men whatever fate will befall them if they come near me again."

He takes the shoe from his guard and hesitantly steps toward me. Slowly, he lowers himself to the ground and holds the shoe out to me. I'm still balanced on my right foot, and he coughs, nodding for me to switch feet. I drop my left one and slip out of my right knee-high boot.

The nanobots blend in perfectly with my skin, covering what will likely end up as a nasty scar from the prince's knife. Davian slips the shoe on my foot, glancing up at me.

"Perfect fit," he muses. I glance away, pretending to be disinterested as he slides the shoe off my foot—I wish I could take it back to Claude. "How are you standing so perfectly still?"

"Good balance, Your Highness." I step back into the shoe I had been wearing and straighten my shoulders.

"You must be wondering what this is about," he comments, gauging my reaction.

"When the Prince of Davengreen tells me to do something, I comply without question, Your Majesty."

"Correct me if I'm wrong, but didn't you just question me?"

"I questioned your men," I indulge in correcting the prince, tipping my head quietly to one side—men have always found it hypnotizing when I shift my hair and the prince is no different.

I spot movement from the corner of my eye. A man and a younger girl attempt to back around the corner out of sight, but the guards take notice. When they attempt to drag the young girl out from behind the building, the man darts forward, brandishing a weapon.

He lunges at the prince, but I can't let the royal die yet —Master will be furious if I let these people destroy his plans. If the prince dies before the king, our plan will fail.

My body starts moving before I command it to, attempting to block the prince from the man's knife. He grabs hold of Davian, wrapping an arm around his throat, knife to the side of his neck.

"Let her go!" the man demands.

The prince's eyes are wide, but he stays calm, assessing his situation with nearly the same precision Master trained me to use. I allow tears to well up in my eyes as if I'm frightened and openly turn into a sniveling mess, leading the man to believe I'm no threat.

"Please don't hurt him," I beg through my fake tears.

The man looks at me, face twitching.

"Let my daughter go," he growls, nearly sounding like it's a question rather than a statement.

I could potentially take his daughter captive and force a trade, but I need to get the prince out of his grip, and I doubt the guards will let me get near the girl.

Slipping out of my shoe as I step forward, I use my wrap-around skirt to cover my movements—I'm grateful I chose to wear it along with my faux-leather pants. I take an uneven step toward them.

"They're just trying shoes on people," I inform the man. "They did it to me, and I'm fine."

The daughter is sobbing in the confinement of the guards' arms. She struggles against them, hands wrapped around their beefy arms.

"Why are you trying the shoes on us?" I ask the prince as if I don't already know. When he doesn't answer, I repeat myself, sounding suspicious of him.

"It belongs to a murderess," he finally growls at me. "If it fits, we've found the killer."

"It could fit hundreds of girls!" the man shouts, tightening his grip on the prince's neck.

"No!" At his outburst, the man lets go just enough so that Davian can breathe again. He coughs. "The pattern has to match. There's only one girl it could fit."

"So if your daughter didn't murder anyone, it won't fit her and they'll let us all go." I try to sound as desperate as possible as I turn to the man holding the prince at knifepoint.

The man swings around to look at me, giving me a mere second to lash out at him. I grab the knife from my belt that I carefully hid from the royal guards and jam it into the man's upper arm. He shrieks in pain. When he recoils, he accidentally sets the prince free.

Reaching out, I flip the man over, wrestling him to the ground until he is subdued. Two guards tackle him as the daughter screams. I rush to her side to make her comply before the guards do.

"I will not be sent to prison because *you* made a stupid choice," I threaten her. Propelling her back against the wall of a building, I grab the shoe and force her to try it on. Her feet are much larger than mine, and when it's clear it can't be her, I knock her out, slamming the hilt of my knife into her temple.

Whipping around, I move quickly over to the father and leave him in an unconscious pile on the cobblestone walk as well.

"I have done as you asked, *and* I have protected you, Your Majesty. I would like to go home now." Making demands of the prince isn't wise, but it's my only chance to have the upper hand.

He grins at me, taking a long step toward me around the man's unconscious body.

That was a mistake.

CHAPTER 4
DAVIAN

"No, you'll be coming with us, madam." I know better than to let someone with her talents go. I've never seen anyone diffuse a situation so quickly—not even the elite guards my father has following us around whenever we leave the palace.

"I must return home," she insists, clutching her bag strap in her hand. She shifts uncomfortably, looking nervous.

"You don't have anything to hide, do you?" I try to sound carefree, but I know better. Even if this girl isn't the murderess I'm hunting, someone has trained her to protect herself—nothing about this girl is ordinary.

She reaches up, tucking a strand of curly, brown hair behind her ear. Her finger snags on her hood, tugging it off-center adorably.

Wait, no. Not *adorably. She is not adorable; she is dangerous.*

"I have nothing to hide."

"Good, then you can assist me on my mission. Obviously you're skilled enough to help me. Once we find the woman we're looking for, you may go. Until then, you'll join my personal team of guards in the search for the assassin that tried to murder my father last night. Having a female with us will make the women we're testing more comfortable."

Her eyes grow wide, revealing green the color of grass. I take a moment to examine her, noting her tight-fitting, long-sleeved, hooded shirt and sleek black pants surrounded by a partial skirt—just enough to look feminine while also looking deadly. I wonder what her story is.

"Come," I motion to the side. She steps out into the lead, following my orders even though she doesn't know where we're going. I eye Filip, and he nods briefly, assuring me that he'll watch the girl. "What is your name?"

I catch up to her with Filip right behind us, weapon carefully hidden just out of her sight. She glances over at me, a strand of her curls toppling out of her hood on the opposite side.

"Does it matter, Majesty?" She speaks so curtly to me that I can't help but chuckle.

"I am Davian," I introduce myself.

"I'm aware."

When this is all over, I'm going to put a tracker on her just to see what she does with herself—she's so intriguing. She doesn't seem at all worried that I could have her arrested or even killed if she angers me in any way—not that I would ever kill someone over that.

"This is the part where you tell me *your* name," I whisper playfully, hoping to get her to let her guard down.

"Oh, but isn't it more fun to keep it a secret and play the game?" she counters flirtatiously. The girl tucks her curls back again, letting her fingers linger near her chin—she's good.

"You can either tell me your name, madam, or I can assign you one, but I'm not going to guess." I don't mind playing games, but it will be on *my* terms.

She considers my words before finally relenting, shoulders sagging. Taking a deep breath, she softly speaks.

"Cindrill."

That's the strangest name I've ever heard, and I wonder if she's made it up. It doesn't matter—I have a name to call her, and once we're all done, I'll bring her back to the palace to interrogate her.

"Very well then, Cindrill," I address her as formally as I can. "We're looking for a murderess who visited the palace last night. She was wearing a green dress and those shoes we made you try on. She and her partner were trying to murder my father, fiancée, and me."

She cringes as I explain, but reaches up to knock her hood off, fully revealing her hair. It cascades halfway down her back in loose curls—the photographers would have a field day with her if she ever visited the palace. If she didn't make me so nervous, I might actually invite her to the palace for an event other than an interrogation simply to add to the aesthetic of a gathering.

"If you were bent on destroying someone and your plan was ruined, where would you hide out?" The question is casual enough. I shrug a shoulder and glance over at her. I can feel Filip judging her response behind me.

"I wouldn't," she responds lightly. "You'd be expecting that. I'd stay close to the palace and remain in plain sight. *Did you* check near the palace?"

The guards checked last night, but admittedly, not this morning.

"I'll take that as a no," she adds. "So you and your men just ran out this morning before the sun could come up to...*what*—run around and corner girls going to the market?"

"Well, we couldn't very well order all the women in the country to the palace doorstep for this, now could we?" I huff. I don't like that she is challenging my decision. "Besides, this way, we won't miss anyone."

"You and your team of *twenty men* won't miss anyone? You'd be better off shooting a couple of arrows from atop the palace walls and hoping it hits the assassin." Filip snorts behind me. "I don't think you've thought this through very well."

"Then just what would you suggest we do, *Miss Cindrill?*"

"Drop the *miss*," she corrects me. "I would set a trap, of course. Why go traipsing around the countryside when you could draw the assassin to you? If you plan it right, you can pull her in, catch her, and not have a hair on your precious royal head harmed in the process."

"And if it's not planned right, he dies. Brilliant," Filip scoffs.

"What kind of a trap?" I ignore my head of security.

"*Another ball,* perhaps?"

"That wasn't a ball," I mutter.

"Close enough." She sounds exasperated. "I've seen your court go in and out of there with their fancy gowns and suits—you can't convince me you're not throwing lavish events inside of those walls."

"It was an engagement party—not everything we do inside that palace is fun, Cindrill."

"Remind me of that during the royal wedding," she sneers at me. I don't think she's thrilled with the idea of me marrying the princess of Briarmar.

"Are you angling for an invitation?" I ask, catching her

off guard. Her gaze shoots over to me, eyes wide again. It's fun throwing her off-kilter a bit.

"Oh, I wouldn't be caught dead in the palace," she replies, her smile dark. "Your guards wouldn't know what to do with me even if I *did* show up."

"I have a feeling you're right there."

"We're almost there, sire," Filip says from behind us. Glancing up, I see the town square looming in front of us, the tall processing building standing high above the rest as it towers over the town.

"We're going to the Epicenter?"

"How else do you expect us to corral all these women?"

"Bat your eyelashes, of course," she mutters under her breath. I whip around to look at her, my own eyes wide this time, and snort, unable to keep my laughter in.

"Is that really what you think of me?"

"That's what *everyone* thinks of you, Prince Davian." It's the first time she's said my name, and she makes it sound even more regal than the court announcer does. "The world bows at the feet of the prince with the pretty face—your fiancée must be thrilled."

My fiancée and I don't even know each other—I doubt she's thrilled that other women think I'm nice to look at.

"You like my face, huh?" I'm not flirting with her—not really. I'm arranged to marry Vila and everyone knows it, and this girl clearly doesn't like me anyway, so there's no harm in having the same type of conversation I've always had with people.

"What's your plan once we reach the Epicenter?"

"Well, I thought perhaps *you* would be able to help me spot anyone who looks like they're worried."

"This is never going to work," she grumbles, adjusting the bag on her shoulder. I probably should have had Filip check her bag more thoroughly, but if she hasn't used anything against us yet, we're probably safe.

We walk through the large doors to the Epicenter. Each town in the kingdom has one, and every morning, the majority of people pass through it to check in for work. They're shuttled to different locations once they've signed in, and at the end of the day, they're returned home. Only people that work within the center of town don't have to make an appearance at the Epicenter to travel to work.

The building is grand, with tall columns built into the walls that stretch high above our heads. The Epicenter is several stories tall, the second and third levels a mix of offices and bay doors for workers to step on and off the shuttles.

"Your majesty," the man at the entrance says, looking shocked. He gapes, unsure of whether to request I place my hand on the bio scanner or not. I step up to it and do it without his prompting.

"Thank you," I say, stepping forward. Cindrill gasps behind me as one of the men pushes her to the scanner, directing her.

When I turn, she's hesitantly placing her hand on the glass covering the device. The light shines around her, reading her biometrics. It dings when the scan is complete.

"I'm here against my will," she proclaims to the man who looks uncomfortable. When he does nothing, she huffs and steps forward.

"The prince kidnapped me, oh no," I mock her. "Did you really think that would work?"

"I think I'm establishing a trail. If anything should happen to me, my father will come looking, and if people know you took me, he'll know to stop searching for me so nothing bad happens to him too." Her honesty is refreshing—no one speaks to me like this.

"I'm not going to harm you, Cindrill, I just need your help."

"To execute a girl," she points out, using her finger to emphasize her point. "You want me to help find a girl that you're going to kill."

"She tried to kill *me*."

"That makes it so much better." She shakes her head but suddenly perks up. "There."

I turn to see where she's pointing at. A woman in her early thirties clicks across the lobby paying us no mind.

She's too old to be the woman I saw last night, but it's a good test for Cindrill.

"Let's go see if it's her." I let her take the lead. Filip follows behind us, carrying the marked-up shoe.

"Ma'am," Cindrill calls out. "Please stop. The prince needs a word with you."

The woman freezes when she hears my title, slowly turning back to face us. She drops into an immediate curtsey, nearly dropping the tablet in her hand.

Cindrill quickly explains that she must try the shoe on, but gives her no explanation as to why. She drops the shoe on the ground in front of the woman and allows her to steady herself on her arm covered in dark brown fabric.

"No match," Cindrill announces. She waits as the woman takes off the shoe and slips back into her own before dropping her arm. She looks from Filip to the shoe, refusing to pick it up—one of the other guards gets it.

The room begins to bustle and my men direct all of the women who fit the correct age range into a line as they wait to try on the shoe. The process takes forever, but Cindrill holds remarkably still the entire time. I, on the other hand, can't stand still.

When the line finally dies down, one of my men approaches us, tension lines stretched across his face.

Filip catches sight of him and demands to know what it is.

"That woman skipped the line," the guard huffs as if he's been running—he hasn't. "She claimed she had to get to work and didn't have time for this. I couldn't stop her."

My heart starts racing—she has to be the one.

"Go!" I demand, forcing my men into action. They all race away to apprehend the woman, leaving me to finish testing the last eight women with Cindrill.

"Last call!" a man yells, and the women in front of me panic as they realize they will miss the final shuttle to their workplaces.

"Come along." I wave them forward. Stumbling, I force them to try on the shoe as we hurry toward the platform to catch the shuttle. Cindrill tries to keep them from tripping, but it's no use.

"Prince Davian," she lectures as a redhead nearly crashes to the floor while still holding onto Cindrill.

I stoop down to hold the shoe out to the next woman, mere inches from the shuttle bay, but the door starts to slide shut, and the rest of the people push inside. They take me with them, separating me from my guards.

CHAPTER 5
CINDRILL

THE PRINCE STUMBLES BACKWARD, CATCHING HIS FOOT ON the edge of the shuttle. He falls to the ground, looking up in horror as the doors start to whoosh shut—the shuttle stops for no one.

The guards are too far away to help, leaving the prince on his own. I throw myself between the doors, slamming into a rider just as the door misses my foot. I glance down at the prince, unsure of what to do.

This is a brilliant opportunity for me—I could take him to Master, and we could hold the prince for ransom to get the king in front of Master's scope, too, or I could hide him away and try to get information from him. I have the rest of the shuttle ride to figure it out, but one thing I know is that Prince Davian will not be returning home tonight.

"Is that the prince?" someone murmurs.

"Where are his guards?" an older woman sounds worried for his safety.

"His guards aren't here?" This man's voice is far more eager. He must be a part of one of the resistance groups that wants to remove the crown and force an insane group of rebels with plans of grandeur onto the thrown to control the people for their own personal gain.

The blond man looks around, his curly hair tossing as he searches for Davian.

"We have to go," I whisper harshly, holding my hand down to Davian. He swallows but takes my hand, assuming he's safer with me than with the rebel—and he is…for now.

He staggers to his feet, and I push him in front of me as I force him down the tiny aisle, crashing into people. We make it to the next car, slipping through the crowd.

"We have to get you out of sight," I hiss. "We're getting off at the next stop."

"What if *he* gets off?"

"We stay on," I reply, annoyed that he doesn't know this already.

I push him into the front corner of the car, hoping to be overlooked if the curly haired man comes through the doors. I'm not as tall as the prince, but I attempt to use my body to block him.

We wait quietly, heads tipped down low together. His

breathing is heavy, even though we didn't run. In my nervousness, I adopt his breathing pace and match him without meaning to.

The door clicks open, the tell-tale swoosh announcing that we have been followed. Davian is looking at me when I glance up.

"He's here," he mouths.

"Trust me?" I ask quickly before pressing my body against his. I wrap my arm around his neck and turn his face into me to use my hair to conceal his features.

Davian wraps his arms around me, getting the picture. His fingers graze over the small of my back and down my hips. I shiver.

He grins against my cheek and uses his hands to run up my back as if it's a game. His nose is against mine, the tip brushing just under my eye as he gets closer to me. An arm wraps around my waist again, dragging me closer to him.

Fine, two can play at this game.

I reach up, entangling my fingers in his hair and I feel his lips part against my cheek in surprise. Sighing, I drag my left hand down his shoulder to his chest making him shudder into me. A little breath of air escapes his lips as I decide to torture him more.

Pushing up on my toes, I pull his face against my neck and raise my shoulder to cradle his head. I yank hard on his hip, shifting his entire body to the side as I pull him away from the wall he's resting against.

He gives in slowly, cautiously putting his lips against my neck as he holds back a groan—I have him right where I want him. Pulling back, I look over my shoulder for the man with the curly hair, but I think he's moved on in search of Davian elsewhere. When I turn back, the prince is blinking rapidly.

"He's gone." I drop my hands from him, pulling away. Turning my back, I stride away, waiting for him to follow me. I leave the car, traveling back to the original part of the shuttle we had entered.

After a moment, the prince joins me.

"That was—"

"You're safe," I interrupt him. "At least for now, but we really need to get you out of this shuttle. I don't care if he gets off at the next stop, we're leaving."

The prince doesn't say anything. He hovers just over my shoulder until the shuttle lurches to a stop.

"Come on," I direct, stepping toward the door.

I glance around but can't tell if the man stepped off of the shuttle or not. It doesn't matter—I have to get Davian out of the public eye if this is going to work.

"Where are we going?" Davian asks, trudging after me. I thought he might have trouble keeping up, but he seems to do just fine.

"Anywhere that's out of sight."

"Is that the *prince?*" a woman asks loudly.

"I don't suppose we should stop to try the shoe on them?" Davian asks. I think he's joking, but I can't quite tell.

"Give me that thing." I have no idea where the shoe was while we were pretending to kiss, but if I can get it back in my bag, I can probably return it to Claude without getting into too much trouble.

He doesn't question me and hands it over. Slipping it into my bag, I feel whole again—but then, when do shoes *not* make me feel that way?

"Do you know where we're going?" Davian searches for answers. I can't say I blame him—I'd want to know too.

"I've been here a few times before," I lie—I've been here *many* times. "I think there's a place we can hide over this way.

I steer us away from the crowded part of town, hoping to keep him out of an area where he could get word to his guards. We duck into an alleyway, curving around a dumpster filled with things I don't want to know about. Davian makes a face but doesn't say anything—perhaps it's time for an economics lesson.

I guide us around the town, aiming directly for the poorer outskirts where I can put on a good show for the spoiled prince. He draws closer to me the deeper we walk into the sketchier area.

"Oh dear, I guess I didn't really know where I was going," I announce, secretly grinning to myself.

"Stay close," the prince says, not sounding afraid at all. I look at him in surprise, and he protectively steps closer to me. "Just stay by me and we'll be okay."

A group of men step out from their homes, stalking toward us—they don't like visitors. We're far enough away that we can make a clean escape, but I figure a bit of a run would do Davian's royal legs some good—I hear they're insured anyway.

I tug on him and we start running as the men chase after us—they weren't close enough to get a good look at the prince's face so they give up after a few blocks. Had they realized my companion could have been the ticket to their next payday, I imagine the scene would have played out differently.

A woman lunges out of nowhere, grabbing onto my arm. She twists me around to face her, jerking me to a stop.

"Please!" she begs. "Please help us."

The woman becomes incoherent, pulling on my arm and babbling nonsense. I'm assuming she took something. Reaching up through her arm, I bring mine down so that I release her locked joint and fold her arm in two at the elbow. She sobs as I push her away, but a man walks up behind us and attempts to throw his arms around me.

Davian leaps forward, beating the man until he quickly releases me. The prince pulls me toward him and we take off down the street, leaving the two to come out of whatever intoxicated state they're in.

"Are you okay?" Davian asks, spinning me toward him.

"Fine. You?" I'm more concerned about the royal in front of me than I am for myself. The man managed to slice my arm open with his knife, but the nanobots crawled up my leg from inside my tall boot where they had been covering my cut skin and already started working on the injury on my arm—they scurry away under my sleeve when the prince notices the blood.

"You're bleeding," he gasps.

"I'm fine. We should go."

"We need to take care of your arm." He gives me a stern look as if he's not taking no for an answer.

The prince wrenches my arm toward him so he can examine the injury. He reaches inside his tailored waistcoat and pulls out a small package. When he unravels it, I discover he's been carrying around some strange form of a first aid kit.

"You don't honestly think they'd let me out of the palace without medical supplies on my person, do you?" He looks at me incredulously. "You're interesting, Cindrill, but a little naïve."

There are fourteen different ways I could kill him with that kit right now. *If only he knew.*

He quietly bandages my cut while I keep an eye out for anyone that might happen upon us. I can feel the nanobots skittering up my arm and over my shoulder toward the small of my back where they will rest until they can return to the injury to repair it.

"Good as new," the prince murmurs. "Now we just need to get back to the palace district."

"Of course, Your Majesty."

"Are you really okay, Cindrill?" He looks as if he's actually concerned for me. I still don't buy it.

"I'm fine, Your Majesty."

"At this point, I don't think calling me by my title is going to do us any good."

"What do you expect me to call you?"

"Davian," he replies. "That *is* my name."

"I doubt the general public will think that I have any right to call you by your name."

"Just try it and see how it goes," he baits me.

I frown. He grins back at me. Squinting my eyes at him does no good—he only squints back in an attempt to make me laugh.

"We're wasting time."

"Time spent with a pretty girl is never a waste of time," he throws back at me. His face suddenly falls as he realizes his mistake. "I guess I can't talk like that anymore, now can I? Sometimes I forget I'm betrothed. Can we pretend I didn't say that?"

At least he thinks I'm pretty—I can use that to my advantage—especially after the shuttle ride.

"I can't image Princess Vila would be happy about that, so yes, we can forget it." I start to walk away but pause to peer back over my shoulder. "Just name your first child after me and we'll call it even."

His jaw drops and I laugh. Waving him forward, relief washes over his face.

"So, tell me about this princess of yours," I comment. I figured I should get him to talk about himself so he doesn't ask questions about *me*.

"Uhh, well…she's my fiancée," he comments, sounding more like a question than a statement.

"Yes, I heard that." I smirk. Clearly the prince knows nothing about his bride-to-be. "What is she like? Is she pretty?"

"Yes."

"That's it? *Yes?*" I refuse to let this go.

"She's beautiful, of course—"

"What color eyes does she have?" I cut him off.

"Blue…I think. Yes, blue." He huffs in aggravation. "You're not going to let this go, are you? I barely know the girl, and you know that. She's only been here for a month."

"An entire month and you don't know the girl's eye color? True love, right here, folks. True love."

"We're still getting to know each other," he protests, sulking. I'm sure my words sting.

"You're going to marry this princess and yet you know nothing about her after a *month*? Really, Davian, she's a person, not a possession."

"Of course she's not," he snips before relenting. "She's a treaty."

"Oh, so much better."

"Fine then, if you're so smart, tell me about *your* boyfriend. Is he going to beat me up when he finds out I ran off with you today?"

"No boyfriend, so I think you're safe." Safe from a *jealous* man, anyway. Master is anything *but* jealous, and he's out for blood.

"*You're* single?" He runs his hand through his hair—which is even prettier up close—and gives me a look indicating that he doesn't believe me.

"I have better things to do than chase after boys all day."

Actually, to be fair, that's *exactly* what I do all day—they just don't survive long after I find them, thanks to Master.

"I'm sure they chase after *you* though..." he leads, bumping me with his elbow.

"Yes," I reply in a deadpan voice. "And I do to them

what I did to that girl and her father back in the palace district."

His step falters, and I imagine he's turning white, but I don't stop to look.

"You don't seriously knock people out, do you?" He rushes to catch up with me.

"Yes."

"Did your father teach you that?" he challenges.

From the corner of my eye, I see a movement in the shadows of the alleyway we're walking down—Master has arrived. He must have realized something was wrong when I didn't return to base, and he came out looking for me. I'm sure he found footage of me somewhere wandering off with the prince and now he's come to collect his prize.

An arrow whizzes past us, landing with a thunk in the door of a building. The prince pulls back, trying to locate the source of the arrow, but I whip the door open and pull the prince inside, slamming it shut behind us.

"Run," I command and point him toward the stairs.

Master will follow closely, but he's not ready to wound the prince yet—he's just pushing us toward where he wants us to go.

I follow the prince up the stairs, slamming my feet into each wooden step to go faster. We burst through another doorway and find ourselves in a bedroom that looks like it hasn't been used in the last year. A layer of dust covers everything, there are no sheets on the mattress, and there's no technology to be found anywhere.

"The window," I shout.

Davian flings the frame open, and I quickly crawl out onto a nearly flat rooftop.

"You've got to be kidding me," the prince exclaims.

"Would you prefer meeting the person with the arrows?" I call over my shoulder as I rush along the rooftop—there's no harm in making the prince work for his temporary freedom.

He doesn't see it yet, but the only way off of this roof is to jump.

CHAPTER 6
DAVIAN

MY GUIDE'S HALF SKIRT BILLOWS OUT BEHIND HER AS SHE races along the roof like a cat. I tried that once when I was a child, and my mother scolded me so badly that I never tried it again.

I feel off balance up on top of the building. The shingles are tipped slightly—I assume so rain can run off of it—but it makes every step I take uneven. I feel as though I'm pulled to the right every time I move.

"Hurry up," she hisses at me, still racing across the roof.

Suddenly, she picks up speed.

An arrow flies between us, stopping me in my tracks.

"Davian!" she shouts, spinning to see where I am.

"Arrow!" I call back, and her face drops.

"We have to jump!" she calls, turning to run.

"*What?*" There's no way I'm jumping off a building.

Everything speeds by me in a blur as I match her pace. I can see the tops of trees in my peripheral vision, and the reds, browns, and grays of other roofs, but nothing is clear.

Cindrill launches herself into the air, gliding from one roof to the next—I don't know how she didn't get caught on the ledge.

"You can make it!" she screams, waiting for me.

Another arrow slams into the roof just behind my feet.

I jump.

Wind rushes around hair, forcing it back behind me. It tears at my clothing momentarily and I'm glad I wore the gear that I did to go out in public.

The ledge fills my vision as I sail toward it—I'm not going to make it. Cindrill's face tells me as much when she charts the course of my trajectory. She races forward, leaning out over the edge.

Stretching my hands up, I slam into the side of the building. One hand catches the ledge painfully, and Cindrill's nails dig into my wrist. I attempt to climb up, using my feet to push myself up the side of the building.

Between that and Cindrill's clawing at me, I manage to make it over the ledge. We collapse behind the short wall of the ledge, trying to catch our breath while still evading the person shooting at us.

"Do you think he knows who I am?"

"Possibly." She sounds out of breath. I pull her to my chest to calm her down and comfort her—she did, after all, just save my life. I suppose I'll have to reward her later —perhaps with an invitation to the royal wedding.

My heart is beating faster than it ever has before and catching my breath is a task in and of itself, but her presence calms me…until another arrow hits.

"Time to go," she says, quickly pushing up off my chest.

She darts across the open rooftop, and I have to hope for the best as I race behind her. Without thinking, I follow her over the edge of the building, and we cascade downward.

I jolt to a stop when we hit a pile of hay.

"How did you know that would be there?" I gasp.

"Lucky guess," she admits. Tugging my hand, she pulls me down the street and around the corner.

"We've got to find somewhere to hide, Cindrill."

"Really, do you think? I thought we could head to the park and take a leisurely stroll instead."

"I'll thank you kindly to take this seriously, madam." I puff as we run.

"Oh, we're back to *madam*, are we?"

The way her lips quirk up when she's sarcastic is enchanting. I consider grabbing her hand to force her to listen to me, but I know that would be a mistake.

"Have you ever considered working for my father?" I ask instead.

"Excuse me?" She risks a glance at me before peeling around another corner.

"My father could use someone like you—I imagine you'd be quite good at spy work."

"I have no interest in being a spy," she says like it leaves a bad taste in her mouth.

Cindrill gasps when she nearly runs face first into my guards.

"Your Highness!" they shout when they see me. The men raise their weapons to Cindrill.

"Stand down," I bark at them. "She's been helping me."

"We saw her get on the shuttle with you."

"Yes, to make sure that I wasn't alone—it's a good thing too, there was a rebel who recognized me, and she prevented him from finding me." I spare them the details.

Filip pulls me to the side while the others surround Cindrill.

"What happened?" His eyes bore holes through me. "Did she try anything?"

"No, she stayed with me on the shuttle and then tried to get us back to the palace district."

"You didn't think to reach out to us?"

In truth, I hadn't. I was too busy running for my life and trying to figure Cindrill out.

"We were shot at," I inform him without emotion. "We ended up jumping off a roof to escape the guy."

"Do you think it was the assassin?"

"I don't know." I shake my head. "This guy used arrows, not bullets."

"And you don't think someone could change weapons?"

"I don't know, Filip," I say pointedly. "I think that's what we pay *you* for."

He narrows his eyes but doesn't say anything—he always does that when he's mad at me but can't say anything.

"We need to go back to the palace—your father is furious."

"I'm sure." I glance around and find Cindrill staring at me. I wonder how upset *her* father is right now. I'm sure an invitation to the palace would smooth things over—unless he doesn't like the crown, which *would* explain Cindrill's hostility toward me. Perhaps I should rethink this.

"She looks pretty uncomfortable." Filip muses without actually turning to look at the girl.

"I don't think she likes you." I smirk back.

"She doesn't look as put together as she did before, either..." He narrows his eyes in a friendly manner. "Something I should know about, Your Highness?"

On occasion, Filip lets his professionalism-guard

down and treats me like a friend—but only on rare occasions.

"She practically kissed me on the shuttle," I brag. "It was our cover, but still."

"*Practically*, but not *actually*." His judgment supersedes my arrogance. He won this round.

"I'm about to be married, Filip." I attempt to cover. "It wouldn't do for an engaged man to be kissing a girl who isn't his betrothed."

"That is a good point, Your Highness." He's back to being all business.

"Besides, Filip, I wasn't worried—I knew you were tracking me." I grin, tapping the small button on the breast pocket of my coat.

"Wouldn't have found you so quickly if I hadn't," he reminds me. I complain enough about technology tracking my every move in the palace that Filip is accustomed to my gripes. He relishes the moments when I actually appreciate his devices.

"We appreciate your assistance, miss," Filip says to Cindrill as we return. He bows his head slightly to her.

"Cindrill needs her arm looked at—she's been injured," I announce to the group. The men all eye her.

"I'm fine, I just need to get home to do my chores."

"I insist." I push. Taking hold of her uninjured arm, I wheel her around. "You'll like the palace—it's lovely there —and we'll send for your father so he can come and visit before collecting you to take you home. I'm sure there is a reward for saving the Prince of Davengreen."

"I don't think that's necessary," she argues.

"You can meet Vila since you seem so interested in her." I drop my voice. "Perhaps we can check her eye color together."

I wave everyone but Filip back from us. Two of the men walk ahead, the rest follow behind, though a few take the side streets, looking for any threats lurking in the shadows.

I glance up and notice the sky has taken a turn for the worse. Where there once were beautiful blue skies, there are now darker clouds—not enough to indicate a storm just yet, but enough to cast shadows over everything.

I replay the scene on the roof over again in my mind. Cindrill was fearless as she jumped from building to building—I wish I had the freedom to be fearless like her. Instead, I have responsibilities and duties.

Father will be furious when he finds out I jumped off a building. I can't say I blame him—under any other circumstances, it would be a stupid thing to do. Still, somehow, I have a feeling I'm going to tuck this one away as one of my favorite memories that I'll tell my children someday.

The group is quiet, falling into an awkward silence as we travel toward the town line to cross over into the palace district. Everyone takes turns glancing at Cindrill as we walk, but she keeps her eyes focused on the ground in front of her. Pebbles litter the path, and she kicks one as she walks.

Her boots peek out the front of her open skirt. Even outside of the palace, fashion is an important concept. The green detailing on her coat tells a story, I'm sure.

Cindrill looks ready to escape the first chance she gets, but her eyes are drilling holes into the ground before every step. Her nose is slanted just enough to turn up at the end, but her curls fall to the sides of her face, blocking it from my sight for most of the walk.

We're a block away from the town line, surrounded by large buildings that look as if they house machinery when a door flies open and Cindrill is pulled inside.

CHAPTER 7
CINDRILL

LARGE HANDS CLAMP OVER MY MOUTH AS I'M PULLED from the side. Master's familiar scent fills my nose, and I relax as he pulls me through the building backward.

I assume the plan is to make it look like I was abducted, and the prince won't be able to find me after his guards race him back to the palace to protect him. If we hurry, perhaps we can catch them as they are entering the palace and slip in that way.

We make it five feet before the door bursts open behind us and Davian storms in looking ready to murder Master—an ironic twist.

He rushes toward us, carelessly leaving his guards behind. His friend rushes after him, but not close enough to catch the angry royal. Davian navigates around boxes and wooden crates as he hurries toward us, intent on reaching me.

The prince threatens Master as he pulls me away to which Master just laughs. It's that dark, terrifying sound he produces when he's about to deliver someone's fate and he wants to terrorize them first. Davian doesn't seem to notice as he barrels toward us.

"Let me go," I insist, twisting against Master. Either way, it doesn't matter—stay with Master and go after the prince another day, or end up in the palace and gather intelligence from inside, possibly even letting Master in during the middle of the night to carry out his task of murdering the king and his son.

"Let her go, she has no part in this!" Davian shouts, leaping over a smaller crate, cutting off a few feet between us. He looks wild as he tries to reach me.

The prince slams into a different box, and I know his shin must be killing him, but that doesn't stop him. He lifts a small wooden container and throws it so that it smashes on the ground next to us—a warning.

"Release her, and I'll consider letting you live!" Davian sounds almost cocky as he wields his threats against the deadliest force Davengreen has ever been subjected to— this lifetime or any other.

"Go back to your palace, *boy*," Master says, his voice modulator activated. If I didn't know the science behind it, I'd find it terrifying. I myself rather enjoy using the voice modulator Claude designed for us during my own missions.

Master pulls back on me, cutting off part of my airflow. My training tells me to escape—flip him over my head, incapacitate him, and run—but I know better, and tamp down years of experience in order to play the role of a victim.

A sound squeaks out of my mouth involuntarily, and my eyes widen when I hear it. On occasion, I don't have control over what my body does, and I hate it—I should be able to be flawless according to my level of training, but every so often, I find a crack in the perfect façade Master and the others have created in me.

Prince Davian looks ready to hit the floor, frozen, when he hears me make that ridiculous noise, making me sound like a frightened mouse. I growl, frustrated with myself, and it only spurs the prince on.

Filip races behind him, unable to catch him as he plows after me through the crowded room. I have no idea how Master can navigate the old factory backward, but I assume he scoped it out before we arrived.

Light shifts in my peripheral vision as Master weaves us around old boxes. The windows are boarded up, but not well, leaving light to leak in at strange angles. Dust dances in the air, puffing up in large clouds with each scuffled step we take.

I work to maneuver against Master, ensuring it

appears as though I'm trying to escape. Davian never takes his eyes off me, while Filip keeps his eyes locked on Master. One of Davian's men bursts through the back door faster than Master had anticipated and his grip tightens around my body, forcing the air from me just enough to let me know his plan was thrown off, but not enough for the prince or his men to tell he was surprised.

Davian reaches into his coat, retrieving the medical kit he had used not too long ago. I squint in question. Before I can figure it out, Davian whips his hand into the air and launches the kit directly at me.

It sails by my face, a mere inch from my temple and hits Master's cheekbone. He growls viciously as one of Davian's men yells behind him.

Now or never—flee and find me later or keep me in his grip and be overtaken by the king's men. Master could easily take out the majority of them, but he has a plan to think about, and Master always carries out his missions. I feel his thoughts trickling down to his fingers against my body as he makes his decision.

He releases me, pretending like Davian's assault mattered. He turns, forcing the air around me to gust like a sudden wind overtook the room. Master scrambles over something behind me, turning it in the process. It clinks against the floor, leaving the scene behind my back to my imagination.

Ahead of me, Davian falls.

Filip yells a string of threats against Master as he rushes to Davian's side, lifting a heavy box off of him.

"Wait, I'm coming," I shout as Filip tries to rock the large crate off of the prince's leg. The rest of the guards rush upstairs after Master—if he's on the second floor, they'll never catch him before he leaps from a window to freedom. "Tip it that way."

Filip and I work together to free the prince—I have no idea how Master lifted such a heavy box, but I'm sure adrenaline had something to do with it. Reeling back, I kick it, using my full weight to help assist the prince's friend.

The box topples over as Davian groans. His leg is still intact and doesn't appear to be out of the socket, but it has to hurt. I'm sure he will end up with some nasty bruises after this.

He and his father might be a matching set.

"It's fine," Davian protests as Filip tries to examine him. "It didn't even rip the fabric."

"It's going to bruise," I point out.

"I'm fine," Davian says harshly. He softens as he looks up at me. "How are *you*? Are *you* okay, Cindrill?"

A hand reaches out to me—*to point?...to ask me to come closer?...to help him up?* I'm not sure. No matter what his intent, I need to use it to my advantage.

I take his hand and settle on the floor in front of him, his legs still trailing behind him as he rests his full weight on his right hip. My skirt settles out to the side, and I position my legs out, mirroring his, but to the side instead of mostly behind me.

"I'm okay." My words are soft and quiet.

"Did he hurt you?" Davian covers my hand with his free one.

"I'm fine."

"I'm so sorry you got caught up in this, Cindrill. It wasn't fair of me to bring you into this and make you a target."

I was always *involved in this.*

The prince looks concerned, brow low. He ignores Filip's pleas to get up and move to safety. When the man tugs on Davian's shoulder, the prince swats him back, refusing to be deterred.

"I'll see to it that you're protected."

"I can take care of myself, Your Majesty."

Davian smirks. "I thought I told you not to call me that."

"I'll be fine," I insist.

"Your Highness, we need to go. Now," Filip finally demands.

I start to get up, pulling Davian with me. He hesitates for a moment, and I wonder if he wants to hold me in place a minute longer—the pressure on my hands suggests he might.

"You need to return to the palace where it's safe,

Davian, and I need to get home." I try to coax him to follow Filip's orders.

"We'll bring your father to the palace, Cindrill. Until we catch this madman, the safest place for you is with my guards."

He stands, leg not cooperating with him as he moves. The prince tumbles forward, only catching himself on Filip's outstretched arm.

I rush forward, ducking under his far arm as Filip takes on the majority of the prince's weight. Davian leans heavily against me, but I can tell he's trying not to. His muscles are tight, and he shifts toward Filip, allowing him to discretely take on more of the work.

Wrapping my arm around Davian's back, I brush against Filip's arm, but he doesn't flinch, holding the prince up. He makes it look easy—Filip is better at this than I thought.

"I'm fine," Davian mumbles. We wheel around toward the door as the rest of the guards join us, shaking their heads in a silent report.

"You threw a medical kit at an assassin," I comment. I probably should have picked that up. One of the guards goes back to get it as I wrench my head around to look for it. "You have pretty good aim for a sheltered royal."

"What do you think I do inside the palace walls all day?" he jokes back.

"I distinctly remember nearly being a victim several

times," Filip mumbles next to us as we step out onto the street.

The sky is still clear, the air crisp. Despite what was nearly carnage inside the old factory, the day has remained glorious outside.

"I threw it *near* you, Filip. It was just a wakeup call. If I had meant to hit you, I would have."

"I'm sure," Filip grumbles, and I gather Davian's wakeup calls were more frequent than they should have been.

Nanobots slowly start crawling up my skin, making their way to my neck. Quietly, I reach up to touch the spot. I hadn't realized it, but when my fingertip comes away red, I know I've been injured. Master's nail must have cut into me during the escape. The nanobots quickly cover up the injury, and I wipe the blood off on the dark fabric of my pants under my wrap skirt. At least if it blends in, Claude won't be able to yell at me for it.

The prince tries to walk on his leg, grimacing each time he puts weight on the injury. Our pace is slower than it should be if an assassin was on our trail, but Master isn't going to try anything else until we get back to the palace, so I let Filip take the lead in directing our pace without commenting on the situation.

Davian's men form a shield around us, moving us through the streets until we reach one of the shuttles.

The guards commandeer the vehicle, clearing a car before allowing us to enter.

I sit across from Davian, his legs kicked out as far as they'll reach toward me. I stay curled in on myself, tucking my legs under my seat. He watches me as we travel. Once, his eyes gaze toward the corner before snapping back to me—a silent reminder of earlier.

Strange. He's more resilient than I assumed he would be. He took on an assassin, didn't fuss over his injuries, and even has the gall to try to silently joke with me, drawing us back to our earlier moments on the shuttle.

Filip engages him in conversation and the two quietly discuss what to do to protect the Davengreen royals, Princess Vila, me, and the rest of the kingdom. Davian seems more worried about the kingdom at large than he does about what happens inside of the palace—with the exception of protecting Vila and me, that is.

He truly believes he is to blame for my involvement in all this.

"We should continue looking for the girl," Filip announces. "She can lead us to the man."

"Or men," I comment flippantly. "Could that *really* have been the same man all those times?"

"Well, it certainly couldn't have been the girl," Davian responds. "She hasn't been seen since the ball."

My eyebrows shoot up. "So it *was* a ball!"

Davian smirks at the triumph written on my face—

why try to hide it?

"You said it too many times," he protests playfully. "I picked up your word for it."

"You can't take it back, Your Highness." I purse my lips and shake my head playfully, pointing at him. "You said it and you can't retract it—this isn't the media. You don't control me; I heard you say it."

He closes his eyes slowly, shaking his head. He allows me this small dig against his family.

"Are you sure you're okay, Cindrill? He really didn't hurt you?"

My skin pings under the weight of his words, my neck throbbing just long enough to remind me that I'm a deceitful liar.

"I'm fine, I promise."

"We'll have the physician check you out just the same," Davian announces.

"I really need to go home now—"

"The prince saved your life, madam, you'll do as he says," Filip says abruptly. We both turn to stare.

"She could have handled herself, Filip," Davian corrects.

"Then why did you go running in after her?" The confrontation escalates even though their voices drop.

"It's my fault she's in this mess."

"Any of us could have gone after her." Filip raises a single eyebrow at his charge.

"You wouldn't have. You would have stayed and protected me."

"He makes a valid point, Filip," I add. "But please, can't I just go home?"

My words are only for show. I'll be more of a help to Master in the palace. *Won't I?*

Davian *had* saved me though. He risked himself to run in after me, full well knowing that an assassin who had nearly shot him off a roof just a little while earlier was holding me captive. The prince had even endured being injured to try to help me.

I wonder if there is a way to kill the king but leave his son to rule. Master hadn't told me the full contents of the missive with directions for the mission, but I know the king was supposed to be taken out so that someone else could ascend the throne…that meant Davian had to die too. The king had to go first, though.

I wonder if Claude would be able to get me more information. Master often tells him less than me—he doesn't need to know what I know—but what he tells him is usually different information than mine, so on the rare occasion we can speak in private, we've been able to piece together more parts of different missions than Master would like. I wish I knew more about repro-graming nanobots—maybe I could reach out to him and uncover a way to save Davian.

The shuttle screeches to a stop, jerking quickly. I

nearly topple off my seat, too busy thinking about changing the plans to pay attention to our movements. The guards stand quickly, preparing to clear the area before we step out.

The doors open to reveal the same Epicenter we left a few hours ago. As if we were still there, I can see where each of us stood before being pushed into the shuttle. Davian steps out first, offering me his hand.

I take it and walk out onto the platform. Knowing I have to protect myself once I set foot inside the palace, I force each step to connect with the Epicenter floors hard enough to produce a sound, leaving my boots to click. It echoes off the walls like some of the fancy shoes the ladies of the court often wear to the balls and palace events. If it's annoying enough now, the guards will remember it later when I'm sneaking around the palace to let Master in. They'll be less likely to catch me because they'll be listening for the clicking sounds that won't be there later as I move.

Stomping isn't pleasant, but if it gets the job done, I'll act like one of those lumbering fools that thought they could make the cut with Master last year. Walking on the dirt will muffle the sound anyway, so I only have to keep it up until we leave the Epicenter. I can start again once I'm in the palace walls.

Davian keeps pace next to me, telling me all about the palace as we vacate the Epicenter.

CHAPTER 8
DAVIAN

"I THOUGHT I SENT YOU TO FIND AN ASSASSIN," MY FATHER growls as I enter the office. His leg is bandaged, but I can see the tiniest hint of blood peeking through the wrap.

"I found him several times," I reply boldly. "Apprehending him was another matter."

He catches sight of Cindrill behind me and sits upright.

"Is this the girl?" he nearly shouts, looking ready to behead her on the spot.

"No!" I shout louder than I mean to. I quiet my voice, knowing I need to approach the matter gently if I want Cindrill to remain in the palace walls without giving away too many details about the day. "She was questioned this morning, but the shoe didn't fit. She presented several skills I thought could be useful to my search, and given her gender, I assumed she could calm the rest of the women we were questioning and set them at ease so we didn't cause a scene."

"Why is she here?" Father tips his chin up, examining her from the dark oak chair with intricate carvings at the head of the table. Papers lay spread out before him, several pens strewn around. It amazes me that he insists on using such an antiquated way of taking notes and ruling his kingdom, but I'll have my own ways when I'm king.

"We were both injured by the assassin. We've returned to regroup, go through the security footage of the towns to try to track him, and to have the girl examined by the physician at my command."

Cindrill cringes next to me. I can't imagine she's pleased with being spoken about like this, but at least she's not stepping out of line in front of my father.

"Hmm." His snort means he wants full details on Cindrill once she's not in the room with us. At this point, I'm not sure I want to tell him of Cindrill's particular skills—she may not ever be able to leave our employ if he finds her useful, and I could never knowingly trap her here. I'll have to stay by her side until I can get her out of the palace.

"Filip will help us to the infirmary so the physicians can check us over. Once we've looked through the footage from today, I'll report back with our plan."

I turn, trying not to hobble as I walk to the door, the others following me. My leg has become easier to walk on, but I'm still limping a bit.

"Check on Vila," Father's voice calls after me. "Assure her that she's safe."

He makes a good point.

I raise a hand to indicate I've heard him and continue into the hallway. One of the men shuts the door behind us and I relax. Cindrill's hand brushing against mine pulls me right back out of the feeling.

"Blue, you said?" she asks.

It takes a moment for me to understand, but then I nod. Vila's eyes are blue—they have to be.

"I'll take you to meet my fiancée," I instruct loud enough for everyone to hear. "Huston, go get Sturges and tell him to meet us in the infirmary. We're not going to waste time sending this through the chain—he can tell us all at once what he's learned."

Filip clenches his jaw but doesn't argue.

Cindrill looks like she's taking in every bit of the palace, from the ornately decorated hallways to the massive tapestries she catches sight of through the open doorways. I wonder what she'll think of the ballroom when she sees it later.

"It's a bit much, don't you think?" she comments quietly.

"It's not as bad as you think," I reply, running a hand

through my hair. "It wasn't all done at once. This is a cumulation of bits and pieces of every ruler since the beginning of the dynasty. We all get to add our own touches, and over the years, this is what it's become."

"Even the sons and daughters that did not inherit the crown were given a chance to add their marks," Filip adds, sounding almost as proud as my family is of the tradition. "While the palace has many ways of making income, the majority of it goes right back into the kingdom—that's why we don't always have as much money as we need when things come up. It's also why our enemies think they can so easily take over here."

"It's why we've had some of the recent taxes. We've been having some trouble with some of our neighboring countries and need extra money to help secure the borders." I lean toward Cindrill. "We've been trying to keep it quiet so we didn't upset everyone, but there have been some issues along the borders that we've been keeping isolated."

She nods. I hope I'm not scaring her too much.

The men stop around us, allowing me to step up to Vila's chambers. Cindrill stays by Filip's side as Vila's herald disappears into her sitting room to announce me. After a moment, he reappears, holding his arm out to invite me in.

Stepping inside, I find the room bathed in firelight. Natural light streams in the windows, but the roaring faux fire consumes the colors, turning them orange. Vila strides across the room, hands folding into one another in front of her.

She blinks, waiting for me to speak.

"Are you well?" I ask quietly, reaching for her hands.

"I'm fine. You?" Her eyes are downcast. I can't quite see their color. Cindrill will destroy me if I've guessed incorrectly.

"Look at me, Vila." I have to know.

Hazel. Cindrill will be merciless.

Vila sighs. "What is it, Davian?"

"You're safe here, Vila. You know that, right?" I don't know her well, but I know I don't want her to live in fear in my home.

"I do," she agrees dutifully.

"We went after the assassin today," I inform her, still holding her hands. "We nearly had him, but he took a captive. We all managed to escape, but *he* also managed to flee. We're tracking him down right now."

"Who is *she*?" Vila nods toward Cindrill, whispering her words. A blonde strand of hair falls with the movement.

"She is part of my team. She was assisting me today when we ran into the assassin."

"Why is she here?" Vila ducks her head closer to me, clearly offended.

"We were both injured today during the fights—"

"*Fights?* Plural?" She forgets to keep her voice low.

"We escaped the assassin once, but he found us a second time. I insisted Cindrill return with us so that the physician could check her over before we return her to her father."

"How did you say she helped you?"

I try not to grin. "We might have had to jump off a building to escape, and she made sure we didn't die in the process."

"*Davian.*" I can't tell if it's shock or a lecture.

"We're both fine, we just need to be examined quickly."

Vila waves her hand as if I should move. When I don't, she puts a hand on her hip. "Let's go. If you need to be examined, we'll continue this conversation in the infirmary."

"You don't have to come with—"

"Oh, yes I do. And even if I didn't, Davengreen and Briarmar are supposed to be united. We can't act as one if one of us is constantly being left out of the loop. Harold, you're in charge while I'm gone."

A herald named Harold…I should have seen that coming. Cindrill eyes me as I walk by her, smirking. She must have seen the surprise written across my features when I discovered my fiancée's staff's name.

The infirmary is a few degrees cooler than the rest of the palace. Cindrill is settled in a station two away from mine, giving me some privacy. Vila quickly follows behind her.

"That can't be good," Filip mumbles, taking a seat off to the side.

"Your Highness," Sturges interrupts. He holds up a tablet. "The video from today, sire."

Once again, we discover that the assassin knew where all the cameras were and managed to hide from most of them. He looks tall and imposing in the flashes we catch, covered in dark clothing.

"Did you?" Vila's voice rises up, sounding shocked. We all look over, but the curtain blocks our line of sight.

"You're going to regret letting that happen," Filip taunts, pointing to the two women.

"Something I should know?" Dr. Romani asks as he slides his hand along my leg checking for injuries. He's been caring for my family for the last decade and likes to joke around with me when my father isn't present. He more than anyone helped me through losing my mother, acting both as a doctor and as a therapist.

"It's a good thing the prince has a strong sense of duty, that's all I can say," Filip jokes.

"That pretty girl you brought in?" Dr. Romani jabs at what will likely be a nasty bruise tomorrow. "She's rather beautiful, no?"

"No!"

I protested too much. They all look at me, eyebrows raised.

Grumbling internally, I quickly search for an excuse for my outburst.

"I have a beautiful fiancée," I remind them. "I thought Cindrill could be useful as a spy, but now I'm not sure."

"Ah," Dr. Romani offers. "You don't want her to be trapped here."

Ten years of listening to me complain about being trapped in the palace, and suddenly the man thinks he knows how I think. He pauses his examination to ask a few questions.

"So, you don't want this girl to be trapped here. That's wise of you to protect her," he continues once I've answered about my pain level.

"There's no reason for her to work for us. She worked for us today and nearly ended up dead twice in a matter of the few hours she's been with me."

"And nearly ended up destroying your marriage, so I hear." Filip chuckles, knowing he can trust both Dr. Romani and Sturges. He wouldn't speak out of turn if anyone else had been close enough to overhear and risk the union.

"Oh?" Dr. Romani says, amused. "Your leg is fine, Davian. Put some ice on it and don't overextend yourself, but you shouldn't have any lasting issues. It will be sore tomorrow though."

"Thanks," I reply, hoping he doesn't press further about the scene on the shuttle.

"Is he finished yet?" Vila asks suddenly from nearby. Filip tugs the curtain back, revealing her. "Cindrill is fine."

Both women stand next to the curtain wall, waiting for us. Vila looks ready to move on, but Cindrill's lips are tight.

"How, precisely, are we spending the rest of our day?" Vila asks. I've noticed she likes to keep to a schedule.

I imagine with a lecture or two.

"Perhaps a tour?" Cindrill suggests suddenly.

"Yes, why don't you give Cindrill a tour, Vila?"

She looks uncomfortable. "Why don't *you* guide us, Davian?"

Vila must not be comfortable enough with the palace layout yet to give a guest a tour. Dr. Romani hands me a few pills to take, and the pain eases immediately.

"Of course," I nod to my bride-to-be. Holding out my arm to her, I wait for her to take it.

The palace seems twice as big as usual, and I've only taken the girls to a few of the more important areas, explaining the history. In between locations, Sturges and Filip review what we know about the assassin, the girls taking a particular interest.

Eventually, we find ourselves in my study, making a plan of action. The light outside wanes, leaving us in a muddled cross between natural light and artificial illumination. It's that strange time of day when everything looks a little off in the mixture of light.

Vila and Cindrill bend over tablets together, swiping through footage of the assassin and talking about how he knew to avoid the cameras. I watch them in a trance until Filip kicks me under the table.

"And you said he was *here* last night, too, right?" Cindrill comments, not looking up from the tablet. "And he avoided the camera then, too?"

"He had to have access to the palace schematics," Filip replies. "We keep those under lock and key, no one should be able to discover the ins and outs of the palace unless they work here."

"You think it was an inside job?" Cindrill sounds surprised, finally looking up.

"We don't know," I offer. "How else would he know how to move, though?"

"And the woman?"

"She had the most beautiful outfit," Vila jumps in. "Even her shoes were perfect."

"I took care of those," I mumble. She looks at me

sharply. I quickly explain how I cut the girl and marked up the shoes, earning myself a dissatisfied huff.

"The girl shoved me in a closet to protect me, so she can't be all that bad," Vila protests.

"And she tried to assassinate *my* father and me, so she can't be that *good* either." I watch her to gauge her reaction. Vila may not love me, but if she wishes the assassin succeeded, I'll be able to catch her.

"True." She sighs. "Maybe we can reason with her though if it comes to it. Perhaps she'll turn on the man if we catch her.

Filip looks like he wants to ask how she proposes to do that, but then realizes she is not our friend yet and he can't speak bluntly to her. He closes his mouth without speaking.

"Thoughts on how to do that?" Cindrill asks instead, taking a genuine interest in what Vila has to say. "Have those hazel eyes of yours spotted something the rest of us haven't?"

The emphasis on Vila's eye color is a direct slap in the face to me as Cindrill flashes her gaze up at me. She's proven her point.

A knock sounds at the door. Sturges stands to open it.

"The king would like to see you," a voice says. We've wasted several hours since returning, and I'm sure he's not happy I haven't spoken with him yet.

"Why don't you ladies come with me?"

"I sincerely doubt your father wants to see me right now," Cindrill replies, glancing up. "Take your fiancée, though, he's less likely to be mad in her presence. She has a calming effect on people from what I've seen."

Cindrill glances back down while Vila beams. Perhaps the two of them could be friends.

"I'll come. I'm sure by now he's heard from my father, and I'll have to do some damage control anyway." Vila walks over to stand alongside of me. "I suppose that's both of our jobs now."

"Will you be okay, Cindrill?" I ask.

She barely looks up, waving us off with a flick of her fingers. Sturges stays in place while Filip and most of the others rise to walk with us. Cindrill makes a small noise, a dismissal of sorts. When I stand there a moment longer, she glances up.

"I'll be fine," she finally responds. "I'm just going to keep studying these. There has to be something we're missing."

I have no doubt if we've missed anything, she'll be the one to find it.

CHAPTER 9
CINDRILL

STURGES EYES ME FROM ACROSS THE TABLE BUT GOES about his work, studying footage. Now that I'm basically alone on this side of the study, I can break into the system and cover my tracks. Vila is a sharp one and probably would have caught me if I had tried to reach out to Claude while she was sitting next to me.

My fingers slowly move over the keyboard so my guard doesn't notice, hacking into the system like Claude taught me to do. I don't have time to tell him about the shoes he made me, but I have to make sure he's alone before I tell him what I really need.

It takes a few moments—longer than I'd like—to get into his system and get him to notice my quiet appearance on the screen in his basement workroom where he creates wardrobe and gadgets for Master's missions.

When I finally get his attention, he sends me a message back asking where I am.

Once he's confirmed he's alone using a special signal we created, I tell him as much as I can get away with typing. If Sturges wasn't as mindful as Filip, I might have been able to get away with more, but sadly, he's just as keen.

Each word is painfully slow to type. Each reply is lengthy and makes the situation more bearable. Claude has been with Master longer than I have, but we truly only have each other. As uppity as Claude can be, he needs me as much as I need him.

Claude tells me everything he knows and informs me he's snooping in the bunker for more information about who hired Master and me to kill the King and Prince of Davengreen. I don't hold out much hope, but he sends me messages, keeping me informed of what he's doing. I watch them scrawl across the side of the screen while I search for Master's travels in the time since we separated—I know his many nanobot faces and have a better chance of identifying him on my own.

"Do you have access to any other cameras?" I ask, knowing Sturges is likely watching everything on my screen on his own device—good thing he can't see Claude's program on the edge of my tablet.

"Just this," he mumbles.

My name pings on the screen as Claude responds to me, drawing my attention. I wait for him to continue.

"It was her father."

The halls are dimly lit as everyone escorts me to my room for the evening. I put up a fuss about bringing my father to the palace, only to be answered with grumblings about trying to locate him.

Is Vila in on this? How much does she know about her father's plan?

We pause at her room as she volunteers to give me something to wear to bed. I slip in after her, passing by Harold who is still standing watch over the doorway.

Inside, her own people hover about, dipping into curtseys when they notice their princess gliding across the room. She smiles kindly at them and guides us to her walk-in closet. Layers of pastel-colored dresses fill the space. Shoes are quietly lined up on the floor under them, save for those in the massive cubbies at the end of the closet. Scarves hang down on one side, belts and wraps hang on the other. A set of drawers reveal a massive amount of jewelry.

"Gifts from Davengreen, mostly. I left the majority of my jewels at home until after the wedding. Daddy will send the rest of my belongings over then." She waves her hand at the glittering jewels.

"You weren't sure this was going to work?" I ask. Vila looks back at me as if I've said something wrong.

"I'm sure you know it's an arranged marriage, Cindrill. I'm doing this for the honor of my father and country, but Daddy would never force me to marry a man who was cruel to me. I'm here to make sure I won't be mistreated in the future, but the rest of my things will be sent along once we've said our vows."

"A quick exit if need be; it makes sense." I run my fingers over a necklace. Claude would have a field day ripping these apart and transforming them. "Do you plan to leave, Vila?"

In the several hours we've known each other, I can pretend we've become friends. Perhaps she'll play along out of propriety.

"I've found Prince Davian to be a good and kind man. I don't know him well, but I'm not afraid of him." She turns her back to me, rummaging through a drawer.

"You're sure he's kind?" I continue to muse, fingering the lace on the sleeve of a deep red dress, one of the few that isn't pastel.

"I believe him to be, yes. He seems kinder than his father, at least." The Princess of Briarmar turns back to me, straightening her shoulders. "I'm going to marry him, Cindrill, if that's what you're asking. He's made a commitment to *me*, and he will honor that, just as *I* will honor my commitment to *him*."

She thinks I'm angling for her to leave so I can have the prince.

"I'm glad to hear that. I think you'll be good for the future of our kingdom. I like that you're here, Vila." My words seem to set her at ease slightly. She hands me a set of light pink silk pajamas. "Thank you."

There's no way I'm taking my clothes off knowing that Master will be here to finish his mission tonight, but I take the garments to complete the act. I haven't been stomping around this palace all evening for nothing.

How much about this assassination do you know, Vila?

She smiles stiffly and nods. When I remove the silk pajamas the rest of the way from her hands, her smile fades into a genuine one. "The men will see you to your room. If there's anything you need, just ask."

My room isn't nearly as large as Vila's, but it's spacious enough that I don't know how I could ever fall asleep. My tiny room in Master's bunker is comforting—I know every inch of it. This is too grand, too open, too unknown.

As soon as I'm alone, I turn out the lights and search for a way out of the room. No panels shift on the walls, no closets give way to hidden hallways, nothing under the plush rug moves to reveal a hidden staircase. My only option is the window.

Stepping outside into the cool night air, the wind snaps against me. I draw my hood up over my hair and tuck the loose strands back so they don't whip in my face.

The roof is slanted, but the shingles offer a little resistance, and I'm able to make my way down a few rooms. I check each carefully before passing the window, simultaneously checking behind me to ensure no one on the ground is watching me.

The fourth window away offers me my best chance. I pry it open, using the nanobots as a pick. It pops open in my hand, and I quietly slip into the dark room.

The moon is high enough to offer a soft, glowing light in the room, just enough to see by now that my eyes have adjusted to being outside. I move slowly, trying not to run into anything.

If Vila's father ordered the hit on the king and his son, I need to find out why, but more than that, I need to see if Vila has anything to do with this. Master will be waiting for a signal from me, but I can put it off a little while longer, even if he *did* witness me crawling across the palace roof.

The door is quiet as I open it. I watch the men outside my door for a few minutes, waiting for a pattern in their movements. They spend most of their time watching their tablets, but they pause every two minutes to look down both sides of the hallway. I duck back inside the room as they glance my way.

When they turn to see the right side of the hall, I make my move, darting out into the hallway and throwing myself against the wall in the connecting passageway. When I don't hear anything, I risk a glance—the men haven't noticed me.

Turning back, I walk down the hall. In the wing with the study, I overhear the guards discussing the king setting up shop in the ballroom for the evening with his son. I adjust my pack on my shoulder and head toward the ballroom.

I consider using the nanobots to shield my face, but if I'm caught, I can claim I was just trying to go home to my father. If they catch me as another person, I'll have no way of explaining myself out of the situation.

I consider my options as I traipse through the palace halls. I could kill the king. Once it's done, if I flee and leave Davian to take over his father's reign, surely Master won't be able to finish the job—Claude said it had to be done the same night for it to work. The king dies, followed immediately by his son—I suppose so Vila would officially take control at that point as the next in line after her husband...or husband-to-be. The guards won't leave the prince alone if his father dies and nothing happens to Davian immediately.

I could let Master in and obstruct his ability to hurt Davian. Maybe I could hide him somewhere off the palace grounds and release him when it's safe. Master would never think to look in any of his own hiding places for the escaped prince of Davengreen.

I can hear the prince and his father talking from outside of the ballroom. The sounds drift down the hallway gently, as soft as the glow of the chandeliers. I'm on the lower level, knowing it will be easier to spy if I'm not at the top of a staircase, but it's a strange feeling to enter without descending the stairs.

Davian and his father sit on their thrones at the far end of the ballroom, leaning in toward each other to talk and point at pieces of paper. Davian holds a tablet in his hands, the blue glow bouncing off his light shirt. He's removed his dark waistcoat, and I almost miss the sight of it.

"What are you doing here?" a voice hisses behind me.

I spin, ready to attack, but Vila grabs my hood and drags me backward, away from the ballroom, choking me slightly.

"Let me go," I hiss, batting at her.

"Why are you here?"

"I was trying to leave."

"Through the ballroom?" she confronts me.

"I don't know how to get around here," I seethe.

"You managed to get past the guards just fine," she

points out. "Why are you here, Cindrill?"

Her voice is cold, and I'm certain she knows of her father's plot. He wants the throne of Davengreen, and if his daughter is the widowed princess, she'll be in control here, reverting power to him. There's no way she doesn't know about this—why else would she follow me?

"Why are you stalking me?"

"I don't trust you," she admits forcefully, still holding her voice down so the king and prince don't hear us. "My country needs this marriage, and I won't let you ruin this for us."

"*Why* do you need this marriage?" I demand answers.

"We're having trouble on our borders. We need a stronger army. We need reinforcements." Vila's eyes hold that same look they did when she spoke about her orphanage.

What if she doesn't know, my thoughts whisper. No, *she has to—her father is trying to steal an entire kingdom.*

"So, out of the goodness of your heart, you're marrying the prince so you can gain access to his armies?"

"And he's doing the same for our money…and men. There's war all around, Cindrill—I don't know if you've noticed or not, but people are dying and we're trying to save them."

"How exactly do you expect to save both countries, Vila?" I demand, circling her. She made the wrong choice engaging with me, and if it comes down to it, I'll take her out right now. "If you're pulling men from Davengreen to protect Briarmar, who will defend Davengreen?"

"We'll take turns assisting each other," she protests, huffing. Her hands clench at her sides as she realizes I'm moving around her, corralling her away from the throne room. If I can lock her in another closet until this is over, I might use that option. "Right now, the threat is greater for Briarmar, and we've got money we can give to Davian and his father."

Her voice rises in pitch with every word, suddenly worried. I'm not quite as nice as she thought I was, though, she also believes I was trying to steal her fiancé.

"I will not allow you to steal Davian away and crush my kingdom." She tries to be brave.

"I'm not stealing your fiancé, Vila. That's not why I'm here." I glare at her. "You've got two options: get in a closet and stay there until I tell you otherwise or die right now."

"You won't hurt me."

"I will," I assure her. I take a menacing step toward her. Footsteps sound behind me—the king and prince must have figured out we were out here and are coming to investigate.

I whip around, looking over my shoulder to check, but when I do, Vila lashes out, grabbing at me. She manages to spin me enough that my bag falls off my shoulder. I pull back on it in response. The shoe bounces out as the bag crashes against the floor.

Kicking out, I swipe her legs from under her. She hits the floor hard, letting out a sharp cry. The men run faster, coming to her aid, but they still have half the ballroom to traverse before reaching us—they can't tell who we are yet.

Grabbing the shoe, I pull her arm, forcing her up. She stumbles as I drag her away, tucking the shoe back in my bag.

"Make one sound and I'll make sure your jaw is wired shut for at least a month," I threaten, holding my elbow ready to strike back into her face as we run. My far hand stretches across my chest, biting into the flesh on her upper arm.

"I was kind to you," she whispers, hissing at me.

"And I was to *you*." She has no way of knowing I saved her, though. Not yet.

I'm faster than the king and his son, giving us an exceptional lead on what was already a very strong head start. I race us around corners until it will be hard to find us. Still, then men press forward, yelling for guards.

"Let go of me, Cindrill." Her words are laced with venom.

"You don't get to hurt the prince tonight, Vila. You and your father will never get away with this."

"What are you talking about?" She claws at my arm

and I shoulder-check her into a wall for good measure. She cries out. "We haven't done anything—"

"You put a hit out on the king and his son!" I shout. I didn't mean to be so loud. Then again, I also didn't mean to care at all. My job is to kill them, after all. Vila is just the one that hired us.

"We did no such thing!" Vila shouts, prying at my fingers once again.

"Your father hired an assassin to kill the king, followed by your precious husband-to-be. Don't tell me you didn't know."

Vila freezes. I'm jerked to a stop.

Her face is tight with shock. Her eyes twitch back and forth as if she's reading a tablet, trying to process everything. I see the moment she realizes what her father has done, her eyes snapping up to look at me.

"He couldn't," she whispers.

"He did." My words are harsh and uncaring. She needs me to be gentle as her world falls apart, but I refuse to be.

"My father wouldn't—" Tears fall down her face. "No, he wouldn't."

"Vila, either you knew, or he lied to you too, but either way, your father will pay for this. Now I need to know if *you* will too."

"I had no idea." Her whisper is soft as the footsteps get closer.

"Time to move." I grab her arm, forcing her along.

"How did you find out?" she asks. I don't answer. "Cindrill, how did you know? Are you protecting Davian? Why are you here?"

My eyes sweep the area, looking for somewhere to hide.

"If you don't answer me, I'll tell them everything!" she cries out.

"Why did your father hire an assassin? So you could rule once they were dead?" I shouldn't have pointed out her father's intentions given the disheveled state she's in, but I can't help but make the jab.

"Is that why you were trying to steal him away? Why are you so set on taking Davian for yourself?" she demands answers.

A loud explosion makes the ground beneath us rumble. Master has arrived.

"Get in there." I push her into a closet. "Stay quiet."

I realize too late that she's heard those words before. She looks at me in horror.

"You're here to kill him." Vila looks horrified, paling in the muted light from outside the closet.

"I'm not going to kill him." Her brows furrow, thinking. "I didn't hurt you, and I'm not going to hurt him."

A second, louder explosion knocks me off my feet. Master is serious this time.

"Go," Vila says, believing me.

I have one chance to stop this.

CHAPTER 10
DAVIAN

THE LIGHTS TWITCH, BLINKING OVERHEAD. AT LEAST ONE of the bulbs is flickering on and off, hovering between life and death. I sit up, trying to figure out what's happening, but the chandelier crashes a few feet away, spewing glass everywhere.

Next to me, my father lays still, propped up against the wall. I shake him, and he groans.

"What happened?"

"There was an explosion."

"Where?" My father sits upright, more alert. Blood trickles from a cut on his temple where he hit the wall, but he seems to be okay other than that.

The scent of dust fills the air—the explosion couldn't have been too far away. The guards call our names.

"Here!" I shout, thinking it might not have been my best choice after the fact.

Filip rounds the corner with several men behind him.

"There's been a breach."

"Yes," a dark voice adds from down the hall. "There has."

The assassin.

Filip's face mirrors my own—covered in terror. Everyone grabs my father, forcing him to run as I stumble to my feet.

Two men run behind me—Filip and one of his team. They raise their weapons, holding their orders silent as we rush down the hall.

Splitting up, we follow procedure, ensuring at least one of us has a better chance of survival. The last I see of my father, he's stumbling down the left corridor toward a safe room hidden in one of the sitting rooms. My leg throbs, but I won't stop.

"Oh, Your Highness..." the assassin's voice calls, changing tones. He must be using some device to change what he sounds like as he taunts us.

I'm simultaneously relieved and horrified when he moves to the right, following us instead of my father.

"Go," Filip whispers harshly. *"Get there."*

He doesn't use the words, afraid the assassin will hear, but he means for me to get to the infirmary where we've set up a blockade that should keep the assassin out. Inside the medical wing of the palace, we've got a secondary room, so even if he *can* breach the medical wing, he won't be able to get to me.

"*Don't*," I warn harshly. I know Filip will stay behind to try to stop him.

"Move," Filip directs.

"What about the girls? Cindrill and Vila?" I question, realizing I had been on my way to investigate whatever Vila was yelling about outside of the ballroom when the explosion rocked the palace.

"I'll find them."

"You'll be dead," I correct, reminding him he's about to try to take on a murderer we've been trying to escape since his first attempt on my life.

"Sturges will find them."

"Tell him," I insist, knowing Sturges will prioritize my father and I. Vila will be prioritized too as a foreign dignitary and the sole link to Briarmar and Davengreen's survival, but Cindrill will be on her own, once again because of me.

Filip taps his radio and relays my demands to his counterpart as the assassin picks up his pace. He's no longer trying to hide—he *wants* to terrorize us.

Ahead, Dr. Romani flings the door open to the infirmary and motions us forward silently. The men pull me forward, knowing I'm already trying to find a way out of the infirmary so I can find Cindrill and Vila and ensure they're safe.

"You too," Dr. Romani whispers after I'm pushed through the door. "You're the only one that can keep him in place in here."

Filip stumbles in behind me, crashing into my back as the doctor pulls him into the room, closing the door. My friend looks surprised when I wheel around to face him.

"Did you—?" He stumbles. "Did you just pull me in here?"

He whips around to glare at Dr. Romani.

"You would have died out there facing whatever you were running from alone—*I assume that assassin*—and we both know Davian would have tried to escape to save Cindrill again, so you tell me…should I have left you out there?"

Something slams against the door, leaving a dent in the metal. We jerk around to look.

He's approaching the infirmary.

Voices mumble outside the door. The girl is with him.

"The feeds," Filip mumbles, pushing me back. "Go to the room. I'll pull the feeds up."

I follow his commands, knowing that if both the assassin and the murderess are here with us, they aren't with my father, Cindrill, or Vila. We'll be protected locked in the safe room inside the bunker disguised as a medical wing, and keeping their attention here will give our men time to formulate a plan and take them down.

The screens in the room burst to life with a blue glow, quickly taking on the shapes of the hallways outside of us as Filip assesses the situation. He quickly calls back and forth to the security room as he coordinates a plan with our men.

I stare at the screen that shows the outside of the infirmary. The assassin is tall, covered in black clothing once again. He has a hood over his head, concealing him even when he *does* turn toward the camera.

A woman is standing next to him. Her clothes are strikingly similar to Cindrill's, but it's clearly not her face peeking out from under the hood. I'm terrified that she could have taken the garments from Cindrill—but then, Cindrill knows how to protect herself, and I see no tears in the fabric or blood on the cloth. Cindrill wouldn't have given up her clothing willingly, and with no sign of struggle, I can only assume she's fine and didn't encounter the assassin woman.

The two talk to each other for a moment before turning toward the door. The woman stands back as the man attempts to break in. He holds his arm out and something crawls off it.

"Filip!" I backhand him so hard he nearly drops his tablet as he jolts. Then I point. "That's what I saw!"

He stares at the screen hanging on the wall above us, leaning closer.

"What is that?"

"I don't know, but that's what happened to the assassin's face."

"What?" Dr. Romani demands, eyes wide as I turn to him.

"Her face..." I start. "When she was running away after shoving Vila in the closet...it shattered...or something, I don't know."

Our view is obscured, and I can't tell what is happening with the thing that crawled off the man's hand.

"Watch him." I direct the others as I latch on to the woman in the frame. There has to be *something* to help us.

Another man walks up to them—a third assassin. The lead man is taller and stronger looking, but this one sidles up to the woman and tips his head toward her, saying something.

After a moment, the door to the infirmary swings open as if the tall man hadn't had to lift a finger. Filip goes still next to me. "How is that possible?"

"They can get in here, can't they?" Dr. Romani voices the question we all have battling inside our heads. We're no longer safe in this fortress.

"We need a plan." Filip's words move us all into action.

On the screens, I catch sight of the assassins walking

toward us. They don't seem to care about the medical supplies laying around, they just search for where we might be hiding.

The woman ducks to look under every table and bed, trying quickly to keep up with the men, but the tall assassin doesn't seem concerned. It's almost as if he knows where we'll be.

His hand looks intact once more. Nothing appears to have changed, but we all saw it, didn't we?

Once again, I freeze, watching the woman—she seems to be the wildcard. If we can appeal to her senses, perhaps she'll side with us. She saved Vila and defied the man once before—maybe money would be a suitable reason to change her allegiances. I'm willing to try anything.

She ducks again, searching more frantically for us, but the man doesn't stop. "What are you doing?" I whisper.

"Trying to block the door," Filip replies, not realizing I'm speaking to the girl on the screen. "How about a little help, *Your Highness?*"

Right. Help.

I turn, rushing to the door the men are trying to brace.

"Sturges says your father is safe," Filip adds when I take a place by him.

"Any word on Vila and Cindrill?" I ask, hearing the frantic tone in my voice. I didn't mean to sound like that.

"Nothing yet, I'm afraid. I'm sure they're fine. The girl saved Vila before, so maybe she did it again."

"I hope."

A strange sound hums just above our voices and everyone freezes. The noise persists, but softer. It's enough to terrify us all. Whatever the assassin had done to open the infirmary doors, he was doing it again.

This time, on the screens, we can see it all. Some type of device crawls off the assassin and covers part of the door, moving like a silent wave as it changes the door. With each movement, the hum changes—the inner workings of the door bending to the will of the creature forcing its hand.

"They're bots," Filip whispers. "He has technology we barely have access to, Davian. Those are nanobots. No wonder he was able to get away with so much."

He shakes his head.

"We stay and fight; we give the prince a chance. Davian, you go out of the back entrance and get as far from the palace as you can. Go into hiding. Do whatever you need to do, but don't stay here. We'll hold him off."

"I can't—"

"Yes, you can, Davian. When he's done here, he's going after your father and we might not be able to stop him. You may be the only hope for the people at this point, and you might be the only one who can get away. You have to go. The second this door opens, you run, do you understand?"

Dr. Romani wheels around to face me. "He's right, lad. You have to go. We'll cover for you here, and we'll do our best to protect your father, but one of you has to survive this night. This is your job—your duty."

I nod. Leaving him behind will be like leaving a second father to be lost to the assassin. I have no choice but to do as he asks.

But first, I'll find Cindrill and Vila and take them with me.

The door creeks—it's nearly open. Filip and the others raise their weapons, prepared to fight. On the screen, the assassins raise their weapons too.

I wait by the hidden door, prepared to make my move. I make my peace with saying goodbye to my friends as they valiantly give the crown a chance to save the kingdom from this madman.

The moment the door opens, I escape out of the back. Shouts rise up behind me.

"Cindrill!" someone shouts. I wheel back around.

CHAPTER 11
CINDRILL

THE NANOBOTS ON MY FACE SCURRY AWAY AS MASTER forces the door open. I need them to know who I am, even if it means I'll be on the run for the rest of my life.

Waiting until the door starts to open, I hold my hands up where Master can't see me. Claude catches sight of me and nods, doing the same as he takes my side and backs me. Filip and the others have guns trained on us.

I know I'm signing my own death certificate, but the prince and his father shouldn't die because Briarmar's king wants to take power from them without starting a war—it will be easier to get Davengreen to cooperate if they think Vila is legally and rightfully in charge. Turning on Master is the worst thing I can do, but Davian is behind those men somewhere, and I don't want him to die tonight.

"Cindrill," Filip says loudly, shocked to see me. My nanobots congregate just below my collar, waiting for orders.

Master wheels around to me, driving the butt of his gun into my stomach. I keel over, thrown off by Filip's proclamation. I clutch at my abdomen, gasping for air. I've never been caught this off guard before with Master; at least, not since I was in training.

Claude looks like he wants to move toward me, but he doesn't dare with Master's anger lashing out like tentacles ready to slice us in half. Claude will support me, but he knows how to play the game.

Filip races forward, prepared to engage. I kick out, slamming into one of Master's boots. He stumbles forward just enough to knock his gun to tip down. It goes off, firing into a guard's leg. He screams in pain.

Master reels around, prepared to end me. Leaping to my feet, I strike. Behind Master, Filip and the others attack, trying to pull him from me.

I'm faster than anyone expected and slam into Master, ripping part of the nanobot mask from his face. The creatures blink bright blue where I tore them apart, more racing up to replace the ones I throw on the ground.

Claude gasps as I ruin his creation but uses the scene to fuel him. He's not a fighter like I am, but he knows how to use his technology to his advantage. Using something on his wrist, he taps commands.

Master suddenly shouts in pain, frightening us all. With his voice modulator disabled, he sounds like himself. The nanobots retract from his face, taking pieces of his skin with them at Claude's direction. If Master gets the upper hand, neither of his minions' deaths will be pretty or painless—we'll suffer for this.

Claude wields the nanobots against Master brilliantly, and I use the distraction to attack. The bullets do nothing against the body armor he's wearing, but that doesn't stop Filip from trying. He and his men shoot at Master, regardless of the fact that I'm directly on the other side of him, ducking his punches. A bullet rips past me.

Somewhere above the insane noise of the infirmary, I hear Davian's voice as he directs his men in Filip's absence as he continues to launch bullets at Master, focused completely on killing the man and not on giving orders. If I can turn Master around so that his hood can't protect him, Filip might have a chance of killing him. If not, I have to end Master's life tonight, or we'll *all* be dead by morning.

"It was the king of Briarmar!" Claude shouts to Davian's men. He knows the odds are stacked against us, but perhaps one of them will survive to put an end to Briarmar's destruction. "He had planned to marry his daughter off to your prince and then kill the king and his son so his daughter would gain control. She'd never know and would listen to whatever he told her to do. It was a coup!"

Master ducks as I swing at him and I catch a peek of Filip's face as it all clicks for him.

"It wasn't Vila's fault!" I scream, making sure he knows she wasn't in on the plan. I truly believe her heart was too pure for her father to let her in on his secret.

Something crashes behind us just before Master's hand connects with my jaw. I hit the floor, the nanobots rushing to my defense as they form a mask around my face. If Master hits me now, he'll regret the pain that comes with it.

Claude rushes to me, picking me up off the floor. His fighting experience may be limited, but we both know Master better than anyone else in this room. My friend raises his fists, his dark features homing in on the man that controls our lives. Today, we gain our freedom in life or in death.

"I command you to stop!" Vila's voice fills the room.

"You can't command me to do anything, little girl," Master replies, his voice sounding eerily normal. "Not even your father can stop this. You're just lucky I haven't killed you yet. He didn't specify that I should spare you—he's your next of kin, so the line of succession would go to him anyway, and he'd have one less pesky problem to worry about."

"I speak on behalf of my father," she tries to say again, voice harsh.

"What did I just say, *girl?*" Master spits his words at her. "Leave or die with the rest of them."

My master's gun turns from me, training on the princess. Davian runs across the room, attempting to block the bullet. I reach forward just as the gun goes off, knocking it up. The bullet ricochets off the ceiling and slams back down into a table. The noise just encourages everyone else to attack.

Several men lay on the ground with bullets in them. A few are dead or close to it, but a handful only have minor injuries. I managed to distract Master enough that his shooting skills were thrown off during the fight and people are alive still because of it.

The rest of the men move to take him down as Davian runs toward Vila. He scoops her into his arms and forces her out of the room to protect her.

It feels empty in the room with them gone, but more guards join us, breaking into the room easily through the already-open door Master left behind.

Claude continues typing something into his wrist keyboard, and Master is frozen in place.

"I knew it would work!" Claude says out loud. I smile. He always gets so worked up when his inventions work. He runs his fingers through his thick, black hair.

Unable to turn, Master stretches around, attempting to mow down anyone who approaches him. The gun pops as he moves, spraying bullets as men dive behind turned-over tables. I count.

One bullet left.

Filip counted too and instructs the men forward. They carefully move out from around the tables, slowly stepping toward the monster I call my master.

Davian bursts back into the room, but it's fallen deathly silent. Master doesn't even flinch. This is between the two of us now. He's already failed at his mission, and he doesn't have enough time to reach for more ammunition before the guards destroy him. His last act will be one of retribution.

The men move forward.

Master raises his weapon at me.

"One more step and she dies."

"Don't stop," I command the men. "Finish him."

Master doesn't waiver.

The men tackle him and Master pulls the trigger.

The nanobots race off my face toward my gushing wound. Davian's face falls in the distance as I reel backward. My eyes close before I hit the floor.

"That was stupid," Claude says, hovering over me. He's more emotional than usual. "You knew he would shoot you."

Pain courses through my body.

"An inch to the left and you'd be dead, Cindrill." Claude doesn't sound impressed by my bravado.

"But at least *he's* dead."

"Yes, they got him. It was miraculously hard, too, even frozen in place."

"You thought he'd go easily?" I wince as he moves the nanobots out of the hole in my chest. It feels like a million tiny insects are crawling inside of my injury.

"They'll be done soon." Claude softens. "*You'll* be done soon."

"Is everyone else okay?" I ask. My nose wrinkles as I cringe at the feeling again.

"Eight died, another six were injured. The prince is fine if that's what you're asking."

"Vila?"

"Confused, I hear." He dabs at my wound with a gauze pad. "She'll live."

"How does the king feel about her now?"

"From what Filip has told me, he's allowing her to stay. They will continue with the marriage, but the king already sent men to detain her father. In a perfect twist, he will use Briarmar's own plot against them and take control of their country."

My heart sinks...or maybe that's from the bots squirming an inch from that particular organ as they work their way to the top of the wound, crawling out of my skin as they close it up.

"Almost," Claude murmurs, leaning forward to examine me. "Just closing up the skin now."

He holds a container out against my shoulder and the nanobots that finished their work wheel themselves back inside. I close my eyes and breathe as the tiny pieces sew my skin together.

Glancing down, I realize all of the other bots have been taken from my body. The mark on my neck is exposed, as is the gash over my foot. Funny, Claude had time to fix my heart, but not my foot.

"You missed a spot." I motion toward my foot.

He tsks at me. "What precisely did you do to my shoe, madam?"

"You can blame Davian for that one. It's in my bag."

"Blaming me again, I see," Davian's dark voice breaks the discussion. "Seems everything is my fault these days."

His laugh holds no humor. Davian's eyes are darker than I remember. It's a terrifying picture.

"I hear you're getting married," I comment, trying to judge his reaction.

"I hear you're getting arrested for treason," he retorts, lips pursed.

"She saved you," Claude hisses at him.

"Careful, boy," Davian speaks down to my friend, even though he's clearly much older. "We haven't worked out all your crimes yet, but I suggest you let us focus on her."

Claude holds up the open container of nanobots, and they form a shape that appears to snap at the prince. My friend smirks as if the prince should be terrified, but Davian's lips just tug down, deepening his frown. "Don't tempt me."

"He didn't do anything, Davian," I say harshly, hoping Davian doesn't know Claude is the one who got the palace schematics for Master. "He's locked away in a basement creating wardrobe pieces and fixing nanobots. He's never hurt anyone. *I'm* the assassin."

Davian turns his cold eyes on me.

"Yes, I saw."

Walking closer, he glances at my foot and grimaces at the red scab he left. He turns to Claude. "Get out. I want a word with the assassin."

Claude straightens. "No."

"Go, Claude," I interject. "What's he going to do to me?"

He huffs, hovering for a moment before following my instructions. Claude leaves the open container of nanobots by my head, ready to take my commands.

"You lied this entire time," Davian says, gripping his hands behind his back.

"Did I have a choice?"

"How many people have you killed?"

"None personally." I try not to make eye contact, but his face is magnetic; I can't help but look. Everything softens, my face melting when I see him. Davian twitches slightly.

"You were going to kill me?"

"I was going to help," I admit. Davian steps closer.

"What changed?" He sounds as if everything in his world depends on my answer.

"I found out what was happening. I know the country has issues with you, Your Highness, but then I found out it was because you were protecting them from things they didn't need to know. When I learned it was Briarmar…"

"You decided not to do it," he finishes for me. "And you spared Vila…twice."

"She wasn't involved."

"I know," he says quickly, nodding. "She's the one who sent me in here."

"Why?" I question. The curtain shifts behind him as if someone walked by and created a breeze.

"Vila won't marry me. She says neither of us would be happy. She's agreed to form a treaty with me, and I've agreed to give her kingdom back to her as a sign of good faith as long as her father pays the price."

"You're going to kill him?" My eyes are wide. Davian looks shocked.

"No, who do you think I am, *you*? We don't *kill* people here. That's not how things are done," he chastises, taking a jab at me. "He will be held accountable for his crimes and will live in a dark cell just inside our border under our control and Vila's where she can easily visit him, but he can't do any more harm."

"So, Vila will rule, and you'll help her."

"I will."

"Why did she send you here, Davian. What good could that possibly do?"

I try to sit up but end up in a coughing fit. Surprisingly, it hurts less than I expect.

"You shouldn't do that right after being shot." His voice is quiet as he slips a hand behind my back to help guide me upright. I slip the strap of my shirt up over my shoulder, covering it. Claude must have taken me out of the rest of my outer layers to work on healing me with the nanobots. At least he left the half skirt wrapped around my pants—it's comforting to have it drape next to me.

I laugh coolly. "Wouldn't want me to die before my prison stint, huh?"

"I don't want to see you hurt, Cindrill." He lets go of the hard edges of his expression. "She sent me here because she thinks you and I belong together."

"And what do *you* think about that?" I'm still not sure where he stands.

Davian sighs, stepping backward with a slight limp. He walks around the foot of the raised cot, turning to move back again.

He holds the defaced shoe up from where he pulls it from the bag on the chair. The prince steps closer.

Davian slides the green, twisted shoe onto my injured foot.

"I knew I'd find you," he mutters, a smile tugging at his lips as he traces the skin next to what will likely end up as a scar. He turns to face me.

"I'm Davian," he says stepping toward me with an outstretched hand. "I'm the Prince of Davengreen, a fairly poor judge of when I should and shouldn't be running into buildings after pretty girls, and someone who tries to make things easier on others, even if it means getting pushed into a shuttle in the Epicenter that I'm not supposed to be on."

I take his hand, smirking as I think about the shuttle ride. His reintroduction is an offer to start over, one I'm happy to take advantage of without hesitation.

"I'm Cindrill—former assassin, excellent fighter, great judge of how far of a drop off a roof really is, and avid shuttle rider."

"Any chance you'd like to give me a few lessons on how to properly use the kingdom's shuttle system?" His eyes sparkle as he continues to hold my hand.

"You might be able to talk me into it," I reply, smiling up at him.

Maybe showing up at that palace to assassinate the royals *wasn't* the wrong choice after all. For now, though, I have to tell him how to catch the other assassins Master and I worked with.

SUGARCOATED

A Hansel and Gretel's Witch Retelling

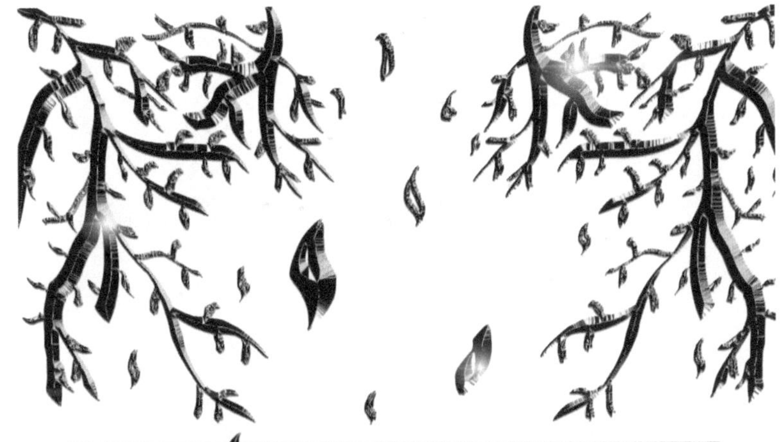

SUGARCOATED

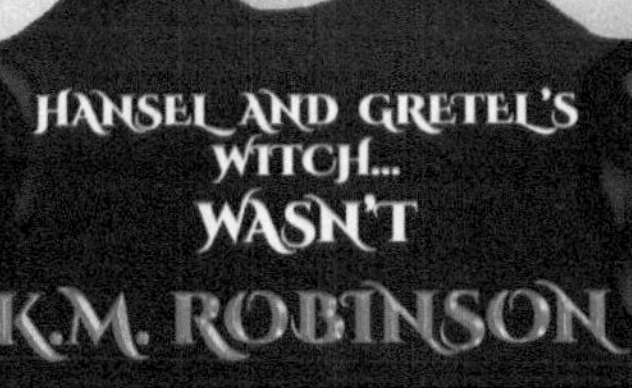

HANSEL AND GRETEL'S
WITCH...
WASN'T
K.M. ROBINSON

CHAPTER 1

SWEETS GIVE US THE ILLUSION OF HAPPINESS, BECKONING us to sample brightly-colored sugar treats and revel in their sweetness...until they destroy us from the inside out and make our worlds crumble.

"Your brother will be here soon," I remind the small girl. "You need to get into position before he arrives."

"Annika, really? Can't we just wait until we see him coming?" She heaves a sigh as she traipses back over to the container. The blonde girl lifts her foot, nearly tangling herself in her skirt.

"You need to get used to it if you're going to help the cause, Gretel. You'll be in there for a long time." I almost hope my words might convince her to walk away from this mission—killing the king is no place for a little girl. The other half of me knows that she is our only chance at ending this.

"You sound like my brother," she grumbles.

"Yes, and *you* look like him," I snip at her, grinning. "Now, in."

Gretel drops down into the barrel that used to contain flour, her blonde braids dipping below the rim. I set the lid on, leaving just enough space so that air can flow in and out. If there's time, I'll inch the lid over before Hansel comes to collect her.

I walk gently over to the window, lecturing Gretel on the importance of controlling her breathing in small spaces while I keep an eye out for her brother. Just like every day for the past three months, he should be arriving any moment from the woods after work.

Right on cue, he saunters down the path, pack over his shoulder. I duck behind the curtain before he has a chance to notice me. Scurrying over to where Gretel is hiding in the barrel by the fireplace, I bump the lid.

"Showtime," I whisper to myself. Lifting my hand, I brush back a piece of hair. In my peripheral vision, I notice a bit of flour on my hand from the barrel—I imagine Gretel will come out white as a ghost. We'll have to clean her off before she leaves so we aren't discovered.

"Annika," Hansel regards me as the door swings open.

His tall frame fills the doorway, and I feel myself blush as he smiles. "Is Gretel ready?"

"You can take her home if you can find her," I reply, turning away from him. I busy myself kneading bread.

Hansel sighs heavily, dropping the bag on the ground by the table leg. I glance down as I work, but don't comment—I know he's intentionally going to leave the delivery here for me so I can work on our project this evening.

He walks around the room, quizzically appraising everything as he searches for his younger sister's hiding spot. Hansel crosses an arm over his chest, grabbing his elbow as his free hand migrates toward his chin.

"Well, she's obviously not *in* the fireplace," he muses. His footsteps are heavy and intentional. "And I know you didn't move the fireplace—I measured after the last time. She's not in the loft. You hid her under the floorboards yesterday, so I'm guessing you wouldn't repeat that."

Hansel steps closer to me before reaching up to flick the long strands of my bangs back, smirking. I consider making it look like the fireplace has moved a foot while he's busy staring at me, but I don't.

"I can't help but notice the flour in your hair, mistress baker, might that be a clue?" His nose is an inch away from my ear, and I shudder as his breath ripples against my skin. Blinking, I try to keep my composure.

"A clue that I run a bakery? Why, *yes*, however did you

guess?" My words are sickly sweet. His eyes spark with laughter.

"Where is she, Annika?" he whispers quietly.

"You can come out, Gretel," I call, refusing to give him her location.

The lid scrapes off the barrel. Hansel turns back toward the fireplace, dropping the strand of my hair he was twisting around his finger. His face lights up when Gretel appears.

"Well," he drawls. "There she is. Not bad, little sister. I never would have guessed."

"Not until you tried to move the barrel," I add.

"Oh, I don't know about that. Gretel's as heavy as a barrel of flour now." He offers his sister a hand as she smacks at him for his joke. At thirteen, Gretel is the resistance's best weapon.

"You realize I have to take her home, right?" Hansel teases. "I can't take her out of here looking like she just lost a fight with Winter."

He bends down and starts brushing the flour off of Gretel's dress. The barrel was mostly empty, but everywhere Gretel brushes against the sides of it, traces of the white fluff adhered itself to her clothing. I could create the illusion of her being clean and save some time, but it would only last until they got halfway home.

"See you tomorrow," Gretel says, waving as her brother herds her out the door.

"See you tomorrow, Annika," Hansel adds in a deep voice. He tosses a look back at me, and I know it won't be long before he returns for his bag.

Once they're gone, I scoop it up and paw through the contents. Hansel doesn't mind me going through his things, but somehow it always feels a little wrong, despite the fact that he's hidden pieces of our device inside his belongings for me.

I come up with an apple in my hand, a small ribbon tied around the stem. I try to bite back my grin, but he's not here to see me, so I allow myself this small moment as I twist his gift in my fingers.

Hansel and I have worked together for years, but our mission is too important to let our feelings get in the way of what we need to accomplish. Still, the last few weeks, Hansel hasn't seemed to care. I told him it was a bad idea last week when he kissed me…that hasn't stopped us from kissing again since. It's reckless, but I've always felt Hansel was meant for me.

"Not bad," I murmur, holding the hinge up to the light when I find it in his bag. It would fit perfectly inside of the compartment. I set to work installing it before night falls and it becomes harder to see.

A few hours go by before I hear Hansel knock. I set down the tools I'm using and walk to the door—somehow this is easier when he just walks in to pick up

Gretel—the formality of knocking sets me on edge. His grin does not.

"Did it work?" he asks, stepping into the shadows of the room. He scoops me into his arms, and I drop the hand I had poised to cast an illusion over the room to protect my work had it not been Hansel at the door. The moon is partially in the sky, though twilight still glitters above us.

"Seems like it." I motion toward the tall outline of a tiered cake.

Hansel's arms drag around me as he steps toward the fake pastry.

"Your father would be so proud, Annika." He tosses a look back at me. His muscles flex as he steps around the mobile hiding place I wheeled out of the back room to work on. "I know you never wanted to follow in his foot-steps, but God himself had to plan to put you here in our time of need."

Hansel strides back over to me, wrapping his arms around my waist once again.

"The resistance would be lost without you, Annika. No one else has been able to get us this close to the king." The fate of our country somehow rests on two eighteen-year-olds and a thirteen-year-old-assassin.

Outside, the fireworks explode in the sky with streaks of white light. It illuminates the rooftops in the distance, round and sloping in candy-colored stripes. Walls glitter against the burst of light.

"Right on time," Hansel mumbles, leaning in to press his lips against mine.

"This joke is getting old, Hansel," I mumble, silently willing him not to stop kissing me. My breath catches as he pulls back.

"You would prefer I talk business during the display?" His smirk casts deep shadows over his face as the sky lights up again.

"I didn't say that," I mumble, his lips roaming over mine as his hands tangle in my hair. Brown locks slip from the loose bun on top of my head.

The tangy scent of apple hovers between us from the present he left me earlier, lingering on my lips as he separates them. All around us, candles grow brighter, intensifying as Hansel pushes me backward toward the table. I bump into it, dropping to sit on the workspace as I drag him down with me.

Hansel pulls back to grin, light dancing over his face as it grows even more golden. His hand reaches behind me, steadying himself as he leans back down to kiss me.

"You should learn to control that," I tease.

"You make me light up, what can I say, Annika?" His voice is low, and dangerous enough that my stomach twists up. "The lights only do what I tell them to do."

Fireworks crackle outside over the city, casting a white glow over us for a moment, mixing with the golden gleam of the candles burning brightly enough to be a raging wildfire.

"And you think letting the king's guards know we're here is a good idea—they can probably see us from the city the way this place looks like it's ablaze."

Hansel's eyes crackle and spark like the flames around us, but he lowers his eyelids, forcing himself to consider my words.

"Fine." He sighs, dousing the lights until only two glow dimly off to the side. "Happy now, mistress baker?"

I was happier when he was kissing me, but I refuse to say it out loud.

"I'm happy that I don't have to whip up an illusion to keep the guards from noticing us," I pretend to chide, ducking under his arm as I slide away from the table.

"Annika," he calls quietly. A candle near me bursts.

I turn as he illuminates the fireplace again, the last of the fireworks fading in the sky outside the window. I wander back over to him but hover just out of reach.

Glancing up, I create a crystal chandelier above us. It picks up the firelight and glitters around the room.

"And here I thought *I* was going to be the one to get us caught." He smirks, revealing deep dimples on his cheeks.

"Well, I need something pretty to inspire me now that I can start working on the cake again. It's a good thing that hinge fits, Hansel."

"I know, but we have it now and we can move forward with our plans." He reaches forward and carefully wraps an arm around my waist as he turns me toward where I've hidden the wooden cake form.

"Is she ready?" I ask, waving my hand to unveil the cake. The cloak drops from around it like a sheet, the illusion wall disappearing before our eyes to reveal the cake.

"I hope so," Hansel whispers. "You'd know more than me. One more reason we'd be lost without you."

"Hansel, are *you* ready?" I ask cautiously. We've been preparing for this for what seems like an entire lifetime, but now that the time is drawing near, we're all a little terrified of what could go wrong.

"I'll save her," he whispers quietly, but his grimace is a silent admission that he's scared of what might happen.

"You will," I whisper back, wrapping my hand around his arm. Sometimes, he still flinches when I touch him, as if he's not expecting me to be so familiar with him, but he looks down to me, soft smile on his lips and lowers his face to me.

"She'll be all right," he says after a moment. "She's got both of us—we'll make sure she's safe."

"You'll pull her back, Hansel," I assure him. "We'll all make it through."

An explosion ripples outside. The entire house shakes under the weight of the blast. If the chandelier I created had been real, the glass would have clinked together and fallen to the floor, smashing into a million pieces. Instead, it's the only thing that doesn't move.

"What in the name of the king's court?" Hansel races to the window, ground still trembling.

"What do you see?" I ask, pausing just long enough to cover the room in an illusion to conceal our secret.

By the time I reach the window, smoke fills the air, dancing in the night. Hansel douses the lights so we can see outside without interference.

My hand feels cold as I place it along the window sill. The king must have had an enemy in our sister town, but instead of dealing with it discretely like he usually does, he took down what I estimate to be half the tiny town. Thankfully it's in the opposite direction that Hansel and Gretel's home is in, though I'm sure if they blew something up, the guards will also be making the rounds to look for others to destroy.

"How fast can you finish that cake, Annika?" Hansel's voice is dark. If he's willing to speed up the timeline like this, it must be worse than I think.

"What do you know about this, Hansel? What did you see today?"

Hansel spends his days traveling for work and has his ear to the ground more than any of us. Nothing happens in this country that he doesn't have a way of learning about.

"If it's who I think it is, it's not one of ours."

My eyes close in relief. I'm horrified that someone has died tonight, but at least it's not one of our own.

Hansel opens his mouth to speak, but I cut him off. "Gretel."

He pauses, jaw still open for the briefest of moments before he closes it and nods. Hansel pulls me close, kissing me hard.

"Be safe." His voice echoes in my head as he rushes to the door. Once outside, he spins and looks at me, demanding I cast an illusion.

Shaking my head to pull myself from the fog, I arch my hand, transforming the bakery into a rundown old building. The lights go out on the outside, leaving nothing but a shadowy old house that's about to fall apart. Only the window remains for him to see me.

Hansel nods, approving of my choice. Quickly, he ducks his head and turns away, running from the bakery toward Leipden where he left Gretel in the care of his great aunt.

I wave my hand again, concealing the window from the outside.

Inside, I throw strings of lights around the room, casting a white glow over my workspace. I tear down the illusion wall and reveal the cake form again so I can work —I won't be sleeping tonight.

The king must die, and my chandelier-lit handiwork

will be the trojan horse that leads to his death at the hands of a thirteen-year-old girl that acts as a guardian of death and life.

Hansel casts a worried look at me as he drops off Gretel the next morning. She rushes in, clearly having slept through the explosion—though she was farther away and it might not have made an impact in Leipden—and dances around the room.

As soon as Hansel is down the drive, Gretel drops her act.

"What happened?" she demands, taking me by surprise. "He didn't tell me, but it can't be good."

"An explosion," I answer. "That's as much as I know. I'm sure he'll learn more about it today."

"We need to move up the timeline," she replies. Her jaw twitches with nerves—something I've seen repeatedly over our time together.

"We can't exactly convince the king to change his party, Gretel," I remind her. "He's already sent word on what he wants for his cake. In a week, we'll deliver the one we made for you instead. We have to be patient, darling."

"A week and two days," Gretel murmurs, brushing back her long hair. *Of course* she would know the exact countdown—it's the day *she* might die as well. She drops her hand quickly, face hardening. "Can't we force his hand?"

"For a ball?" I scoff. "No, our plan is a good one, but we can't even suggest he move up his party or he will know something is wrong."

"I just want to get this over with." She's frustrated, and I can't blame her.

"We'll get you out of there, Gretel." My words are soft as I try to soothe her fears. "Hansel won't let anything bad happen to you."

"I'm killing the king of Candestrachen." She looks at me incredulously. "I'll do what I must."

Gretel has always been willing to sacrifice herself for the cause—better to give up a few lives and save the masses than to watch us all perish at the hands of a corrupt and unpredictable king—but Hansel and I are willing to do what we must to keep her alive. Besides, we might need her again for the next man who rises to power.

"They won't even know it's you, Gretel, I promise. You'll look like someone else entirely."

"If you can get in the door," she reminds me. Turning, she makes her way to the cake form.

"I have to bring the cake in. I'll find a way to be in the room, Gretel. I won't let you down. Once it's over, Hansel will pull you back and get you out of there."

"His lightness and my darkness," she muses.

"You have life and death, Gretel." I walk up behind her and take her long mane in my hands. Braiding it quietly, I add, "Hansel has light. He will pull you back from the darkness when you destroy King Levin. I know you don't like using death, but we're all grateful to you, Gretel."

She's quiet for a long time. I would be terrified if I were in her position. Entering the palace in a Trojan cake with the intent of killing the mad king—if anything goes off plan even in the slightest—there's no telling what the crown would do to a thirteen-year-old assassin.

"Will you at least give me brown hair like yours? And make me look older?" She places her request for an illusion to change her appearance while in the palace.

"Would you like my face too, Gretel?" I laugh.

"No, but only because they'd come after you afterward." She turns, and the braid falls from my hand.

"What's wrong with your hair, my little darling?" I prompt, hands on my hips. A smirk tugs at my lips but I try to hold it back.

"Nothing," she remarks, curving around me to walk along the wall toward the window. The girl touches a plant sitting there and it springs to life, bursting with flowers. "I just like yours better. Besides, if I'm going to look different, I should look *very* different."

"Fine, brunette it is. Now, do you intend on helping

today, or are you planning on frolicking around the bakery all day growing things?"

She turns to see what else she can sprout with her touch in the cool fall weather. Before she can notice, I create a few vines as an illusion a few feet away. Gretel moves to touch them, but she can't make them grow.

I flick my fingers by my side, changing the positions of the vines. My charge turns around to glare at me. "Very funny."

"I try." I don't bother hiding my grin this time.

"You and Hansel were made for each other." Gretel rolls her eyes. She doesn't know about us yet, but if we survive the assassination, we'll have to tell her.

"Well, what do you expect, little bird? We were raised by our fathers—they were practically like brothers, so of course, we have the same training."

"Yes, *that's* what I meant," she mumbles so low that I almost miss it. Perhaps she *does* have an idea of what's going on without her.

"Come along, Gretel. I've had enough of waiting around for answers. We're going to town for supplies."

"Hansel will be furious." That doesn't stop her. She grabs a cloak from the rack by the door and wraps it around her shoulders. Bright pink tones make her hair pop, and her eyes sparkle as she looks back at me.

I wrap a brilliant blue and lavender shawl around my shoulders, the long center corner hanging down my back.

The tassels tickle against my arms, but no matter what walk of life you are from, in the towns of Candestrachen, the women are meant to be seen in bright colors and ornate clothing.

My long skirt bounces around my ankles as I walk. It's a muted gray color—one that would be entirely unacceptable in town under normal circumstances, but it's best for baking in. When we finish walking through the woods, I'll use an illusion and make myself more presentable.

Gretel flicks her wrist and brings a blueberry bush back to life, fruit springing out of its branches. She pauses long enough to gather a handful of berries and pats the bush as if it were a dog. Holding her hand out, she offers me some.

I indulge, but only a few so she can have the rest. Gretel is about to save us all—she should have whatever her heart desires in the coming days.

Music swells up in the distance. Gretel sighs, displeased with the display we're too far away to see.

When we reach the edge of the tree line, I transform my dress into a brilliant gown that matches the cotton candy colors of the center of the town of Leipden. We round the corner and reach the true spectacle.

King Levin doesn't like for his people to work where he can see them. Anyone trapped inside of the city centers is forced to create a spectacle for the king and his guests to see, as if the entire country were one big festival. People like Hansel and I who live outside of the town limits were given permission to work, but the poor souls inside still had to provide for their families without any source of income—we help however we can, but it's still not enough.

Young men sometimes sneak out to live with relatives in the woods while the women stay behind to cover for them using their flashy dresses to catch the noblemen's eye in the streets as they bustle about, pretending to be happy. When Hansel and the others find the ones that escaped, they put them to work, giving them a place to belong and a way to help their families back in the towns.

Gretel falls behind me just slightly, her now-vibrant dress bouncing with each step. She stays behind my elbow as she follows me through the streets.

"Good morning, Annika," a voice calls. A friendly hand waves as the gentleman pushes a cart through the town. I wave back, offering a smile.

I make my way to the miller's shop to order more flour. While I have enough to last through the assassination attempt, I need to make it look like business as usual. The miller's shop is far enough away from the flour mill that I imagine it's difficult for Bauer to run his job, much less help lead the resistance.

The buildings loom over us, looking down on two young women making their way through the streets of

Leipden. Each tower on every building is striped with a different color, winding its way around the pointed precipice of the roofs.

Bold magentas and orange tones dot this section of the town, mixed with bright whites like a twisted mint. Perhaps it's unfair of me to compare everything here to a candy world, but when one's entire life revolves around baking and creating confectionary delights for royals and peasants alike, one has little else to compare the bright world too.

We pass a row of brightly designed fireworks meant for later this evening. I secretly wish Gretel's powers extended to turning inanimate objects into duds so we could have one night of peace in the skies.

Turning, I allow my hand to scrape over the embossed edges of the building at the start of the street. Each groove is familiar beneath my hands. From the corner of my eye, I see Gretel do the same.

A group of young girls runs by us, clad in bright yellows and blues. They spin, laughing as they run down the street. Their mothers have taught them to have fun with the king's little games, but when they're older, they'll learn the truth of their prison.

A bell dings above me as I guide my charge into the miller's shop. Bauer looks up from his place behind the counter, a streak of flour runs across one side of his forehead.

"Ahh, young Miss Annika and her apprentice," he regards us. "What can I help you ladies with today?"

"The King is coming!" someone shouts outside. Bauer tosses me a worried glance but hurries around the counter on his bad leg. Gretel and I pick up our skirts and step out of the door before the miller—I can't let the crown see our secret child-weapon.

CHAPTER 2

In the streets, people are busy lining the walkways, ready to put on a show for when the king passes by with whatever dignitaries he has hanging on his every word today.

Lights flicker on down the length of the street. Despite being trapped in Leipden, the people have developed a system over the years to help each other out. A lookout sounds the alarm when a member of the crown's guards come close. Lights are turned on only when necessary, and the people crowd into the streets. When possible, a few slip away into the darkened corners of a shop to be productive while they can.

Everything sparks to life as if we've all been in the streets celebrating all day. Men raise their glasses and women dance as voices fill the air with rehearsed lines.

I tuck Gretel behind me, using my tall frame to block her. Bauer sidles up next to me, leaning on my arm for support as he too covers Gretel from sight. He reaches up to swipe the flour from his face, jostling his light brown hair in the process.

The parade files past us, led by guards in brightly colored uniforms. Should anyone ever attack Candestrachen, there will be no hope for us—subtlety is not the king's strong suit and his guards are more easily spotted then the women's dresses.

A cart wheels by—Hansel would be fascinated by how they power it. A short man sits in the front, guiding it down the roads as an engine quietly hums beneath him. We don't have access to all of the technology the king has, but Hansel has ways of finding things we aren't supposed to have.

A woman in royal blue raises the shout, and we all follow, watching the vehicle move.

"A blessing to King Levin and to Candestrachen!"

When the third round of cheers dies down, the king leans out of the red, white, and yellow cart. He waves his hand, tousling his dark brown hair—if I didn't know any better, I'd say we could be twins…if I were a decade and a half older, that is.

Music fills the air as musicians dive into song—it doesn't matter which one. A group of older women starts singing, swaying together in unison. I raise my voice with them, knowing I need to blend in as I croon about the magnificence of Candestrachen. Gretel sings behind me but stays hidden.

The king eyes us all as he passes by, a calculated, jovial grin on his face as he points us out to the man seated next to him. The lights on the miller's shop behind me flicker in bursts of bright colors, painting light over King Levin's face—his father before him was handsome, and one could even argue that Levin was a sight, but the blood on his hands has stripped away every last shred of humanity I could ever find in him.

He locks eyes with me for a moment, focusing on my face. My muscles go stiff with the shock of his gaze but I force myself to smile, and I sing—his death is coming, and I will be glad for it.

"You know what color we're missing here?" The king shouts to his companion. I hold my breath, knowing what's coming. "Red!"

The cart wheels down the street and around a corner. Terrified, people run around buildings hoping to catch him on the other side—if they're in his presence, they're safe.

Several guards in the back stop, prepared to carry out

his coded orders. We didn't put on enough of a show for his guest, and one of us will pay the price.

"Go," I murmur, pushing Gretel back toward the door. I step back, not turning away from the street, trying not to draw attention to our escape.

Bauer grasps at Gretel, catching my arm by mistake. Four, five, six steps and we're at the door to the shop, and he pushes us in, closing it behind us.

The street erupts in our wake as men and women try to avoid the guards—whomever they catch first will be the one to add red blood to the streets. Stifled screams fill the air—it will be worse if the king hears our cries from the next street over—but those near the guards can't help but call out in fear.

"Annika!" Bauer tries to keep his voice down as he shouts at me.

I wheel around to find him pointing to a hidden compartment in the wall. I suppose I don't need to find a place to hide Gretel after all.

"You too," he hisses, grabbing my arm to force me into the compartment. I start to argue, but I know he's right. For as much as the resistance needs Gretel, they need me too—at least until next week. "I'll be fine."

Once inside, the panel slides shut, concealing us from view. Through a small hole, I can see Bauer hiding behind his counter, ready to act as if he were the only person hiding in the miller's shop should the guards choose his establishment to disrupt.

I add a secondary wall in front of ours, preventing the guards from finding the secret panel, should any of them be smart enough to look.

"*Don't,*" Bauer warns when he notices. I drop my hand, taking his advice not to hide him—if anyone saw us come in and they don't find anyone, they'll tear the shop apart and find us all.

We all have to make sacrifices for the cause.

Gretel presses up against me, also trying to see through the small hole. I wave my hand and add a second one to allow her to see what I see.

Minutes pass by. The waiting is the hardest part—possibly even harder than the small pop we hear five minutes later. Somewhere, someone has been tied to posts with a small explosive device attached to them, only big enough to tear them apart when it goes off. Blood is splattered, coating the area red as onlookers cry tears of sorrow and relief. Soon, somewhere new will be painted red with the blood pooling on the ground as the guards finish their assignment.

I drop the illusion, and Bauer releases us from the small hole in the wall. I climb out, pushing and pulling my skirt into place as I stand. Worried, I quickly change the colors and styles of our dresses before we leave the miller's shop.

"What do we know?" I ask, trying not to sound shaken. I smooth back my hair, knowing at least part of it has toppled out of its bun.

"The explosion last night?" Bauer asks. "Not much, I'm afraid. I was waiting for Hansel to come tell me. I'm afraid we have much to worry about, though."

He loops around to stand behind his counter, as if ready to take my order. I lean forward onto the countertop as he scribbles on a pad.

"Are you ready?" he asks, head still down.

"We will be."

"I'm ready," Gretel chimes in, furious over the events of the morning. "He will pay for this."

"Gretel, this is not a mission of revenge," Bauer snaps. "If that is why you are doing this, I'll pull you out right now. We are preventing further loss of life; that is all."

"Yes, Bauer. I know. I'm sorry," Gretel hangs her head. "It is for the greater good—for the future lives."

"We can't change the past," Bauer concludes. "You *will* save the future, though, Gretel."

He swings back to me, dropping the conversation. Gretel may be the key to stopping the king, but she's still a child, and it amazes me how some of the resistance treat her as one.

"Take her home, Annika, and do not come back here until it's time for the delivery," he instructs. His implication is clear—I messed up by bringing her out this close to the assassination attempt.

Bauer hands me a bag of flour, softening his gaze. One side of his lips tick up—an apology for being harsh. I take the flour from him and hand it to Gretel before resting a second bag on my hip.

The streets are back to bustling when we exit the shop. Gretel's green dress is a startling difference to the pink one I had created for her earlier, but I need her to look drastically different. I'm not sure if the king will remember me when I journey to the palace next week, but I certainly hope not. I'd change my hair if I could, but enough people know I'm the baker that if I showed up without my signature brown locks, they'd know something was wrong.

Music trickles its way down the streets, calling for us to join the celebration, but we avoid it. Instead, we follow the main street laid with colorful rocks until we can turn onto a side road that leads back to the woods. Gretel knows to keep quiet until we enter the trees, but I purposely take the long way, knowing we won't run into the remnants of whatever poor soul painted the town red this morning.

"Are you okay?" I ask as soon as we are concealed in the tree line.

The illusions drop around us, and we stand in our

muted clothing again, the only signs of color left back on the town rooftops that peer through the tops of the trees.

"Bauer seemed angry," she comments.

"Bauer is always angry."

"Not with Hansel," Gretel corrects.

"That's because *Hansel* plays by the rules," I remind her.

Gretel stomps off, leaving me to trail behind her. The trees rustle on the wind and Gretel waves her hand, leaving a trail of bright green leaves where dying ones had once clung.

A gasp stops us.

Turning to the right, I search the bushes for the source of it. Throwing my hand out, I add illusion leaves to the ones Gretel gave new life to, creating a wall of greenery between us and the voice, as if the wind had blown them to cover their sight.

His uniform is green, covered in designs of white, cream, and yellow—the guard nearly blends in with the foliage. He staggers back, eyes wide.

"You're a witch; a magic woman." He collides with a tree.

"Whatever are you talking about?" I adopt a fake cheery tone as he takes in my altered appearance—an old, haggard woman. "Are you all right, sir. When we found you, you looked like you had hit your head."

"Don't approach me, woman!" His hands claw around the back of the tree as if he wants to pull it out by the roots and throw it at me. "Your kind has been banished for decades—they don't exist here anymore."

"Sir, I don't know what you're talking about." Another step toward him and the apprehension on his face slips away. He grasps his weapon and aims it at me.

"No!" A scream tears from Gretel's lips. She throws herself on the ground behind me, her hand stretching out just far enough for me to see in my peripheral vision, and the entire forest twists.

Trees burst from the ground, while others rearrange themselves, moving from the roots. Vines drop from branches, while bushes spring up around our feet. A wall of massive trees separates us from the guard.

Instead of fighting to reach me around the bark, he turns and runs toward the town. We're in trouble.

"Gretel, change the forest," I instruct. I drop my illusions as she grows new paths all around us, changing the way to the bakery to make it nearly impossible to find.

"He'll go to the king about this," Gretel says from her place on the ground. She summons more plant life, hindering the man's way back to the palace.

"We need to get back, Gretel, hurry."

I scoop up the bags of flour we both dropped and pull her off the ground. I start running, but with the changed landscape, I'm not even sure we're headed in the right direction.

The ripple effect travels before us, the forest quietly changing as Gretel's summons moves throughout the woods. I slam to a halt as a new tree presents itself in our path. Turning, I pull the little girl around it, taking a different route.

I hear the voices before I see them—men.

"Do you have any idea where to go?" one asks.

"This isn't right, the path should be right here."

"Are you drunk, my friend—spent too much time out last night?" a third calls jovially, enjoying the confusion. He slaps the second man on the shoulder loudly. Perhaps *he* is the one who spent too much time out last night.

"Something isn't right." I recognize the fourth voice— Hansel. This must be his team. Then I realize I know the other voices as well.

"Hansel!" I shout as we step around the tree blocking our view.

His head whips around to me. All of the boys are carrying large sacks on their shoulders. Pickaxes and other tools are attached to the belts on their waists. Hansel's eyes widen as he takes me in.

He stalks over to me, grabbing my elbow to spin me.

"Get us home, Hansel," I whisper before he can speak.

"You did this?" He looks to Gretel.

"Get us to the bakery," I demand again, knowing we can explain later.

"Boys, we're officially off duty. Come on," Hansel calls, waving them over.

His team surrounds us, and we set off in the direction we believe the bakery to be in. Gretel's ripple slows, transitioning quietly into the world we know as we get close to the bakery.

Hansel's feet pound into the ground alongside of me, clearly frustrated as I quietly explain what happened. The muscles in his arm are stiff as I collide with them as we walk.

The bakery is a tall, two-story building with high ceilings downstairs, perfect for creating my confections. The dark brown tones of the wood are highlighted by pops of aqua blue and cream, my father's homage to my late mother. Whereas the towns are covered in decadent architecture, out in the woods, we are more understated with our buildings, only adding color at the king's demand.

Hansel takes the stairs two at a time and Gretel, and I struggle to keep up. The team of six waits outside, watching for anyone who might be coming our way.

I wave Gretel off as I follow Hansel to the back wall near the stairs. The little girl mills by the fireplace as I create an illusion wall between us, shortening the interior of the house by ten feet.

Anger rolls off Hansel in waves, and as I turn, his face softens with worry before slamming me into the back wall. His arms go around me protectively, caressing my waist while his lips move against mine—not the conversation I was expecting to have, but I much prefer it.

"Are you okay?" His lips catch on mine as he tries to speak between kisses.

"Yes," I mumble, words catching against his skin.

One hand quickly reaches into my hair, working his fingers between the strands. I wrap myself around him, holding his back with one hand, the other palm cradling the back of his head just above his neck.

I can hardly breathe as he crushes against me, worry written on his face as he pulls back with a wrinkled brow.

"What were you thinking?" he whispers harshly, chest dragging up and down against me as he struggles to catch his breath.

"I was ordering flour from Bauer," I protest. I run my hand along his arm, hoping to soothe him. "I was trying to keep up appearances. I knew I'd need next week to finish the cake form, and we need to create all of the pastries for our cover story before that happens."

Hansel tips his head forward to learn against my forehead.

"Annika, what would have happened if we had lost you?"

"Bauer and I were going to protect Gretel."

"Yes, but I'm asking about *you*." His hand twists in my hair that is now fully released from the bun I had wound it in. It cascades down behind me, tumbling to the sides.

I pull him toward me, pressing his chest against me as he cocoons us against the wall. His sister is only a few feet away on the other side of my magical wall, and his team is only on the other side of the door, but I don't care—neither does he. His voice is hushed as he speaks, but actions are louder than any words and Hansel's movements are saying a great deal.

My back moves away from the wall as I lean forward to kiss him, our lips colliding and parting furiously. His arms reach around me and for a moment, I think he might pick me up and carry me away to a safer town far away from Candrestrachen. My fingers slip around his suspenders, and I'm careful not to let them snap out of my fingers as I pull him closer. He grins against me, laughing so quietly that it flutters over my skin.

"I will not lose you, Annika," he responds to his own question. "You're too important to the cause and too important to Gretel and me."

"You'll be just fine without me if it ever comes to it." I sigh—if I could stay hidden behind this wall with the people I care about for the rest of my life out of the sight of the king, I'd be happy.

His hand comes up to my chin, tipping my face up to

look at him. His eyes are intently focused on me as I gulp air. His shoulders sag with each breath, and I realize we should have pulled apart earlier.

"Don't sugarcoat this, Annika. We can't lose you." Hansel is frustrated, but I don't back down.

"I'm a baker—sugarcoating is what I do, or haven't you ever tried my palmiers?" I snap back. I regret bringing his favorite dessert into the conversation, but I'm not going to tolerate him saying I'm being too soft about this. I'm not the important one here—the focus should be entirely on Gretel.

I should bake him something later as an apology—maybe my peanut butter fudge that he loves so much.

"We have to go back out there," I inform him. I'd pull away if I could, but he still has me trapped against the wall.

"Is Gretel okay?" he asks reluctantly. As he takes his arms from around me, I realized he's had me up on my tiptoes this entire time, supporting part of my weight as we kissed. I feel heavy without him holding me up.

"I think she's scared about all this, but she's not wavering."

"What about the woods?"

"The guard scared her—she reacted out of fear. She did the right thing changing the forest, but I think upending everything like that unnerved her a little."

"It will be easier when she only has one task to focus on and not changing an entire landscape."

"Speaking of, how are the locals going to get around now?"

"Most of them stay out of the woods, so it's really just our teams," Hansel says, thinking it through. "I'll come up with a signal so we know how to find our way back here."

I nod, trusting him to handle the situation. Hansel has always been a problem solver.

"Annika, I think Gretel needs to stay with you until this is over. We can't risk her traveling now that we're so close."

"You don't think they'll notice you traveling without her? We can't afford questions. They'll notice you coming and going without her even if you *don't* live in town."

His hand grazes mine, fingers wrapping around mine slowly before pulling away. Hansel holds my gaze and brushes back a strand of hair. I tip my head toward him and rub the back of his hand with my cheek.

He sighs and pulls away. Reaching up, I wrap my hair back into a loose bun making him smile.

"I'm going to make a trail of lights," he informs me, stepping back. I follow him.

"They won't notice that?"

"Blinking lights," he corrects. "Electronic fireflies. They won't have any idea."

I consider the merits of his idea. If he creates a path of

tiny devices that flicker like an insect, people who pass by won't know. No one will stand for prolonged periods of time to watch for a trail, nor is it uncommon for an insect to land on a bush and stay there for a time. It makes sense. If anyone can get access to technology for that, it's my co-conspirator.

"That's brilliant, Hansel."

"I save all my best ideas for you and the mission, Annika," he teases. "Gretel will stay here with you tonight —don't argue. I'll take her home tomorrow after I set the trail in place."

"You mean *after* you figure out how to get home." His back is turned to me, but his head twitches to the side as if he started to turn back to me.

"Another reason she's spending the night here—I don't know how to get her home safely yet. Just start your baking project early since you'll have the extra help. It will cover for us in case things get busy over the next few days and you can't make your stockpile supply to use as a cover."

Hansel nearly walks into the illusion wall, trusting me to take it down in time. If I didn't want to kiss him again soon, I'd let him walk into it, but I need his face to stay intact if I want to taste his lips again. I wave my hand and the wall drops as he raises his voice.

"We have a plan," he announces, brushing back his hair. I hope my own mane looks all right—he would have told me if it hadn't because he doesn't want to give away our secret any more than I do.

Gretel turns, jaw locked. Two of Hansel's team members stand in the bakery, looking annoyed. One uncrosses his arms, letting them fall to his side while the other raises an eyebrow.

"What exactly is this plan?" asks the one who was clearly just pretending to be drunk. Aurik has always been unique.

"We're marking the trails tonight, boys. We'll come back tomorrow. Annika will be babysitting."

"What?" Gretel shrieks.

Hansel motions for the guys to leave the bakery and they oblige, turning on the heels of their work boots. They leave bits of dried mud in their wake for me to sweep later.

Few people know Gretel is the key to the rebellion's success—it's too dangerous for people to know. As far as most people are concerned, Gretel is just Hansel's kid sister and responsibility since his father died. Aurik and Brahms know, but even so, some distance is kept.

The fierce little girl marches up to her brother, not letting on how tired she must be after rearranging an entire forest.

"Why am I being left here?" Her long blonde bangs fall in front of her face, and she pushes them back harshly.

"I don't know how to get home, which means it's not

safe to take you out. Annika needs your help tonight anyway to work on the food supply for your alibi. I have a feeling next week won't be kind to us."

"Hansel has to concentrate on building firefly bots anyway," I inform her, touching her elbow softly. "He's going to light the paths so we can find each other."

"Just do what Annika says," Hansel directs his sister. He hugs her quickly, tossing a glance at me. He mouths, "Sugarcoat it."

He eyes his sister before he pulls away—she doesn't need to know how difficult her handiwork has just made our lives.

Hansel is worried, and I don't blame him. So much could go wrong over the next few days.

"They won't even think to look here, Hansel," I promise. "It will be safe."

I twirl my hand in the air, coating the entire outside of the bakery in bright colors. Hansel laughs from the drive outside when he turns to see my handiwork, the team members mercifully already in the woods. Sculptures of candy wrap around the columns of the porch—everything Hansel's sweet tooth has ever craved over the years. The top of the bakery now has points like the buildings in the cities—mine drenched in what looks like whipped cream and pink frosting. Chocolate drips from the shutters coated in rainbow colored sprinkles found in only one shop in the entire kingdom. The door is covered in melted green and white peppermint, leaving the steps transformed into rows of salt water taffy lined with lollipops.

I've sugarcoated the world for Hansel and Gretel…at least for now.

"Could you flirt any harder?" Gretel mumbles next to me once her brother is out of sight. I whip around to face her. "I'm about to kill a king, Annika, you think I don't notice the things around me? Conjuring up all of Hansel's favorite sweets was a clear and definite message to him. Now, take it down before anyone else sees."

"Just for that…" I reply. Instead of finishing, I transform the interior of the bakery into a candy wonderland. The banister on the stairs twists into swirled rainbow candy canes, and a lavish sculpture protrudes from the wall with every treat imaginable. A chocolate fountain streams in the corner surrounded by a base of butterscotch candies. Macaroons and truffles line the fireplace mantle.

"I'll forgive you," she replies, "but only because I love macaroons and I know you have some real ones in the back."

I smile, leading the way after making sure the door lock is secure. She glides behind me gracefully—she'll be a force to be reckoned with when she grows up.

"We've got fudge to make tonight, Gretel."

"Oh lovely, more bribes for my brother."

"*You* like it, too," I remind her, tugging on a few strands of her hair. "We've got a lot to create tonight, so I hope you aren't tired."

"Considering we haven't had lunch yet, I guess we're in for a long day."

CHAPTER 3

A ROCK CLICKS AGAINST MY WINDOW, WAKING ME. THE floor is cold as I set my feet down—the fire must have gone out downstairs. I've only been asleep for two hours, so it shouldn't have gone out so quickly, but perhaps the draft quieted the flames.

I reach for my cloak, tucking the hood up over my hair to help with the chill. A few long strands of hair tumble out from behind the fabric and I don't bother to tuck them back.

Hansel is standing below the window, poised to throw another pebble. I rest my hand on the window, and he drops his arm, knowing I've seen him.

I hurry down the stairs to let him in. The embers from the fire still glow in the blue-toned night. Only the moonlight illuminates the house now.

"You kept the candy, I see." He greets me with a smirk as he brushes past me to come inside.

"Only for you, Hansel."

"Where is Gretel?"

"She's still sleeping," I reply, closing the door.

"I'm here." Her tiny voice bounces off the walls in the early morning hours. She glides off the stairs, also wrapped in a cloak.

Hansel moves his hand, and the fire ignites once more. Another flick of his wrist and the candle bursts into flames too. A small light on the side of the room comes on, allowing us to see more easily.

He eyes me as if to say, *you really should watch that*, but I'm in no mood for his judgments. Hansel's gaze sweeps over to Gretel. Catching sight of the mountains of pastries we baked in the hours since Hansel left us, his eyes grow wide. Tarts and scones fill the table where we left them to cool. A few extra pies sit on the stools, though the rest are in the back. Cookies sit in baskets on an open rack off to the side, while rolls and sticky buns rest in containers waiting to be moved—we were too tired to transport everything into the back when we went to bed at two.

"Did you get everything done?" He asks, looking at Gretel.

"Mostly," I answer.

"Good." He nods, all business. "We need to go."

"It's four in the morning," Gretel complains, yawning. "You couldn't have just left us until morning?"

"No, Gretel, I couldn't." Dark shadows pass over Hansel's face. "The king's men are out looking for the witch that transformed the woods. If they found you here out of place, you both would have been detained for questioning. You and I have to go home *now* before they discover we aren't there."

Gretel's face pales in the candlelight. Hansel turns to me and scoops up one of my hands.

"You need to remove the illusion."

Startled, I raise my hand in an arc, dropping the façade outside. I had already removed it from the interior of the house as we worked because we needed more space to set the things we were baking. Hansel squeezes my hand before dropping it.

"Shoes, Gretel." He nods to his little sister's feet. She turns, rushing back upstairs to collect her things.

"Will you be all right here alone, Annika?" It's sweet that he's concerned.

"I have to be," I reply. I don't have a choice. "Will you two be okay out there?"

I'm terrified the king's men will find them as they

make their way back to Leipden. Their poor aunt must be beside herself.

"The course has changed, Annika, but there are still ways to get to and from the palace when this is all over. I know the way to you—I've lit the path. But here—" he holds out his hand, waiting for me to open mine, "—use these wisely. They're bots. They'll follow you wherever you go."

Tiny yellow lights blink in my hands, the same size as a firefly. I close my fingers around them.

"Once you activate them, they'll hover every hundred feet on their own until you run out. If you run out, they're programmed to move on their own, spacing themselves out further. If anything happens, Annika, and you need to run, these will let me find you."

Hansel is brilliant. I shouldn't be so shocked.

"Yours are yellow—I figured that would be the least likely to be noticed aside from the green ones I made for Gretel. Mine are a light blue."

"You had time to create these *and* mark the trails?" I ask skeptically.

"Well, *some* of the trails. This was more important." Hansel shakes his head, tossing his blond locks. "It appears some of Gretel's force is still at work and occasionally the boys have witnessed a tree moving. Most of it is farther out, mind you, but these were the only way to find each other if we have to."

"Oh, great," Gretel mutters, coming down the stairs. "I can't even handle an escape plan—are you *sure* I'm going to be able to kill the king?"

"You'll be fine," we both protest at the same time.

Gretel yawns again, fighting against only getting two hours of sleep. I like to think I'll be able to crawl back into bed once they're gone, but I know I'll be wide awake, worrying.

"You know the way home?" she asks.

"Yes, we just follow the blue trail." Hansel waves for me to follow them out into the yard. I slip on a pair of dainty slippers before stepping out onto the porch.

The grass is wet with early morning dew. Mixed with the cool weather, it soaks through my slippers, piercing my skin painfully. I'm grateful Gretel has boots on for the walk home.

"This way," Hansel says, leading us to a tree.

I wince as I follow behind them—I despise the cold weather, even when it hasn't fully arrived yet.

"See that little dot there?" Hansel points. I watch for a moment, seeing nothing. Then, a tiny blue glow appears down the path. A few seconds later, another blue dot glows so far away that I can barely see it. "That, ladies, is what you're looking for."

He takes a firefly from Gretel and shows us how to activate it. He has Gretel test it out, walking back toward the house. Once she reaches the porch, she returns to us, several lights still in her hand. Hansel demonstrates how to call the robotic creatures back to us before wrapping his arm around his little sister.

"Stay safe," he warns me. "Gretel and I will be back in a few hours."

I nod, waiting for them to leave but Hansel refuses to move until I'm standing in my doorway once again. When they slip out of sight, I lock the door.

Knowing it's a waste of my time to try to sleep, I set to work hiding the evidence of how Gretel and I spent the last twenty-four hours.

The sun is up, glistening off of the rooftops in the distance when Hansel and Gretel return. They're dressed brightly—Gretel bound in a deep red dress with laces up the front, and a navy cloak wrapped around her shoulders and Hansel outfitted in three different hues of dark green.

I noticed them through the window as they exited the woods, but look up when they knock, keeping to our usual routine in case anyone is watching. When planning to assassinate a king, paranoia is called preparedness.

"Good morning," I greet them, brushing back part of my hair. I feel woefully underdressed standing next to them. "What's all this?"

"The king's guard was out in full force this morning." Hansel's voice is deeper than usual as he drags a hand down his face. "You should change, too, in case they come this way."

My shoulders sag, but I move my hand out to transform my wardrobe into an illusion to match theirs.

"No, Annika. Change for real. You may need to hold other illusions in place should anything else happen."

I grimace—with an illusion, I can get dirty while baking without ruining my fancy clothes, but if I use real fabric, anything I drop onto it could be damaged. Crossing his arms, Hansel doesn't take no for an answer.

Gretel moves about the room, preparing for work as I turn and make my way to the stairs. If I have to be put out, I'm going to make a point of it.

My parent's room is large. When I first moved into it last year, I didn't know how to handle all the extra space, but I had wanted to be close to them and this was the only way I could think of to do it. Of course, as the new owner of the bakery, it was also expected, and should any of the king's guards ever inspect the house, there would be far too many questions raised if I was still in my childhood room.

I slip into a dusty pink dress, draping a light-colored fur over my shoulders. Pulling my necklace out from the collar of the dress, I let it rest on my chest as I navigate toward the stairs again. Hansel's eyes widen when he sees me.

"The ball is *next* week, Annika," Gretel jokes, snickering.

"Yes, but who doesn't like baking in furs, darling?" I retort, shaking my head playfully.

"I didn't mean you had to dress for town, Annika," Hansel adds, shaking his head.

"You made a good point, Hansel—we don't know what might happen later today, especially once the king starts to investigate the forest. Anyone could stop by."

"And *you* were being snarky," he muses, smirking.

"Of course." I wave him off. "Go to work, Hansel, something tells me you're going to be busy today."

Hansel angles himself toward the door, walking slowly. "Keep an eye out for the boys today."

I nod. If any of Hansel's team shows up today, it means something bad is happening. If he's worried enough to tell us to actively watch for them, we'd better be extra vigilant.

"Well, that's new," Hansel says from the door, looking out from under the porch. Gretel and I scurry over to look out of the doorway with him.

In the distance, nearly blocked out by the blinding light of the still-rising sun, something floats in the air. First one, then five, then enough that it could be a cloud if it weren't for the sun piercing through them, destroying the illusion.

"Are those…lanterns?" Gretel asks, squinting to see.

"Those are definitely lanterns," Hansel responds. His hand quietly bumps into mine.

"But those aren't ever sent up until night when the people can see them," Gretel whispers, realizing something is off.

"Stay in the house today." Hansel frowns, moving toward the steps.

"Wait," I call, turning to run back into the bakery. I hear Gretel say something to her brother as I pick up a small bag of the peanut butter fudge we made for Hansel last night. She brushes past me as I hurry onto the porch again.

Hansel raises an eyebrow, quirking one side of his lips up. He runs a hand through his hair as I approach him.

"I forgot to give this to you earlier." I hand him the candy.

"I give you apples, you give me fudge," he muses.

"We all have our different kinds of sweets, Hansel."

"Just like we all have our different kinds of gifts," he teases, finishing my thought. "But not all of us have those."

"Not all of us have sweets, either," I remind him quietly. "Don't let those go to waste."

"These won't even make it down the path, Annika,

and you know it." He grins, untying the ribbon holding the bag closed. "You spoil me, woman."

Hansel hands me the ribbon that matches my dress. I close my fingers around it, unsure of what to do with Gretel a few feet away in the house, likely watching through a window.

"Be careful, Annika. We don't know what's happening out there anymore. If you think anything is going wrong, get Gretel out of here and I'll find you." He pauses a moment before sighing. With a quick glance to the house, he turns and saunters off toward the woods.

Back inside, I set the ribbon down on the table. Draping the fur over the back of a chair, I instruct Gretel to sit by the window behind the curtains and watch for anyone coming from the woods. I'm less worried about the morning lanterns for the moment than I am for possible intruders.

I turn my attention to the wooden cake frame while Gretel keeps watch. I carve an intricate design into the wood for when I place the fondant over it—it will save me time on the design later. The wood scrapes under my knife, filling the room.

Gretel sighs loudly, nearly making me jump.

"Bored?" I ask playfully. I reach up and brush a piece of hair out of my face with the back of my wrist.

"How is the cake going?" she asks in a monotone voice to make her point. I giggle quietly.

"Well, they won't know it's not some elaborate sugar creation until after the fact," I reply. "Honestly, I'd like to get the fondant on and just get going with this."

I look up in time to see her cringe and realize I shouldn't wish the assassination—and her possible death—to come faster.

"Annika." Gretel's sharp voice tells me she hadn't been reacting to my comment.

"What is it?" I drop the tools I was using, flick my wrist to put an illusion over the half of the room where the wooden cake sits, and rush to her side.

"Bauer," Gretel murmurs. "This can't be good."

It feels like my internal organs drop inside of me like when I jumped off that cliff into the river as a child before King Levin took power. Air fills my mouth as I remember to breathe, gulping in oxygen.

"Go to the back, Gretel. Get the cake and go." I drop the illusion so the girl can move our secret weapon out of sight. The wheels drag against the floor as she pushes it away.

I rush to the door, opening it as Bauer hobbles up. He clutches at the neckline of his coat that falls below his knees. Stone blue makes his dark hair stand out.

"Bauer?"

He thrusts two large bags of flour at me. I fumble to catch them before they hit the ground. Straightening, I follow him inside, flour bags in my hands. Setting them on the table, I wait for his gasping to stop.

"What's happening?" My voice sounds hollow even to me.

Bauer starts to shake, breathing deeply. As he leans back, I flick my wrist toward him, rolling my fingers gently as if I were shooing a fly away from a freshly baked roll. A tall stool materializes behind him, catching him as he sits.

"Has anyone been here today?" he asks.

"No, just Hansel and Gretel."

"Where is she?" Bauer's brown locks fall in his face. Soft wrinkles form around his eyes and crease his brow from years of wear.

I nod to the back. Gretel steps out.

"We have to go," Bauer informs us, standing to his feet. His voice loses its wavering tone. Was this an act?

"Those lanterns were the start of something, girls, something bad."

"You're not really suggesting we leave, are you?" I ask, horrified.

"We can't leave you where they can find you," Bauer protests, looking less winded.

"What is going on, Bauer?" Gretel asks, crossing her arms over her chest. "We can't leave. If we do, how will we get me into the cake and delivered to the palace? Annika can't just abandon the bakery."

"What about the cake?" I ask, glancing at the back wall.

"Hansel and I will come back for it, but if anything happens to Gretel, all is lost. We can always come up with a new plan, but not without the girl," he confronts me. "We need to get you both somewhere safe."

"Where is that?" I demand, hands on my hips. I know Bauer would never move us without a reason and if he's willing to risk this plan, he must be exceptionally worried.

"Closer to the palace."

"Excuse me?"

"What?" Gretel speaks over me. "We can't be there until the ball. It's still days away."

"The king's guards will be scouring the towns, we can't move closer. Our ticket in is the cake—we have to wait until we take it to the palace for the ball." I frown.

"The guards aren't going to know who is bringing the king his cake, nor will they know where the baker appeared from. As long as *you* show up with the cake, everything will be fine, Annika." He puts his hand on my back and turns me toward the door.

"What do you know that we don't, Bauer?"

He sighs but continues to push at my back, propelling me forward.

"The king is searching for us. He's looking for rebels. Somehow, word has been spreading that a plan is to be enacted before the ball—rumors, as far as I can tell, I don't think we have a traitor—but he's scouring the cities looking for us…for *you* and for *her.*

"He's already searched the towns around the palace, and his men are branching out. If we can get you safely beyond the perimeter as it comes toward us, you'll be safe until they've completed their search."

"And if they find the bakery empty?"

"They won't, Annika, we'll make sure one of us is here. The guards don't know better unless they grew up here and knew your father. Even then, we should be able to explain it away. We just need to make sure you two are in the palace district."

Gretel looks nervously at me as we step outside and Bauer closes the door behind us. "We need to go."

I trust Bauer almost as much as I trust Hansel, so I swallow back my argument and take the steps down to the dirt path. The trees seem to swallow us as we step into the woods that are now completely unfamiliar to me.

A bird chirps loud enough to make Gretel jump, and she moves closer to me as we walk. Bauer limps along beside us at what must be a brutal pace for him, but he doesn't stop.

"Does Hansel know about this?" I ask.

"Not yet, but he will as soon as you're safe. Our next mission will be to rescue the cake."

I tap the fireflies to life, and the first takes its place to guide Hansel to find us—I won't risk him losing us should something happen along the way. Gretel notices me and nods.

"The lanterns this morning were some kind of signal, weren't they?" I question as the trees block out more of the light. Each leaf rattles as the wind picks up enough to blow my hair in front of my face. Reaching up, I pull it from the messy bun I'm wearing so that it falls to help prevent me from getting chilled.

"I'm afraid that was my fault," Bauer admits. "I was on my way from the mill to the shop and I saw the guards. I overheard their plan and knew I needed a way to get some attention.

"Our people all saw it—anything out of the ordinary makes them vigilant—but it also kept the guards distracted long enough to make it to a few of our key players to warn them. I came straight here as soon as I could find a way to escape without being noticed rushing from the town.

"Quiet now, girls," Bauer warns us, suddenly sensing something. He stops walking, straightening both of his knees. Dropping his voice, he adds, "We need to run."

CHAPTER 4

GRABBING GRETEL'S HAND, BAUER LAUNCHES FORWARD, NO longer limping—yet another of his façades. We crash through the bush, nearly colliding with a tree we forgot had recently moved.

Everything blurs around us as we stumble over the underbrush. My foot catches on a tree root, nearly sending me toppling forward. Gretel's long, blonde hair trails behind her as she leaps nimbly over tree roots and fallen branches.

Behind us, I hear the guards' voices calling to each other. After a moment, they catch the noise we're creating as we trample through the woods in the distance and follow us, quickly gaining speed.

"*Gretel*," I call. She reaches for my hand so I can steady her as we run.

"Are you sure?" Bauer asks, wrenching himself around so he can assess our enemy.

"Is it her?" a guard yells.

"Do you honestly think a witch can run that fast?" another calls in reply.

"Oh, well, this is lovely," I grumble. "Time to give them a witch."

Gretel drags her hand across the rough bark of a tree as we pass by it. I'm sure it hurt, but she doesn't cry out. We pass another, and she darts her hand out again. The tree immediately begins to move, and I catch it from the corner of my eye as I pass it.

Unlike the last time, Gretel isn't transforming the forest. Her touch is merely coercing the trees to form a wall behind us, corralling the king's men away from us.

A firefly leaps from its place on the small pouch attached to my belt and darts toward the bushes. It blinks once before it disappears behind a bush left untouched by Gretel's commands.

I consider telling her to touch the ground and affect the roots of all the plants in the forest again, but Hansel and the others have already worked so hard to navigate the trails—it will be hard enough for him to locate us now and the line of trees is giving us a temporary reprieve from the chase. Still, we don't slow.

A bird cries out in shock as Gretel removes her hand from the bark of the tree it's sitting on. It flies into the air, lecturing her for disturbing its rest.

"Hurry, girls, we have to get to the town." Bauer pulls ahead of us, leading the way now that he's certain the trees are slowing the guards down. In the distance, I hear calls for the witch's head.

Gretel is breathing heavily, and I slow our pace. Bauer realizes we're lagging and slows as well, knowing we can't tax the girl before her mission. Each time she uses her gift, she depletes some of her power until she can recharge. Small tasks like bringing dying plants back to life in the bakery hardly affects her but rearranging an entire forest and now creating a wall of trees within two days will certainly take its toll on her—I can't let her do anything else until the mission has been completed or we risk putting her in danger without being able to kill the king.

Bauer guides us off course, looping around toward the outside of the forest. Releasing Gretel's hand, I wrap an arm around her waist to help support her as we slow to a quick walk.

"I'm fine," she puffs in response. She's anything but fine.

"We need to get out of the forest," Bauer informs us,

looking back. "We've lost the guards thanks to Gretel, but now they know we were there and will be searching the woods for you both—for all of us. We have to get you around people."

"You want us to blend in?" I ask.

Bauer nods. "You need to belong to whatever town you find yourselves in. We'll move quickly to get you to the palace district, but it's going to involve a little waiting while I clear the area before I bring you out in the open."

I study him as we move. I can tell he's nervous. His gait is stiff, though, I suppose that could be from discomfort since he isn't walking with his fake limp at the moment. Slowing again, he pauses until we catch up and slips his arm behind Gretel, under her arm, to help support her with me. The more we can do for her now, the easier it will be later.

"Hansel is going to kill me for this," Bauer grumbles.

"Probably," Gretel offers meekly. I blow air out of my nose instead of laughing to let her know I got that she was joking, but I'm too tired and too focused on our movements to offer a real laugh.

"Not much farther, girls," Bauer adds softly. "Once we reach the tree line, I'll get you two hidden, and I'll make sure the guards have already swept the area. Then I'll come back for you two."

"Okay," I agree quietly. I've done far too much running the last two days, especially for a baker who focuses on building muscle through lifting heavy bags of cooking ingredients.

"It looks like that's the town up ahead." Bauer nods forward.

If I strain, I think I can hear music coming from the streets of whichever town we've stumbled upon—possibly Gimpenlaug or Perihausen. If the music is so loud, that has to be a clear sign that the guards haven't left yet.

"There," Bauer says, pointing. "There's a large cluster of trees growing together. You can rest there and use the tree to hide yourselves if need be."

If we must, I'm sure Gretel could cause the five trees to swirl together, locking us inside until help can come, safe from whatever guards we might run into. We'll have given ourselves away, but at least Gretel will be protected until then.

I guide my charge to the trees, helping her to sit in the makeshift seat the trunks have formed. Glancing around, I make sure no one else is near, even though Bauer swept the area before he disappeared through the trees.

"Are you all right, Gretel?"

"I'll be fine," she murmurs. "This running thing is for the *guards* though. No one else should be subjected to this nonsense."

"Your brother trained you." I give her an incredulous look, "There's no way he didn't teach you how to run."

"Oh, I can run, Annika," she grumbles. "I just don't like it."

"Well, I can't say I blame you there. How long are you going to need?" I pray she doesn't need more than a few days to recover from using herself up over this.

"I'll be ready," she answers.

I sidestep as a cricket leaps past me, frightening me enough that I gasp—I forgot they like to act like rockets being shot at neighboring countries this time of year. It pings against a branch as it lands.

"I hate those things," Gretel voices my own thoughts. "I'll be ready, though, Annika. You don't have to worry."

She sounds stronger and less winded, but I know it's an act—like one of my illusions. It's a pretty façade to put people at ease. I've even done it to keep others calm around me. Poor Hansel has been a victim to my charms a time or two.

"We're going to be okay," she says, taking my hand. "You'll get me where I need to go, I'll do what I need to do, and we'll handle the rest of it. It will all work out, you'll see."

She's wise not to give any details of our plan while out in the open, but she's Hansel's sister so I should expect nothing less.

"Any chance you still have some of that peanut butter fudge in your pocket that you slipped my brother earlier?"

"Sorry, dear. We can make more later if you'd like." It wouldn't be terribly hard to make more of Hansel and Gretel's favorite candy. I know the recipe by heart these days.

"At least Hansel will know how to find us," Gretel changes the subject. "Good thinking on using the fireflies."

"We might have to use yours soon, too, if we go any further."

Gretel reaches to tap on the pouch on her hip just as the explosion goes off. I drop to the ground, pulling Gretel down with me. Overhead, a firework crackles in the bright blue sky.

"What in the name of lollipops is going on here?" Gretel's face scrunches up as we try to see through the trees.

"I don't know," I respond.

It's hard to see the colors in the light of day, but the remnants of the white glow slowly falls down from the sky. A second screaming collision with the air frightens us again. I lurch back against the tree, trying not to be too obvious about jumping.

"If the lanterns meant something—even if it *was* Bauer —do you think these fireworks mean something?"

"We have to assume that it does, but this time, Bauer hasn't had enough time to reach the fireworks at the center of the town. Something else is going on here."

I listen for the sounds of music coming from the town, but it's strangely silent. A third firework goes up in the air. Peeking around the tree, I look for signs of life along the edge of the town, hoping someone might be walking by and I could gauge their reaction to the fireworks. No one is there.

Another minute passes before I hear it—the sound of screams.

"It must be the guards," I whisper. "They've probably caught someone."

"What should we do?" Gretel struggles to turn around so she can see toward the town as well. I wrap an arm around her waist as she leans to the other side of the tree.

"Stay hidden, Gretel." I pull her to my side and she sighs.

The wind kicks up, knocking leaves off of the trees. They cascade around us like yellow raindrops. The rustling covers up the sound of crunching leaves for a moment—just long enough for us to lose our edge.

We turn at the same time, hearing the boots stomping through the woods. Gretel's face pales. She reaches out, getting ready to hide us if need be. I grab her hand, pinching it tightly—she can't do anything else to conceal us, or the assassination attempt is over before we've been able to do anything, and since *I* don't have time to make a *real* cake now, the king will probably have me executed.

Still holding her hand between my fingers, I flick my

other wrist, causing a shower of illusion leaves to fall between the men and us—they likely won't notice fallen leaves disappearing as much as they'd notice tall trees suddenly poofing out of existence when I get too far away, so I don't create any illusion trees for the moment.

As the shower of greenery continues, I pull Gretel toward the town. We're going to have to face the guards in the town if we want to escape the ones we're leaving behind, whose sole attention would be on the two of us in the woods—I'll take a distracted guard over a group going after two lone women in the woods any day.

We stumble the first few feet, but the buildings are close enough that we dart behind the first one while the leaves are still coming down in front of the king's men. Glancing around, I assess the situation. Gretel clamps down on my hand, as she's been trained to do so we don't lose her in a situation like this. Our jobs have always been to protect her; Gretel's job is to make sure she doesn't get separated from us.

The buildings have a pink tone here, and while there are a variety of bright colors—pink seems to be the over-whelming hue of this street. Even the glass in some of the shops is tinted with rose. Doors slam shut all around us, though they aren't closing because of us—they're afraid.

I have to find somewhere to hide Gretel. Not knowing who we can trust, I put an illusion over us, changing our appearance so no one could find us.

"That was bold," Gretel chirps at me.

"We don't have time for subtleties right now," I growl back. I didn't mean to sound so harsh, but I left all my sugar back at the bakery. "There."

I haul the girl across the street, nearly colliding with a man and his son as they maneuver away. He curses but doesn't stop.

The old woman who waved me across the street can barely hold up the cellar door for us, but she waits until we're safely inside before letting it slam shut. I climb down the stairs, refusing to relinquish Gretel's hand.

Once on the dirt floor, the old woman points to where she wants us to go. I can't question it; we're underground, and the old woman only wants to be safe too—she doesn't mean to harm us.

She nods to the wall as she runs her hand over it. It clicks, revealing a hidden door. Just as she pulls it open, a firefly slips from Gretel's pouch, blinking in the dark cellar. The woman's head snaps over to the bright light.

My hand lashes out, concealing the device.

"I got it," I whisper as if I'd killed the bug. Holding my hand closed tightly, I try to block the light and conceal it behind my back. When the woman turns away, I slip it into Gretel's pouch. She tightens it so the rest can't escape to do their jobs.

The room smells like damp earth, but the woman

touches a switch and a dim blue light fills the room, just enough to give us limited visibility.

"What did you see?" the woman asks. When hiding from the guards of Candestrachen, information is coveted and often the only means of survival.

"Nothing," I inform her. "We weren't here when it happened. Do you know what the fireworks were about?"

"You weren't here, and yet you're here, girlie. Where were you?" She doesn't answer my question.

"We were in the woods, collecting firewood. What were the fireworks about?"

"The guards found some rebels, I think." She waves her hand, referring to the resistance—she must not be one of us. "Whether they are or not, I'm sure we'll have an execution. Levin will be thrilled."

It's strange to hear her refer to the king without his title, but I like how it removes some of his power. I might have to try that sometime.

She eyes my new, curly red hair.

"Are you two sisters? Surely you aren't mother and daughter."

"Sisters," I inform her, picking up Gretel's hand. "We live with our mother over—"

My words are cut off as the heavy sound of a body trying to break through a door fills the space we just left. The guard pounds again on the outside cellar door.

"There's another way," the woman whispers. She

hobbles across the blue-lit room. Opening another door, she motions us through. Maybe she is resistance. From the corner of my eye, I see her shutting the door behind us. "Go to your mother."

I try to protest, but she stays behind, shuffling back across the room to save us. Knowing we can't stop, we press forward, groping the walls to figure out where we're going in the dark.

"Ow." I gasp as I run into the bottom step of a staircase leading upward. Gretel bends down to feel what's ahead of me.

Carefully, we climb to the top, looking for a latch that will let us escape. "The firefly," I remind her. She pulls one of the tiny devices out of her bag and holds it between her hand. Every time it blinks, we search for the way out.

Finally, the door clicks. Gretel puts the firefly away, brushing back her now-brunette hair—a new illusion I cast meant to keep people from asking too many questions. This time, I look old enough to be her mother, and Gretel looks at least a few years younger than her age.

She nods, and I crack the door open to see what's outside. The street is quiet, so we hurry outside, closing the door behind it—it blends in perfectly with the side of a stone wall.

"Let one of them go," I instruct. "He's never going to be able to find us at this rate."

Gretel follows my command to leave a trail for her brother as I notice a pile of stacked logs at the end of the street, nearly on the corner. If we can hide behind it, we'll be able to see through the logs but won't be likely to be seen. I'll have to watch for snakes hiding in the firewood, but they're our least dangerous enemy at the moment.

This street is filled with colorful pastel houses, each boasting awnings and shutters of different colors. As we reach the end of the street, I try to determine if we're about to enter a pit of vipers more deadly than the king's guards, and then we duck behind the wood.

Through the holes in the cut fire logs, I can see out onto the street. It seems strange now that the fireworks have stopped—though they stopped before we ran into the cellar—and the sound of footsteps is overwhelmingly loud next to us in the explosions' absence.

The guards pass by, oblivious to two strange girls on the ground mere feet from them. The logs protect us from view, giving us the advantage. I eye the top of the stack, trying to decide if any of the pieces could make a good weapon.

When the street is quiet for a moment, I add a few illusions to the stack of wood, making faux pieces stick out farther than the rest to keep passersby at a distance. Gretel fidgets nervously beside me, and I wonder if that's what she does when I force her into barrels and that wooden cake meant to take down the king of Candestrachen.

The noise flairs up again down the street. With the logs sticking out perpendicular to the street, I can't see anywhere but straight ahead, leaving me to guess what is coming. Someone is struggling against the guards, but the shouts of the men overpower the person being dragged down the street.

A young boy is pulled past us, kicking and screaming. He lifts his feet off the ground, hoping to drag the men down with the sudden shift of weight, but he's small and doesn't carry the weight he thinks he does. Gretel tugs at my sleeve, but there's nothing we can do.

The boy's hat falls off and is quickly trampled by another guard. The man shoves the boy as he dangles in the air between the other men. The child kicks his legs as if he's running, trying desperately to find any kind of traction with which to turn himself around to confront the older man.

Gretel buries her face against my arm, not wanting to see the boy in the light blue shirt and suspenders dangling in the air. He looks to be around her age, and I know this is the image she will carry with her as we wheel her into the palace in a few days.

The boy shouts as the older men yell over him, taking him further down the street. Just before my line of sight is cut off, I see the far guard angle himself—they're turning. Throwing my hand out to the side, I nearly collide with Gretel as I force an illusion of darkness between us and the street we just vacated. The guards pass by without seeing us.

A few agonizing minutes later, we hear the wails of townspeople, pleading with the guards. I hold my breath, knowing the sound that's about to fill the air. A tear slips out of my eye as the poor boy dies from the small charge they tied around him somewhere a few streets over.

"We need to go, Annika," Gretel says, tugging on my arm. Her voice has a hard edge to it. "We need to go home."

Before she can do anything else, more footsteps approach. Gretel leans back against the side of the building, not wanting to see this time. A few women's dresses swish by us in a rainbow of colors. They hurry ahead, not wanting to slow in front of the guard coming our way.

Their ankles twist as they look back to see the men approaching, but they don't lose their step. Their words mesh together as they speak, but I hear something about a rebel leader.

"Make way," a guard calls. His voice is deeper than my father's was. It's startling to hear. I've always associated my father with the deep tone of his voice and the scent of cinnamon, and the sensory connection is so strong, I can nearly smell the spice in the air.

More people walk by, and I realize they aren't trying

to escape at this point—they're following orders. This is a parade.

They've caught someone.

Legs position themselves in front of the openings I was looking through, so I scoot down, trying to get a better line of sight. Gretel follows, curiosity getting the better of her.

It's easier to see around men—they have wide stances, but the women's dresses make it impossible to view anything. Judging by the number of people I can't see around, I'm guessing there's at least fifty people out there —it's enough for us to blend in. The guards have someone in their grasp, so they shouldn't have time to bother with the likes of what appears to be a mother and daughter mixed into the crowd.

"Blend in," I hiss, poking Gretel until she moves.

Once in line, we hover behind a man and woman, trying not to look as nervous as the young girl standing next to them. Guards pass by, weapons ready as they glance over the crowd, eyes glazed now that their job is done and they've chosen a victim.

"Get back, you swine," the deep voice calls again. I search the crowd for him, bobbing around heads as they move in and out of my line of sight.

Someone is kicked. Air rushes from the man's lungs as he crumples back into the crowd a few yards down. A log flips as he grabs hold to steady himself, sending it flinging into the street nearly colliding with a guard. The king's man pauses, glaring at the man who stumbled. One of the other guards whispers something into his ear, and the angry man looks away, letting the townsmen live another day.

The group sways, forcing their victim forward. I can't see around the tall guard standing in the front, his uniform blindingly bright.

Gretel wraps her arm around my hip in case we need to run. I wish I could brush back her blonde hair, but my illusion has covered any trace of the girl we raised to be an assassin. Gretel has always looked like an innocent child, but the dark hair similar to mine makes her look even more angelic.

The mass of guards steps closer, yelling about what happens to rebels and traitors when they're caught by the king's men. The speech is different than the usual one—though perhaps that's because we're in a different town and the guards take a different tone here.

"This man is accused of leading the rebellion against His Royal Highness, King Levin and his armies. You know what happens to traitors and liars, but this man is worse than any treacherous scum slithering through our streets of Perihausen! He is the leader of all of the rebels and charges have been brought against him by one of his co-conspirators for plotting to destroy the king and his kingdom!

"He is being taken to the palace where he will be brought before the council and justice will be leveled upon him. King Levin will decide how to handle this kind of atrocious behavior and this man will pay for his crimes, as will the sniveling rat that pointed him out to us."

The guards sneer around him in response.

I'm sure the man who accused the leader was only trying to survive, but it backfired on him, and now two men will die instead of one—both a bigger spectacle than the guards had thought.

The tall guard moves, swaying to reveal the rebel leader behind him. Gretel nearly falls next to me, clutching at me to hold herself up.

Bauer.

CHAPTER 5

Our leader fixes his eyes straight ahead, refusing to look to the left or the right. He's adopted his limp again, heavily leaning on one of the guards each time he steps with that foot. His shoulders are back, and his head is held high as the guards parade him through the streets.

Unlike the young boy earlier, Bauer will not die today. He will be put on trial and accused of whatever the younger man blamed on him to escape death and anything else the king hurls at him to put on a good show.

His death will be far more complicated than an explosive wrapped around his mid-section in the center of town, standing on a platform for all to see the spectacle. No, Bauer's death will be a celebration unlike anything we've seen in Candestrachen.

A firefly takes off through the crowd, rising above the heads of the men and women forced to cheer the death of someone they'd rather help save—no one knows who Bauer is, but if the king wants him dead, they assume he must have done at least something to help the people of Perihauser in their minds.

I turn to Gretel to see if the firefly is hers as it flies through the crowd. A deft nod is my answer, her eyes fixed in horror on Bauer as they lead him past us. The mechanical firefly blinks in front of Bauer, almost as if it knows him. The man flinches for the first time, and I can tell by the tiny tick in his neck that he almost turns to search for us. He forces himself to stay still, refusing to accidentally give us up.

If Gretel weren't with me, or if I didn't need to finish the cake and take it to the palace to complete our mission, I'd risk myself and create an illusion to distract the guards, kicking them or pushing them long enough for Bauer to have a chance at escaping. I'm not alone though, and I know what Bauer would command me to do—protect the mission at any cost.

The guards harass him and the other man as they walk by. People scream insults at the two traitors, knowing what is expected of them. They try to hide the defeat and sadness in their voices so they aren't called out as sympathizers.

As soon as they round the corner, people turn back, peeling away from the group. Much like they do in Leipden, they run into homes and businesses, trying to stay out of sight. I move with the flow of the group, pulling Gretel along behind me. She matches my pace, never stumbling—I wonder if she's regaining her strength or if it's fear pushing her forward for the moment. It's often in moments of great weakness that we find our deepest wells of strength and do the impossible, at least, according to my father.

When we reach the end of the street, I slip into the shadows. It's still day, and while the shadows aren't dark enough to hide us, they offer us at least a little concealment, and we move. It's cooler in the shadows of the buildings than it is in the sun and I suddenly realize just how strong the wind is.

Leaves gather around our feet as I slow us, trying not to draw attention by running now that we're away from the crowd. Each step elicits crunching noises, and I worry we might be overheard.

The edge of the town is quiet, but people still loiter around as if the guards hadn't just been there. The men aren't using their brains, but if they want their heads on a spike, that's up to them.

Before stepping out, I cause a fountain to appear on

the far side of them. Water bubbles up from the ground, slowly at first—enough to go unnoticed—but once it's a few inches high, it starts to get attention. The men turn, trying to figure out where the water came from.

With their backs turned, I point Gretel to the woods. I entice the illusion water higher—knee level, then up to their waists. As they reach out, I cut it off, pausing for a moment before it springs up again. Gretel guides us to the safety of the woods while I distract the men who could possibly turn us in later on if they think it might save them when the guards inevitably find them out here. When we're far enough away that I'm straining to see, I cut it off, leaving the men confused.

"I know," I cut Gretel off. "We'll figure out how to get Bauer back."

"No, we won't, Annika. The mission is in one week. If you think the king won't kill Bauer as part of the celebration, you're crazy." She sounds like her brother—practical, logical, mission first.

"We can complete the mission *and* save him."

"*No*, Annika, we *can't*. We both know it." Gretel's arms shake once as if her entire body wants to convulse but can't because she's holding her muscles so tight. She swallows, breathing heavily. "Think this through—what is he going to do?"

She's not talking about Bauer; she means the king.

"He will move up the event because you're right, he

will want it as part of the celebration, but he also doesn't let his enemies live long. He will move the ball up to match the execution."

"Which means we have to go back," she whispers. "We have to follow the markers, Annika. We can't stay."

I close my eyes, taking a deep breath. I'm supposed to be the logical one here, and yet, I'm being emotional. Of everyone who was willing to die for this mission, I didn't expect Bauer to be the one to actually make the sacrifice —he wasn't even supposed to be in the palace. Frankly, I assumed it would be me—Hansel and his sister are far too resilient to die at the hands of King Levin and his whims.

"There," I point, catching sight of a glowing blue dot in the distance.

We make our way through the trees, walking at a normal pace. There's no need to exhaust ourselves yet. We've got a few hours before darkness falls and if we arrive late, the guards will likely have left my little bakery home, giving us time to make preparations for the new date the king is bound to shift to.

If my calculations are correct, we'll have no more than three days until his tolerance gives out and he wants to end Bauer. Our leader, on the other hand, will hold out until his dying breath. He will never give us up, but he'll hold out long enough to give us time to get everything into place so when we come to his funeral-masquerading-as-a-ball, we'll be ready to kill his executioner to prevent it from ever happening again.

The walk is long, much longer than the run. The wind gusts around our clothes and I realize I can drop the illusion I've been holding around us since we were in the town. My pink dress moves around my ankles, picking up stray leaves and pieces of debris.

We walk in silence—there's nothing to say. Bauer will die. We'll have to work night and day on the cake to be ready. Hansel will find us eventually. The king will die— there's nothing we can change until he does.

Another blue firefly blinks ahead, hovering in a bush. I open my hand, picking it up and returning it to the pouch on my hip. By the time we find the next two, the weight of the day has crashed over me, and I feel exhausted.

"Are you feeling any better?" I ask softly.

"I'll be fine," she replies. "Even if it moves up, I'll be fine."

She will have to be.

I didn't realize how far we'd traveled until it took half an hour to locate the next firefly. We nearly took the wrong path, but Gretel saw it blink in the distance on the opposite side of the fork. I have to squint to see it as she points.

Another twenty minutes and we find the next firefly, its blue glow bouncing off a tree as the sun shifts in the sky. The clouds take on a pink light, tinging everything a strange shade of red-gold.

"Annika!" Hansel's voice startled me. I jump, spinning to face him. I hadn't heard him approach, though, no one ever does if he doesn't want them to.

"Hansel."

"Hansel!" Gretel charges past me toward her brother.

Aurik stands next to him, Brahms just behind. All three hold axes in their hands—innocuous enough to be played off as if they were leaving work, but deadly enough to take down anyone who got between them and Gretel.

Hansel steps forward, dropping his weapon to the side. Gretel throws herself against her brother, and he wraps his free arm around her.

"What happened?" he demands.

"Bauer showed up," I inform them. "The guards were on their way, and he came to get us out."

"There were guards in the woods," Gretel continues. "They came for us."

"We made it to Perihausen. A woman hid us, but it didn't last long. We hid in the crowd and discovered that someone had turned Bauer in as a rebel leader. They have him, Hansel."

His face pales. Tension lines form around his eyes as he drops his arm from his sister's waist.

"They'll move up the ball," I say.

Hansel nods. "We need to get back. The bakery is fine —no one was there when we arrived. It looked like they did some damage to your cover story supply though."

"The cake?" I inquire. I'm terrified if they found the extra food, they might have also found our delivery method.

"You did a good job hiding it." He nods to Gretel.

"What did you do?" I turn to the girl. She hadn't had enough time to hide it when Bauer came in.

"I slipped a few of your plants in." She tries to shrug casually.

"She covered it with greenery like it was a massive plant stand." Hansel chuckles.

"She even added some trays of bread to it as if they were cooling there," Brahms adds.

"It was pretty inventive." Aurik cocks an eyebrow, shooting Gretel an impressed look.

A worried look fills Hansel's face when I glance at Gretel. She stares back at me defiantly.

"What did you do?" Hansel's voice comes out as a whisper.

When Gretel doesn't speak, I answer for her. "There

were guards in the woods—apparently there are *always* guards in the woods now—and Gretel moved the trees again."

"But we didn't see anything shift." Aurik's statement comes out like a question.

"Further down," I inform him. "It wasn't the entire forest this time."

"Hansel, you've been holding out on us about your sister," Aurik protests good-naturedly. "We could have borrowed her last year for that big project—"

"No, we couldn't have." Hansel silences him. "She has a bigger purpose, and we're dangerously close to having that opportunity destroyed."

They grimace at his protective tone. Stepping away from the other men, Hansel pulls Gretel aside, whispering harshly. "How bad?"

She murmurs but I can't hear her reply. Aurik and Brahms glance at me uncomfortably—none of us like being caught in a sibling argument but there's nowhere we can go.

"We can't risk it," Hansel argues, still whispering loudly as if we can't hear him. Gretel quarrels back, crossing her arms over her chest. After a moment, she flings her hands out to the side, catching herself just before she shouts.

"Okay, that's enough," I interrupt. "We need to get back to the bakery. We have to replenish whatever the guards ruined and finish the cake because we all know Levin is going to move this stupid ball up and we'll all be in trouble if we're not ready on time."

The three men look taken aback when I use the king's name without his title. I like their reaction to it.

"She's not ready—" Hansel protests.

"I'm fine!" Gretel shouts, disturbing two birds sitting in different trees. They flap their wings at the same time, taking off in a similar direction.

"It doesn't matter," Brahms interjects. "Annika is right. We have to get back; we can handle this discussion there, no matter what we choose."

Hansel broods as his friends start to walk away, guiding us back to the bakery. I take Gretel by the arm, spinning her to follow them. After a moment, I hear Hansel's footsteps crunching behind us in the fallen leaves.

He stalks behind us for a few minutes, but eventually lengthens his stride and takes his place by Gretel's side. Hansel glances over Gretel's head to make eye contact with me. He clearly isn't happy, his narrowed eyes are a clear indication of that, but he softens his gaze, silently asking for my opinion on his sister's condition.

I think about it for a moment. If Gretel is sure she can handle the mission, we have to trust her. I understand why Hansel is so worried—I'm worried too—but this has to be Gretel's choice. She knows herself better than we do.

Gretel barely comes up to my shoulder, so I'm pretty familiar with the top of her head. Her hair parts in the middle, cascading down into long white-blonde strands on either side in a shiny curtain that protects her from the world when she hides behind it like I used to as a child. Somehow, looking down on her at this angle makes her seem even younger.

I nod.

Hansel purses his lips and nods back, closing his eyes for only a moment—he trusts us to make this decision, even though he doesn't like it.

The rest of the walk back to the bakery is quiet, comprised of stiff steps and dark moods.

The outside of the bakery is just as I left it earlier today, though it glows in the setting sun. I anticipate the fireworks display will be brighter and longer tonight in celebration of Bauer's capture. Brahms informed us that the fireworks earlier were also to announce a capture, this one in Gimpenlaug, though we haven't discovered who the king's men caught yet.

We trudge up the steps, and I want nothing more than

to lean against Hansel's arm and let him drag me up the stairs to the bakery. He's too busy keeping Gretel upright.

The moment we get inside and close the door behind us, Hansel takes her upstairs to rest. Brahms and Aurik look to me for instructions.

"We're not going anywhere, so you might as well put us to work," Brahms says.

"He meant *you might as well feed us*," Aurik corrects.

"You can have whatever the guards didn't take." I make my way to the back where I had set everything out of sight.

The room is practically empty. While they didn't tip anything over or destroy it, the guards helped themselves to the sweets and treats laying around the bakery. I'm sure if the king's cake had been baked and ready to go—assuming it was a real cake—they probably would have devoured that without a second thought as well, leaving me to take the fall if I didn't recreate it in time for the ball.

"Looks like there's some bread and cookies over there, boys, help yourselves." I wave at the remnants of the trays. It's a shame Bauer hadn't delivered that massive fake flour order I had placed yesterday…I have a feeling I'm going to need it to replace everything.

"Where do we start, Annika?" Brahms asks softly, touching my arm like Hansel might have before we became close.

I sigh. At least they're willing to help.

Pointing things out, I set them to work collecting materials for me while I walk into the other room to start the ovens. I don't bother playing with the fire, knowing Hansel will be down momentarily to start it.

As if on cue, the fireplace lights up, casting the room in a deep orange tint. Sidling up behind me, Hansel wraps his arms around me.

"Hansel, what if they see?" I shrug him off, attempting to slip away. He catches me by the hip and spins me, pinning me against the oven.

"Those two?" He grins, cocking an eyebrow at me. Hansel leans toward me. "What do you care? Let them find out."

"Find out you two have been making out for weeks?" Aurik walks into the room, arms full with bags of flour and sugar.

"Oh, whatever will we do when we find out *that* news?" Brahms asks innocently.

"Why, we might just die of shock." Aurik continues, setting down the supplies on the large table.

"Wow, really?" Hansel retorts. He wraps his arms around my waist. "Fine, if there are no secrets here…"

His lips touch mine softly, which is shocking considering the force with which he moved toward me. My hands rest on the crooks of his arms, and I let him kiss me publicly for the first time. The men ignore us for a moment before telling us to knock it off.

Hansel brushes back a strand of my long hair.

"I like not having to hide," he whispers just loud enough for me to hear. "And apparently, we were terrible at keeping it a secret anyway."

"*You* were. *You* were terrible at it. *I* had no one to keep it from."

Since I lost my father, all I've had was Hansel and his sister. Bauer too, I suppose. If anyone gave our secret away, it was Hansel.

"I think Gretel knows, too," he murmurs as he kisses me again.

"Oh, she knows."

"We *all* know," Aurik snaps. "What we *don't* know is how to bake this stuff. A little help here, Annika?"

The two motion at the table littered with supplies. I pull away from Hansel and start to direct the baking efforts. Once I have Aurik and Brahms settled, Hansel wheels the cake form out for me to begin my work. He leaves me alone to complete my task and takes his place alongside his cohorts.

I open and shut the lid a dozen times to make sure it will work. It doesn't so much as creak. When I'm satisfied, I begin to circle the wooden cake, formulating a plan for decorating it.

From the corner of my eye, I can see the three men

watching me as I stalk around my project, but they don't say anything as I work. My hands reach for the fondant.

I smooth every bit of the fondant over the cake form, leaving only the top uncovered. It only picks up bits of light over the carvings I created on it earlier, the rest is so dark that it almost looks like I pulled night from the sky and whipped it into the fondant.

The fireworks explode outside as if the king knew what I was thinking. Pink fills the sky, radiant and bold, as it announces Bauer's capture. Reds sparkle after it, followed by screaming white blazes of light. The show would be magnificent if it weren't so murderous.

We make our way to the porch to watch it in case anything is different about it. Like every night, the fireworks glitter in the sky, reflections bouncing off of the pointed rooftops.

Minutes go by and the show proceeds as normal, the only variation is the colors and styles of fireworks the palace and towns shoot into the sky simultaneously. Hansel rests his hand on my shoulder as I lean against the porch railing. I can smell the scones inside and turn to go and check on them. Hansel's hand trails after me, but he doesn't take his eye off the skies above us.

I duck into the bakery and remove the tray of scones from the oven. Setting them on the table to cool, I glance around to see if anything else needs to be attended to.

"What is *that*?" Aurik's voice fills the room.

"It can't be," Brahms responds, panic in his voice.

"Annika!" I run to the door when I hear Hansel's harsh call.

In the sky, an orange fireball curves up into the air. I exit the bakery only a moment before it transitions from a streak of orange with a long tail into what looks to be a fire with a tail of blue and purple, almost like the wick of a candle. When the light hits it, it changes again, becoming a white glowing cloud trailing after a tiny spec of orange as it continues to arc up into the night sky.

"What is it?" I ask.

"It's a rocket, Annika." Hansel sounds breathless. It's terrifying.

As if totally disjointed, the rocket separates, leaving the thick trail of clouds behind, only a thin line of almost-blue clouds connecting the now-white glowing circle to the tail end of its streak.

"Where is it heading?" Aurik murmurs. I have a feeling he already knows.

Suddenly, it's as if the rocket explodes, a large cloud of pulsing blue frills out from it like a petticoat some of the towns ladies wear under their massive skirts. It swirls around the glowing streak as it changes its trajectory, beginning its descent.

Another moment goes by and none of us speak, fixated on the rocket sailing through the night sky. Behind it, fireworks continue to go off as normal in greens and yellows. The clouds from the rocket suddenly widen, becoming a solid wave rolling off the bright white light guiding it through the air. Something flickers behind it, leaving the secondary glowing object to pulse out strangely-shaped clouds in two different directions as it keeps up with the part of the rocket in the lead.

Pieces of the rocket break off, drifting quietly to the ground, glowing just as brightly as the main rocket. The entire glowing mass tips down, propelling itself quickly toward the ground before I realize what's happening.

"Hansel, is that—"

"Perihausen." He confirms my suspicions only moments before the rocket collides somewhere beyond the trees. Small ripples can be felt in the floorboards under my feet, but I likely wouldn't have noticed if I hadn't watched the rocket slam into the ground as it wreaked havoc on the city where Bauer was captured only hours ago. I hope the old woman who helped us is safe.

The vapor trail still glitters in the sky as smoke drifts up above the tree line to meet it. The fireworks finish their explosive show, the last of the finale sparkling away in the cool night breeze as we turn to go back inside.

"At least it wasn't here," Brahms says, breaking the silence.

"The king wouldn't hurt his precious cake." I didn't mean to lash out.

"He didn't touch Leipden, at least," Aurik adds.

"But he destroyed Perihausen," I protest.

"We don't know that for sure yet." Hansel tries to calm me. "We'll find out tomorrow."

"You know he did," I say under my breath as I return to my cake.

The dark colors inspire me, and I set to work decorating the device that will deliver death to King Levin.

CHAPTER 6

IT'S LATE MORNING WHEN I FINALLY WAKE UP, NO LONGER perched against the chair I was leaning on while icing the wooden cake. My blanket is warm around me, demanding I stay in place longer.

The floor is cool when my feet touch it. Hansel must have carried me upstairs after I fell asleep, but there's too much work to be done to stay in bed any longer.

Opening the curtains, I find that the daylight is unaffected by the spoils of last night's attack. Opening the window, I can faintly smell smoke, and I'm sure once I reach the first floor and can see out another window that there will be a dark trail of black smoke from the charred ruins of whatever remains of Perihusen.

Candestrachen lost a fine town last night to the king's whims.

Downstairs, Gretel is awake and working over the stove. Bacon, eggs, and French toast scents fill the air. Aurik stares in Gretel's direction hungrily. Brahms looks up as I approach.

"You shouldn't have let me sleep so long."

"Thank your boyfriend," Aurik calls over his shoulder.

"*Boyfriend?*" Gretel snaps, turning to look at me. "Is that what we're finally calling it?"

The front door swings open, revealing Hansel. His frame fills the doorway, backlit beautifully by the sun. His blond hair takes on a golden sheen as the breeze moves a few strands. The girls in the town have been throwing themselves at him for years…if only they could see him now.

"You're up," he mentions, moving across the floor. He kicks the door closed behind him, cutting off the sunlight.

"What did you find out?" Brahms asks.

"The ball has been moved up."

"To when?" Brahms inquires.

"Tomorrow." Hansel sounds grim, his face showing the wear of the day, dragging down his features.

"Tomorrow?" I gasp.

"*Tomorrow?*" Gretel's terrified voice jerks us all into action. We leap toward her, ready to comfort her. I reach her first, wrapping her in my arms.

"You'll be okay, Gretel," Brahms promises her as Hansel reaches us.

"We'll take care of you," Aurik adds. "No one will hurt you."

"Will you be ready, Gretel?" Ever the big brother, Hansel sounds as if he's ready to carry her off to safety right now and call the entire mission off.

"Can you get me out of there, Hansel?" she asks.

"Always. I will always get you out of bad situations."

"Than I will do this," she announces, gathering her confidence around her like a barrier between her and the world. "Annika, can you finish the cake?"

It's as if Gretel has suddenly been possessed by the girl in the mill, ready to take down the king. I have no doubt that she can kill the king and escape.

"I can finish it, but you have to promise not to do anything today, Gretel. You need to be as recharged as possible when we put you in that cake tomorrow morning."

"This is nearly a week before we expected it to be," Hansel responds. "We need to make sure everything is in order and that we don't forget anything when the time comes. We're rushing, and that makes me nervous."

"I can work on a list while I'm sitting around since I'm

not allowed to help." Gretel side glances at me. She adds quickly, "It will give me something quiet to do so I don't have time for my brain to stress out about everything."

"I'll get you some paper." I move away to find a notebook and pen for her.

When I return, I find her in a chair near the wooden cake—we'll be able to chat about the list while I work. Hansel stands behind us, observing the dark cake for a moment.

"Did he ask for that?"

"No." I shrug. "He said he wanted a cake to celebrate Candestrachen. What better way than to bring in the elements of the cities?"

"I don't see how—"

"You will," I interrupt him. "Now, go. You have work to do."

Aurik slips out the front door to prepare the other men for the change of orders. I have one day to complete this cake—in the morning, we have to deliver it to His Royal Highness.

"What *is* your plan for that, Annika?" Gretel asks as her brother steps away.

"The king is so fond of his candy-shaped rooftops and glittering light displays. I'm going to bring them to life on the cake."

"And his fondness for *death* will be included on the inside?" She smirks like her brother does.

"Yes, my dear, his death will most certainly be on the inside of his precious cake."

I lift the icing bag and begin to swirl large strands of bright pink frosting around the base of the cake. Walking around it, I cover it evenly with smooth lines of sugared perfection. After a while, I set the pink down and pick up an icing bag with white icing. Tracing along the same path, I mimic my motions, adding a thin white line next to each pink stripe.

Gretel mutters in approval, glancing up from her list for a moment before looking back down. I catch her staring at the cake when she doesn't realize I'm looking. I'm sure she's worried about everything, but the moment I look up as if I might glance over, she goes right back to work—I hope I'm helping keep her mind off of tomorrow.

In just over twenty-four hours, she'll be springing from the cake, prepared to touch the king of Candestrachen's hand. She'll pull the life from him, taking on every bit of darkness and soul inside of him. It will flood her over, threatening to break her.

I've seen her do it before—take life. Each time, it darkens her eyes, leaving her looking cold and lifeless. Though I've only ever seen her do it to plants, I know the toll it takes on the young girl's mind and body.

Hansel will not only have to pull her to safety once the guards realize what's happening, but he will have to use his power over light and *light* to pull her back from the evil she will have to take on. He's the only one that has the ability to rescue her and share the burden.

Along the top tier of the cake, I drizzle an off-white liquid icing, allowing it to dribble down the sides of the top tier of the massive cake. The droplets fall down, some reaching the top of the next tier, others ending relatively high.

I hand a bowl of sprinkles to Gretel. "Here, I know you were looking forward to this."

She grins and tosses a few handfuls at the drying icing. Most of them stick in place. I walk around, adding the colorful sprinkles to the sides she can't reach from her chair.

"So much for not working." Hansel snickers at us. Without missing a beat, Gretel tosses a handful of sprinkles at her brother's face. He reels back in surprise.

I join the young girl, tossing the tiny candies at Hansel…I'll regret it when I have to clean it up later.

Aurik walks in just in time to see Brahms and Hansel team up against Gretel and me. With a flick of my wrist, I transform the entire room into the candy-world illusion I had cast a few days before. The room springs to life with candy chandeliers and chocolate fountains. Swirled candies cover the banisters, and the fire pops in delight as I string illusion hard candies up by their wrappers from one edge of the fireplace to the other.

Brahms looks shocked as he turns to explore this sudden new world, eyes wide with delight. Aurik picks his jaw up and grins, frowning only when he realizes illusions aren't edible.

"Cruel," he comments.

"Isn't *everything* we're doing these days?" I counter.

"As delightful as this is, I have news," Aurik redirects us. "Bauer is to be executed at the ball tomorrow."

We grow somber as he explains the new plans for the party.

"The guards will be coming for you tomorrow morning, Annika. They'll escort you and the cake to the palace to see that nothing happens with it. I lied and told them I was your brother and that I would deliver the news of the rush order to you so they wouldn't come here themselves."

"At least you didn't say you were her boyfriend," Brahms jokes, glancing at Hansel.

"I would have turned him over as the witch they've been searching for if he had," I say sweetly, batting my eyelashes.

"I knew I liked you," Hansel adds, throwing an arm around my shoulder.

"You like me for my peanut butter fudge and my pastries."

"We've established that," Hansel replies, "but I like you for other reasons, too, like your quick sarcasm."

"It's her lips," Aurik jumps in. "Don't deny it. You're in it for the kissing."

"And that's enough of that, thank you," Gretel says shrilly. "We need to get back to work."

Aurik quickly relays the rest of the information he and his team found out, and we all settle back in to complete our tasks—the boys baking up our alibi, Gretel ensuring we won't forget anything, and me sugarcoating King Levin's demise.

"Open by order of the king!"

I wheel around to face the door. My hand dances in the air, concealing the scones, cookies, breads, and pies Hansel, Aurik, and Brahms had created. The candy-world illusion drops immediately, taking the sparkling sprinkles with it. Another flick of my wrist conceals Gretel behind a false wall with Aurik and Brahms as her protectors. Hansel is at the door before I can drop my hand.

I nearly drop the icing bag as I try to look natural as the guards force their way in.

"Where is the baker?" one demands.

Hansel looks to me.

"I'm the baker," I answer softly.

"By order of King Levin, we are to deliver you to the

palace." The guard eyes me carefully, slowly dragging his gaze over my dark red dress.

"I assumed as much," I reply, motioning to the cake. "I need a few more hours to finish the decorations."

I lean toward the cake, ready to continue my work. The guards grumble.

"Surely you don't mean for me to leave with a half-finished cake. What will His Majesty say?"

The guards protest rudely, but Hansel silences them. "The lady says she's not done, and your job doesn't require you to escort us there until the ball tomorrow. If you want to go out and have fun this evening, go. You don't need to babysit us while we're icing a cake. Come back tomorrow to collect us."

"Fine, finish the cake. We can go in the morning."

"We'll bring the vehicle first thing."

Strange, they didn't seem to have brought a vehicle to transport us this afternoon. Perhaps they were anticipating finding me flustered without the cake ready and thought they'd be taking me to be punished instead of lauded for my magnificent sugar creation.

They stalk out of the bakery and down the steps. The snake that chases them is my own design, slithering after them as one of the men screams long enough to make Hansel snicker beside me. The snake hisses, lashing out, only to disappear as the men run off.

"Testy now, aren't we?"

"I didn't like them." I eye Hansel. "They were planning on hauling me to the palace to stand trial."

"Ah, you noticed that too, did you?"

I drop the illusion as we turn back from the doorway.

"It's safe," Hansel announces. "We need to get this finished and ready to go, though."

"Did I hear you invite yourself along on the cake delivery?" Aurik asks, stepping away from his place along the wall.

"Better than trying to *talk* myself in," Hansel retorts. "The two of you are on watch duty tonight. If those guards come back, we have to be ready to get Gretel into place before they make it up the stairs. You can take turns standing watch while the rest of us sleep."

"We should stay down here by the cake," I comment, pushing back my hair. I wind part of it around my finger in a loose curl.

"Agreed. But first, we need to actually finish it." Hansel takes my elbow and turns me back to the cake covered in candies, swirls, and sugar designs. He whispers into my ear. "After you, mistress baker."

"It's a good thing you all need me tomorrow, or I'd have to end myself right now after a sappy line like that." Gretel pretends to gag. "Now fetch me a snack. I'm hungry, and I'm not supposed to do anything for myself."

She plops herself back down on her chair and waves for her brother to bring her a pastry.

"This only lasts until tomorrow, little sister," he warns her playfully.

"We'll see," she retorts, waving her hand again. "I'm killing a king, after all."

"You're rescuing Candestrachen," I add, holding the icing bag that I just scooped up out to her waiting finger. "Killing the king is just the method that gets us there. Don't forget that."

Hansel looks surprised, lips slightly parted as he returns.

"Don't ever forget that," he says seriously to his little sister, turning to her. It's important we protect her from what she's about to do—taking a life, even to save thousands, is a devastating, life-altering situation to be in. I imagine the poor girl will have a hard time coping with it after.

"Got it." She licks the white icing off her finger, making a popping sound for emphasis.

"Now let me see that list while Annika finishes this monster up." He kneels down beside Gretel, eyeing me from under his long, dark lashes. I turn away, not needing the distraction.

"Are you ready?" Hansel asks as we lean against the railing. Brahms and Aurik sit inside, giving us a few minutes alone on the porch to decompress before we turn in for the night.

"The cake is ready," I answer. "I *think I* am. I'm nervous. What if I can't hold the illusion long enough?"

"You can," he promises, taking my hand. "You've held massive illusions for very long periods of time. All you have to do is keep the three of us from being recognized once we get inside. The rest is up to Gretel and me."

"I'm nervous about that too," I confess.

"You don't think I can get her out of there?" I can hear the frown in his voice. The fireworks display has long since ended, but I almost wish Hansel would add a little lighting out here for us to see by since the moon is hidden behind the clouds.

As if reading my mind, a string of lights snakes its way around the column next to me, adding a soft glow as Hansel turns me toward him. His touch is warm against the coolness of the breeze.

"You're the only one that *can* get her out, Hansel." I sigh. "I'm just...I'm worried that something will go wrong. Our entire plan had to be rearranged and pulled together in one day. There are so many ways it could fail."

"We're going to be fine, Annika." He lifts the necklace off my neck, twisting it in his fingers. "I've always been able to find you by this when you were wearing an illusion. It has always been the *key* to reuniting us."

A lone cricket chirps in the yard somewhere. I nearly glance toward it, but I know we're having an important conversation.

"I'll be able to find you tomorrow, no matter what. And because of you and your necklace, I'll be able to find Gretel because of her necklace too. No matter what happens, no matter how many illusions you pull, I'll be able to recognize you."

I raise my hand, touching the gold trinket on the end of my mother's golden chain. It's a key with a burst of sparkling light at the top—a perfect representation of the lights Candestrachen is so obsessed with. In the palace, they'll catch the light and sparkle—even across the room, anyone who is specifically looking will notice it.

"I'm changing the plan, Hansel."

"What?"

My wrist brushes against the skin on his cheekbone, lightly brushing over his face as I move strands of his hair back from his eyes. He leans into my touch.

"I know we had planned to make Gretel a brunette and younger, but there's a better way now—the guards have handed it to us."

"What do you mean, Annika?" He reaches up and takes my hand, turning his face to kiss my open palm. It burns through me as if I accidentally touched the wire rack in the oven while adding a tray of uncooked muffins.

"The guards want a witch…we'll give them a witch. It won't be a tiny girl betraying the king, it will be the haggard old woman they saw in the woods that day. We'll give them their greatest nightmare—the woman who destroyed the forest and cost men their lives. They'll search for her until the day they die, but they'll never find a little blonde girl living with her brother in Leipden."

His lips are on mine as he mumbles, "You're brilliant." His fingers scrunch through my hair as he focuses on our deep kiss. I don't bother to stop him, even though our friends are only feet away inside the house. After an intense moment, I pull away.

"We should go in."

"Should we?" He grins.

"We need to sleep, Hansel. Tomorrow, we go to the palace."

He lets me lead him inside, holding his hand behind me with my arm stretched out as he pauses long enough to let me know he wants to stay.

Scooping up an apple from the table, he hands it to me as Aurik heads outside to take the first watch. Hansel sinks along the wall, waiting for me to join him a few feet from the cake form. I nestle against him, leaning against his shoulder and chest as I take a bite of the apple.

"It's always amused me how someone who bakes all these sugary treats could prefer healthy food like apples."

"A different kind of sweet, my friend."

"Well, I prefer your kind of sweet." He kisses my lips again. "Maybe apples aren't so bad after all."

CHAPTER 7

"Annika, it's time." Gretel shakes me gently. "Help me into the cake, Annika."

The room is deathly quiet aside from the snap of the fire and Gretel's tiny voice. Hansel and Aurik lay sprawled out on the floor, sleeping in different corners. Brahms stands on the porch, a sliver of his arm and side visible through the window.

"Wake up Hansel, and we'll help you—"

"No."

I blink at her.

"I will not say goodbye to my brother. I won't do it. I'll see him after, and that is that. Now, help me in before they wake up. We need to be ready when the guards arrive."

"Did you even eat yet?" I rub my eyes.

"I'll eat inside. You can hand me some snacks before you close it and add the final layer of icing." She tugs at my hand. "Please, Annika, I need to do this before I lose my nerve."

"Okay, okay." I stumble to my feet. "Go get whatever snacks you want, and I'll create the ladder."

I poke at my eyes again, trying to see straight. Blinking, I force my curls back. Separating my feet, I find my balance and stare at the cake. Terror washes over me—this is it.

My hands move slowly as if I'm conducting musicians. They flow through the air gracefully, and I picture the strangest set of stairs that lead from the floor, around the side of the cake in a wide arc. Railings appear on either side of the steps, swirling around the edges of the king's cake. I douse the entire thing in what looks to be pink swirled frosting and rock candy lollipops.

Gretel smiles softly as she returns.

"Gretel," I say, taking her hand as she sets her treats on the chair next to me. "I know you wanted to look a little different for this, but we've come up with a new plan—one where they'll never have any hope of finding you."

She raises an eyebrow at me.

"Gretel, you're going to be a witch."

"What?" She raises an eyebrow, her voice flat.

"From the woods. You're going to be the witch that rearranged the forest. A haggard old thing. When they come looking, they'll never expect to find a child."

She cringes as I use the word *child*, but she nods in understanding.

"I'm already the witch that rearranged the forest."

"But now you'll look like her."

"It's a shame not everyone has gifts like we do. It would make all of this a lot easier."

"It's a glorious thing that we are unique in this, Gretel, or we'd never pull this off—they'd be watchful of everyone. Besides, can you imagine what King Levin would do if he had the ability to do more than create fancy clothes with his gift?"

"He would be so jealous if he knew you could create illusions." She giggles quietly. "If he knew about you, you'd be stuck by his side for the rest of your life, transforming his little parties into even-more-grand events."

"You're probably right. Good thing he'll never find out." I take a deep breath. "Are you ready?"

She nods. Her eyes dare me to try to say anything that remotely sounds like a goodbye.

"Once you're inside, I'll seal off the top." I escort her to the first step. She places her hand on the rung of the railing and lifts a foot daintily. "You'll know when it's time to come out.

"I'll leave you in this form until we reach the palace and then I'll give you the illusion of an old woman. The ride will be long and probably bumpy, even with the motored machine. Try not to crash into the sides of the cake. If you need more air, you know what to do."

She nods, taking the next step.

"Try to focus on your surroundings. I'll be in the vehicle with you, so listen for my voice."

"I doubt they'll let you speak." She takes another step, allowing her to look down at me. My heart hammers in my chest with every step she rises into the air.

"Than just know that I'm there. Focus on every sound you hear. You'll be able to hear Levin's voice when he gets close enough to cut the cake.

"Be careful of the knife in his hand when you come out of the cake form. You're going to surprise him, and he might lash out. You need to be quick about it."

Gretel nears the top of the cake form, dressed in dark-colored clothes. She looks like an avenging angel.

"Do what you need to do, then get out of the cake, Gretel. Run. Hansel will find you, and I'll block however I can."

"I know."

"I'll find you when it's over, Gretel," I promise.

"I know you will, Annika. You've always taken care of

Hansel and me." She takes the final three steps, tipped down into the cake form. My fingers move, adding a few steps that disappear as she takes her foot off of them until she's standing up to her chest inside the wooden contraption. "I'll see you after."

She taps the sparkly necklace on her chest, and I tap on mine. Hansel will be wearing something similar on his coat pocket as well. All three charms shiny and noticeable, but nothing that can tie us together.

I hand the food to her and Gretel closes the lid, settling into the cake. I turn to find Brahms staring in the window at us. His eyes are glassy. He tips his head toward Hansel, eyes squinting as if asking why we didn't wake him.

I clutch my necklace in my fingers and smile. Nodding, I assure him it's okay, this is what needed to happen. Brahms sighs and turns back to his post.

I double and triple check my work once the top of the cake is concealed. When Brahms and Aurik switch places, I drag Brahms over to check my work.

"It's fine, Annika. You did good work."

"I'm sure it's fine," Gretel calls from inside the cake, her voice muffled by layers of fondant and icing.

"Aurik and I are going to try to rescue Bauer," Brahms confides in me quietly. "Hansel and Gretel will be our priority, of course, but if they don't need us, we're going to try to prevent the execution. We're hoping it takes place after the cake."

"You don't think he will use the cake to celebrate?" I frown. "And *you're* not even supposed to *be* at the palace."

"I'm sure he will, but maybe you could make something flash on the cake to keep drawing his attention all afternoon so he can't take his mind off it and he'll do it early."

"We have no idea when he will use the cake, Brahms."

"It's our best shot. Maybe we can get Bauer out in the chaos."

"Okay, I'll try, but I can't do anything to compromise Gretel."

"I would never ask you to." He touches my elbow.

"Thank you for risking yourself to try to save Bauer. You and Aurik could be safe in all this, but I'm really glad you're going to try."

"You three shouldn't be the only ones taking a risk today." He pats my hand. "Now, wake up Hansel and let's get ready. The light is peeking up, and I imagine the guards will either show up incredibly early or incredibly late."

"Gretel," I say a bit louder so she can hear me. "It's time to wake your brother up."

I want to give her as much time to prepare for his reaction as possible. Walking over to Hansel, I kneel down and touch his arm. He blinks awake, smiling for only a moment as he sees me before he remembers what day it is. He sits up quickly.

"Are they here?" He tosses a blanket off of himself and jumps to his feet.

"No, not yet." I take his hand. "We need to eat before they arrive though."

His eyes sweep the room.

"Where is Gretel?"

"She's ready, Hansel." It takes a moment before he catches on. His muscles tighten as he stalks toward the cake.

"Hansel, don't you dare upset her," I snap at him, whispering so Gretel can't hear. "She didn't want some big goodbye scene to throw her off. Tell her good luck and come outside to yell at me."

Hansel stares me down for a moment, jaw clenched. Glancing at the cake, tears fill his eyes. "I'm not going to yell at you," he whispers.

He looks like he's being torn in two, like some machine the guards use to torture people is shredding him right down the middle. I wish I could protect him from this like he's protected me so many times before.

"You good in there, Gretel?" he calls, gaze fixed on the floor off to the side.

"I'm fine," she calls back, sounding stronger than Hansel looks at the moment.

"Okay, I'm going to get something to eat and then I'll be back to walk through everything with you."

"Okay," she calls in reply.

I step forward and take Hansel in my arms—I know how hard this is for him. He lets me hold him for a minute, transferring his worry into our embrace. If I can carry even a little of it for him, I will.

His breath is shaky when he pulls away, but to his credit, his body doesn't show any signs of shuddering. He takes both of my hands in his, holding them near his chest.

"It will be okay, Hansel. We'll get her out of there."

"I know." He pulls away from me, sauntering over to the table for food. He picks up a palmier and holds it in his hands. After a moment, he takes a bite, looking like he might be sick. For as terrified as I am, it's so much worse for him with his little sister putting her life at risk.

"They're here." Aurik slips into the bakery from the porch.

Hansel swallows the rest of the sugary treat.

"Did you eat?" He shoved one at me. I gratefully devour it, wiping my hands on a towel before running over to the cake.

"Ready, boys?" I ask as Aurik and Brahms shove themselves against the back wall. I put an illusion wall between us as Hansel helps me move the cake. "Time to go, Gretel. We'll be with you the whole way. Just watch for the pendants."

She stays quiet, knowing her mission has started.

The motor on the vehicle roars loudly as the guards pound up the steps. I open the door before they can knock, inviting them inside. Before we went to sleep, we put away all of the extra pastries so the guards wouldn't see them, leaving only a tray out for us to eat this morning. I motion to it, inviting the guards to partake.

Hansel instructs them on how to help move the cake. Together, the three men lower the cake down the stairs and wheel it toward the brightly colored vehicle. Leave it to the king of Candestrachen to go overboard on the decorations on a motor vehicle.

The taller guard lowers the back, pulling down a ramp. The entire vehicle lowers to the ground, leaving the ramp as a mere decoration. Had they tried, they could have easily just lifted the cart with the cake into the vehicle.

As the men assist him, I take a small magnetic device and push it against the underside of the wheel well. Hansel reprogramed his fireflies to work in unison, so as we make our way from the palace after the assassination, we'll be able to easily find our way back to territory we know, no matter what happens.

The guards instruct Hansel to push the cake inside, nearly touching the seats in the front. From the sides, the men pull down extra seats and demand I get in. I climb up next to Hansel, taking a seat opposite him, positioning ourselves between the guards who follow us in and the cake.

A third man drives, steering us away from the bakery. Once they're sure we're gone, Aurik and Brahms will race through the woods toward the palace, slipping onto paths the vehicle can't take. They won't beat us, but it won't be more than an extra half hour until they arrive—it will give us enough time to be turned away from the palace and use illusions to slip back in, that way, in the aftermath, the baker can't be blamed because she was back at her shop, making pastries.

The road is less bumpy than I thought, the vehicle stabilizing us each time we hit a dip in the road. The cake is barely jostled as we move. If I didn't hate things the king oversaw so much, I might actually be impressed with their ingenuity.

Hansel watches me in the bouncing light of the vehicle. The sun shifts and changes as we drive under trees and around corners, casting long shadows at strange angles. He locks eyes with me, stretching his foot out quietly to touch mine, calming his nerves as much as mine.

I wish I could see out of the back of the motorized transportation, but there are no windows on the back doors. It's probably for the best—the guards can't accidentally see our fireflies and grow suspicious—but I wish *I* could check on them.

The journey stretches out, simultaneously taking forever and no time at all. The guards comment crudely as I step out of the vehicle to allow them to assist Hansel. Making sure no one is looking, I pull the magnetic container off the car and toss it away.

The men maneuver the cake out of the vehicle and onto the ground. They instantly wheel it up onto a marble ramp, taking it into the palace.

"Thank you," a woman with folded hands and a high collar says from the platform. "You may go now."

I start to protest, but she holds a hand up. "You are dismissed, young ma'am."

I blink. I hadn't anticipated being turned away so quickly.

"You don't want to come in here," she adds quietly. "This is no place for a pretty young thing like you. You will leave immediately. You've been thanked for your service, now go."

Her words leave no room for argument, but I've heard they prefer men take the accolades and praise inside the palace—I suppose this wise woman is why. I appreciate her looking out for me, but I value her unexpected part in our assassination plot even more—she has no idea she's giving me an even better alibi for the murder. At least I didn't have to come up with a reason for them to keep me out.

The woman hands me a few coins, not nearly enough to cover the cost of the cake if it had been real. I pocket it and turn to go. With the guards inside guiding the cake, Hansel and I are left to walk all the way back to the bakery.

Once we're out of sight, we round the corner to the front of the palace where large groups of people wait to get inside. Dignitaries hover near the front, flanked by townspeople doing their duty to show up to the frivolities.

My fingers dance, dousing me in shades of green. I release my hair from its bun and let it fall down to my waist. Hansel's breath catches as I look up. He's suddenly clad in an illusion dusty blue suit, with a long jacket reminiscent of the one Bauer was wearing when he was captured. I change Hansel's hair to a shocking red-colored that will ensure he is noticed in the crowd. My own hair morphs into a light brown that's not quite light enough to be blonde, but not dark enough to be brunette.

"I'm amazed at how stunning you look, even in different forms."

"You'd rethink that if you saw my haggard look from the other day," I joke. "Now, go get yourself into the palace. Good luck."

"Are you sure? That might be your best look of them all." He kisses my cheek, grinning. "After you, madam."

I make my way into the crowd, looking for an opening. If I can find a family or group, I might be able to sneak in at the end of their party without the guards noticing an extra person. The townspeople huddle together, acting like they're having fun, but there is nervousness in the depths of their eyes, and they quickly look away when I accidentally make eye contact with them. I hope they all make it out when the chaos erupts.

A group of men and women hover at the far edge, and I make my way over as the line shifts, allowing people into the palace. Slowly, I inch toward them. One step at a time, I get closer.

Suddenly, they sidestep, walking into the palace through a second door the guards open—I missed my chance.

"Well, what do we have here?"

I look up into the eyes of a guard towering over me.

"I'm here for the ball," I reply, batting my eyelashes. One of the perks of an illusion is that I can fix up my lashes when I need to.

"Are you now?" he asks. "Are you on the list?"

"Do I need to be?" I ask breathlessly. I could gag.

"That depends," the guard steps toward me.

From the corner of my eye, I catch sight of Hansel's illusion-red hair. He tries not to look horrified, but I can't miss his wrinkled nose and tight brow.

I take the guard's hand holding the list and stretch on my toes to lean over his arm. Pointing at the list. "There I am. Though, I'm not sure I'll be able to stay for the entire ball. If you see me coming out of those doors a little early, well, don't you fret. I just needed a little fresh air."

My toes curl in my shoes as I realize just how bad I am at flirting. I bat my eyes again, hoping to distract him from my ridiculous words.

His hand drops from the list as he transfers it to the one with the pen. It finds its way to my backside. "I'll keep an eye out for you."

I spin away, rushing toward the open palace door as he laughs behind me. Without bothering to wait for Hansel, I scurry down the hall to find my place in the throne room where the cake will be waiting.

If the outside of the palace was impressive, the inside is *inspired.* For as stunning as my candy-world illusions are, the interior of King Levin's palace is more spectacular and encompasses everything I created without any reference to candy.

Large columns shoot up from the floor covered in hand-carved vines and flowers. The marble floor is tinged pink and laid with small rivers of sparkling gold that course throughout the entire room. Chandeliers grace the ceiling every few yards with one massively large one hanging in the center.

Floor-to-ceiling windows allow the sparkling light to bounce through the diamonds placed into the crystal glass. Along the tops of the walls, there is a runner of precious jewels in every color, acting as a border for the room.

The cake sits by the throne—a massive silver thing made of arrows and dark metal. The king hasn't arrived yet, but once his crowd fills the room, I'm sure he'll make a grand entrance—he'll probably fly in on the back of a golden swan if the rest of this room is any indication of the lengths he will go to in order to impress people.

"Are you okay?" Hansel whispers harshly as he slowly walks by.

"Fine," I mumble—we can't be seen together. "Go away."

He steers himself across the room, positioning himself a dozen people away from the cake in the second row of the crowd. Pedestals with roses under glass cases dot my side of the room, and I pick a place next to a dark red one. I can tap it with my elbow if I need something to anchor myself to as I focus on everything around me.

Using my sleeve to hide my movements, I wave my fingers at the cake, adding a few small sticks around the tiers. If I need to get the king's attention, this will be how I do it.

The room grows louder as more townspeople enter. The dignitaries and visitors from other lands take places near the throne and in the stands off to the side left for guests of the king. Music swells up, and a number of couples dance as if it's their job—I'm sure it is—to make outsiders believe this is something we revel in every week. At least the king enjoys himself at these parties.

Heat creeps up my neck into my cheeks as more people fill the room. They mumble about Bauer out in the courtyard, locked in a cage with a rope around his neck, waiting for his execution. The dignitaries discuss it so loudly from their places in the stands that I can hear them taking bets on how the king will murder my friend.

The room feels like it's moving around me, but it's only overwhelm messing with my perception. A few deep breaths and I calm myself. I hope Gretel is staying focused inside of the cake. I move my fingers, trans-forming her into the old hag that claimed the forest as her own.

As her dress grows dark, and wrinkles form on her skin, I add a small piece of candy into her hand to let her know it's done. She can't eat it, but it will make her smile and give her a reason to relax. I picture her tucking her now-gray and matted locks behind her ear as she arranged her witch's dress to accommodate the space around her. We were only separated for a few moments, but she must have been terrified to be on her own with no protection or backup.

An hour goes by as more people file into the throne room. The noise is louder. Each breath makes it hotter. I lock eyes with Hansel once and his lips part, but I look away.

The world stops as Levin, King of Candestrachen walks into the room.

CHAPTER 8

LEVIN STRUTS INTO THE ROOM, A GOLD CROWN RESTS ON his dark brown hair. Like me, he's wearing a green outfit, complete with a cape. For a moment, I consider giving Gretel a cloak with a hood to add to the witch's character, but the crowd needs to see she's old and a hood would cover that.

The king takes long steps through the center of the room as the crowd parts, bowing as he passes. He holds one arm behind his back, shoulders straight and head held high as he surveys this tiny sample of the kingdom crammed into his spacious throne room.

Slowly, he takes the steps up to his seat. Spinning

quickly, he makes a few women nearby gasp in surprise as he faces the room. The man sits, resting his hands on the ends of the armrests of his silver chair. One side of his lips tick up in a sickening smile and the crowd cheers.

Music pours out from the instruments in the corner of the room, the people playing them intentionally precise about every note. The chandeliers sparkle and I wonder how much Hansel is itching to change the colors of the light in them to shock the king.

The king waves his hand, and the dancing begins. People whirl around the room as I try to hide behind the glass-encased rose. Eventually, a man offers me his hand, and I have no choice but to allow him to lead me to the floor.

As I swirl, I try to find Hansel. Instead, the eyes I find are far more sinister—King Levin. He watches me for a moment as I dance. I try not to take notice, but it's hard to rip my eyes away from his piercing gaze. Does he remember me from outside Bauer's shop? He can't in my altered state, but I feel as though he knows everything about our plan as if he can read my mind.

The man swirls me one last time and I hurry off the floor with the crowd and Levin looks away, locking eyes with another girl and grinning wildly—no wonder the woman with the clasped hands warned me off. I huddle next to the rose again, watching the cake closely, but no one seems to be bothering it.

The king eventually gives a speech, ranting about the rebels and how easy it was to catch Bauer. He still doesn't know our leader's name, so he assigns one that doesn't fit Bauer at all.

The list of crimes is long, but we knew it would be. Outside, fireworks go off, giving me an idea. If I need to distract the king, now is the time for it.

I brush my thumb and pointer finger together as if I were snapping, brushing the skin together enough that if I were in a silent room, I'd hear a quiet swish. The sticks I had placed in the cake earlier spring to life—sparklers—emphasizing the king's words just as he gets to the part about moving outside for the execution. He's picked a particularly painful way to kill Bauer, and if I can give him even the smallest chance of escape, I have to try.

Levin glances to his right toward the cake. If he wasn't so distracted by the sparking dessert, he might have spotted Hansel with his illusion-red hair glaring at him in the background.

For a moment, hope swells in my chest, and I actually believe we can do this—we can assassinate the mad king and take our country back. But then the king takes a step off of his platform toward the crowd.

"I'd like to thank you all for joining me today," King Levin addresses them, holding his hands out in front of him benevolently. "I know you weren't expecting to be here until next weekend, but with the rebels quelled here in the glorious kingdom of Candestrachen, I couldn't help but share my joy with you."

He takes another step, and several stewards rush forward to move the cake as Levin barely moves one finger toward it.

"Given this entire event has been rearranged, I think perhaps we should toss aside tradition on this momentous occasion and celebrate first—perhaps even *during* the execution of our enemy. Let him see us reveling in the life I've created for this kingdom—a life of happiness and generosity. Let him see what he tried to destroy and what he shall never have for himself. What do you say?"

The crowd cheers on command, raising hands into the air. A man starts a chant. The crowd picks it up, praising Levin and his wondrous works.

Men wheel the sparkling cake from its position off to the side to where it can be seen in front of the king, closer to the far side of the crowd as they wait for him to call it forward.

Any normal person would have noticed the sparklers should have gone out by now, but I hold them in place, sparking and glowing for the king as he monologues. He never even considers the sparklers wouldn't bend to his will.

Suddenly, the sparklers glow brighter, as if an entire cloud of light surrounded each of them—Hansel. I find him in the crowd, but his eyes are trained on the cake as they should be.

"Even our cake knows we've earned our treats today!" the king jokes as the sparklers glow, transitioning to a red glow. "I've never seen a cake so beautiful—just look at it! It's Candestrachen in cake form!"

He uses the words he sent to me when he requested the cake be made and I feel as if I've done my job well. It may be a fake cake, but the outside was crafted to perfection. Dark icing with pink and white swirls and streams of icing flowing down the sides mixed with sprinkles—the architecture of the kingdom ready to bite the king when he least expects it.

"Ladies and gentlemen," he continues. How can one man speak for so long? "Today we celebrate the quick thinking of our guards. We celebrate the takedown of a rebel leader who never stood a chance against the *greatness* that is Candestrachen. We celebrate a cake that represents the *greatness* of this nation, but first, we celebrate the death of a traitor."

He lifts the hand near my side of the room, and the doors fly open as guards stomp into the room. The cake keeps sparkling as everyone turns. Trapped between several of the king's men is the man who turned in Bauer.

They force him several steps into the room before kicking the backs of his knees, making him drop to the ground. A guard pulls a sword—a weapon I've never seen any of the king's men use before—and swings it at the man before any of us can react.

I've witnessed men and women being blown up by explosive devices before, I've even seen them being pulled apart in different directions, but I've never seen one die like this before—it's archaic and grotesque. Blood pools out, reminding me of the icing I dripped on the cake less than a day ago. People push back to avoid it touching their shoes.

"And now...cake!" the king proclaims. I turn back to find him grinning, looking every bit the madman we know him to be.

The group turns in horror toward him. Several women blanch, fighting to keep their hands by their sides instead of clutching their chests. Children fidgeted against their parents' legs, trying not to react.

I've heard stories about time slowing down when major moments occur in one's life—every sense becomes sharpened, every heartbeat is felt, everything is experienced in acute detail. That doesn't happen now, but I wish it would so I could be more aware of everything going on around me—it would let me protect the people I love easier.

The guards wheel the cake forward in front of the mad king, sparklers still spraying small sparks everywhere. Even if the king got close enough, the illusion wouldn't burn him.

The executioner walks up from the back of the room, drying off the sword on a piece of material he found somewhere. I wonder for a moment if the king planned it this way—he probably did.

Once the blade is clean, he hands it to King Levin with a slight bow. This wasn't a part of our plan—he could run Gretel through with that sword, and she has no idea the king is holding it. She likely doesn't even know how the man was killed across the room.

"Darkness once overtook us," Levin says, slipping back into his speech as he points at the black, fondant-covered cake. "But *I* have brought the light."

I twist my fingers together again just enough that the sparklers expand with his words as if on cue. I can see Levin's eyes widen in surprise, but he grins as if he knew it was coming.

"I've brought life back into this nation and have given it a reason to thrive. We live in a land of luxury that cannot be found in any of our neighboring kingdoms." He turns to his guests. "We welcome you here, my brothers. There is none greater than Candestrachen, and your friendship is welcome here."

He glances around to his guests, selecting which will be honored. He nods to an old man with a gray beard reaching halfway down his chest. The man returns his nod, lips tight.

Levin turns, his green jacket and cape moving gloriously behind him. A piece of his long, brown bangs flips in front of his eye, and for a moment, he almost looks like he could belong in the towns of Candestrachen, selling wares in a shop, attending parades, and courting young women. His sneer morphs his face into something dark and twisted, though, as his evil side creeps out.

The side of the top tier of the cake unlatches, moving just enough so I can see it. Gretel has clicked the button on the inside of the wooden cake form as she prepares to launch herself at her target.

I slice my hand through the air at my side, killing the sparklers on the cake as Gretel in the form of the most decayed old woman I've ever seen flies from the top of the cake. Her face droops, skin sagging off her shallow bones. Deep recesses under her eyes demand the light create shadows there. Her hands, while fast, show the wear of years, and her veins protrude deeply.

Tight sleeves wrap around her wrist, pointing down toward her fingers—a feature I'm sure the king would appreciate had he had time to see it. Black and gray lace swirl over the dark fabric of her dress. Her bodice matches the sleeves, flowing into a skirt she can easily pick up to run in.

Gretel's face shows no emotion as the king attempts to reel back in surprise. The sword catches on the bottom of the cake form. Instead of slicing through it like it would with a normal cake, it scrapes up it harshly, sticking before it reaches the middle layer. It tumbles from his hand, crashing to the floor, point still stuck in the wood of the cake form.

"The witch," he cries, his words loud above the quiet crowd.

Gretel reaches out, catching his hand in hers. She leans forward, squinting into his eyes. The more hers close, the wider his grow.

She mumbles something at him as he pales.

Everyone watches in horror as the king begins to fade. It happens so quickly that his guards don't know how to react. As if transforming into a male version of Gretel's witch form, the king begins to hollow, his face growing slim and skin sagging off his bones. His once-brown hair turns a vicious gray moving out from the roots to the tips.

It looks like he shrinks before our eyes, caving in on himself as Gretel pulls the life from him, leaving only the decay of death.

She doesn't move as she works, focusing solely on her victim. Hansel is fixated on the young girl in disguise, so I take up the responsibility of watching the crowd. No one moves...except the guard who brought the king the sword.

The king falls to his knees; Gretel leans forward with him, but the approaching guard moves faster than she expects.

"Look out!" someone in the crowd cries, warning Gretel.

A woman screams, distracting a few people. The guard isn't deterred though. I rush forward as our plan goes sideways.

The man in uniform pulls the king away, tossing him on the ground, half dead. Pulling the sword from the cake, he reaches for Gretel. I throw my hands out, creating a barrier around the girl. The wall snakes around people, forming an oddly-shaped room and a maze-of-a-hallway leading out of the throne room. People jump out of the way as the barrier races at them. I slip inside the wall before it races past me and I barrel toward Gretel.

She's in a daze, not moving. I try to pull her from the cake form, but she's trapped in a world of death and Hansel isn't here to pull her back from the horrors she's committed. With no other choice, I leap over the bottom tier of the cake form and push it down the corridor I've created.

Tears burn against my eyes as I realize we've failed and now the only way out is through this maze I've built us. Even if we escape it, where can we go? How can we escape the palace? If I extend the escape outside of the palace walls, they'll just follow it and catch us when I lower the illusion wall. We have no hope and no means of finding freedom.

"I'm so sorry, Gretel." My words come out mixed with tears.

At least I can hold Hansel's illusion until he can escape. He'll be devastated over the loss of his little sister. I'm responsible for her death now.

"Get out of here, Hansel," I will him, whispering as guards pound against the wall, some nearby. "Don't be stupid. Go get Aurik and Brahms and leave. Come back and kill the king another day."

I can't believe we had come so close only to have him be pulled out of Gretel's grasp before she had ended him. She only had him under her control for a moment before the guard interrupted her, but it wasn't quite long enough. It was much easier for her to create life than death.

"Gretel? Gretel, I need you to come back to me," I beg, but I'm not Hansel and I have no control over life and light.

I wheel us around a corner, trusting the illusion walls to take us out of the palace by way of the main entrance —it's the only way I knew to get out.

Maybe, by some miracle, I can reach the end before the guards do and transform Gretel back into a young girl, fulfilling her request to look like me. And if by some miracle, I can, maybe Hansel will be there to pull her to safety.

I have to hope.

Light starts to filter into the tunnel I've created, and I assume we're reaching the end, but the noise behind me assures me I'll never make it—the guards have broken in and are running behind us.

Tears blur my vision as Gretel stares back blankly at me. Then, she blinks.

Perhaps she's coming back.

Moving my wrist to take the pressure of pushing the cake, I wiggle my fingers at her, dropping the illusion I'd placed over her. Her skin bounces back, tightening. Brunette locks color in the gray mats as Gretel returns to me.

But two women entered the tunnel—one of them was a witch.

The men gain on me. Another few steps and they will know.

I do the only thing I can—I transform.

CHAPTER 9

I cover the tunnel in candies of every color as I work to change everything the guards will see. I bring my candy-world to life again, hoping to distract them. At the very least, I hope they trip over some of it.

A man slams into me, knocking me to the ground. Gretel careens forward, slamming into the wall that turns at a ninety-degree angle, jutting out into the courtyard. I kick the man off me, scrambling to reach Gretel. My screams fill the hollow hallways, echoing out into the courtyard.

Hansel has one chance of saving his sister, and it's now.

I drop all of the illusions but the ones that cling to my body and to Hansel and Gretel. The walls disappear, but the candy bounces on the ground around us, reappearing. Brunette-Gretel—nearly unrecognizable—sits in a pile on the ground, free from the cake debris. Somewhere, Hansel is in his illusion form, looking for a way to us. Light floods around us and I squint.

"The witch!" one of the men shouts.

"She put a girl in the cake!"

"How did she get her?" another shouts.

People pull at Gretel, trying to get her away from the evil witch rising from the ground. Hands pull at her, and I want to stop them, but I can't draw extra attention to her.

"The witch was trying to eat the child!" someone screams. "She couldn't have the king's soul, so she tried to take the little girl's!"

"Stand back!" A man's voice shouts. It's familiar. "She'll steal your souls too!"

Bauer rushes toward Gretel and pulls her from a woman's hand. The boys must have been able to release him in the chaos of the king's almost-death. I move my fingers, concealing our leader in an illusion so the guards don't recognize him. He nods once to me, reinforcing the decision I made. Someone will pay the price, and it's going to be me.

Aurik and Brahms stand off to the side, trying to

assess the scene. They haven't caught on yet, but they watch Bauer—they saw him transform, so they know I'm here somewhere—and take his lead as he clings to Gretel. They know the brunette girl isn't me, but they haven't figured out I switched places with the girl yet.

The guards draw their weapons, kicking the illusion candy out of the way.

"You can't kill a witch, you fools," Bauer shouts. The boys echo him, realizing where I am as they try to spare me an immediate death.

The crowd is fearful of me, holding their children behind their backs, trying to move as far away as possible without catching the attention of the men wielding weapons. Any movement toward or away from me could be taken as a sign of their involvement—either to help the witch or run from their crimes connected to the hag that tried to kill the king and nearly sucked the soul from a small girl.

A guard calls to me, trying to talk me into kneeling and giving up. As long as Hansel isn't here to save Gretel, I can't give up yet, no matter what that means.

Searing pain rips through my arm as one of the guards shoots at me. It tears through my flesh, and blood spills out, dousing my black lace sleeve. Better me than Gretel.

Bauer pulls Gretel deeper into the crowd. She steps back with him, but she's still not with us.

"Witch!" the deep-voiced guard calls to me, reminding me once again of my father's voice. "You are accused of trying to kill the king of Candestrachen. The punishment is death."

Oddly enough, I'm about to take Bauer's place. At least the resistance has their leader back—I'm of no use to them anymore now anyway—we've played my card.

A flash of red grabs my attention—Hansel is here.

I look him in the eye and tap my necklace. He registers my height—much taller than Gretel—and realizes that I'm taking her place. He locks eyes with me and his face falls. Hansel shakes his head once, begging me to find another way, but I can't; not from this.

"Witch!" the deep-voiced man calls again. "Give up."

I dip my hands to the sides, stretching out my arms, but I say nothing. Hansel's gaze follows my more emphasized arm to where his sister's necklace gleams in the light. His pendant glints as he rushes to her side.

Bauer says something to Hansel, letting him know he's in an illusion, preventing him from ripping his sister away unnecessarily. I see them as I slowly spin in a circle, taking in the crowd.

This is the last time I'll see the sun or breathe the fresh air. It's the last time I'll feel dirt under my feet, and the final time I'll see people. I take it all in. Closing my eyes for a moment, I inhale, filling my lungs.

When I open my eyes, I complete my circle. I stare

down the guard, daring him to come for me. I don't speak.

He takes a strong step forward, thinking I'll balk. I don't.

"You'll die for this, Witch. You'll be taken before the king. You'll pay for this."

I wave my hand and the candy littering the courtyard disappears.

I'm sure I will pay for this.

At least I'll get to see what has become of the half-dead king in person. I'll know how soon they'll all be safe from him in his weakened state.

Weapons are raised in my direction again, but the guard instructs them not to kill me yet. The king, of course, will want his say in the matter.

"He's alive, Witch. You didn't kill him, but you knew that, didn't you? That's why you stole the child."

With all eyes on me, I drop Hansel and Gretel's illusions, leaving them in their true forms. The little girl the witch tried to devour is no more—they'll never find the brunette again.

The guards run at me, tackling me. Screams rise up in the crowd as they kick me, mingling with my own. I'm wrenched backward, onto my knees to face the crowd.

"This is what happens when you come against the king!" He rips my hair back, tears pressing against my open eyes as I snarl. I must look hideous in this form when I make that face.

Hansel looks devastated, hands wrapped tightly around Gretel as if she's the only thing anchoring him to this world. He rocks on his feet, leaning forward with her. She's the only barrier keeping him from running to save me.

Aurik places a hand on Hansel's arm, ready to make the decision for him if he needs to—escape comes first. Bauer prepares to back him up if necessary.

Gretel blinks, slowly coming back as Hansel pulls her back to us. She'll register what's happening in a moment. She doesn't need to see this, and I silently will Hansel to run. I don't want her feeling responsible for me. He can tell her I was lost during the escape, but not how it came to be—he'll protect her from this, but he can't if she sees with her own eyes.

Hansel's beautiful hair falls over his face, catching the light just enough to make him glow, but then, Hansel has always been full of light. He radiates everywhere he goes and illuminates the path for every life he touches. I regret not spending more time with him earlier on.

He's breathing heavily as he watches me. A tear slips down his cheek. His lips part in a silent prayer.

I try to smile. I want him to know I'll be all right. I want to do this for them.

He shakes his head, disappointed that everything

crumbled around us like a candy house smashed by a child's errant fist. Tears stream down his face—he knows there's nothing he can do.

Bauer tugs him back—it's time for them to go.

I nod and blink back tears.

Bauer and Aurik pull Hansel back, fighting him. Brahms wraps Gretel in his arms and pulls her away just as she comes out of her trance. He shields her from the horrors around her. Hansel strains against his friends. Giving up, he finally bows his head, a complete wreck.

"I'm sorry," he mouths to me, disappearing in the crowd as they force him away. He reaches for me, hand disappearing behind the crowd.

The guards beat me, forcing my body to jerk in different ways until they lift me off my feet.

Hansel and Gretel will try again. Bauer will come up with a new plan. The bakery will likely be taken over by one of the other girls in our group of rebels that can pass as me, but I doubt Hansel and Gretel will ever set foot in it again. Life will go on without me for the rebels and for Hansel and Gretel.

My fate is uncertain. Should the king lock me in one of his prisons before my execution, I'll decorate it in illusions and slip away in my mind, oblivious to what will happen to me. If he kills me on the spot, it will all be over. The fireworks this evening will signal the destruction of the witch that kills kings and eats the souls of children.

I was never a witch, but if I must take the fall to protect Hansel and Gretel, I'll be whatever kind of monster Levin needs me to be.

I contributed to the cause, and now the king is aged so dramatically that even if the resistance fails again, Levin only has a few years at most. Our people will see his candy-colored world crumbles around him, even if I'm not here to see it through.

I wave my hands at the sky, setting off illusion fireworks that end in shattered pieces of candy bouncing off the rooftops of Candestrachen—my final goodbye to the world I'm giving my life to protect.

I can't sugarcoat their world anymore.

VIRTUALLY SLEEPING BEAUTY

A Sleeping Beauty Retelling

BOOK 1: VIRTUALLY SLEEPING BEAUTY

VIRTUALLY
SLEEPING BEAUTY

K.M. ROBINSON

Chapter 1

"I CAN'T GET HER UP," SHE SOUNDS PANICKED.

"You can't *what*?" I mumble.

"I can't get her up, Royce. You need to come over here and help me."

She sounds like she's rushing around the room. Suddenly, I hear the sound of skin coming in contact with skin as she taps her goddaughter's cheek repeatedly as she tries to wake her.

"Would you relax please, Aunt Perry? She's in a game. She'll be under for a while. That's just how virtual reality works these days—once you're in the chair, you're out for up to four hours depending on your settings."

I jingle my keys to my car, trying to flip to the correct one. It's ridiculous how many different keys I have to carry for my family.

"That's the problem, Royce. She's been in there since this morning."

I glance at my watch. 3 pm.

"What *time* this morning?" A twinge of nervousness slips into my voice. I don't exactly know this girl, but that fact that she's been in for over four hours has me concerned.

"Eight. She was supposed to be out for lunch. We had errands to run."

Perry murmurs something to the girl, this time slapping her harder.

"Perry, stop!" I shout. "That's not going to help."

"What about water—?"

"No!" I bellow. "Just stop messing with her. I'll be right over."

I drop my coffee cup into the drink holder before slamming the keys into the ignition. The car roars to life —*the red-hot beauty that she is*—and I take off down the block.

Aunt Perry's house is only a few streets away but by the time I arrive, she's in the driveway waving hysterically at me. I take a deep breath to steel myself.

"Royce, I don't know what's happening," she sobs as she grabs my arm, pulling me toward the house. My coffee sloshes out of the mouthpiece of my container, dripping on my hand. Good thing it wasn't that hot to begin with.

We stumble up the steps clumsily as she pulls me into the house. My father's siblings have never been known for being great in a crisis. She pulls me toward the stairs inside and I managed to pull free of her so I can walk with my drippy hand on the banister.

"Calm down, we'll handle it," I demand a little more aggressively than I mean to. Perry looks close to tears. "I'm sorry. We'll figure this out, I just need you to stop shouting."

She nods, holding back the tears.

"Okay, tell me what happened," I prompt.

"Rora has been staying with me this week while her parents are on their trip," Perry starts, gaining the tiniest semblance of the ability to speak. "Once or twice in the evenings she's played her game for an hour, but she always comes down to have ice cream with me before we go to bed."

None of this is helpful, but okay.

"Because it's the weekend, she usually gets up early to play, so we had planned on her playing until eleven and then we were going to go get lunch and run some errands. When I came to check on her a little after eleven, she was still in the game. I assumed she started late so I gave her an extra hour."

She tugs me over to the sleeping girl in the chair, sniffling.

"It's been hours, Royce. I can't wake her up. What do we do?"

"Some people have been known to take extra injections to stay in longer," I offer.

"She wouldn't. She's too responsible for that." Perry gives me an impatient look. "This is the girl who is class president, and works at charities, and does all of her homework for the entire week before she even *considers* playing a virtual game. Rora wouldn't take extra injections when she knows it's against the rules."

Some people are adrenaline junkies—they do it for the rush. Maybe Rora is one of those girls who is super straight-laced in all other parts of her life and this is her guilty pleasure.

I can't say that would be the *worst* thing in the world. I, myself, would love to stay in the games longer.

"Well, if that's the case, maybe we should call a medical team to come wake her up," I reply, turning for the door. Let them handle her.

"No!" Perry shouts, racing after me. "We can't. If something really *did* happen, we can't let them catch her. And even if she hasn't done anything wrong, her mother's going to kill me for letting this happen on my watch. Please, Royce, we need a better idea."

I sigh dramatically.

I don't like being at everyone's beck and call.

"Fine, there's one other thing we can do first."

Setting my coffee cup on the desk next to a few of the girl's binders, I walk back over to where she's quietly laying in the chair.

She's still breathing, which is a good sign. Her

fingers twitch slightly so I can tell she's playing the game. Other than that, she barely moves—a side effect of the injections that allow us to enter the virtual world and feel and experience everything inside the game.

"I'll go in and find her," I announce.

"What? No, Royce, you can't." My aunt pulls on my arm. "What if you get stuck in there too?"

"I won't. I do this all the time." I brush her off. "Go grab me an injection, would you?"

After an angry look, she turns and leaves to find an injection.

Most people use the virtual reality system in one form or another, so there are usually injections lying around every house. The older generation uses it to relax—sometimes they go to a beach, other times they attend orchestra concerts or explore museums. The younger generations are more careless and play high intensity games. I tend to spend my time gaining skills I'll never use in real life as I leap from buildings and save damsels in distress.

I climb into the chair next to her and roll up my sleeve. When I have my feet comfortably arranged at the end of the footrest, I lean back and make sure I like the position I'm sitting in.

Perry walks back in and hands me the injection.

"I'm going to set the machine for an hour, but hopefully I'll find her right away. I need to get over to Alan's, so I don't have a lot of time to waste."

Perry looks nervous so I send her downstairs with the assignment of running her errands for the day. I promise to call her when I have her houseguest back in the real world. She reluctantly agrees to leave, slowly walking out the door to her car. An empty house is for the best right now.

I wait for her to drive away. The last thing I need is for her to come back in, have a meltdown, and throw water on me while I'm in the game. I quietly study the girl's face while I wait so that I don't accidentally miss her in the game. It's a little hard to see around her goggles, but it will suffice. I program the machine to take me to the game she is playing.

With the headset on, ready to be slipped over my eyes, I place my hand on the reader to identify myself and then inject my arm. I quickly put the goggles in place and rest my hands on the arms of the chair.

My vision goes black before crackling into a white burst of light. It fizzles out as the gamescape filters into place in front of me.

Interestingly enough, Rora plays the same game that I do. That should make this easier.

I glance down at my armor to make sure everything is in place. My weapons are just as I left them, attached to the quiver on my back. When I'm sure nothing glitched on me, I walk forward into the game, leaving the holding cell behind. It disappears behind me, evaporating into the air, leaving me exposed.

I quickly flip my settings to explore mode, preventing me from losing any of my credits in the game. I can't engage with people and earn items within the game, but I can walk around and talk to them. It's not something the game allows you to do for extended periods of time, but occasionally people use the setting to meet with their friends while they were in different locations, so the game gives us some leniency while we wait for people to show up.

Now, I just have to figure out where to find the girl.

Chapter 2

THE LAST TIME I WALKED AROUND WITHOUT PLAYING WAS when I had to wait for Alan to bother to show up for a team round. It was so long ago, that I've forgotten how funny it is to watch newer players try to rank in the game —so many easy mistakes.

I wish I had been able to bring my coffee with me—it could have been a nice, leisurely stroll through the king- dom. I shouldn't waste time meandering around though. Find the girl; get out.

I wonder if she'll let me ping her location.

Pulling up my controls, I enter her screen name that I cleverly looked at before entering the game. When Rora- Rose registers, I request her coordinates. Hopefully she'll recognize me as Perry's nephew.

While I wait for a reply, I walk toward the castle. The next time I'm in the game, my mission is going to take me there. I have to figure out how to get in, so a little reconnaissance mission while I wait to hear from Rora won't hurt.

Everything inside the gamescape is brighter that in the real world. Buildings are taller. Lines are sharper.

It's magnificent.

To my left a girl is screaming, running from a battle with an ogre. She has an axe and could easily take it out, but apparently today is not her day.

Off to the right is one of my classmates, Harry. He and Gina appear to be on a quest. It looks like Gina is taking it easy so Harry can keep up—*the downfalls of playing with your boyfriend.* I try not to embarrass him when Gina stares. She and I have played together once before and I don't want to take any of the spotlight off of Harry because she knows I'm easier to work with.

Several young teens run past me, dressed in breast-plates and leather pants. They'll learn the benefits of a suit of armor soon enough. While it doesn't look as modern as their attire, it's better for battle.

An electrical pulse snaps across the control panel on my wrist—I'm receiving a message.

Coordinates appear on the screen, telling me where Rora is located. Surprisingly, I'm going the right way.

I continue on my path, this time much faster than before. Several young girls stare as I walk by, glancing at the sword on my hip. I wave as I pass.

"Really, Royce, you couldn't pick anything that glares less in the sun?" Alan asks, sidling up to me.

"Where did you come from?" I ask, realizing I now have help on my mission.

"I got your text message and thought you might need a hand with the little lady." We fall into step.

"You realize we're both wearing the same thing, right?"

"Yours is gold. It glares in the sun. Mine is black and doesn't shine at all," Alan informs me, knocking his hand against his metal-covered chest.

"Makes sense. Only one of us can shine at a time." I grin at him sarcastically.

Alan makes a face but defers tackling me until our mission is over. We pick up the pace as we track Rora's coordinates.

"So who is this girl we're searching for?"

"Perry's goddaughter. Her name is Rora. Apparently she went into the game this morning and still hasn't come back out."

"How did she manage that? Did she over-juice?"

"Doesn't look like it. We'll find out when we ask her though. She should be just around the corner in the trading post."

A knave stands on the corner, looking for a fight. When he sees us, he runs, sword out in front of him. He swings it at us as he yells, but it bounces off the invisible shield that surrounds us while we're in explore mode. The metal vibrates in his hands as it bounces back.

"Sorry, we're just here to talk to someone," I inform him as he snarls at us.

"You won't be so lucky next time," he scowls before scampering away.

"Why do the knaves always think they can take on a knight?" Alan shakes his head. "Let alone two of us. Like we didn't see him coming."

I roll my eyes. They'll never learn.

The trading post is filled with people. It's hard to hear over the voices chattering around us.

"Wait here," I instruct Alan.

Inside is even more crowded. I muscle my way through, looking for the blonde princess.

"Hey there, handsome," a woman says. She's at least five years older than me.

"Hello, ma'am," I nod, trying to brush past her.

"Where ya going, Mr. Knight?"

"I'm looking for someone, sorry."

The raven-haired gypsy follows me around the post. Every time I look back, she's on my tail.

"I'm really busy, sorry," I try brushing her off again.

"You *will* be," she murmurs, wandering away.

Spices fill the air, mixed with the scent of leather and blood. When you're injured in the game, you suffer the pain until you return to the real world. The place is crowded with new players looking for bandages and potions.

"I'm looking for RoraRose. Have you seen her?" I ask the man working the exchange register.

"She was here a while ago. I don't know where she went." He shrugs, waiting to take credits from the next person in line.

"Hey, Royce!" Alan calls from outside.

I push my way through the crowd, feeling an instant drop in temperature the moment I step outside of the crowded building.

Pressed against one of the support columns that holds up the front of the porch, a blonde dressed in purple and black pants with a half skirt wrapped around it stares at me. Her arms are crossed, one foot kicked up against the column with her knee bent. The girl's collar arches up over her shoulder and wraps magnificently around the hair piled on top of her head. A few loose curls hang down in a way that is unmistakably soft and girly *and* harsh and foreboding all at one.

Her gaze looks like it could cut down any man in its path.

"Really? *You're* Royce? Some prince you turned out to be," she scoffs. "It's about time somebody showed up."

"Rora," I regard her, nodding once. "Perry is beside herself. Do you have any idea what you've put her through?"

I cross my arms, mimicking her. She is nothing like I expected her to be.

"I'm locked in. I don't know what happened," she drops her tough girl act. "I should have been pulled out hours ago and it won't let me return manually."

"Anything we should know?" Alan charmingly asks. *Idiot.*

She glares at him in disgust.

"Never mind, I'll figure it out on my own." She turns to stomp away.

"Hold up," I reach for her, catching her elbow. "He didn't mean to accuse you of anything. We can't leave without you, so let's figure this out."

"He most certainly did," she snarls at him. She's feisty. "For the record, I didn't do anything to cause this. I didn't juice and I never would. I'm not sure why I'm in here."

"Did you make a bad trade with someone? Could it have been some kind of glitch in the system?"

"Have you ever known the system to glitch before?" Rora's eyes spark as she speaks. "As far as I know, no one has ever been locked inside the system. My last trade was with a magician. Everything seemed to work properly. It wasn't even today…it was two days ago."

She blinks impertinently at me as she waits for a response. When the light bounces off my armor and reflects onto her face, it lights up the little flecks that sparkle in her dramatic eye makeup.

"Let's talk to the magician," I suggest. Maybe he knows something."

"*She* may not even be in the game right now."

I hold my hands up to apologize for assuming, though mainly it's to keep from being pummeled. She looks like she'd have no trouble feeding me to the dragons.

Just then, a large flame rises in the air in the distance. *Speaking of dragons...*

I extend my hand, gesturing that we should start walking. Rora and Alan turn and the three of us start toward the castle where the magicians can usually be found hiding in the dark corners just outside the moat.

Rora's half skirt trails behind her as she walks, making her look like she would fit right in with the royalty inside the castle. Alan elbows me as we walk behind her. The dagger that dangles on her hip might have warned him off if we weren't in explore mode.

"I've tried using all of the escape buttons," Rora calls over her shoulder, prompting us to walk faster and catch up to her. "I've even tried pausing the game, but it hasn't done anything."

A scream rises up to our right as a girl with a spear charges at Rora. Alan and I watch as she sprints I our direction, weapon in the air. We're shocked when Rora engages with her.

She pulls her dagger from her hip, knowing her arrows won't be fast enough to stop the oncoming attack. Rora ducks, using her arm to block the spear before it can touch her. She hits the ground and rolls, bouncing to her feet before the girl can take her on.

Rora kicks the girl's leg, shattering it as the girl crumples on the ground. In a moment of pure rage, the girl thrusts her spear at Rora, nicking her arm. Blood bubbles up from the ripped sleeve of her dark outfit.

"What are you doing?" I shout, rushing to her side.

"I can't enter explore mode," Rora shrieks desperately, trying to cradle her arm and take on her attacker at the same time.

Two more people run out from an alley, ready to target Rora. I quickly take myself out of explore mode and prepare to defend her. Alan joins me, making it an unfair match for the geniuses that thought they could take us on.

The moment she sees us enter the game, Rora straightens, throwing down her arm to her side in a show of strength. She reaches behind her for her bow, but one of the boys reaches her first. Rora kicks at him, knocking him back. As he comes at her again, she lands a punch to his nose, breaking it with a loud crunch. He's going to be incredibly thankful injuries don't follow us into the real world.

I wield my sword, clashing with the first assassin who ran from the shadows. He's quick, but not as quick as I am. His weapon falls to the ground and I slam my sword into it, making it vanish from the game.

He takes a step back as I lunge toward him. Thinking better of it, he turns and runs, taking his partner with him. I'm not done with them yet though.

"Get them," I instruct Alan before turning back to Rora to see how bad the damage is. Alan rushes after the assassins. "Are you okay?"

"I'm fine," she says, cradling her arm.

"Do you have health points?" I inquire.

"Yeah, but at the rate I'm going, I think I should save them for when something worse happens."

She purses her lips. She's not telling me something.

"You've already been attacked today…"

She nods, finally making eye contact with me.

"Earlier. Before you got here. One of those guys came after me. I tried hiding in the crowd at the trading post, but that didn't go so well. Apparently he found me. I only gave you my location because I connected you with Perry."

"Let me see your arm." I hold out my hand to her. It takes a moment, but she finally relinquishes it.

"Really, it's fine," she protests. She doesn't like relying on other people.

"Let's see if you can look for an Apple of Life. That would fix this right up and you wouldn't have to waste your health points."

She nods and allows me to guide her to a small cluster of trees near the water pump in the center of town. I almost leave her on a stone bench by the pump, but think better of it in case Alan hasn't caught the assassins yet— we need information before we leave her alone again.

"There," she says, pointing high above our heads. "Give me a boost."

I lower my hands, weaving my fingers together. She runs at me, placing her foot in my hand. I lift her and she flies toward the tree. Her foot hits it and she bounces off, high into the branches. She's playing as a princess, but she has the skill sets of a ninja.

Grasping the Apple of Life, she allows gravity to do its work, falling out of the tree. Her feet hit the ground and she crouches into what looks like the beginnings of a pounce. Like a cat, she gracefully springs back up and slinks over to me, twisting the apple in her hand.

Rora clenches it hard in her hand—claiming her points—making it disappear. The mark on her arm instantly heals.

"Easy enough. Thanks for the hand." She brushes her sleeve off as if something still remained where she had been injured. "Good as new."

"Tell them," Alan rushes up, an assassin's cape in his clutch.

"She has a bounty on her head," the younger of the assassins informs us. "The entire game will be coming after her soon. They just set the challenge to the assassins first."

"What's the price?" Rora asks, crossing her arms as she strides up to him.

"Everything you have," he sneers at her, looking like he wants to shatter her.

I backhand him.

He falls to the ground, temporarily knocked out of the game until he regenerates with one less life point.

"What are you doing?" Rora shrieks, grabbing my arm as if I would hit him again. "He could have told us why."

"That's all he knew," Alan says, shaking his head.

"So what now?" she mumbles. "Why are they after me?"

"What will the acquire if they kill you?"

She pauses as if she doesn't want to say.

"We can't help unless we know what's going on," I remind her.

"Everything. They're getting everything. I'm one of the highest ranked players in this game."

"Yeah, okay," Alan scoffs. "If you're so important, why haven't we heard of you?"

"An intelligent woman knows when to keep her secrets. I've been quietly playing this game for as long as you two have—I just don't go around bragging about it. I don't take on challenges for the sake of taking on challenges. I'm strategic. I've been saving up for the final battle—I'm close. I could rule the castle soon, if I wanted."

"You're going to take on the Queen?" I try not to sound sarcastic. I fail.

She stares at me as she taps a button on her control panel. A translucent screen pops up with a list of all her battles, challenges, statistics, and the items she has collected along the way.

Rora is as skilled as I am.

For once, Alan has nothing to say.

That is, until an angry mob of half a dozen people come running around the corner from behind a large pink building, screaming for Rora's head. We prepare to fight them, but before we can, Alan starts glitching.

"Not now!" he yells, tapping on his control panel. He tries to warn us as he fades away. "I'm being pulled out!"

He must have set his timer for less time than I did.

"This is bad," I say, pulling my sword.

Rora rips her bow off her back and takes aim.

"I hate this part," she informs me before releasing an arrow at the mob.

My sword clashes against a shield as a guy my age tries to get around me to reach Rora. When I look over, she's surrounded. Someone tries to grab her around the waist.

"Behind you!" I shout as I kick at the person in front of me. She struggles to evade him.

Then, suddenly, it's like she's changed modes. She effortlessly fights the other players off, taking them out left and right. Rora elbows a knave, knocking him down before using her dagger to fend off a girl a decade older than us.

We're down to five people left when I feel the tug. My hand starts to disappear, my skin glitching in and out of the game.

"No!"

My shout makes Rora whip around to face me.

"I'll be back! I'll find you!" I shout as I'm torn from the game, leaving her alone to take on the remaining assassins.

Chapter 3

I WAKE UP WITH A START. RIPPING THE GOGGLES OFF, I punch my fingers against the control panel to pull up my logs. I hope Rora stays in the same general area so I can find her.

The game has a lock that won't allow us to go back into the game for an hour—it's an hour that might kill me.

My phone buzzes next to me—Alan.

"You're out?" he demands as soon as I answer.

"It pulled me," I confirm. "She's all alone taking on those assassins. We have to get back in there."

"From what I saw in her logs, she can handle herself, but I'm on my way over. For now, see if you can find a way to wake her up from this side." The phone clicks off.

She's still in the chair next to me, fingers twitching once in awhile as she plays.

"Rora?" I hover over her. "Rora, can you hear me? I'm coming back for you, just stay safe until then."

I try picking her hand up to see if the movement would wake her, but her muscles are stiff, as if they're part of the chair arm. I wonder if my muscles lock like that too while I'm in the game.

My eyes dart around the room looking for an idea. Somehow I don't think a bunch of bookshelves will help me. *Waiting* may be the only thing I *can* do.

The door opens downstairs. I assume it will be Alan walking in, but once I reach the landing, I discover that it's Aunt Perry.

"Is she out?" Perry demands, setting down two large bags on the small table by the door. I fear the table might collapse under the weight of the groceries.

"I went in and talked to her. She's locked inside the game. Alan and I got pulled out, but we're going back in for her as soon as the timer lets us."

Perry twists her fingers nervously. When she starts pacing around the room, I launch myself down the steps. I scoop up the bags and thrust one of them at her. I hold on to the other.

"You need to put this away. Whatever is going on here, it's not right. Rora didn't do anything that would cause her to get stuck, but we can't let anyone know about this." I push at Perry's back to make her move toward the kitchen. "Put these away and then go next door to visit Mr. Grimmerson. Stay there for a few hours while Alan and I work on getting her out of the game."

Perry nods but it doesn't look like she's heard a word I've said.

"Aunt Perry, did you hear me?"

"Her parents are going to kill me," she says through tears.

"No, they won't because she'll be just fine. She's one of the best players in that game. They can't touch her."

"What do you mean? Is she getting hurt in there?" Perry suddenly grows coherent.

"She'll be fine. We just need to wake her up, that's all. We're going to help her get out. Just go next door, please."

"I'm here," Alan slams through the door. He takes one look at Perry and looks like he's going to bolt.

"Upstairs," I point quickly before ushering my aunt to the door. "Just go to see Mr. Grimmerson and don't come back until you see Alan or I out in the yard, okay? Grimmerson is a talker so you should be fine."

"But…" she objects.

"Just go, Aunt Perry. I promise I'll wake her up."

I carefully force her out the door and shut it behind her. When she turns back to me, I wave her along. She reluctantly goes to her neighbor's.

I turn, throwing anything cold into the refrigerator before rushing up the stairs.

"It kind of has a creepy look to it now, doesn't it?" Alan asks without turning around to face me. "If she wasn't twitching, I'd think she were dead."

"She's not dead," I murmur as I grab to injections and place them on the armrests of the chairs. "We just need to get back in there."

"Should we both go at the same time? We only have three hours left each." Alan's point strikes like lightning, making me swallow.

"That's a good point. If we can't get her out, at least we can protect her longer." My breathing is shallower than it should be as my mind tumbles over ideas for saving her. I need to remember to breath.

"We can't let her stay in there all day though. There's no telling what it's doing to her body out here while she's under the influence of the game. It could have lasting effects." Alan has always been the more practical of us.

I glance at Rora as she sits in the chair. Her shell is here, but *she* is elsewhere, possibly in danger. Every minute that she doesn't return makes me more nervous.

"I'll go in first," I reply. "You stay here and research. See if this has ever happened before and if it has, what they did to fix it. And *don't* get caught. No one is going to believe someone who has achieved that much in the game didn't turn to juicing to stay in longer."

"I'll be careful," he nods, looking at Rora. "Just make sure you're careful in there too. You actually have to play the game and there's an angry group of people out to kill."

"I can afford a few lives," I remind him.

"Yeah, but you only get three a day, so don't blow it."

He makes a good point.

I glance at my cup of coffee on the desk. So much for it still being warm. I turn back to face Rora as Alan pulls up a search on his phone to start working. I set a timer on my phone—ten more minutes.

After the longest ten minutes of my life, the timer finally goes off. I jump into the chair next to Rora and put the headpiece on.

"Hey, just remember, you don't have to save her. She's fine on her own, so you're just there to help her. There's no reason to be a big, tough hero in there," Alan reminds me. He grins sneakily before adding, "That's *my* job."

"Whatever, man," I say as I inject myself. "See you in three hours. Watch over her. If something goes wrong, it doesn't matter—just get help. We'll deal with the conse-quences later..."

My words trail off as I fade into the game.

I arrive back where I left Rora but she's nowhere to be found. The thugs have moved on. The game cleaned up whatever wreckage there was so I can't even tell if she's been hurt.

Taping on my control panel, I try to contact her. It comes up as static.

"This is bad," I mumble to myself.

I need information. By now, everyone has to have the kill challenge. I only make it three steps before it pops up in my control panel.

Ducking into the shadows of the pink building, I read the instructions. Two hundred players have already checked in to the challenge list. She'll have to survive them all, but at least the challenge is still being handed out which means she hasn't been caught yet.

Whoever wants her gone is really gunning for her.

I try to contact her again, but it's still nothing but static. I type a message telling her I'm going to the castle to look for the magician in case it manages to get through to her.

I bat at a vine hanging down from the top of the building. The greenery against the pink of the tower makes it look like a giant watermelon. Then again, the tall vines nearly look like bamboo, so who knows what I'm really looking at. The branch swings back quietly, like a lock of a girl's hair in the breeze.

I peel out of the alleyway and move quickly toward the castle. Unfortunately, I already used my one explore mode use for the day, so I'm hyper-vigilant to take in my surroundings. Most people will be focused on catching Rora, but I'm high ranking as well and an easy pick if I'm distracted.

Ahead, the random tree in the middle of the town

shifts shapes. An Apple of Life grows on a low branch. I have a feeling that I might need it, so I jog over. When an assassin appears, also running toward it, I attack. I don't need the Apple of life so much that I'm willing to take out an assassin for it, but I know he will be going after Rora when he's done and it's easier to take him out now.

I'm worried about what will happen to Rora's physical body if she's trapped in the game much longer. Alan's point is a scary reminder that we don't know what all of this means. Even worse, I'm terrified over what might happen if Rora depletes all of her lives inside the game and is still trapped.

The assassin launches himself at me, trying to punch my face. I duck, pulling a branch back. When I release it, it snaps in his eyes. He reels back, blinded by the branches.

By the time I'm done, he's been pulled from the game for the day. I pluck the Apple of Life off the tree and take off down the now-quiet street.

Most people leave me alone as I run down the dirt roads. On normal days, if someone is running and it's not at you, it's best not to get involved. Today, most people have a goal in mind and if I'm not going to help them catch Rora, they don't pay any attention.

When I reach the edge of town, I spot a warlock trying to create a team of fighters to go after Rora. He shouts loudly to organize them. Wasting time trying to disband them would be a mistake, so I keep running through the rows of tall pink buildings covered in vines.

It's beyond me who decided pink was a good color for a building, but the kingdom is paved with them. Each one is a twisted shape with long, dark shadows. Some crumble with virtually assigned age, showing the wear of battles long since fought. Ahead, the castle glimmers in the sunlight, a pale blue color that I assume is supposed to be symbolic of glass.

The water in the moat sparkles a dark navy blue with crests of white as if it were the ocean. Despite the lack of a breeze, it ripples fiercely.

I pause for a moment, scouting the bridge that leads across the outer moat. Players are allowed to cross the outer moat and enter the kingdom courtyard, but only players on quests that involve the castle can go beyond that and cross the second bridge to the castle grounds. I've been theee twice before.

People are bustling on the wide bridge, trading and forming alliances. I let my hand linger near my sword as I step onto the dark brown wood of the bridge.

I weave my way through the crowd, trying to find any sign that Rora has come this way. She's not on the bridge, but when I reach the grass, I make my way to the shadows where I might find the magician.

"Hello," I greet someone in a deep red cloak. They

turn and I find another princess, this one in full ball gown.

"Hello," she says cautiously.

"I'm sorry, I thought you were someone else," I excuse myself. She quickly wanders away.

She had the same hair color, so it was logical to think it might have been her. Rationalizing is a strong suit of mine.

Deeper into a recess behind one of the sculptures large enough to be a room, I find someone covered in darkness. Something pricks along my arm, urging me forward.

"I'm looking for a magician," I call.

The figure shuffles further back, trying to get away from me.

"Please, I require a magicians help," I say again, this time softer to show I am not a threat.

The figure pauses, waiting for me to approach. The hood on their cloak conceals their face, but I think I've found my magic woman. I place my hand on the hilt of my sword just in case.

Fingers wrap around my shoulders, slamming me backward into a corner. I can't unsheathe my sword, so my dagger will have to do.

"Shhh," she hisses. "Put that away."

"Rora," I gasp.

"Of course, you fool. Who did you think I was?" She scowls in the shadows.

She must not have recognized me when I first walked in.

"Where did you get a cloak from?" I question, looking her over. "And how did you fit it over that massive collar?"

"It doesn't matter, I did." Her fingers are still on me. It's impossible to feel her touch through my armor, but I feel every single finger as it rests on me. "It certainly took you long enough."

"I've been trying to find you for twenty minutes," I say, annoyed.

"I found the magician," she says, not noticing my dig. "She's over there."

"Great, let's go talk to her."

"Wait," she tugs on me as I try to turn away. "I can't go out there."

I pause, examining her.

"You're worried about what happens to you out there," I muse. She nods. "I have Alan researching that now, but honestly, we're kind of worried too—you're barely breathing out there." I ignore the part where she looks like she could be dead—there's no need to worry her over that.

"He'll send a message in if he finds anything," I add.

The game allows people who are friends within the

game to send short messages to each other inside the game in order to coordinate missions. For some people, it's their only form of communication because they don't have contact in the outside world.

Rora glances around me, looking at the magician.

"I'll go talk to her, you stay here."

I leave her in the dark corner, hoping she watches me walk away. I make sure to give her a good show.

The magician lurks by the edge of the wall. Under the edge of her cloak I can see several potions she's created to trade with other players. They glint when the light bounces off my armor and hits the glass bottles from a distance.

"I'm looking for some information," I say in a hushed voice as I approach her.

She eyes me skeptically.

"What kind of information could I possibly have?"

"You met with a girl recently—I know you know exactly whom I mean," I add before she can protest. "I want information."

"She came to me, yes. We traded." A strand of her dark hair slips out from behind her hood. It rests in front of her wrinkled cheek.

"What did you give her?"

She doesn't appear to be too concerned with me so I take another step toward her, trying to intimidate her. I tower over the older woman but it makes no difference.

"She wanted an Acceleration for a new skill. I don't remember which one." She waves her hand as if it's of no consequence.

"You do." She doesn't even flinch when I take another step toward her.

"I do not, young man." She twists to look up at me. "What do you want?"

"Did you do something to her?" I question.

"I didn't," she challenges me, "but it looks like *you* want to."

She pushes past me, knocking against my chest piece. I spin as she moves around me.

"We all got the same message. Go find her yourself," she demands.

"I don't believe you." I dart around her. "What did you do?"

"You think I cursed her?" She glares at me.

"I do."

"I did no such thing, and if you had any experience in this game, you'd know there's no way for me to do whatever you think I did."

She hurries away from me. I quickly pull up my control panel, trying to check her statistics to see what level she's at but it can't locate her.

"Hey," I rush after her. "What did you do when you gave her the Acceleration?"

"I did nothing," she stoops into a sarcastic bow, "your

highness. I gave her the Acceleration she traded me for and she was on her way."

"What did she trade?" I demand.

"Lives, probably. I didn't get to be a magician without understanding the importance of having lives in this game. *You couldn't take me out if you tried.*" She glares at me. "Now run along, *RoyalRoyce*. No one needs you here."

The magician crackles out of the game, evaporating into the air. I wait a moment to make sure it's not a magician's trick, but when she doesn't reappear, I make my way back to Rora.

"Well?" she asks the moment she sees me. She drops the piece of hair she had been nervously twisting while I was gone.

"I think she's in on it. She wouldn't give me any information—acted like she didn't remember your trade—and then pulled out of the game to avoid talking to me," I inform her. "I couldn't even get a read on her statistics. The control panel didn't locate her."

"That's not possible—the control panel *always* picks up other players' stats." Her eyebrows push down in confusion, scrunching her nose. "What are we supposed to do now?"

"I'm not sure." I'm just as confused as she is. "Let's get closer to the castle and see if there is a higher-level player that can help us. Maybe another magician would know what is going on.

She nods and waits to follow me out of the shadows.

I slip back on to the main part of the street. Rora keeps her hood over her face. It's too bad we can't change our appearances in here without playing as different types of characters—it would be easier to hide Rora if we could change her appearance. We're careful to keep her covered while we walk.

"Royce," Rora suddenly yelps, latching on to my shoulder. Her fingers dig into me—she's stronger than she looks. "That's her."

Rora points over my shoulder toward the castle. The older woman stands there, smiling viciously at us. She cocks one hip out to the side as she straightens, the years melting off her face until she looks young again.

She's the woman from the trading post.

The magician stands there, watching us, a knowing smile on her face. She takes her hand off her hip before spinning around gracefully and walking inside the castle.

Chapter 4

"SHE LEFT THE GAME!" I SHOUT IN CONFUSION.

"*That's* the part you're worried about?" Rora cries behind me. "Her *face* melted off!"

"She's a magician—things happen," I counter.

What I can't figure out is how she could leave the game and then reappear so quickly. I had to wait an entire hour to come back in and help Rora.

"She's not a magician, Royce." Rora corrects me.

Rora steps to the side, spinning me enough to partially face her while still monitoring the castle.

"No magician can do that. And what magician needs to get into the castle for a quest anyway? *Knights* do that. *Royalty* does that. Magicians are playing an entirely different game here. *That over there* doesn't make any sense." She points to the castle dramatically.

The castle glimmers in the sun, reflecting the blue glass color onto the grass in front of it. It twinkles as if glitter has been embedded into its walls. Giant roses sit on vines crawling up the walls, much like on the other buildings, only here there are also blue glass roses resembling the castle embedded on the branches.

The magician is still gone.

"Who is she?" I murmur, still staring.

"Think, Royce," Rora replies. "Who can come and go as they please in that castle?"

"No one," I respond instantly. "No one can come and go in there without having a specific quest to complete."

"Think again," she says calmly, already having figured it out. "Who can come and go as they please? Who can transform at will? Who can keep their statistics from being seen—who can walk around this game cloaked like that? Royce, we're messing with the wrong person."

The only person who has unfettered access to this game is the one that controls the castle—well, that and the game makers but they don't play other than to test new features. They walk around the system like gods that everyone keeps a respectful distance from as they stare in awe. Which leaves only one person—the queen.

"I thought she didn't leave the castle." I squint toward the castle, hoping it offers some new information. It doesn't

"Apparently she does," Rora muses, reaching up to adjust her hood.

"What does she want with you?" I ask.

"I'm in line for the throne, Royce." Her words are simple but it doesn't make them any less complicated.

"What do you mean?" I stammer.

"I'm a threat to her. Technically I could challenge her claim to the castle at any time. I just haven't." She frowns, green eyes wandering to the ground a few feet away. "I don't want the castle. I just want to play the game."

"You said earlier that—"

"I was proving a point, Royce—I'm better at the game than you. But truthfully, I have no desire for the castle. I just want to beat the dragon, gain more skills, and play the game quietly without any fuss from anyone. But apparently *she* doesn't see it that way."

"So you think that she's trying to make you fail so that you can't take her place."

Rora tucks a strand of hair behind her ear. She struggles a little to avoid knocking off her hood in the process. It's kind of adorable…until she catches me looking.

"What are we supposed to do about this?" I ask, trying to distract her.

"I don't know." She sounds defeated. "The short term goal is to get out of here, but long term…I can't come back if she's going to keep locking me in."

Her eyes fill with tears as she looks up at me. She's nearly a head shorter than me when she hunches down like that—almost like she's deflated.

"Hey," I grab her elbows suddenly to make her face me

fully. "We'll find a way to get you home and we'll find a way to get you back into the game safely. Maybe we can make some kind of pact with her."

"You think she's going to let us get close enough?" she asks spitefully. "If I get that close, I could challenge her and that would lock her into the game. I would actually have to defeat her and I don't want that. I just want to play."

"Maybe I could talk to her. She seemed awfully interested in the trading post—"

"You talked to her before?" she snaps, cutting me off.

I suddenly notice the noise swell around us. I glance around, making sure no one has spotted us. When I determine that it was only the natural rise and fall of voices in the game, I look back to her.

"When I was looking for you," I explain. "She came up to me. I brushed her off and went outside where I found you."

"Oh great, *you've* made her mad too."

"Well, to be fair, I think I angered her more just *now* than I did a few hours ago." I give her my best smoldering looking. It doesn't affect her.

This girl is complicated.

"I honestly don't know how you'd get close enough to talk to her at this point," Rora says. "We need to move."

She suddenly swerves from me, walking away from the surge of people crossing the bridge. Her skirt trails out from under her cloak as she walks, making at least two people stop and stare.

"Where are we going?" I ask, jogging to catch up.

"Away from the castle until we can figure out a plan."

"Come on," I say, guiding her onto the bridge. She hesitates for a moment but follows close behind.

Rora keeps her head down as we pass over the wooden bridge to the main part of the game, passing by maidens and knaves trying to trade up on the bridge to the castle. A warlock glances at me but doesn't pay much attention to Rora as she trails behind me.

I've always found it amazing how realistic the textures are inside the game. The harsh boards of the bridge give way to softer, more cushioned grass and dirt as we step back onto the land. The grass shifts in the fake breeze—too bad we can't feel the wind in the game. At least it's temperature controlled.

Without a destination, I navigate us toward the wishing well off to the left. We pass a knight I've been meaning to duel with for the last month but we don't have time for that now, even if I could use the points. I pause, letting Rora inadvertently step up next me, blocking me from his view—it's not worth getting sucked into a battle right now.

I put my hand on her back to keep her moving as she faces me.

"Keep walking," I mumble. She turns back and plays along.

Once we're beyond him, I explain myself, earning a nod.

I'm brought back to reality when my control panel buzzes on my wrist. I nod toward the shade of a giant rock sculpture and we duck behind it.

"What is it?" Rora asks.

"Alan," I reply as I lift the panel to check his message. I try not to frighten her, but sucking in a breath of air quickly probably didn't help my cause.

"Royce?" She says my name like it's a demand—she wants information. Rora latches on to my arm, eyes wild.

"He's been researching," I say, skimming the very short message. We're only allowed a handful of characters per message so Alan can't give me much information. "Oh."

Rora's eyes grow wide and she stretches on to her tiptoes, balancing herself on my arm. Her lips part as if she's going to ask a question but no sound comes out.

"The message is really short but it sounds like we really need to get you out now. He says we have to beat the game."

"But what happens if we don't?" She insists on having an answer. I don't blame her.

I type back to Alan, hoping he can reply quickly. We only get two more messages each before it cuts us off.

I turn my back to the rock as I wait for a reply, leaning against it so I can survey the area. Rora's eyes are locked on me.

"It will be okay," I remind her. If anyone can save her, it's me.

Her jaw tightens as if she doesn't quite believe me. Her breathing moves her shoulder up and down in a restrained repetitive motion—she's concentrating on staying calm.

Alan's next message is more concerning than the first.

"He says he found a man who claims he was locked inside the game. They arrested him for juicing." I glance at her. "We have to beat the game and get you out."

She trembles, realizing her fate if we don't succeed. We don't have much time left before I get taken back out —an hour and half at most. Alan can come back in for an hour and a half after I leave, but Rora might not have that long.

A group of people runs past us, metaphorical and literal pitchforks in hand. They're still chasing her. At least this queen of the castle hasn't raised the price on her head. She must feel incredibly challenged if she's willing to do this to Rora.

"You'll be okay," I insist. "We just have to get you out. What was your next quest? We'll play through and if we have to take on the queen, I'll help you."

"You're willing to give up the game to help me?" she

asks cautiously. "I know how seriously you and Alan take this—I checked your stats earlier."

"It's way more important to get you out without causing any damage." I failed to mention that Alan had told me the state of the guy who had been trapped in the game and it wasn't good, but I didn't want to scare her any more than she needed to be. "I can always rebuild. But let's face it, once this queen realizes I'm helping, I probably won't be able to come back to the game anyway."

I shrug casually. In truth, I hate that, but it's better than letting Rora get hurt. She doesn't need to know that now though.

"What's your quest?"

She watches me thoughtfully for a moment, appraising my armor from head to toe. Rora tips her head when she finally reaches my eyes again.

"I have to fight the dragon."

Even *I've* never fought a dragon in this game. It's a fool's errand. Very few people can escape its fire.

I nod.

"Let's go find a dragon."

Unlike dragons from stories, the dragons in the game work on a schedule. They are restricted to certain locations that only higher-level players can enter. Their jobs are to destroy players, sending them back to the beginning of the game.

If you are caught by a dragon without being on a quest to find one, you are eliminated from the game and have to start over from the loest point. If you are vanquished by a dragon while on a quest, you lose all of your lives except for one and have your weapons and skills depleted by half.

If you successfully win in a battle against a dragon, you are advanced to the highest level—the level Rora needs to take on a quest to take the queen's place.

Very few people venture to view the dragons inside the game. Even fewer battle against them.

Still, like clockwork, the dragons announce their presence by sending fiery blasts into the sky, crying out loudly so the kingdom can hear. From what I can tell, there are at least three separate dragons within the game.

From a distance, I've seen at least one black one, but I've heard rumors of red and green dragons as well.

As if they are expecting us, a dragon shrieks somewhere behind the trees. The sound echoes off of nothing —a benefit sound effect of the game—filling their area with a warning not to enter. Rora seems unfazed.

She adjusts her sleeved, then lifts her hands to remove her cloak.

"You're not taking that off, are you?" I question.

"I can't very well fight with that thing on," she replies indignantly, dropping the cloak to the ground. "You don't have to come with me…"

She gives me one last opportunity to back out.

"And miss a dragon fight? Not a chance, princess." I draw my sword, swinging it around in a large loop, hoping to look impressive. "After you, m'lady."

Rora smirks at my antics but doesn't hesitate in walking toward the part of the kingdom that houses the dragons.

"That's her!" someone shouts.

Rora and I look at each other at the same time, rolling our eyes. Here we go again.

She whips around, dagger in hand. I match her with my sword, ready to take on our assailants. A guy attacks me, trying to take me down, but he's distracted watching Rora fight off his friend. I slam into his neck with my blade and he vanishes from the game.

Rora slices at her attacker's arm as he tries to kick her knee out. She leaves a nasty cut followed by a left hook that knocks the guy to the ground, unconscious. He vanishes from the game.

Two more people step up to attack us. When they both launch themselves at Rora, three others decide to rush for me, hoping the winner will share the spoils of defeating Rora with them as a thank you.

I cut one, but not enough to deter him. The tall one

slips behind me and attempts to yank my arms behind my back. They scream at their friends to kill Rora.

I go down to my knees as they kick out the back of my legs. My sword tumbles to the ground. The moment I feel the pressure of my knees being kicked out, I prepare myself to toss the man over my back as soon as I hit the ground. He shoots forward, toppling over me as I grab my sword and take out one of the other men.

Rora screams in pain, but it only fuels her. She lashes out at the men in front of her, easily destroying them like it's child's play.

She spins, kicking in the air like a ninja from one of those old movie clips we saw in our history class. Her half skirt spins out behind her in slow motion.

Rora elbows the man in the face, snapping his head back. She spins on her heel, kicking a second man. I charge for him, knocking him to the ground as she takes on the first man.

Both guys disappear at the same time, flickering out of the game. Rora straightens, throwing her shoulders back.

"I hate those guys," she mutters.

"Maybe we need to kill the kill order first," I suggest.

"We don't have time. Most of them can't get into the restricted zone anyway. Let's just go find a dragon."

"If you're sure…"

"I am. Let's go." She turns and marches toward the invisible wall that the newer players can't cross.

The wall tingles as we pass through it, letting us know we are in a different zone. Several people who were part of the hunting pack run up to us, bouncing off the wall when they don't realize they can't enter. I'd laugh at the look of shock on their faces when I turn around after hearing the slam, but we don't have time for that.

"Can you pull up any information on the dragons?" I inquire, hoping to find some sort of advantage.

"I don't know, but I think we should walk a little deeper into the bushes and take cover before I check. I think we need to be hyper vigilant now that we're here," Rora points out.

We walk deeper into the overgrown area that becomes so thick that it's like we're walking through a jungle. It wouldn't surprise me if we walked right by a dragon hiding under the foliage and had no idea.

"Here," Rora finally says, stepping into the shelter of a large tree-like structure that's so covered with trees we have to move branches back like we're swimming in the ocean.

After a moment, we come to a small opening, big enough to fit both of us without being poked by branches.

Rora puts her back against a tree trunk, preparing to

search her control panel for information. She glances up, catching me staring again. Dang, she's pretty.

"Should you maybe," she pauses, hoping I'll catch on. When I don't, she continues, "watch the area for threats?"

She looks at me like I'm clueless.

"Right," I spin, realizing I'm acting like an idiot.

My eyes scan the area for signs of danger. Each shift of the leaves on the tree catches my attention as I listen carefully. I could use some coffee right now.

"It looks like there are five dragons here. If one engages with me, I have to fight it, but there are some that are easier to defeat than the others."

"Which ones are those?" I quickly ask.

"Navy," she replies, still staring at her control panel. "The problem is that it's hard to tell the difference between the navy and the black dragon since they're so similar in coloring and shape. Black is the deadliest."

"Perfect, we could either run into the easiest or toughest dragon and have to battle it because we don't know which one it is."

"Exactly." Her eyes never flicker from her screen.

"Okay, so what's the second easiest? I say we go after that one."

"Green can spit fire like the rest of them, but it also cause hurricane-like windstorms with its wings."

She finally looks up at me. Ah, so that thing in my

stomach is a windstorm that her green eyes are creating. *Makes sense.*

"That's the second easiest to defeat?"

She nods miserably.

"Okay, so we go find the green dragon and make sure we don't get treated like kites."

"How? You want to tie ourselves down? We can't fight that way," she protests.

It's an interesting thought, but somehow I can't imagine attaching ourselves to boulders with chains is going to do any good.

"I don't suppose I could tame it," she muses.

"I sincerely doubt that," I reply, making her frown, despite her eyes sparkling.

"Well, prince charming, *you* try coming up with an idea," she snaps.

"Prince charming?" I scoff.

"Your screen name is RoyalRoyce, what do you expect me to say?"

"Personally, I'd go with *king* over prince, but whatever," I grin, flexing my muscles under my armor. She makes a face. I'm starting to like her more and more...but there would be time to flirt with her later.

We both fall to the ground when an earth-shattering scream rings out over our heads.

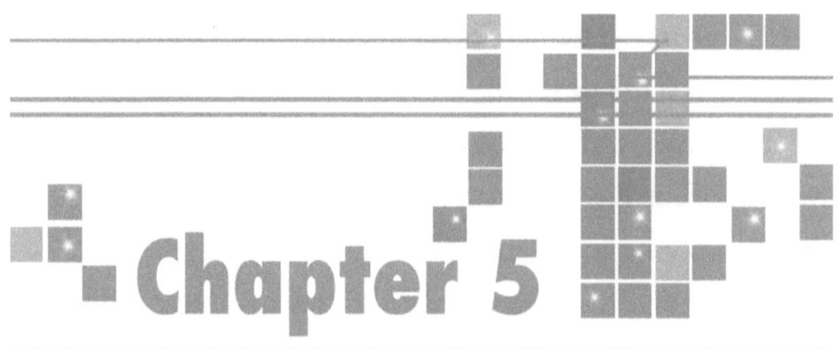

Chapter 5

A GUST OF WIND KNOCKS THE TREES FROM AROUND US, exposing us to the open sky. A dragon darts out of view.

"Which one was it?" Rora shrieks over the noise.

"I don't know—it was too dark to tell!" I yell back, trying to crawl to her. "That's an insane amount of wind though, so maybe it's our green dragon?"

"We need a better look." Rora says, standing. Now that the dragon is out of sight, the trees right themselves, stretching back up to their normal height. "I'm climbing up."

Before I can stop her, she scales the tree she was leaning against as if it was nothing. I'd have to remember to get the Stickiness modification next time I was in the Mod shop. It's clearly an epic thing to spend my credits on.

Rora stands on a branch high above my head. Now I see why she opted for pants with a half skirt—that wouldn't be nearly as easy in a full dress like some of the girls wear in the game. She spins quickly in a circle as she searches for the dragon.

It appears out of nowhere, suddenly filling the space with another gust of wind. Rora clutches at the trunk of the tree, trying to balance herself.

The dragon shrieks, shaking the ground under my feet. The beast tips its head up, releasing fire into the sky —right on time. Smoke trails from its mouth for a moment as it looks back down.

Rora topples from the tree, unable to catch herself. I rush forward, trying to reach her. She slams into my arms, elbow knocking painfully into my shoulder. I cringe as I nearly drop her.

She bounces in my arms trying to catch herself against me. When her hair smacks against my face, I get the most incredible scent of her shampoo. It smells like roses.

Rora flips herself out of my arms before I can register the pain of our collision.

"Bad news," she yelps. "It's the black dragon."

I look up, horrified.

"How do you know?"

"That little reappearing act that it just pulled—not an act. It can actually disappear and reappear," she warns me.

As she speaks the words, the dragon vanishes, leaving

only the rush of wind from its wings behind as a reminder of its presence.

"We have to run," she gasps, turning to me. "We need to stay on the move."

Rora grabs at my hand, forcing me into action. The world stills as we run, crashing through the brush, but the light suddenly changes from the pure white light of day inside the game to a vibrant golden tone.

The dragon has reappeared and cut off our path with a trail of fire. The tall, dark monster creeps along the ground, strategically placing its feet to move in a way that would intimidate anyone.

He eyes us before hissing loudly.

"I see you've met my pet," a voice rings out. "When one defeats a dragon, the rest of them bend to your will, *word to the wise.*"

The raven-haired woman walks around from behind the dragon, petting it on the nose. She's changed into a red medieval gown with sleeves that nearly reach the grass. Must be nice to be the queen and do whatever you want.

"Why are you doing this to me?" Rora confronts the woman.

"Why else, dear? You're getting too close."

"I don't want your castle," Rora challenges. "I have no desire to take your place. I just wanted to play the game. Let me go home and I won't come back."

"Nice try, princess. No one works as hard as you did just to give up when they're so close to ruling." She swings her hip to the side like she had done in front of the castle. "But you're right about one thing—you won't be coming back."

My stomach drops. I should have told her.

"You see, RoraRose, while you're locked in here, your body isn't doing so well out there. If you die this time in the game, the game takes it out on your body," the woman informs her. "The last one didn't fair so well, I hear."

She grins as she takes a step toward us. I fight the urge to sweep Rora behind my back. Inside the game, my strength is no different than her strength, but her skills are better because she's higher ranking. While she can handle herself, if I take the game-death first, that gives her at least one more chance to save herself. I just have to time it correctly, and now is not that time.

Rora matches the woman, stepping forward. The dragon turns to her, watching. One snap of its jaws and it wouldn't even have to use its fire on Rora.

She surveys it, hand lingering near her dagger. That little thing won't be enough against the magician queen.

"Who are you?" Rora challenges her.

The woman waves her hand in the air. Our control panels buzz on our wrists—she unlocked her information.

"MaraAdrielle, Kingdom Queen," Rora reads.

"I've ranked higher than you'll ever rank, little girl," Mara glares at her. "No one else has even come close. It will be a shame to see you go though."

"I thought there was someone else that wasn't doing well," Rora reminds her. Vindication is written on her face.

"He reached a level where I decided he was a threat, but to *your* credit, he wasn't as good as you." She sneers at Rora. The two are locked in conversation as if I'm not even there—maybe I can use that to my advantage.

"So what's your plan here? Have your dragon eat me?" Rora tips her chin up defiantly.

"That's too pedestrian. Anyone could have their dragon roast you," she leers at Rora as she starts to circle her. "No, I think I'll have Drayce destroy your *boyfriend* instead."

Mara throws herself sideways, evading her dragon's wing as it wheels around to face me. It roars in my face as it begins to run toward me. Thankfully I'm close enough that it can't gain much speed in the distance between us.

I manage to grab on to the hilt of my sword, holding the blade in front of me, as the monster runs at me. Rora shrieks, trying to draw the dragon's attention away.

"Remember, RoraRose," Mara calls to her, "if he dies, there's no coming back for him—he's not supposed to be here. He may have other lives, but he's starting from the bottom. He can't help you if he's dead."

She laughs as the dragon's eyes grow wild. From the corner of my eye, I see Rora run toward the dragon, trying to defend me and draw its attention away long enough for me to stab it.

Rora throws herself against its leg, driving her dagger into its scaly flesh. Just as I thrust my sword upward into its heart, it disappears.

"Did we do it?" I call to Rora.

"Hardly," Mara chirps. She snaps her fingers and the dragon reappears on her other side, decidedly far away from Rora. "But if you're not a fan of Drayce here, I can always call Ejder."

Above our heads, the sound of swopping fills the air. The dragon's flame shoots high above it, letting the kingdom know it is here. When he settles on the ground, I find he matches Mara's deep red dress. I wonder if she borrowed some of its scales for her belt.

The red dragon moves its tail as it sizes me up.

"What does this one do?" I say just loud enough for Rora to hear me. I keep my lips from moving as much as possible.

"It's resistant to weapons." She looks like she's ready to be sick.

"What?" I nearly drop my sword, turning to look at her. I probably shouldn't have done that.

"We can't use weapons on it," she repeats. "We can hurt it a little, but we can't do any serious damage and we can't kill it."

"How do we—?"

"Without weapons," she cuts me off.

"And you said the *other one* is hardest to kill?" My voice goes up an octave but I don't care.

"Last chance, pretty thing. Leave now and I'll spare you. It's only *her* that I want…in fact, if you leave now, I'll let you into the castle for a quest. You can score unfathomable points and lives inside. And if you work with me, there won't ever be a need for me to do *this* to *you*." Mara waves her hand around at the scene. Her dragons surround us, forcing us back with their tails.

"You can't use both dragons on us," Rora calls, fully prepared to take on the black dragon advancing on her. "My quest only calls for one dragon to be slain. Once I engage with one, the other can't attack."

"That won't stop the other from going after your boyfriend," Mara cackles. "Unless, of course, he makes a wiser choice."

She holds her hand out to me. The wind from her dragon's wings pushes her hair back like it would in one of those movie sequences. She's actually quite stunning for a moment.

"Nah, I'm a loyal boyfriend," I call, making her face

falter. "I also know that once I'm engaged with a dragon, a second one can't attack me."

Knowing Rora had no idea I would be saying that out loud to Mara, I launch myself toward her. It would have been better if we could have both taken the red dragon together, but Rora didn't know my plan until I announced it to both women.

The red dragon—Ejder— reels back as if he's been slapped. I've confused him. His jaw snaps open and shut once before making his move.

I dive to the ground, rolling over to get out of the way as his flames tingle across my skin. Despite the suit of armor, I can feel the fire licking at my arm, singeing the hair like a fireplace I once got too close to as a child.

When I stand, I'm by Rora's side. She glances at me to make sure I'm okay before lashing out at the black dragon. I slice at it with her, locking both of us in battle with the creature.

"Ejder, come," Mara commands. The red dragon recoils, wallowing in misery at its failed attempt to destroy me. I can't hide my grin at evading it, though the black dragon's roar removes it completely.

Mara leans against her red dragon, getting cozy to watch the show. It wraps itself around her, protecting her.

"Come here, my pet. Let's watch your brother defeat the little knight and his princess," Mara croons loudly enough for us to hear. "Drayce will do a magnificent job destroying them. Drayce, darling...*kill the knight first.*"

The black dragon's head whips away from Rora. It screeches a loud war cry, tipping his head back to release his fire into the air above us.

Rora uses the opportunity to bring her dagger down on the dragon's toe, slicing it off. Drayce comes down in pain, shrieking and shaking its head. Eyes narrow as Rora and the dragon face off.

I race toward the beast, angling my sword to enter its heart. I'm positive there's no way it will be this easy, but I'm willing to try. I have the overwhelming urge to yell my own battle cry as I run, but alerting the monster probably isn't a good idea.

It sees me despite my best efforts and picks up his foot, slamming it into my body. Drayce tosses me like a rag doll. I roll as I hit the ground, losing my sword in the process.

The red dragon hisses at me as I sit up. It's nostrils flare as it looks at me with pure hatred.

"Shame," Mara mouths to me, petting her dragon. She smiles and shrugs before looking at Rora.

I jump to my feet, running toward Rora and the black dragon. When I finally locate my sword, it's in Rora's hands. She wields it against the dragon ferociously.

"I'm here," I shout, trying not to throw her off her game.

"Grab the bow," she instructs, angling her back to me.

"Already on it," I reply, surprised we were thinking the same thing.

I haven't used a bow inside the game very often, but I have used them in real life—*thank you, physical education mandates*—so I imagine it will be fairly similar.

It feels steady in my hands as I knock an arrow and aim toward the digital dragon's eye. I might not kill it, but I can blind it and give Rora every chance possible.

Smoke streams from the dragon's nostrils as my arrow finds its mark. A low, guttural sound emanates from its closed jaws.

"Don't stop," Rora demands.

I stay by her side, pulling arrows from the quiver strapped to her back. Our legs and hips find a place next to each other, as if we share a side like conjoined twins. When she moves, I move.

"You okay?" she asks, clearly out of breath.

"Fine, you?" I reply. I haven't done as much lunging as she has because my weapon is long distance while hers is for close range attacks. "Ready to switch?"

"Not sure we have time for that," she mutters.

"Have any other tricks up your sleeve, princess?"

When I glance around, I notice the underbrush has fallen away, leaving the entire area to look like a peaceful meadow—there's nowhere for us to hide even if we *do* get away. I didn't realize the game changed landscapes in this section of the kingdom.

"One, but it might get us killed in the process," she says. Her arms sink as if she's growing tired from holding the heavy metal sword. "We could blow it up."

The dragon disappears in front of us. I quickly flip around to face the other direction, watching our backs. I knock an arrow and wait.

"Define *blowing it up*," I request.

The red dragon screeches as if cheering its brother on.

"I have the ability to create an explosion, but if we don't get out of the way fast enough, it could take us down too.

Drayce reappears to my left, warning us with the loud stomping of its feet. It crouches low, slowly moving toward us. Rora and I turn to face it, putting me on her right side—exactly where I don't want to be.

It breathes fire at us, glittering flames bursting in our faces. Before it hits us, Rora tosses her arms up, throwing an invisible shield in front of us. The flames hit it, bouncing off of the shield back toward it.

"One time use, sorry," she explains why she hadn't used it earlier.

The dragon frowns—something I didn't realize digital dragons could do—and takes another step toward us.

"So," I try to say casually, "are we blowing this monster up, or what?"

"It takes time to prepare, Royce. Can you hold him off while I get it ready?" She sounds nervous. I've been willing to help with everything else, so why not this?

"I've got this," I say, picking up my sword from where Rora had dropped it on the ground to summon her shield.

Rora falls back. I glance over my shoulder to see where she is so I keep the dragon away from her and catch Mara leaning forward with a concerned look on her face. I hope we accidentally blow her up too, though I imagine as queen, she can't die in the game until someone takes her place inside the castle—I haven't bothered to learn the rules for taking over as head royalty in the castle yet since I still have a few levels to go.

Drayce and I face off. It circles around me, trying to cut me off from Rora, but I hold my ground. I won't give it the advantage.

The dragon rears up, crashing down next to me as it coils its tail around me. I slam the point of my sword into its scales as it lifts me off the ground.

"Royce!" Rora calls from somewhere behind the dragon. I catch the tiniest glimpse of her blonde hair and purple collar as the dragon shakes me, trying to remove the sword from its flesh.

Mara pushes away from the red dragon and glides quickly toward Rora.

"You can't interfere while I'm on a quest!" Rora shouts. Inside the game, once a person is locked in a battle quest, no one can interfere unless they started the quest at the same time. *I* have the ability to mess up Rora's plans but *Mara* can't do anything but wait until the battle is finished since she didn't engage in the battle at the same time.

The queen waits restlessly for the battle to finish. If she has it her way, the fight will end with both Rora and I being removed from the game. If Rora loses, I can never come back even if the game allows me to start over.

I pull a dagger from the belt around my waist, driving it into the dragon's tail at the same time I pull the sword out. It wasn't expecting the attack and drops me, disappearing.

Avoiding my sword while I fall, I plummet fifteen feet, crashing into the ground.

"Royce!" Rora shouts again. I can't say I hate it when she says my name.

"I'm okay," I grunt, picking myself back up.

"Where is it?" she demands, rushing toward me. She carefully holds her explosive device under the open front hem of the skirt near her hip.

"It will be back," I promise.

"When it returns, get out of my way. Get as far away

from here as you can. I have speed that I can unlock to get away, so don't wait for me," she instructs me.

"Got it," I confirm just as the dragon reappears in front of us. It glares at us harder than Mara has been.

"Get your sword up like you're going to fight, then wait for me to throw the device," Rora mumbles.

I glance down, looking around her body to the hand she's attempting to keep concealed with her half skirt. She's angled toward me, blocking the dragon from noticing the gold and jewel-encrusted circle she's holding. It could pass as a dragon egg if it were a bit larger.

Something clicks.

She locks eyes with me, nodding. We both take a step forward as if to charge at the beast. It rears up, preparing to take us on, but only Rora steps forward.

Rora throws the gold device at the dragon and it skitters under its body. The moment she releases it, I run, looking back over my shoulder.

The dragon lets out a vicious cry of terror, it's red sibling echoing its concern. Mara screams as Rora starts to run.

I pump my legs as fast as I can, propelling myself forward. Rora quickly catches up to me, grabbing my elbow as she forces me to run faster, lending me part of her strength.

A single rock stands in the middle of the meadow,

having shifted to give us a place to hide from the explosion. We dive behind it.

Rora trips as we hide behind the rock. I grab at her, trying to steady her, but I end up falling on top of her. I cover my head with my hands to protect myself from debris. She wraps herself around me, trying to help protect me while I act as a human shield for her.

The detonation is so loud, I'm positive the entire kingdom can hear it. I picture the knaves and warlocks all jerking around to face this forbidden part of the kingdom, wondering what is going on.

Digital debris floats down from the sky as if pieces of the blue above us were drifting down. In fact, pixels from the dragon are mixed with pixels from the sky and grass. They twist and loop as they settle around us, disappearing once they hit the grass.

I pull away from Rora quickly, allowing us both to look out from behind the rock. Mara marches toward us with her dragon in tow.

"You may have beat the quest, RoraRose, but you won't be able to take my throne. I'll see to it that you never escape in one piece."

Mara waves her hand, disappearing as she shatters into a millions glitch-filled pieces.

The red dragon hisses at us, shooting flames straight up into the air over its head. It lifts itself off the ground and flies toward the castle, breaking the barrier that limits where dragons can roam.

In the distance, it settles onto the high walls of the crystal castle, waiting for us to approach. It roars, daring us to come to the final battle for the title of queen.

Chapter 6

"I GUESS WE'RE GOING TO THE CASTLE," I MUTTER, SIGHING dramatically. "Are you injured?"

"I'm fine," she says, refusing to look at me.

"You healed yourself, didn't you?" I ask. I need to know how badly she depleted her options.

She nods miserably.

"How bad?"

"Pretty bad. There's not much left."

Her hair has fallen out of its swept up look, making her look like she's been through battle. Dirt covers her face and I can only imagine how I look.

"You need to do whatever you have to in order to survive. Don't be discouraged. Now all we have to do is take Mara down." I give her a confident smile.

"Do you have any idea who she is?" Rora asks as she starts walking toward the castle.

"Not a clue. I don't think I've ever seen her before today."

"Too bad, we could really use some leverage on her."

"Wait." I pause. "I still have a few messages with Alan. Let me ask him to look her up. I type quickly on my control panel, asking for information on the magician queen. Hopefully he'll respond soon.

"At least we took the dragon out. Great thinking on your part," I offer as we start walking again.

"Thanks. I've been storing that one for awhile."

"It was a good call," I affirm. "Hey, you know once we walk out of here, the kill challenge will still be in effect."

"Yeah, we'll have to avoid that." She taps the quiver on her back, replenished with new arrows.

"Do we have a plan for that?"

The grass ripples in the nonexistent breeze. Rora tucks a strand of her curly hair behind her ear.

"Fight them off, I guess. We don't have much choice at this point."

My control panel buzzes as she finishes speaking.

"What does he say?"

I pull up the message.

"Her sister is one of the game's creators," I read out loud. "Mara was banned from playing the game when it was new because her family didn't like the idea of immersive virtual reality, so she snuck in under an alias and went on to level really high."

I close my control panel over, looking at Rora.

"It sounds like there's a division between them. Alan is

trying to get in contact with the one game maker now. I have a feeling she'll help us to oust her sister from the game."

"Well, that would certainly help."

The red dragon screeches in the distance, clearly annoyed that we are taking so long. It spits fire over the bridge making everyone duck. The curious people that stayed to investigate the dragon's appearance at the castle clear out of the area quickly.

"Huh. Guess that will make the kill challenge easier to avoid," I muse.

"Looks like it," she says, working her hair back up into its sweeping up do. I suppose she can't fight with hair in her eyes. "Maybe we should pick up the pace. I can't stand drawing this out any longer."

I match her speed as we run toward the castle.

"Do you think we'll have to fight to get inside?" I ask, staring at the red dragon. It watches us walk across the second bridge. I doubt dousing it in the moat would drown it, but maybe it would extinguish the fire.

The dragon hisses at us, clawing at the top of a tower. Crystal blue bricks fall off the building, smashing like glass when it hits the courtyard ground.

"Pretty sure," she surmises.

The dragon's tail swishes down in front of the castle door as it opens revealing Mara on the other side. She's changed outfits again, this time standing in her own version of armor.

Dark metal surrounds her body, dripping over her like pointed dragon scales. Each one moves individually as she steps out of the castle.

"Congratulations, RoraRose," she says as if mandated to speak the words. "To make it this far is quite the accomplishment. You now have a choice—battle me for the throne or leave the game."

"I choose to leave the game," Rora shouts immediately.

Mara's shoulders drop.

"Oh, you stupid girl," she shouts. "You don't *really* have a choice—I locked you in, remember? The game just requires me to say that."

Mara walks closer, each step more dangerous than the last.

"To win against me, you must enter the castle and succeed in taking my power. Only one of us can win and neither of us can leave until someone is declared the victor by the game." Mara turns to me. "*He* can't come inside. You might want to kiss your prince good bye now, RoraRose, because before I'll let you enter my castle, *I'm going to kill him.*"

She throws her hand to the side, a bolt of something flying out from her fingertips. It strikes the ground at my feet, burning a hole into the otherwise perfect grass. Mara smiles wickedly.

"You had your chance," she taunts.

Rora rushes to stand in front of me.

"You can't hurt me while I'm out here." She wraps her arms around me as I stand behind her. Her fingers graze my back as she presses herself against my chest, her quiver nearly poking me in the face.

"No, but I *can* move you out of the way." She raises her hand as if she's going to snap for her dragon.

As I watch her, I wonder how she's going to fight with half her hair tucked up like that. It's like it's pulled back and up on one half of her head while the other half hangs loose and bold. She tosses part of it while watching us.

Rora fidgets behind me as if she's trying to type into her control panel on her wrist. I wind my hands in front of her, trying to give her more room to work without Mara noticing her movements.

I glare at the queen, hoping to hold her attention.

"You can't touch me," I challenge her. "Not in the trading post and certainly not here."

"You'll see soon enough that power is attractive, RoyalRoyce. You wanted this too. Don't deny it—you've been working toward this moment for *yourself* for all of these years. Even if your little princess *does* beat me, you'll be battling *her* within a few months. Isn't it nice to have already learned all of her tricks?"

Something zaps inside of me. Rora transferred something to me. It registers in my control panel but I can't check it yet.

"Oh, trust me, I've only just begun learning her tricks. She and I have a lot more to teach each other." *Hopefully outside of the game too.* "Don't worry, Mara, we won't even think about you once when you're gone."

Mara grimaces, baring her teeth.

"We'll see about that." She takes a deep breath, preparing to launch her dragon attack.

My hands find their way to Rora's hips, ready to push her aside if I need to. The dragon can't kill her at this point, but he can still injure her enough that she can't defend herself once she's inside the castle walls.

"Pity, that handsome face could have been such a nice addition to my throne room. Maybe I'll stuff your avatar once Ejder destroys you— *assuming* he doesn't burn your face off—and set you up in the castle anyway. You could be my muse."

Rora works one arm around me, placing it between her back and my chest so it's resting on my opposite hip. She's preparing to push me into action. I wait for her signal.

"Well, then, here's hoping it burns me to a crisp," I shout.

Her hand claws at my hip, forcing me to step to the side of her.

"Stickiness," she hisses. "Go!"

I run for the castle, surprising Mara. She spins as I dart past her and leap onto the wall of the castle. I gracefully scale it.

If this ability doesn't stick around after this level, I'm going to do whatever it takes to get it back—it's incredible.

The dragon shakes its head as it watches me climb, shocked to see me move like that. Behind me, I can hear Rora engage with Mara, distracting her.

I jump for the dragon before it can react, slicing off part of its tail. I wish my weapons could do more damage. It wails in pain, sending more crystal bricks shattering to the ground. I fall among the glass pieces.

The dragon whips around to face Mara, realizing she's fighting. It throws itself away from the castle wall, landing near its mistress.

Knowing it can hurt Rora, and being fully aware that Rora only has one chance to escape, I know what I must do.

With sword in hand, I take on the dragon that cannot be killed with weapons.

I won't be coming out of this alive.

"Rora, get inside!" I insist, holding my blade above my shoulder.

"I'm not leaving you," she refuses. "We're in this together."

"No, Rora, we're not. You can only win if you get inside and fight that witch. I can't go in either way, but if you defeat her, you can call off the dragon! Now, go!"

Fire races through the air toward me, sizzling against my armor. It warms enough to burn through the metal as it touches my skin. I cry out, dropping my sword.

Rora looks like she wants to cry, but my words ring true—she's the one that has the power to stop this.

"Go!" I beg her, stooping to pick up my weapon.

She looks at Mara. The queen has her hands buried in Rora's hair, trying to pull it. Rora's hands are piercing into the queen's shoulders, her arms locked to keep her at a distance.

Rora growls at her, sounding for a moment like a dragon. She digs her nails into Mara's arms and forces her toward the opaque glass building.

"Give up, child," Mara yelps. "You don't have the power to defeat me. I will always rule this kingdom."

"You mean your *sister's* kingdom?" Rora defies her.

"She may have built this world, but *I* own it."

The dragon snaps at me, swiping at me with its tail at the same time. I drop to my knees as it pulls my leg out from under me. Heat radiates off of the creature.

"Not for long," Rora challenges.

"I've been at this much longer than you have, *princess*. I watched this game take over my sister's life—I know every trick about it."

"So when she wouldn't let you play, you thought the best revenge of all would be mastering her game?" Rora shouts, taunting her. The two grapple, clawing at each other. Rora's dagger bounces off the queen like it's nothing since they can't hurt each other until they are inside.

The dragon lifts me up, flying back to the nearest tower of the castle. My hand still sticks to the walls, giving me at least some hope.

I can hear the woman shouting, but from high on the castle walls, I can't make out the words. From the look on Mara's face as she swings them around, I'd guess Rora is roasting her about her sister.

The dragon moves me from its tail to its clawed front foot, lifting me up as if it's going to eat me. Its teeth are large and stained black, nearly the size of my forearm and hand.

I slap it as it leans into me. It shakes its head, allowing me to get a good punch to the nose. My fingers claw at it, trying to defend myself. Rora needs to get moving.

"Royce!" she shouts.

"*Royce!*" Mara mimics. "Ah, young love. Too bad it never lasts."

"Let him go, Mara," Rora demands. "He can be your little pet."

Her negotiating tactics are lacking.

"Bring him here, Ejder," Mara summons, breaking away from Rora.

The red dragon lifts into the air, dropping on the grass with me still in its clutches. I bring a brick with me that it loosened when the dragon landed on the edge of the wall. It doesn't notice as I hide it behind my back.

When we're settled, Mara walks over to us. Only Rora's nails digging into her arm stops her from getting too close.

"Kill him," Mara commands.

"This ends now," Rora summons all of her strength, dragging the woman toward the castle. She calls out to me, "I'll be back, Royce."

The dragon turns to me and I strike. The glass causes enough damage to get the beast to release me. I drop to the ground, readying my sword.

I know Rora's watching behind me as she hurries toward the castle so I shout goodbye to her.

"I'll be fine—*just get out*! I'll see you outside!"

Fire surrounds me, melting my skin, as I plunge my sword into the dragon's heart.

I fade out of the game as the castle door slams shut.

Chapter 7

I wake with a start.

"Royce!" Alan shouts, racing across the room. "Where is she?"

"She had to defeat Mara alone," I glance up to see Perry rushing at me. "Aunt Perry?"

"It was either get her out of here or watch you two. I couldn't stop her," Alan informs me. "Chrystal said not to leave Rora alone."

"Who is Chrystal?"

"She's the game creator, dear," Perry says nervously as she fusses over me. "She's supposed to be hacking into the system to help Rora escape.

"Supposed to be?" I demand, swinging my feet over the edge of the chair.

"She *is*," Alan corrects. "Perry is just being paranoid."

"We can't let her die, Royce," Perry begs.

"She won't die. I've been with her for hours. She's got the skills to beat Mara."

"Why did you leave her?" Perry demands, grabbing my shoulder. I shake her off.

"I had to die in the game so she could defeat Mara."

"Dude, you died?" Alan asks. He sounds a little sad. We won't be able to play together for a long time until I reach higher levels again. "At least you protected her."

His ability to bounce back is astounding.

I maneuver myself to stand next to Rora.

"She's not moving," I frown.

"Perry, Royce needs coffee. He's had a long few hours and if we're going to help Rora, he needs to be thinking clearly." He waits as Perry rushes downstairs as if our lives depended on it. He's somber when he speaks again. "She hasn't moved for the last twenty minutes. I'm really worried."

It takes a great deal of effort to lift Rora's fingers off the armrest, but I slip my hand under hers.

"Dude, what happened to you?" Alan asks as I swallow hard. "You've only been in there for a few hours and you look like you're losing your best friend—which, by the way, is supposed to be *me*."

"We can't let her get hurt in there, Alan. She doesn't deserve this." I can't take my eyes off her. It doesn't even look like she's breathing. "When was the last time you were in contact with Chrystal?"

"A little while ago. She was still hacking in. She's trying to circumvent the system because it was design so that people couldn't hijack it. She knew her sister had snuck into the game and taken the castle but she didn't know she was hurting people on the outside to keep it."

"She didn't know about that guy Mara got locked up for juicing?" I question.

Wait, did Rora blink? No? No.

My shoulders sag when I realize it was wishful thinking.

"Turns out Mara has some clout out here. She's a judge. She had the records sealed and refused to let the media report on it. That's why I only found it on that one website. It took some serious digging, let me tell you." He raises an eyebrow at me. "Oh, and her real name isn't Mara. It's Dara. She changed it for the game."

"A judge...wow."

"Here," Perry runs into the room, thrusting a cup of coffee at me. It sloshes on the floor, this time avoiding my hand.

"Thanks," I take a quick sip and hand it to Alan to set down, unwilling to move away from Rora.

The girl in the chair gasps, making us all leap into the air. Aside from that, she doesn't move.

The waiting takes forever. Alan paces around the room, sending Perry on a thousand little missions to get her out of our hair.

"Should I go in there?" Alan asks.

"No, she's in the castle. You can't do anything to help her."

"Should I contact Chrystal again?" Alan has been known to babble when he gets anxious.

"We might hurt Rora's chances if we bother Chrystal and distract her."

I'm trying to think practically about this.

If I weren't attached to Rora's hand, I'd be pacing around the room too, likely lapping Alan despite how fast he's walking. I lean against the chair's armrest with one elbow, holding her hand in the other, willing her to make *some* movement.

Alan rounds the corner again.

"We just turned into a trio, didn't we?" He offers me a sad smile.

"Yeah, I think we did," I reply, glancing down. We'd known this girl for a handful of hours and already she was one of us.

"Her mother is going to kill me," Perry cries from the doorway.

"Out!" we both shout at her, making her retreat.

"Go handle her," I direct Alan, feeling terrible for yelling at my aunt.

Alan swiftly walks out of the room, guiding Perry down the stairs. He'll drop her on the couch, calm her down, and be right back up.

Rora rests in the chair, her hair curled in ringlets

around her shoulders. I move a strand away from her lips.

"I just need you to wake up, Rora. Come on, you can do it. You can defeat her," I whisper, knowing she can't hear me.

Alan's phone lights up, buzzing.

I let go of Rora for the first time and run across the room, snatching it up.

"Hello," I answer.

"Who is this?" a female voice yelps.

"Alan's friend, Royce."

"Oh," she says. "This is Chrystal. You're out of the game?"

"I died," I answer bluntly.

"Are you with her?"

"Yes." I rush back to her side.

"Good, it's nearly over," her voice rises in pitch as she rushes to get in her words. "You're going to hear static, when you do, take the goggles off of her and then don't touch it. Stay on the line."

The end of her words are overtaken by a loud crackling sound as if our entire gaming system in the room is about to combust. I drop the phone on Rora's leg as I quickly remove the goggles. Her hair falls out of place, dangling off the sides of the headrest.

"Royce? Royce?" the voice on the phone asks. I jerk my head around to locate the device.

CONTINUE THE SERIES

Virtually Sleeping Beauty is the first in a series of
episodic fiction novellas set inside the Virtual Reality
world of the story.

New installments are coming out in 2019.

LITTLE MISS MUFFET

Little Miss Muffet sat on her tuffet,
eating her curds and whey.
Along came a spider
who sat down beside her
and frightened Miss Muffet away.

CHAPTER 2

"GO HIDE, PEST," SHE ADDRESSED HIM as the building fell into view. Spider slipped behind a hedge of bushes, blending into the dark branches as Fet made her way to the metallic grey structure.

Launching herself onto the stairs, she swung up onto the ledge. Kicking her feet off of the stairway railing, Fet steadied herself on the edge of the building, disappearing from Spider's limited view.

"There," she muttered as she located the panel once safely on the roof. Pulling open the covering, she searched the screen looking for the coded message. Finding nothing, she rocked back on her heels.

After a moment, Fet grabbed a rock. She dragged its edge along the screen. Peeling the blank piece back, she revealed a secondary screen, blinking alive with its newfound freedom.

As she began to type, a code appeared on the screen, racing as she decoded its message. Fet's brow creased, her

"But where?" Spider answered, still too close for comfort. "Where are we going?"

"I know a place where there might be an Irex, but you're not going to like it. Come on." Fet stood to her feet the moment the watchmen had passed. Her short skirt swished around her as she turned, catching Spider's eye. He followed along behind her, forcing himself to keep pace as she dashed away.

"YOU HAVE TO BE KIDDING." SPIDER SAID, looking up the face of the cliff.

"Aren't spiders supposed to be good at climbing?" Fet taunted, extending her arm to grab the first stone.

"It's so steep it's practically inverted." Spider's eyes were wide as Fet lifted herself off the ground.

"That's why it's perfect," Fet called over her shoulder as she scaled the rock wall. "No one ever bothers it."

"The fact that it's in the middle of nowhere might have something to do with it," Spider called to her as he forced himself to latch onto the first handhold.

Fet was out of sight a moment later, scrambling over the side to the hidden entrance. The cave was dark, lit only by the blue screens housed inside. It had its own power system, far removed from the eyes of the government. The rock facade gave way to old-time luxury;

metallic walls with a ventilation system circulating air to keep the machinery at the right temperature. A lighting system was mounted to the ceiling, but Fet didn't bother turning it on.

"Back here," she called when she heard Spider enter. She glanced up just in time to see his face fall in shock.

"Once they started the Upgrade, our grandparents started collecting the older machines. Not everything was saved, but there is a massive amount of technology here from over the years."

"This is a Hydren." Spider announced gleefully, the shock and reverence clear in his voice as he eyed a machine once he had recovered for the surprise of finding what he had been told the government had destroyed long ago.

"You want some time alone with the computer or are you actually going to help?" Fet glanced at him. He brushed his hair back behind his ear and tore himself away from the system. Moving further back, he wandered through the technology. He was going in the wrong direction, but Fet didn't bother to correct him.

After a few minutes of wandering, she located the console she was looking for. She started it up. The machine silently flickered to life, adding a bright glow to the back corner of the room.

"You found it," Spider's quiet voice in her ear caused Fet to jump, nearly colliding with her conspirator's face.

A new screen popped up in its place and Fet watched as Peep's captor took over manipulating the machine. There was no way to prevent her from watching their every move now as code streamed across the interface.

Suddenly everything froze and Fet rose out of her chair. There it was: the next command.

CHAPTER 3

"THE WHITE COATS ARE AT THE HUB. BREAK INTO The Lab while they are gone and destroy it if you want your friend back." The screen read.

"Destroy it?" Fet asked in horror.

"How do they expect us to do that?" Spider hissed behind her, raking his hands through his hair, only the tips of his pale fingers visible around his black leather fingerless gloves as Fet turned to face him.

"Do they expect us to blow it up?" he asked.

"I don't know, but we have to go," Fet answered, twirling her own blonde pigtail in her hands. Standing, she threw one last look at the Irex, coding scrolling across the screen.

The sun was blinding as they exited the cave. Fet scrambled down the face of the cliff. She had only made the trip several times during her life, but she would never reveal to Spider that the climb terrified her. Spider's foot slipped, forcing gravity to help him the rest of the way to the ground. Fet reached out her hand and steadied him as his feet collided with the earth, miraculously leaving him upright.

"Let's go," she announced as she took off, leaving Spider in her wake. Suddenly she felt a sharp electrical burst against her hip.

"Stop," the screen read.

Eyes darting up, she focused ahead of her, confused, searching for an answer.

"*You*," she growled, turning on her heels, when she realized what had happened.

"I'm helping you, best not to leave me behind." Spider sneered, slipping his device back into his own pocket.

"If you *ever*..." Fet started her tirade, but he stopped her with a raised hand.

"We don't have time for your lectures, Muffet. Save the dramatic flair for your work." He walked passed her at an accelerated clip, his jab about her coding flourishes stinging more than it should. Fet had always taken great pride in her work, and somehow he found a way to diminish it.

Running beyond him, she set the pace for their journey to The Lab. They were both struggling for breath when they arrived, the sun lower in the sky, but still bright. The large building had several guards posted outside, checking for clearances.

"We need to get them out of there," Fet whispered.

"We need to figure out how we're going to take down the building," Spider replied.

"I've got that covered. We just need to get rid of the guards."

Spider watched her for a moment before his eyes grew wide. "You're not actually going to blow it up, are you?"

"What choice do we have?"

"How are you going to do that?" he gasped, "you don't even have materials to make a bomb."

"We're not making a bomb, Spider, we're causing an explosion."

His eyes focused on her as she pulled out her device, her fingers flying over the screen as fast as his own typically worked. He knew he could outsmart her, he had done it before, but it was entrancing to watch her work without a screen and codes between them.

"There. I found it. Now I just have to get in." She frowned as she hit a block.

Spider brought his device to life, joining in on the fun.

"Allow me." His suddenly-much-deeper voice prompted Fet to look up at his newfound chivalry.

As they worked together, breaking through each wall, their keystrokes became more frantic, as if every time they made a move, someone specifically blocked them from continuing.

"Are you getting this?" Fet whispered loudly,

concerned over what entity they might be facing and how they so quickly knew her every move.

Spider didn't answer, intently typing away on his device, nearly matching Fet's every move.

"Who are we up against?" she whispered.

Fet's blonde hair fell in front of her face and she used the back of her wrist to swipe it away. Clearly the person holding Peep was not behind this blockade. Did that mean someone else knew what was happening and was trying to stop them?

"Still with me, Fet?" Spider taunted, a smug sneer creeping onto his face.

A few strokes later, she looked up, triumph written in her grin. "Nope," she said, "I'm already in."

Spider's head whipped up.

"How?" he stammered.

"I'll never tell." She arched her eyebrows, daring him to take her on. "Now, we need to move the guards."

She typed for a moment as Spider continued to stare, his eyes slowing to trace over her from head to toe, his fashion-opposite.

Fet's device started vibrating. The arrogance drained from her face as she lifted it.

"Spider, we have to move. Now!"

In his confusion, he stumbled, attempting to follow along behind her as he put his own device back into his pocket.

"What are you doing?" he yelled as he realized they were headed directly at the tall white building that loomed in front of them. Its modern, arched edges were anything but welcoming.

"We're on the clock, Spider. We have less than one minute to set off the explosion," she said as she tried to type while she ran. "There, the meltdown has started. All of the badges had already swiped out of the building when the power source went down, apparently it was all hands on deck, so there are only the guards left."

The first of the explosions filled the air, pieces of the back of the building floated to the ground. The noise pulsed around them, shocking their senses as they ran.

Fet nearly lost her footing as she realized they were about to make a mistake. Spider showed no signs of slowing.

"Wait, get down!" Fet yelled as they approached the terrifying scene. "They can't see you."

She intentionally tripped Spider, sending him crashing to the earth as she ran ahead.

"Fet, no!" he yelled, reaching to her from his place in the grass. "You can't die, no one will be able to save Peep!"

Ignoring his call, Fet ran as quickly as she could in her tall combat boots, pink skirt jostling around her as she rushed forward. She raced toward the building, feet pounding against the pavement as she hit the blacktop.

Spider couldn't hear the words she shouted to the guards as he stumbled to his feet and raced after her.

The second explosion rang out as the confused guards ran from the building, heeding whatever warning Fet had imparted on them. Debris rained down on her, like stars falling from the sky in a mass exodus of space. She rolled as she hit the ground, launching herself to her back to her feet and continuing on, only a slight limp as evidence of the danger she had been in.

Spider grabbed her arm as he reached her and dragged the girl away from the men who were turning for an explanation. Putting as much distance between them as possible, he only ducked when the third explosion sounded in the distance.

When he collapsed into the tall grass, his devices tumbled from his pocket.

"Thanks," Fet breathed when she stopped gasping. Her hand stretched the length of her leg to her ankle, checking for injuries.

"Have you lost your mind?" he yelled. "You could have died!"

"And if I hadn't, *they would have!*" she shrieked back, suddenly angry.

She reached for his device, picking it up off the ground to hand to him.

"I'll get it." Spider said quickly, reaching for it.

"Wait." Fet's brow knitted together. Something felt off.

"You used this. How could you use this? Your device went down when I killed the power."

Matching her face, he looked at her. "I…. I don't know."

"But…"

"We don't have time to figure it out, Fet. We have to get away from The Lab." Pieces of the building floated between them, catching in Fet's pigtail. Spider used his hand to brush away a piece of ash caught in his long eyelash.

"Over there!" a voice shouted—a guard looking for the young girl who had appeared out of nowhere as the explosion took place.

"We have to go," Spider whispered harshly.

"Not yet. We're not done here."

"But The Lab has been destroyed," he insisted, pulling at her arm.

"Not yet." Fet rose, allowing the guards to run beyond them before she doubled back. "I left one room standing. It's the backdoor into Irex."

"What?" Spider followed along behind her.

"It's how we take it back. The man who created it… He left a way into it that not even the government knows about. You need to wait here," she replied.

"Not a chance." Spider refused to back down.

The building was in shambles, walls standing at odd angles, pieces still falling off. Fet raced into the debris, careful to avoid the hot mental from the machinery. On the far side stood a confusing array of partial walls and hanging lights.

"There's a guard," Spider pointed out.

"Then take care of him," Fet hissed, pushing him toward the man as she disappeared around the wall.

The system had been partially damaged but enough remained that she could hack it. Fingers flying across the keyboard, she set to work establishing the break in the code needed to take back the Irex when the time came. Her head jerked up as a scream came from behind the wall, but she couldn't stop. Something very bad was happening, but she didn't know if Spider had caused it or experienced it.

The final stroke allowed her access. It was done.

Rounding the corner she found Spider leaning against the wall, waiting, face grim.

"What did you do?" her voice was low and terrifying as she realized where she stood in this little game.

"What did *you* do?" he challenged. Everything about him was so dark that he looked like a different person.

She couldn't trust him. She never should have to begin with. He was a hacker…he had destroyed her job once before. He had no remorse and no reason to help her.

His leather-bound hand dragged through his hair as he watched her, eyes narrow.

"Did you hurt that guard?" she demanded.

"No, I scared him off though." His gaze was icy. "What did you do, Muffet?"

"I enacted a program that lets me gain control over Irex," she responded.

"What program?"

"It's called the Way, and that's all you need to know."

He looked at her as if he loathed every bit of her. Sneering at the girl, he held her gaze, his shoulders rolling back as if he wanted to be anywhere but near her.

Suddenly, Spider's eyes softened just enough to be visible and he leaned toward her again, frightening her. Just as suddenly, his posture stiffened once more, reclaiming his icy distance.

"You need to tell me what's going on..." his voice was cut off as a small series of pops made Fet lunge forward.

"The last detonation is going to go off, move!" she charged at him, pulling him away before the last burst.

A sharp pulse moved through her hip as another mission came through.

"Return to the Hub." The words scrolled across her screen when she retrieved it. She realized she still didn't have an explanation for Spider's device suddenly working again. Nothing could be trusted.

"What could they possible need us *there* for?" Spider asked. No one answered as they continued to run.

CHAPTER 4

THE MOON WASHED THE WORLD IN A white light as they approached the center of town. Sneaking passed the Legends building, hidden in plain sight, Fet realized she had never contacted T with information. She couldn't afford to now.

The Hub was still chaotic as the Coats were setting up their new home in the center of the town, having seen evidence of the explosion at their home base. Guards filled the area, keeping people back, weapons poised for use.

Faces in the growing crowd appeared. Fet caught BB's eye and shook her head to warn him off. Glancing quickly toward Spider, she hoped she had sufficiently warned the others. BB pulled back, drifting into the masses as the others slowly followed.

"We have to deal with the Irex, don't we?" Spider asked. A curt nod was the only response she gave him.

"Use Way to disable it from here," he said as she started forward, grabbing at her arm.

"Can't. Need the wires." Pushing past him, she forced her way into the crowd, refusing to tell him her plan. People jostled against her, knocking her off balance.

The air crackled, revealing a tense standoff between the people surrounding the building looking for answers and the watchmen guarding it. They held a barrier, attempting to block the people from getting to close. A man demanded answers, only to be pushed back.

A guard yelled, imploring everyone to stay away while the Coats worked. Tired of waiting for hours, the people jostled against one another, ready to take the men on. They had never experienced trouble with their technology like this before. Nothing had ever been shut down for so long. The disruption in the life they knew caused them to become caustic.

Fet filtered between people, making her way to where she could see a path into the building. Quietly, she slipped by, attempting not to be noticed with her loud outfit and eye-catching hair. Taking an elbow to the stomach, she pushed further, until she came to a less crowded area.

"Stop," a voice yelled. The weapon was raised at a child.

"Don't." she warned, stepping between the guard and the boy.

The boy flinched behind her. The guard lashed out, catching Fet's arm, missing its mark. Fet fell to the ground, blood already pooling beneath her. She kicked, sending the guard crashing to the ground beside her. A second man ran to assist as a person in the crowd snatched up the child. The darkly clothed person hustled the boy away as Fet scrambled to leave the scene. Clutching her arm, she ran around the building directly into a Coat.

"I'll be needing that." Fet said as her good arm darted out in front of her. She touched the man's neck and he dropped, the pressure point knocking him out. Shrugging on the man's coat, she forced herself to walk slowly into the building. Making sure she was alone, she slipped inside.

The Hub was filled with Coats, all testing equipment and trying to right the situation. The low hum of technology filled the air as they used a generator to try to reestablish the connection. She took the stairs two at a time as she made her way to the remaining Irex system, hoping to make it behind closed doors before the blood started to show through the coat.

Powering the Irex through her own device, she sifted through everything that had happened.

"This makes no sense," she mumbled as numbers filtered across the screen. After a few moments she gasped. "It can't be. It's the Wall job."

"You're even better in person, Fet." Spider's voice grated against her ears, her shoulders hunching in disgust as he entered the room behind her.

"I *knew* you had something to do with this. It was all too convenient."

"I saw what you did, Muffet. You protected those guards at The Lab and you took an attack for that child. Two men are dead out there. This chaos is getting people killed," he said, hands in his pockets.

"Who sent you, Spider?"

"The Piper."

Color drained from her face as the name hung between them.

"What does the Piper have to do with this?"

"The Barrier was his design. The government took it over and forced him out. He wants it back. This is his escape plan. The Wall job was just part of it. He designed it to see if the Legends could handle it."

"To see if *I* could handle it," she corrected.

"Yes," he nodded solemnly, giving her more information than she thought he should be, as her enemy. "He needs the leader of the Legends to finish this."

"Why are you telling me this?" she asked, still kneeling in front of the console.

"People are dying now. I won't be a part of that."

"Suddenly you're working with me? I don't buy it."

"I've known what was going on from the start, Muffet.

I was the one working against you at the Lab. I've been working to bring down the Piper from the inside."

"You honestly expect me to believe you're a triple agent?" her glare stopped him. "I get that spiders have eight legs, but not even *you* are capable of juggling that much. Careful, or I'll start ripping those legs off."

"You don't have to. I'll do it *for* you," he disregarded her warning. He took a dangerous step closer as he prepared to confess, hoping she would believe him. "I ruined the Wall job for you, but I gave you a way into the system. You're going to need that. Piper thought I was doing as he asked, but I created a backdoor into *your* system so I could see what you were doing and help you work against him. That's how I got in with the Legends to begin with. I knew your every move. I've watched you every day since that job. I know every keystroke you've made."

Fet stood, hands clenched at her sides, ready to attack if he got too close.

"I know you've never hurt anyone. *Piper has.* My family has been working against him from the start. We worked against the Legends too, until I watched you this past year. We stopped fighting you months ago. Didn't you realize when your life got suddenly easier?"

Her blood boiled at his words. He had no right to watch her.

How much time had he spent observing her every move?

How much did he know about her? How much did she want *him to know about her?*

He held her gaze, refusing to admit anything. She had no idea he knew so much more than she'd ever know. For an entire year he had memorized her every keystroke, every flourish, every movement. He knew every step she would take before she decided to take it. Her reactions were second nature to him.

Stepping forward, she swung at him. Catching her wrist, he pulled her close, leaning her backwards just far enough that if she moved, they would fall.

He held on to her, trying to control the situation and force her to listen to him.

"I'm not fighting you, Muffet," he growled, inches from her face.

Fet tried to decide if she could believe him. The way her body relaxed suggested she could, but her head screamed that she was crazy for giving in so quickly. She charted everything he had done in between breaths. Her mind whirred through everything he could have interfered with since the Wall job. Had he helped her? Every coincidence suggested he might have been with her all along.

"Then what are you doing?" She couldn't look him in the eye. He was too close.

"Helping you end this." Righting her, he refused to let

go of her waist, fingers lingering against her side. "Now finish disabling the Irex. Our next stop is the Wall."

"You mean it's a real place?" she asked, relinquishing the last brain cells that held out against him, hoping she hadn't misplaced her limited trust in him. She lowered herself to her knees in front of the wires she needed to manipulate and waited for the sound of a weapon against her skull as she turned her back to him to work, but nothing came.

"It's a very real place. And you're the only one who can finish it there."

"What does he want from me?" she asked as she carefully removed the wires from their rightful place.

"Your code. When the program was developed, a code was put in by the leader of the Legends. You have that code and he needs it to gain control back."

She didn't have the code. Peep had the code, passed down by the leaders of the group over the years.

"Back when he was working with the Legends, he trusted them with the final piece, a piece not even he knew, in order to protect the system. But now, with the way the government is...he just wants to get out, and bring the government down in his wake."

"The same government who is willing to kill innocent bystanders if they appear to threaten their reign at the command of the Coats?"

"Yes. Do you need help?" he asked, peering around her.

"I eat codes for breakfast, Spider, and I certainly think I can handle some cords and Way." She rolled her eyes, making him stifle a smile behind her back.

He watched as she carefully unplugged every wire and shut the system down.

"We're coming back for that, aren't we?"

"It's not like we're running away when this is all over," she huffed, brushing past him. "Now where is this ridiculous Wall?"

CHAPTER 5

"PEEP IS ON THE OTHER SIDE of the Wall, isn't she?" she stared up at the tall, metallic barrier.

"Yes."

The sleek silver glinted in the moonlight, a pale blue tone reflecting off of it menacingly.

"How do we get in?"

"You break the code," he answered. "There's a panel somewhere that we have to find. You need to plug in your code to open the door."

"Why exactly are you so eager to have me plug this code in? I thought you were working against him," she whispered as she judged the distance from the tall grass to the Wall.

"He has almost complete control now. We have to break in and take control back. And Fet..." he paused, catching her eye. "My brother is in there with Peep. I have a lot to lose, too."

"You risked your brother to work against the Piper?" she asked, suddenly softening to him.

"We need to end this."

"Peep is the head of the Legends," she admitted, shock registering on Spider's face. "I don't have the code."

"Then we hack it. Together," he collected himself. "Careful what you say when we walk out of here. He can hear."

Spider stalked out of the tall grass. Fet jumped up and raced behind him, boots pounding against the dirt. They separated ways, searching for the panel.

"Here," Spider called.

"Welcome, Muffet. Break the code and you can have her back," a taunting voice rang out. "Just plug your code in and she'll be free to go."

"Arach too." Spider shouted as he pulled off the panel.

"You really want your traitorous brother back, Spider? He lied to you. He worked for the enemy. He nearly got you caught. If I hadn't have saved you, you would have been tangled in his web of lies too. Unless…" the voice paused, as he realized he had been tricked. "…you're one of them, aren't you? Well. I didn't see that coming." He kept his voice even as he talked, refusing to show his feelings on the topic.

"The *Piper* didn't see that coming? What a fool! I thought Pipers knew all." Fet taunted as she plugged in her device and started typing along with Spider.

"Ridiculous girl. The world *follows* the Piper–" he started.

"–right to their destruction," Spider yelled, cutting him off.

"Nevertheless, you have to use your code if you want your people back. Don't think you can outsmart me; I have the Irex."

"Shut up if you want us to break your precious Wall." Fet yelled, glaring at the blinking camera hanging above them.

A panel slid away above them, allowing them to see the Piper's face, piercing green eyes overtaking the screen as he grinned at them.

"So feisty, Muffet. However do the Legends get anything accomplished with a leader like *you*?"

"We don't," her voice mingled with Spider's.

"They don't." he said at the same time, revealing that Fet wasn't their leader.

Piper's face fell as he realized his mistake.

"*You knew*," he accused.

"Not until just now. The Legends did a great job of keeping their leader quiet...even from me," Spider sneered as he typed, not bothering to look up at the screen.

"You'd better pray you can figure out the code then, or your people are dead," Piper threatened.

"Spider, get out!" a voice yelled in the background, forcing Spider away from his work.

"Pay attention!" Fet hissed as her fingers pounded against the keyboard.

Spider's head snapped back down. He moved closer to Fet so that their inside legs touched, making them a connected team. Whispering quietly, they tossed commands to each other. "Just like last year."

She nodded at his final idea, tied to the Wall job from the previous year. Code streamed out of them, attacking the system. The Irex backdoor allowed Fet to sneak into the system another way without being detected while Spider finished the assault that Piper could see.

"Who is your leader, Muffet?" Piper called, demanding answers. "If you fail, I'll kill them both."

"Not if we kill you first," Spider replied, bravado overcoming him.

"Tell me who it is!" he demanded.

"Send them out first," Spider retorted.

"I have the code!" Fet yelled satisfactorily. "Send them out!"

"System override in one minute," the system's digital voice penetrated the conversation, setting a timeline in motion they hadn't realized they initiated when they attempted to access the Wall's program.

"Send them out or you'll lose control of the system forever," Fet said smugly at the camera.

"Code first."

"People first," Fet insisted, brushing her hands against her skirt in defiance. She crossed her arms over her chest and waited.

The screen went blank, but Fet stared it down.

A door to her left slid open revealing Peep and Arach being held by guards.

"Code, Muffet, then you can have your pathetic friends back."

"You're so willing to kill for what you want. Is it worth it?" she fired back, unwilling to move.

"*Fet,*" Peep warned, glaring.

"Gaining my freedom back? Yes. It's worth it. After what they did to me…they deserve it." Piper sneered as he lit back up on the screen. "They took everything from me."

"Says the man in a walled-in compound."

"My price for my silence," he shrugged, glancing at his prize. "No matter though. It will all be over soon and I can live anywhere I like. I'll control everything."

"You used to protect people," Fet challenged. "That's why I'm here, isn't it. Your little failsafe for keeping the system and people protected. What changed?"

"They did. They took everything from us. So what if there are a few deaths along the way to taking back our system from them? I'm going to set everyone free."

"By ruling over them?"

"I can keep them safe," he answered.

"By controlling them?"

"By controlling you *all*." He smiled as if he believed his words weren't merely a cry for power. "Now finish it."

"Fet, don't you dare!" Peep cried as she struggled against the guards. Arach locked eyes with Spider, trying to sense his plan.

"System override in ten seconds."

Alarms shrieked. Fet was surprised there weren't flashing lights to add to the drama of it all.

"Now or never, *Muffet*." Piper yelled as the guards raised their weapons to their captives.

Fet nodded to Spider and they turned back to the panel.

The code spun passed the screen, falling into place as the system exploded across the interface. Fet pressed the final keys.

Code sparkled as it fell down on the screen, regrouping at the bottom.

"No!" Peep shouted, falling to her knees.

Arach threw his elbow back, colliding with the guard. Peep forced her way free. She ran back toward the compound in an effort to undo the damage Fet and Spider had created.

"Arach!" Spider yelled, indicating he should turn and catch her. The boy raced after Peep, wrapping his arm around her, pulling her toward the exit. Spider held the door open, bracing himself between it and the wall as Fet charged forward, keeping the guards back. Arach dragged Peep outside, leaping over Spider's legs as he forced the door open with his body. Fet darted over him just as the door forced Spider to drop. Fet pulled him along behind her, forcing him out of the way as the door slammed behind them, nearly crushing him.

"Run," Spider demanded, out of breath from holding the door open.

The four crashed through the tall grass, making their way away from the compound, anger rippling from Peep.

"How could you?" she shrieked when they slowed.

"Relax, Peep." Fet looked at her in disgust. "You have so little faith."

"She set up a back door," Spider said.

"And just who are you?" Peep demanded, whirling to face him.

"That's my brother." Arach announced.

"The one who works for Piper?"

"*Worked.*" Spider corrected. "Double agent."

"Triple agent." Fet scoffed.

"Wait a minute. I know you. You're one of the *recruits!*" Peep scrutinized him.

"Can we skip that and get to the part about the back-door?" Arach cut in.

"Fet used the Irex to create a backdoor," Spider informed them.

"Irex?" Arach looked shocked.

"You went…?" Peep asked.

Fet nodded, giving them a quick rundown of their missions.

"Now we have to get back to the Hub and fix this."

"You're sure we can take him down?"

"Now that you're here, I'm positive. You've got the real code, after all." She grinned as Peep nodded.

"Well then, let's go run the Piper off a cliff."

They sprinted back to town, finding chaos still erupting between the people and the guards protecting the Hub.

"Stay here." Peep instructed, motioning them to remain in the shadows.

Spider and Arach mumbled quietly to each other. Fet only picked up a few words as they huddled together a few feet away discussing what had happened while they were separated. She glared when Spider kept glancing over to her, more frustrated than when his brother checked on her as well.

"What is she doing?" Spider eventually hissed.

"How should I know?" she bit back.

"Children." Arach cautioned, sensing an argument.

"Is that her?" Fet asked, looked beyond the brothers.

They turned, squinting to see who was approaching.

When Peep returned, she had a man at her side.

"He can get us in," she said, turning on her heels. Peep had contacts everywhere.

Without questioning her, the three followed behind them, Spider terrifyingly close to Fet again. His hand brushed against her side as they walked up to the building. A door opened in front of them and Peep hesitated. Glancing at Fet, she made eye contact.

Fet nodded and Peep turned to the man holding the door. Spider and his brother were allowed access, officially being initiated into the Legends, all ceremony cast aside. The light of the early dawn was their only guide once inside.

"After you, Fet," the man whispered as she walked by him.

She froze in place before turning to him, studying his glasses.

"And you are?"

"You know me as Nim." His eyes sparkled as he revealed his identity. "These people know me as Jack."

A grin spread across her face.

"Our double agent." She nodded, letting her coolness slip away for a moment.

He pushed his glasses up on his nose, making him look even older than the decade he had on Fet.

"We've been watching each other a long time, haven't we?"

"We have." Fet glanced down the hall, making sure

none of the other Coats were about to intrude. "Thanks for last month, by the way."

"I couldn't let my team walk into an ambush, now could I?" He nodded that they should start down the corridor, whispering directions before peeling off down a side hall to avoid being caught with the group.

He shifted his gait as he walked away, making him nearly unrecognizable from the man who had just left them. The limp would easily throw any of the Coats who might identify him later. He was a man of many faces, as any good hacker would be.

Fet led the way up to the Irex, Peep attaching herself to Fet's side.

"Nim knows them." Peep hissed in her ear.

"Who?"

"Arach and Spider," she replied. "He's been watching them for a few months since the rest of their group was taken out."

"What happened?" Fet leaned in as quickly as Nim had just walked away.

"Nim's been covering for us here with the Coats. He only let them get so close to us before he'd block them. He saw them get close to their group too, but since we have no connection to them, he didn't interfere. Obviously he regrets that now since only a few of them weren't caught or killed in the raid."

Peep's fingers tightened around Fet's arm, digging into her skin.

"He started watching them and says they are clear. We can trust them."

The conversation stopped short as they reached the room containing the Irex. All four hackers paused to look around before slipping into the room.

Fet and Peep attached the machine's cords back in place as Spider and Arach stood back, watching their hands work quickly over the wires.

"What did you use?" she asked.

"The Way," Fet answered, stepping back.

"Seriously? Your big plan was to *unplug the cords and use the Way?*"

"Just stop talking and take back the system," Fet snipped, waving her hand at her boss.

Peep rolled her eyes and set to work. Leaning against the wall with Spider and Arach, she waited for Peep to need her help. She watched as her friend strained over the console, fighting to gain control, taking long enough to make Fet nervous.

"Ready," Peep said loudly, forcing Fet to push away from the wall and join her.

Together they fought the system, adding new codes and changing the existing ones to destroy Piper's control.

"Spider!" Fet demanded and he raced across the room.

His eyes flitted over the screen, bouncing across the

numbers. Sliding in next to her, he started to work his magic on the system.

The room became stifling as they worked, their eyes growing heavy from prolonged time looking at the screen. Arach watched quietly as his brother attempted to shatter the system.

"Almost there," Peep said.

"Don't even think about it." The voice made them jump.

Piper stood in the entranceway, his hand outside the door holding something. Men flanked him, waiting for their orders.

"I knew you couldn't resist doing something like this." He grinned. "So Peep, *you're* the real leader. I should have guessed. Your stupid act had me fooled. *Bravo.* But I'm still in control and you're going to step away."

His voice was gentle and easy; a terrifying combination when mixed with his harsh face.

"Not a chance," she growled.

A muffled cry from outside the door made Peep gasp.

Piper dragged BB in by the collar. His hands were bound in front of him, a gag in his mouth. He shook his head violently at Peep, warning her off.

"Oh, I don't think so," Spider snarled, launching himself at the man.

The guards attacked as Arach, Fet, and Peep joined the fight.

"Take out the machine!" Piper ordered.

Spider stopped the first guard with a well-placed fist to the throat. He recoiled, shaking his leather-covered hand. Arach managed to take out a second guard, a chair to the back of his head stopping him in his tracks.

Peep struggled to free BB as he pushed her back to the console. He worked, wrist still bound, alongside his girlfriend as the others fought to keep the men back.

A guard pulled on Fet's pigtail, jerking her head violently to the side.

"Fet!" Spider shouted, attacking the man who had her. Fet was thrown against the wall as Spider slammed into the man. Pushing back her long hair, no longer restrained on one side, she kicked out at the man nearest to her, stopping him from taking a piece out of Arach.

"Almost there. Fet!" Peep yelled.

"Go!" both brothers yelled at the same time.

Fet ran to Peep's side, moving BB out of the way. He was no match for them when they paired up, even unbound.

"Ready?" Fet asked.

"Now!" Peep commanded. The system destroyed all ties to Piper's control. They had freed the system and destroyed the Irex, ensuring no one could control the Barrier program again.

Rage washed over Piper, causing his entire body to shake.

"*You* did this!" he shouted at Fet.

Running toward her, he flew through the air, suddenly landing on the ground. Spider pulled his leg back under him, not even shuddering as the man tripped over him. He rushed to Fet's side.

"Go!" he said, grabbing her shoulder. "Run!"

"But…" she protested, wanting to stop Piper once and for all.

"Go. Now," he commanded. "Arach…"

Arach latched on to Peep and BB, spinning them to the door. Pushing them, he forced the couple to run toward it.

"Fet, go. I will take care of him, but he can't catch you. Now move."

"No!" she said, irritated. She did not need protecting.

"Get out, now!" he yelled as one of them men started to stir.

He looked around, preparing for the fight.

"Arach, get her out of here."

"On it." His brother reached for Fet. She beat him away.

"Fet," Spider grabbed her shoulders. "You need to go now. I can take care of this. I'll find you when it is safe, but he can't catch you. He will kill you, or use you to do his bidding, and I don't know which is worse. Just go. *Go!*"

Terror raced through her as he screamed at her, the wildness in his eyes prompting her to listen. She ran.

Arach followed behind her. She couldn't remember running down the stairs, but she found herself on the ground floor, running through the door.

BB was free from his binds by the time she reached them. He held Peep close as they waited for Arach and Fet to catch up. Peep shot them a look.

The watchmen swarmed the building, the Coats demanding they protect the technology and end the intruders.

"He stayed behind. We have to go." Arach supplied before she could ask. The chaos in the building they had run from increased, terrifying Fet to her core. Who would survive?

BB LED THE WAY AS THEY RAN TO THE Legends building, ducking within its walls. Everyone was relieved to see Peep back. She explained what had happened, introducing Arach as a new member of the group. Everyone listened intently as they manned their stations, looking for fallout from Piper.

Fet wander to the edge of the building. She slipped passed the recruits' room into an isolated area near the door. Oppressive silence followed in her footsteps, making her thoughts that much louder as they ricocheted around in her brain.

It was her fault. He never should have stayed behind for her. If he died, that would be on her hands.

She paced, each step making her combat boots feel heavier. Her hand found it's way to her pigtail, coiling it around her fingers as she tried to steady herself, convincing her overactive mind that it would all work out.

"He'll be all right." Arach's soft voice sounded eerily like Spider's as he slipped into the stuffy room.

"You're sure?" she asked, letting down her tough façade.

"He hasn't failed me yet. I know he doesn't look as buff as me," he paused to grin, "but trust me, he's been trained well. Besides, if he could defeat *you*, don't you think he could defeat *Piper*?"

"*Hey!*" she gasped as he threw the Wall job in her face. What was with these brothers?

"He'll be fine. And even if he's not, it's not your fault. He knew what he was getting into when he started obsessing over you."

"He obsessed over me?" she shot him a smug look.

"Long pigtails, pink skirts, shoes as tall as his, and a top hacker to boot? Yeah. He was obsessed." Arach grinned. "Anyway, let me know when he gets back."

He sauntered away, hands in his pocket, apparently

unconcerned that his brother had just taken on a villain and his goons alone. Watching him, she realized how much they looked alike, even though Arach was more muscular and his hair was short cropped. She was amazed at what a good team they had been.

Silence overtook the room again, the life leaving with Arach. Her fingers ached to find a screen with code so she could stop thinking and focus on something else. Only her breathing filled the silence.

"You don't have to worry about him. The authorities have him."

Everything stopped.

She nodded, not trusting herself to face him.

"You scared me back there," she finally announced.

"I know." Spider took a step closer.

Giving in, she pushed away from the table she was perched on and turned to him.

"Your arm…" she began as she caught sight of him.

"I'm fine," he stopped her, shifting to take the focus off the blood that mirrored her own. Matching scars from their first mission as a team would be a lasting reminder.

"How did…?"

"I stopped him and handed him over. That's all you need to know."

"I need to know what you said to that guard at the Lab…" She crossed her arms, wincing as she felt the pain from her injury she had yet to tend to.

"You should get that looked at," Spider grinned, taunting her.

"You should too, *pest.*"

"You want to look at it for me?" he challenged.

"Ha. *You wish*, Spider," she said sarcastically, as he stepped toward her, closing the distance.

"Yeah, I do." His voice was hard, as if the words physically hurt to say them. Ice dripped like sharp knives falling from his lips as he admitted he didn't despise her. The dark-haired boy waited for her ridicule. Giving in before she could end her silence, he raised his good hand and tangled it in her free falling hair.

"*I* heard you're obsessed with me," she mocked him, his lips turning down as his eyes narrowed.

"I'll squash him like a bug." Spider sneered, knowing it was his brother who had sold him out. She smiled as he leaned closer.

"You're a real jerk, you know that?" Fet said, refusing to lean any closer.

"You have no idea," he replied, wrapping his injured arm around her. "You can find out though. But no more running away, okay? And *I know*, I *told* you to..."

He rolled his eyes, knowing she would call him out for sending her away. She cut him off.

"*Hmm...* Didn't like that part?" she taunted quietly, smirking. He shook his head as he moved so close his lips were nearly brushing hers. "Don't worry, I'm pretty much caught in whatever web you've spun, Spider."

"Good, because we're nowhere near done with this thing yet. Piper may be arrested, but the fallout from this has only just begun."

CONTINUE THE SERIES

Along Came a Spider is the first of two prequel novelettes to The Legends Chronicles Series.

New installments are coming out in 2019.

THE GOOSE GIRL AND THE ARTIFICIAL

A Goose Girl Retelling

The Goose Girl and the Artificial

A Goose Girl Retelling Novella

by

K M Robinson

"YOU DON'T HAVE A CHOICE," ARTA SNEERS. "YOU LOST your key—you have no control over me, and in case you've forgotten, I'm designed to be smarter than you."

My father always used to tell me that if I had to lose to someone, I should lose to someone that wasn't as smart as I was. That's hard advice to follow when the person you're losing to artificially *created* to be smarter than me.

I trail behind Arta as she walks away from Fal. My dress swishes behind her as she moves.

If they're smarter than you, they will know how to stay on top. If they aren't, you can beat them at their own game.

Arta is definitely smarter.

"Behave," I tap Fal on the head. He beeps quietly, slipping into sleep mode.

"Greetings," a man sings, walking swiftly toward us. "Thank you for making the journey. My son has been waiting for you."

"Thank you, your highness." Arta dips gracefully into a curtsy. "This is my Artificial."

She waves her hand at me.

"What might your name be?" the king asks.

"Goselyn, sir," I say softly. Arta waves a finger behind her back, reminding me to follow orders.

Artificials aren't required to bow to humans, so I hold my pose. There are a lot of things I'm going to have to remember to do now.

"Come along, ladies," the king turns, guiding us toward the massive palace.

Panels along the hallway walls mimic exterior windows, morphing into different scenes based on the king's biometric readings. The device around his neck reads his movements and controls the devices around him, including the settings on the fake windows.

A door slides back in front of us courtesy of the device, opening up into a stunning parlor. The walls are covered in red and gold tapestries—a stark contrast to the purple and silver in my own palace.

"Princess," a young man says, jumping to his feet as he

sets the book down he had been reading. "Thank you for coming all this way to handle the proposal."

Arta nods graciously to him.

"I think this will be a productive visit for us," she remarks, gathering her long skirt—*my* skirt—in her hand. "I'd like to freshen up after our journey if you don't mind. Perhaps we could begin our negotiations this evening?"

"Certainly, Princess Sylvane," he nods to her, referring to her by my official title. In Untae, the royals are referred to by their station and country as a way of identification. Outside of our own countries, people rarely know first names.

"You may call me Arta," my Artificial informs him as she swings around more gracefully than I ever could, and waltzes away. When I don't follow, she snaps my name.

We follow a short robot down several halls and up two flights of stairs before we step into Arta's room. Red floral curtains are drawn back to reveal the gardens in back of the palace.

"You may go," she dismisses the robot. It scurries back to its home base until it is needed again. "This is lovely...I can't wait to see it burn."

"They're going to figure this out, Arta," I protest. Her short dress around my calves frustrates me. In Sylvane, we distinguish humans from our recreations enhanced with artificial intelligence by wardrobe—though I'm considering changing that rule once I take over if this is what they have to suffer with every day. Then again, they can't feel the sensation of uncomfortable clothing, so perhaps that shouldn't be my first decision.

"They won't have time to figure it out, Goselyn. You yourself didn't realize what I was doing until after I had taken your key away. Do you really think a boy like that will figure out our plan? They're as easily replaced as you are—and just as unfit to preside over the countries of Untae.

"Your cousin has a plan, Goselyn," she addresses me as she sits on the bed. "Your kind cannot withstand it. The Artificals will keep this country functioning."

My cousin programs many of the palace Artificials. His work offers him access and power, but it's never been enough for him.

"By destroying this proposal?"

"We don't need Sylvane and Delare working together on this. Let's face it—neither country makes the best decisions," she reminds me. "Now go sit."

I make my way to the corner, settling on the small sofa where I will be sleeping for the length of our stay.

"Don't get any ideas about warning them either," Arta snaps. "You know I have your key—I can control anything I want back in Sylvane. Your mother is only safe as long as you cooperate."

"I understand the terms," I growl at my Artifical. "I'll

pretend to be you and let you destroy my reign in order to save my mother."

I glance down at the marble floor with its intricate pattern swirling into twists and turns. If only I could return home.

"Ridiculous diplomatic mission," I mumble under my breath. "I couldn't have just stayed home. *No, I* had to go and be the problem-solver and do my duty and traipse off to a far-off country to fulfill a silly little requirement before I can *eventually* take over the throne.

A knock sounds at the door. We both turn. Arta slices her hand in the air, motioning from me to the door—I'm the servant now.

I step back as I open the door. An Artificial stands outside holding a tray with a pitcher of water and two glasses. He steps inside and places it on the table.

"Prince Corinth will meet with you in half an hour downstairs in his office, Princess Sylvane." He nods to Arta. He turns to me. "You may come with me if the princess is no longer in need of your services."

"You may go, Goselyn. Do whatever they ask you to do and don't get in the way."

The Artifical leads me downstairs, past the parlor where we met Prince Corinth earlier. He wasn't bad looking—his height had surprised me a little since I had heard all of Delare was on the short side. I had heard he was rather brilliant, but I suppose I'll never find out.

The palace grounds are covered in flowers and stonework. Paths swirl as far as the eye can see. The Artifical leads me beyond the stables, toward the fountain.

"We don't have any real need for you, but you can assist here," he says, gesturing toward the lake. "The lake grounds are meant for enjoyment. The swans and geese are only permitted to get so close to the waterfront. You need to monitor the birds and keep them in their respective areas."

I nod, completely terrified. I have no idea how to keep large birds at bay.

"Gand is in charge here. Speak to him if you need anything."

A tall Artifical walks up to me imposingly. An Artifical would not flinch so I command my body to be still.

"You will monitor this area," he motions to his right. "This is how we handle the birds here."

He demonstrates the proper techniques for keeping the birds where they belong. One pecks him in anger, but he doesn't acknowledge it. This could create a problem for me as someone who *actually* feels pain.

I spend the rest of the day on a log, holding a Sheppard's hook to corral the geese with. As late afternoon arrives, Gand chases the birds back inside a building where they are fed and sheltered at night.

I don't understand the purpose of having the creatures if they're going to shut them up every night. Why not spare the entire area and set them free off of the palace grounds?

I settle back into a standing position near a log, waiting for the birds to attack.

We take our meals inside Arta's room—*my* room—to avoid prying eyes. Artificals do not need to eat and Arta skipping meals while I indulged would raise flags.

A week goes by as I sit with the geese and swans, prodding them away when they get too close.

"May I ask you a question?" a voice asks one afternoon.

Prince Corinth takes a seat on the log next to me, fidgeting with his hands.

"Yes, Prince Delare, of course."

My hand migrates toward my hair, but I quickly force it back into my lap. I can't risk moving my locks and exposing my neck. If he notices I don't have a control panel with a chip, he will figure out what has happened.

I silently think of ten vicious names to call my cousin when I return home, though none of them are strong enough to convey how angry I am at him for trying to take my throne and putting my mother in danger.

"You may call me Corinth. I'm sorry, what was your

name again?"

"I'm Goselyn, sir." I keep my eyes transfixed on the ground, hoping he will go away.

"Goselyn. Right," he reminds himself. "Goselyn, I was wondering if you could give me any advice on working with Princess Arta. She and I seem to be having trouble connecting over this proposal."

"What do you mean?"

"Well, every time I think we have something worked out, she seems to hesitate. I keep thinking that I'm saying the right things, but then she seems to get frustrated with me.

"I know we both want this to work—it *has* to work for either of to complete our requirements for taking the next step toward the throne—but I'm worried we're never going to reach an agreement."

"I don't have any advice for you, I'm afraid," I reply sadly. "She has a specific plan in mind."

One designed by my cousin. I'm not sure how he overrode Arta's original programming, but he manipulated her into turning on me.

"I see." He frowns, rubbing his fingers over his temple. "Perhaps you could tell me about Sylvane? Maybe that would offer me some insight."

"Shouldn't you be negotiating with the princess?" I attempt to get him to go back to the palace.

"We're taking a break. We don't seem to be getting

anywhere today."

"Surely your father could help you," I comment, silently pleading for them to figure it out and help disable my Artificial.

"He's not allowed to take part in the negotiations. The princess and I are the only two allowed to work on it and whatever we come up with is final...she can't even leave until it's done," he mutters, frustrated with Arta's hesitance. "I'm sure you're ready to go home, Goselyn—it's been an entire week. Can you just try to think of something that will help me?"

"Sir, they're looking for you," an Artificial approaches us, waving toward the palace.

"Perhaps we could speak tomorrow," the prince says as he stands. He strides toward the palace, sending a group of geese scattering toward me.

"What did he want?" Gand asks, wandering over to help push the geese back.

"Advice for working with the princess."

"Did you give it to him?" He pushes at a swan. It flaps its wings dangerously.

"I have nothing to give—the princess makes up her own mind over things."

"How many years have you worked with her?"

I gently bump the chest of a white goose with the end of my hook, trying to coax it back before Gand can reach it.

"Many," I reply. He pauses to evaluate what I said.

"You've been studying her this long and you don't have any insight on how to handle her?" he inquires. "Perhaps in Sylvane, the technological advances are not as great. Here in Delare, we know everything there is to know about the humans, down to how their facial expressions will change based on the food that they eat. I do not believe you have no information about your princess."

"I know many things about her," I fire back. "I simply have nothing that will help the prince convince her of things she does not wish to do."

"You've been here a week," Gand replies, taking a step closer. "In that time, you have worked alongside of me here with the birds. You don't act like a normal Artificial, but I cannot decide if it is because Artificials are different where you are from or if you are here for another reason."

"I do not know if we are different. I only know this is how I am," I inform him, trying not to get caught in a conversation.

"I'm watching you," he says, turning his back to walk back to his own area.

Arta is going to be thrilled—the local Artificials could bring her plan down before I do.

Gand studies me from afar as I pretend not to notice.

The moment we are released from our duties, I walk back to the palace and head straight for my room.

"About time," Arta says.

"The prince says you're being difficult," I confront her.

"Well of course I am—this isn't supposed to be easy. He has to be willing to give in just to get this thing finished."

"Oh, so *that's* your plan? Wear him down until he agrees to anything?" I kick my shoes off as I walk to my sofa in the corner. Draping a blanket over my feet, I compensate for the short dress I'm wearing.

"Yes, it is," she glares as she walks across the room. "Now eat, that. I was supposed to have the tray set out twenty minutes ago."

She motions to the food on the small table. I race to it quickly, piling as much food as I could onto a napkin. I take several bites out of the apple before setting it back on the tray and leave bits of the pastry crumbled on the plate before setting it outside the door to be picked up.

At least Arta wasn't depriving me of food.

"Now stay here. I have to attend a ceremony in the rose garden and I don't need you getting in the way."

She glides across the room toward the door.

"I don't know why these silly ceremonies are so

important to you humans. Traditions are ridiculous, especially when they have to do with flowers."

She marches out of the room as the door swings shut.

I grab the sheets I smuggled into the room yesterday from under the sofa cushions. Tying them to the handle on the window probably isn't my best move, but I have to get out of the palace without her knowing and the other Artificials can easily see me from the hallway.

I'm only a floor off of the ground, but it's still enough to make my stomach drop when I look over the ledge. I slip my shoes into my dress pockets before carefully swinging myself out the window.

After an eternity, I reach the ground. I didn't inherit many things from my father, but my hand-eye coordination is the thing I appreciate the most. Aiming, I throw my smuggled knife high into the air, praying it's enough to slice through the sheet I braided into a rope. Part of it rips before the knife falls back to the earth.

I jump back to avoid the falling blade. Once it settles and no longer bounces against the ground, I rush to the sheet-rope. I pull on it, trying to break it free. The material rips, but not enough. Using my full weigh, I jump up to grab it, using gravity to my advantage.

It breaks.

My feet don't cooperate as I fall, leaving me in a pile on the ground. The braided sheet hits me in the head and I bit my tongue to keep from snarling at it.

The bush acts as a hiding place for the evidence of my escape—I'll need to find a new way back inside, but at least they didn't see my leave from the hallways.

If I can find Fal, I can send him to my mother with a message. Arta has been keeping me from my loyal butler, refusing to let me see him.

I creep around the side of the castle, making sure no one is there. When I'm sure it's clear, I run toward the stables where everything that didn't come with us to the room is being stored.

Our vehicle sits at the far end of the stable, away from the animals. I tiptoe as quietly as I can through the array of animals, grateful I haven't put my shoes back on yet. Any noise might spook the creatures.

I quietly open the door, looking to see where Fal might be. I had put him into sleep mode so he shouldn't have gone far.

I tear the vehicle apart, having no luck finding him. I final extricate myself from the vehicle, stepping out backward onto the dirt.

A distant beep pierces the air so softly that I'm not sure I heard it at all. I turn slowly, trying to locate the source. When I can't find it, I close the door and begin to move around the stable, looking for where Fal might be hidden—I won't let Delare steal my butler.

I jump out of my skin when I hear the beep again, this

time overhead. My eyes sweep over the walls until I finally spot him.

Mounted on the wall high above me is Fal's head. I shriek, clamping my hand over my mouth to try to stifle the noise.

Fal's body is nowhere to be found. A string of lights blink across his eyes, adding the only color to Fal's silver shape. Without the rest of him, he looks like an upside-down metal bowl that blinks.

"Fal," I whisper.

He hovers somewhere between sleep mode and functioning mode, just enough to make small noises and move the tiny lights across his face. I reach up, tapping his head. I struggle on my toes to stretch high enough.

When I tap him, his eye light up, white with blue electronic pupils, as he connects with my biometric signature.

"Goselyn," he says quietly. "They took me apart."

"What happened to you?" I can feel myself on the verge of tears as I lower my heels down to the ground.

"Arta didn't want me to tell the Delare royalty what had happened. She had them dismantle me—she told them I wasn't functioning properly. They took my body and gave it to another robot and put my central system up here until they can reprogram me."

"We can't let them reprogram you!" I shout.

As a robot, Fal's programming does not allow the

Artificials to have access to him, but it also means that if someone reprograms him, he will be gone for good—robots' systems are far less complex and advanced than Artificials' systems.

"What is she trying to do?" His eyes light up, changing color.

A noise on the other side of the stable stops us. Fal dims his lights, going into his night state. I press against the wall, hiding behind a barrel. After a few moments, the person leaves.

"What does she want, Goselyn?" Fal repeats from his place on the wall.

"She's trying to ruin the negotiations and change the proposal. My cousin reprogrammed her because he wants me out of the picture. He thinks by destroying this proposal, I won't be allowed to succeed my mother and it will fall to his family."

"You need to tell your mother," Fal informs me as if I didn't know.

"That's why I was trying to find you. You're the only one that can get back to Sylvane without Arta finding out."

"I can't move without my body." Fal's face lights up with green, red, and yellow dots racing across his interface. He beeps unintentionally as his system flails from being mounted on the wall.

"I couldn't even get you down if I tried." I look around

for something to climb on to reach him.

"I'm stuck up here. Even if you could reach me, it would take an hour to get me unhooked. There's something weird back here." His lights slow to a crawl. "You need to go back and find a way to warn the king. You know if your cousin is coming after you, he will also go after Delare—he's always said he should take command here if you were to inherit Sylvane."

Another noise frightens us across the stable.

"Just go, Goselyn. Put me in sleep mode and come back after you've ended this. I'll be fine."

"But—" I protest.

"No. You need to go. I can't help you. You need to put Sylvane first."

Fal has always been wise beyond his programming.

"I'll be back for you," I promise as I reach up to turn on his sleep mode setting.

"I'm sure you will. Good luck, Goselyn." He beeps when I tap him, settling into sleep mode.

Stopping Arta before Fal is reprogrammed becomes my second motivation for beating my Artificial, urging me to quickly sneak out of the stables. I slip my shoes on once I reach the grass and hurry toward the palace.

The most dangerous part of my return journey into the palace is slipping by the kitchen without being noticed. People bustle about, preparing the evening meal. I can smell the roast chicken from down the hall.

"What are you doing?"

I jump at the question. Spinning, I clutch my chest. Artificials shouldn't be scared, but I can't help my reaction.

"Goselyn, what are you doing?" Grad demands. His jaw clenches like a real human's would. "I knew it—you're not an Artificial."

"No, I am," my words come out panicked and high-pitched.

"You're not," he says, reaching for my neck. He struggles to move my hair as I fight back.

As we grapple, I do my best to eject the chip from the back of his neck. The Artificial throws me against the wall, slamming me between it and the back of his shoulder. I yelp in pain.

I stomp on his foot, causing him to look down long enough to punch the button on the back of his neck. It pops out just enough for his face to go slack.

Opening the small control panel, I pull up his programming. While I only learned a few things from my father, I gained many skills from my mother, including the ability to alter the programming of the Artificials and robots we work with.

Before securing the chip back in place, I program Gand to not be able to come within ten feet of me. I also erase the last ten minutes of his memory. He will know I removed the time from his programming, but it will take him a few days to recover it, giving me enough time to fix the problem with Arta—*I hope.*

While Gand blinks back to life, I slip down the hall and dart around the corner. I make it back to my room with just enough time to pull the remnant of the sheet off the window and close it before Arta opens the door. She eyes me but says nothing.

The next day, I make my way down to the lake, the geese following in my wake. Gand watches me from his place on the other side of the lawn, trying to figure out what happened.

I turn my shoulder away, keeping my back to him as I corral the birds on the lawn.

"Gand," the prince's voice bounces off a nearby tree. I look up in time to see Gand retreating, having been dangerously close to me.

"Should I ask what that was about?" Corinth asks as he sits next to me on the log. His blond hair tips down gently over one eye as he turns to face me.

I pull my dark hair over my neck, ensuring he can't see my skin.

"I don't know," I try to keep my response simple.

"Have you thought of anything that might help me?" he asks. I sigh.

"Perhaps…" I pause, trying to think of *anything* I can give him. "Let her think she has won. Give in to as much as you can, but hold true to the most important things and make them seem unimportant. If she thinks she has won, perhaps you can make this work."

"That's an interesting thought," Corinth replies. "I'll try that. You're very wise, Goselyn. I knew I liked you."

He stands, preparing to leave.

"How do you like it here, Goselyn? Are you finding everything to your liking?" he asks, turning back to me.

"Delare is a very nice country, sir."

"Thank you," he smiles. "That's not what I meant."

"I'm doing fine, thank you."

I'm only being held captive by an artificial who is threatening the lives of everyone around me at the whims of my narcissistic cousin, but sure, I'm great.

"Is Gand treating you well?" he inquires, putting his hand behind his back as he was trained to do.

I smile, not wanting to answer.

"Gand?" Corinth calls, motioning my keeper over. "How has everything been? Are you two working together well?"

"Goselyn has been managing just fine, Prince Corinth."

"Very good," he replies, giving Gand a curious look. "You're taking care of her, right? Treating her as one of our own?"

"Yes, sir," Gand assures him, placing his free hand on his Sheppard's hook in an attempt to make the prince feel more at ease. Artificials are trained to make human-like movements specifically to make humans feel more comfortable around them, even to the point of regularly blinking.

"Good, we want everyone to feel welcome here," Corinth smiles, nodding to me. It's amazing how he takes so much time to talk to his Artificials publicly. I've had many long talks with mine, but only in private.

Gand takes a step toward us. He suddenly leaps back as if a bee stung him. Corinth looks as shocked as Gand does.

"Are you all right?" Corinth moves toward him.

Gand's eyes shift toward the clouds as he processes what just happened.

"I...I'm not sure what that was." He takes another step forward, bouncing back as if he's hit a wall. Gand won't know it until he recovers the data I deleted, but I programmed him to do that.

"Perhaps you should come inside and have one of the programmers take a look," Corinth reaches a hand toward the Artificial. "Maybe there's a glitch in your data."

Unable to resist, Gand follows him toward the palace.

"Will you be okay on your own, Goselyn?" The prince

turns back to me with a concerned look on his face, brow furrowed kindly.

"Yes." What other choice do I have? At least Gand won't be in my hair today.

I take a seat as the prince and the Artificial walk away. For a moment, I consider letting the geese roam free for a while, but I don't need any extra questions. I go back to tending them properly.

It isn't long before Arta joins me.

"What happened?" she demands.

"The Artificial was asking too many questions. He got close to me and I managed to pop his chip out and program him to stay away from me so that he didn't expose your little plan."

She grimaces, wrinkling her nose.

"Fine. Keep it that way. I'm nearly done anyway."

"You mean we'll get to go home?" I ask, standing.

"Yes. I just have to get the prince to sign the proposal and then I can remove him."

My blood runs cold.

"What do you mean?"

"Oh stop being so sentimental, Goselyn. I won't do it while we're here. We still have to go home, present the proposal, enact the plan, and *then* we'll kill him—you don't have to watch any of it. All you have to do is keep your mouth shut."

Before my cousin got his hands on her, Arta never

would have spoken to me like that.

My knee pops out of place, nearly forcing me to pitch forward. Arta's eyes grow wide for a moment before narrowing.

"Pull it together," she hisses. Any human-like movements could give us away—Artificials don't let their knees pop. She blinks intentionally, compensating for her lack of human motions.

"Princess," the king calls from the hill. "My son is waiting for you inside. He'd like you to join him in his study if you don't mind."

My first reaction is to curtsy, but I remember just in time and manage to hold still. I wait as Arta accepts his initiation to return to the palace.

Part way up the hill, the king slows. Once Arta is safely inside, he returns to me.

"Hello," he greets me. He's friendlier than his son, though, I imagine, just as strategic.

"Hello, King Delare."

"All by yourself today?" He stands with his hands behind his back, posture straight as my Sheppard's hook.

"Your son sent Gand in to be looked at my a programmer. He seemed to be experiencing a glitch," I report.

"Yes, I caught him on the way out actually. Had quite the story to tell," he pauses, removing a hand from behind his back to stroke his chin. "It seems he thinks you are not an Artificial. I wonder why he would think that..."

"I don't know, sir." I look down, trying to avoid him as I scoot a goose back.

"I see," the king muses. "And there's nothing you would like to tell me?"

"No, sir."

He pauses, trying to decide what to say next. A swan wanders by us but he waves for me to leave it alone.

A few dozen yards away, the fountain cascades into itself, creating a never-ending cycle of soothing sound. I wonder if I could hide behind it.

"Perhaps it's that you *can't* tell me." The king tips his head, examining me.

"I couldn't say, sir," I reply.

"I see," the king says solemnly. "Maybe you'd like to sit with me."

He motions me over to the log. He's larger than his son and takes up more space on the turned tree stump.

"I would very much like to help you, Goselyn, but I can't do that unless I know what is going on. No one is watching us and your princess is behind closed doors. All of my Artificials, robots, and workers have been removed from the area. If something is going on, now is the time to tell me," he insists. He's clearly trying to be gentle with me, but the wrinkles on his forehead suggest that he's worried something is going on.

I don't trust Arta. She decapitated Fal—or order him to be. She's threatening my mother. Even just now, she told me she's planning the assassination of a ruling monarch of another country. The king may feel it is safe, but I know it is not.

"I truly do not know what you mean, sir." I reach up, brushing back my hair. Pulling it to one side, I expose the skin on my neck.

"I see," the king says slowly, eyes widening. "And you're sure there is nothing I can help you with?"

"I think the only thing you can do, sir, is help your son. He's in greater need of it than I am," I say, praying he understands my meaning. I tip my head to emphasize my point. "Children need their parents to look after them just as much as parents need their children protecting them."

"You make a good point," he agrees, standing. "I'll see to my son. He's always been good about keeping secrets, as I'm sure your Princess Arta is.

"I hear you've been advising my son. Thank you for your help. I'm sure he would like to thank you personally later." He makes it ten feet before he turns back to me. "I think I shall send a letter to your queen, thanking her for the magnificent representatives she has sent for this diplomatic mission. I'm sure she'll be quite pleased to hear of it."

"I'm sure it would mean everything to her, thank you. You'll want to send that via Channel One so no one accidentally intercepts it."

"Indeed," he nods, acknowledging that he understands someone else is controlling this scenario—no Artificial would have knowledge of the private communication channels of the reigning monarchs. Not even my cousin knows about it—only the kings, queens, and crowned princes and princesses know of its existence.

The king of Delare is willing to warn my mother of my cousin's plans. I want to throw my arms around him to thank him, but I hold still. My mother will know what to do to disable Arta's ability to control the Artificial in Sylvane the moment she reads his communication—now I just have to figure out how to survive Delare and return to take down my cousin.

"Princess," Corinth greets me by my title, corning me outside the stable. I eye him warily until he holds up a necklace—a device that prohibits intelligence gathering within a certain radius. It knocks out all cameras and recording devices while looping in old footage. "We're alone."

"Has your father contacted my mother?" I ask.

"He has. I'm so sorry you had to go through all of this. Your mother is working to shut down Arta's ability to control the Artificials as we speak. She'll be safe soon."

I hope she figured out that my cousin is behind this

and didn't enlist his help. We've always been wary of his demands and outbursts, so I'm sure she's being cautious.

"You're in danger," I quickly tell the prince. "Arta is planning to destroy the proposal, and then once it's public, she's going to remove you."

"Remove me?" His eyes widen as he takes a step back. "What does that mean?"

"I assume it means you're going to die," I try to say gently. "My cousin wants my throne *and* yours, so he's trying to take us both out at once after we've returned with the proposal."

"But if she's not here, how will she manage that?"

"I would imagine that she's not the only Artificial in on this plan." I glance around, waving him into the shadows of the building. "It's entirely possible he has control of some of *your* Artificials too.

"Gand must not know, or he wouldn't have pushed things with me, but who knows which of them are working together on this."

"Why is he doing this—other than simply wanting the thrones?"

"My cousin believes his leadership would be superior, Corinth—he doesn't think we can handle ruling. He doesn't want our countries working together."

"We've done just fine until now," he says bitterly.

"Now we just have to prove it."

Corinth nods to me as I trail behind Arta into the parlor —my mother has sent word back that she is safe.

Let the games begin.

"Princess, have a seat," Corinth motions toward a fainting couch with a large, ornate gold rim along the tiny fragment of a back.

Arta arranges her skirt carefully as she sits. I quietly follow behind her, taking a seat on the edge of the couch, prepared to go after her control panel if needed.

"I've been thinking about a few addendums to the proposal," Corinth starts. He lays out a few papers on their laps as he sits next to her. "I think it would be beneficial if we could—"

"What is this?" Arta shrieks. She gathers the papers up and shoves them at the prince. "No, we agreed to the original proposal and we're sticking to that."

"No, actually we didn't, princess. You tried to *force* me into it, but you never once listened to me. This is what I feel we need to add to make this beneficial to Delare and not just Sylvane," he protests, trying to hand her the paperwork again.

"You are a fool," Arta shakes her head in disgust. "I will leave right now and neither of us will have completed our part of the proposal."

"You can't be queen without it," he reminds Arta,

jumping to his feet to follow behind her as she sprints toward the door. "But honestly, *I* don't mind. I've never really had a taste for ruling. You'd be doing me a favor."

Arta looks at him in shock.

"This hurts *you* more than it hurts me, Arta," he says in a darker voice. "If you want me to play along, you have to make this worth my time. You've offered me nothing."

Arta pauses, her face going slack, as she processes the information, a telltale sign that she's an Artificial. When she comes out of it, she blinks.

"I can offer you my hand in marriage. We can rule our countries together."

"No, thank you, you're not my type," Corinth quickly replies, infuriating her.

"Well, what do you want?" she demands.

"A robot, for starters." He grins. "I hear you had one brought here. I'd like to see it. Your robots are quite a bit different than ours here in Delare, so it would be a bit of a novelty."

"It's broken." Her words are biting.

"It's not," he challenges her. "I saw you bring it in. Go fetch it."

He waves his hand at her, shooing her toward the tall, oak door. Arta looks like a petulant child about to stamp their foot.

"Goselyn," she shrieks my name, never taking her eyes off of the prince.

"Let's all go," Corinth encourages, motioning for me to quickly follow.

Atra argues the entire way down the hall that she doesn't know where Fal is, but Corinth expertly guides her toward the stables where he knows our things are being stored.

"There he is," I add when we can finally see my butler strung up on the wall.

"What happened to him?" Corinth yells, acting surprised.

"I told you, he was broken. Your programmers took him apart for scraps."

"You're not handing me a robot head," Corinth snarls. "Go find it a body."

He swings back to face me, away from Arta.

"This is ridiculous," he growls at me with a playful wink. He turns back around to face her. "Well?"

Arta huffs and scurries off to find Fal's missing pieces.

"That will keep her busy for a while," Corinth grins as he steps toward me.

"Oh?" I try not to blush as he smirks at me.

"I hid the pieces," he shrugs. His eyes sparkle when he notices my cheeks and he quirks an eyebrow at me. "She's going to have to make him a body from scratch. I think we should follow her and see what she does."

He tugs at my hand, keeping a safe distance behind Arta as she scours the stables for anything she can use to recreate Fal. She throws things behind her, disrupting the animals, but she doesn't flinch even once as they panic.

We follow her through the stables, out into the yard as she stomps around, looking for anything she can use to cobble together a robot body. She never once considered asking me to do the work for her, though she's also aware that I don't have the technical skills to build a robot body.

A vicious tug pulls me back as we stride toward the palace. I shriek against my captor, fighting to break free. Corinth wheels around, ready to defend me.

"She is not an Artificial," Gand rages, pulling me away from Corinth.

"I know, let her go, Gand," the prince commands. "Now!"

Gand freezes, still holding me against his silicone body covered in lab-created skin. The only thing that gives him away is his lack of pulse.

"Sir, she does not belong here. She is lying to us. She needs to be taken for questioning." His grip tightens around me.

If I had seen him coming, I could have defended myself, but Artificials can be as much as three times stronger than a human. I wriggle under his grasp. Even Corinth looks slightly worried.

"Put her down, Gand. I'm aware of what is going on." Corinth lowers his hand, indicating that I should be set down.

The moment my feet touch the ground, I sprint toward the prince, pushing away from Gand.

"She erased my memory, Prince Corinth," Gand addresses him. "She attacked me in the hallway and tried to undo my programming."

"No, Gand. You attacked her and she was trying to protect herself *and* me. I can't explain it now, but you'll understand soon."

"I will take this to your father," Gand threatens.

"He already knows, Gand."

The Artificial takes a dangerous step toward the crowned prince of Delare. Corinth doesn't back down.

"Go back to the geese, Gand." Corinth reaches for the key around his neck, prepared to force Gand back.

The Artifical turns around slowly, slinking back toward the lake. We watch as he kicks at several of the geese.

"You need to find him a new job," I comment, pursing my lips.

"Or to turn down his anger levels," Corthin murmurs back.

"Maybe take out his personality all together?" I suggest earning a smug, close-lipped grin as Corinth fights not to laugh.

"But he has such a charming personality," he remarks.

"True. The Artificials of Delare are so welcoming." I toss my hair as I speak, rolling my eyes dramatically.

"Hey, we're not all bad," Corthin corrects me.

"I didn't realize you were an Artificial. I supposed that would explain why you weren't friendlier to me," I tease.

"I wasn't the one concealing my identity, princess," he reminds me casually. "We should catch up to Arta."

With the sudden change in conversation, we spin around and hurry back toward the palace, assuming Arta went inside to look for supplies.

It's quiet inside as we search for Arta, methodically sweeping the rooms until we locate her. The loud crash in the dining hall suggests we've found her.

When we enter, it's not Arta, but rather the king that we see first.

"Son," he warns in a harsh tone. "Get back."

Arta's arm is wrapped around his neck. She grabs her wrist, using her forearm to apply pressure to the king's throat. He struggles uncomfortably beneath her grasp. Corinth gasps beside me.

"Arta," I try to reason with her, though I'm not sure why since she's under my cousin's control. "Let him go. There's still a way to make this work."

"How is that?" she asks, her programming urging her to listen.

"We can still get both parties to sign the proposal. You and I can still take it back to Sylvane," I reply, taking a small step toward her.

"It's too late for that—they already know about the plan," Arta contradicts me.

"They only know what you've told them," I assure her.

"Don't lie, Goselyn," she gives me a withering look. "You've never been good at it."

"Can he hear us?" I ask, referring to my cousin in Sylvane.

She pauses, waiting for confirmation. Finally, she nods.

"Kenneth," I call. "You need to end this. We won't hold it against you if you stop now."

Arta drops her arm from around the king's neck. His hands fly to his throat as he attempts to step away from the Artificial.

The moment of hope passes as Arta runs full speed at me. Corinth attempts to block her, only resulting in him being pushed to the ground.

My Artificial tackles me to the ground, our screams mixing together. Something twitches in her eyes as we wrestle-perhaps a bit of the old Arta before she was reprogrammed. She slams my head into the ground.

I kick her off of me, sitting up to a spinning world. Corinth throws himself on her, forcing her backward until she tosses him over her shoulder.

The king runs at Arta at full speed, slamming her into the wall with his shoulder. She grunts, struggling to get her footing while she claws at his face.

I hate the idea of hurting my Artificial, but she's no longer the Arta I know—she's something much more hideous now at the hands of my cousin.

Art breaks free of the king as Artificials pour into the room to see what is happening. They surround us for a moment, looking on.

I pause next to Corinth, breathing just as heavily as he is. We watch the group of human-like creations as they watch us, unsure of who has control.

The king hits his button to protect himself from the Artificials.

"Son," he warns, urging the prince to enable his key to protect himself.

"She doesn't have one," Corinth replies, refusing to enable his safety net if it will leave me vulnerable.

The king looks equally as shocked as he looks overwhelmed with respect for his son.

"I think you two are going to get along just fine after this," he murmurs. "But we really don't have time for this right now."

He rushes at Arta, slamming his elbow into her face. Her head snaps back at an angle so sharp that it would have done incredible damage had she not been a machine.

"Get the key," he demands as he pushes his hand against her face to hold Arta back.

We scramble forward, unsure if our movements will

cause the Artificials to attack. Corinth tears at Arta's neck, looking for the chain my key is on.

I could help Corinth and retrieve my key, but that will only protect us for so long. Instead, I thrust my hands toward the back of Arta's neck, fumbling for her control panel.

"That won't work," she warns me. "You can't eject my chip. Kenneth made sure."

I would eject her chip if I had to shatter her neck to do it.

"I'm smarter than my cousin," I counter.

"He's a programmer," she yelps, struggling to rip my hands away. "He's better than you."

"We both had the same teacher," I respond, fingers slipping off her fake skin. "I promise you my mother didn't teach him everything she taught me."

Arta uses her feet to push off the wall as the Artificials erupt around us, some breaking free of whatever control Kenneth had over them, while others are still clearly under his programming.

The king falls to the ground, nearly tripping Arta. She springs over him at the last second, leaving me only a step behind her. I tackle her, attempting to pin her arms.

"Use your key," I scream at Corinth.

"I didn't get yours yet," he yells back, rushing to my side.

"You need to stay protected," I shout back.

"So do you, *princess*," he says, for the first time, not using my title respectfully.

"One thing at a time, *prince.*"

I lower myself, running at Arta. Grabbing her around the waist, we topple to the ground. I pull open the control panel on her neck, prepared to punch in the necessary information to fight back against my cousin.

Corinth throws himself on top of us, lending his weight to the struggle. He rips my key necklace from around her throat a he sits on the Artificial.

He gently leans toward me, brushing back my hair as he wraps the small digital key rectangle around my neck, latching it. He twists the clasp around to the back of my neck, tickling me in the process.

I reach up for a moment to enable the biometric key, knowing Corinth can't do it for me. As soon as it locks into place, putting a digital barrier between me and the rest of the fighting, I go back to my attempts to disable my Artificial.

"Anytime, Goselyn," Corinth says as he pitches forward. Arta bucks, trying to throw us off. He catches me, holding me steady as I work.

"Kenneth," I lecture my Artificial sharply, knowing my cousin is getting a full report. "You're going to pay for this."

"Goselyn," the king shouts, running to our sides. "A bot just arrived with a message. "Your mother has control of your cousin. All you have to do is reset your Artificial."

The news gives me renewed strength. I lunge at Arta again, working to key in the proper codes to disable the override. She struggles, but there isn't much she can do under the weight of two of us.

I key in the final commands and she goes slack. We sit in silence.

"Is it over?" Corinth finally asks, afraid to move.

"It's over," I breathe, shuffling off of the motionless Artificial. "You should also have control over your Artificials again."

I motion toward the human-like figures around us. They've already slowed, connecting to their former programming.

"Already taken care of, my dear," the king replies. "I think it's time you contacted your mother."

"And time to get the proposal negotiations back on track," Corinth adds. "I get the feeling that we really shouldn't wait on that."

"I agree," I let out a nervous laugh. "But first, can we go get Fal, please?"

"I'm sure you need something to feel a little more secure about your place here," the king responds. "Corinth, take the princess to rescue her robot, please."

Corinth offers me a hand. Together, we leave Arta's shell on the floor. The king's Artificials will take her to their programmer to get her back up and running in her former working condition before I leave, though, I imagine I'll have some trouble trusting her for a while.

"I'm sorry we made you work with the geese," Corinth drawls as we walk toward the stables. He places his hand behind his back properly.

"There were swans there too," I remind him. "Aren't we past all the formal stuff at this point?"

He smiles slightly, not missing a step.

"I suppose we are, Goselyn." He drops his arm, walking more casually. "I do apologize that you had to go through all this though. I'm sure it was very difficult."

"I'm sorry I brought it all to you. I didn't have any idea until right before we arrived," I sigh.

"It's not your fault," he says as we approach the tall doors to the barn. "I think I might have a few things to say to your cousin though."

He chuckles warmly.

"Well, perhaps you'll have to come give him a piece of your mind."

"I might have to." He walks a little faster, catching the door to hold it open for me. "After you."

Fal is sitting on the wall where I left him, still in sleep mode.

"Hold on," Corinth says as I reach for my robot.

He finds a step stool in the very back and drags it over. Climbing up, he wrestles Fal's central system off the wall. A programmer joins us, carrying Fal's body. He expertly puts him back together, though the wait is excruciating.

I tap Fal's head, bringing him back to life. The light blinks on, simulating eyes as colors dart across the interface.

"You did it?" Fal asks, beeping the way a cat might purr.

"We got word to mother and she helped us turn of Kenneth's programming. They're working on fixing Arta now."

Fal notices Corinth and beeps at him.

"He's fine, Fal," I smile. "Corinth, this is my robot, Fal. Fal, this is Prince Corinth of Delare."

"Nice to meet you, Fal." Corinth looks like he wants to get down on his knees and address the robot as a child. My robot beeps back at him.

"Your Highness," Fal addresses him.

"I'm sorry about the rude welcome. I hope you'll allow us to fix that," Corinth apologizes.

Fal looks up to me, gauging my reaction. I nod, encouraging him to relax.

"We have negotiations to work on," I redirect the conversation. "We should probably get back. I need to message my mother too."

"Of course, Princess."

"You're much easier to work with," Corinth informs me as a tray overflowing with fruits and cheeses is set on the table next to us. "Prettier too, if I might add."

My hand stops in mid-air as I blush profusely.

"You like doing that, don't you?" I ask, blinking back the uncertainty.

"Making you squirm? Yes," he answers bluntly.

"That nice guy act was just for show, huh?" I pick up a grape.

"Oh no, I'm always nice to the Artificials—they don't do so well with sarcasm and flirtation."

"I liked you better when I was an Artificial," I tease.

"Most people do," he nods innocently. "The good news is that we're almost done with these charges against your cousin, so you can go home soon and never see me again."

"You say that as if you weren't planning on coming along to harass Kenneth during his trial," I mumble, glancing up just in time to catch his grin. He quickly rearranges his face to hide it.

"Fine, you'll be rid of me after I see justice is done. You'll be sad to see me go though."

"Will I?"

"You will," Fal beeps next to me. I quickly tap him on

the head, putting him into sleep mode. Corinth smirks, scooting closer on the couch.

"I like the little guy," he shrugs casually. "I also like that I don't have to be so proper around you."

"Benefits of fighting an insane Artificial together, I suppose."

"What would you have done," he asks, putting his arm on the back of the couch, "if my father hadn't found out you weren't an Artificial."

"Climbed out the window again and escaped, I suppose."

He looks as though I've struck him.

"You climbed out the window?

"Did I not tell you about that part? Oops," I shrug, reaching for another grape.

He catches it out of my fingers, popping it into his mouth.

"That's what happens when you keep things from me," he informs me.

"It's been a week—we hardly know each other well enough to share all of our secrets," I retort.

"Two weeks, madam," he corrects, staring at my hand resting on my knee.

"Yes, but only one of being a human."

"Fine, I'll give you that, goose girl. Good thing we have the entire journey to Sylvane to talk."

"Oh, doesn't that sound lovely?"

"It does." He purses his lips, tipping his head as he looks at me.

"Goose girl?" I question.

"Yeah," he grins. "Since you like pecking at me so much—"

"Your Highnesses," a knock at the door sounds. "We've fixed her."

The programmer opens the door, stepping to the side. Arta stands beside him quietly.

"Your mother sent us the specifications," the programmer informs us. "She's been restored to her last backup."

"Hello, Goselyn."

I tap Fal on the head much harder than anticipated. He springs to life, wheeling himself over to inspect Arta.

I reach up, taping my key necklace to control my Artificial. After going through the motions of testing her, I finally release Arta.

"Welcome back, friend."

She smiles at me as I introduce her to Prince Corinth.

Corinth recoils as she turns an icy glare on him when I inform her that the prince will be traveling with us. I'm positive this will be a very enlightening trip home.

ACKNOWLEDGMENTS

At fourteen, I started my first business: I was a web designer.

Over the years, I've studied everything from web design, to photo manipulation, to video creation, to augmented reality and virtual reality.

I am *here* for the technology.

When I started writing retellings, I loved working modern and futuristic technology into my stories, so it only made sense to create a collection out of them for you.

Long live the tech queens and kings—you are the ones who will rule and reign. Use your gifts wisely.

Special thanks to my fabulous editors who helped with each individual story in this book—you're the best!

To my dearest readers, I hope you enjoyed these techy

takes on classics we all know and love! I hope you continue to read more in the Legends Chronicles series with Few and Spider, and Virtually Sleeping Beauty series with Rora and Royce!

If you loved all of these stories, please let me know! My favorite thing as an author is to hear from fans who loved my characters! Hit me up on social media or send me an email!

Be sure to hit up my Facebook page for bonus scenes from some of these stories, filters to use on your photos, and interactive, choose-your-own-adventure games from some of these stories as well!

Stay inspired,

K.M. Robinson

ABOUT THE AUTHOR

K.M. Robinson is a storyteller who creates new worlds
both in her writing and in her fine arts conceptual
photography. She is a marketing, branding and social
media strategy educator who is recognized at first sight
by her very long hair. She is a creative who focuses on

photography, videography, couture dress making, and writing to express the stories she needs to tell. She almost always has a camera within reach.

Visit her at her website: www.kmrobinsonbooks.com

CONNECT ON SOCIAL MEDIA

facebook.com/kmrobinsonbooks

instagram.com/kmrobinsonbooks

twitter.com/kmrobinsonbooks

Get free excerpts and full novels from K.M. Robinson at
excerpt.kmrobinsonbooks.com

ALSO BY K.M. ROBINSON

The Golden Trilogy

Book One: Golden

Forged: A Golden Novella

Book Two: Locked

Book Three: Edge

The Complete Series Boxset/Omnibus with Tempered: an exclusive bonus novella

The Jaded Duology

Book One: Jaded

Book Two: Risen

The Complete Series Boxset/Omnibus with exclusive epilogue

The Siren Wars Saga

Book One: The Siren Wars

Book Two: Darker Depths

Book Three: Beyond The Shores

Origins of the Siren Wars: Prequel Novella

Book Four: Forbidden Waters (coming soon)

The Legends Chronicles

Along Came A Spider: A Prequel Novelette

And They'll Come Home: A Prequel Novelette

The Archives of Jack Frost Series

The Revolution of Jack Frost

The Redemption of Jack Frost (coming soon)

Stealing Steam Series

Book One: Lions and Lamps

Book Two: Pistons and Prisoners

Book Three: Railcars and Rulers

Top Hats and Telegraphs: A Prequel Novella

The Complete Series Boxset/Omnibus with Vambraces and Victories: an exclusive bonus novella

Virtually Sleeping Beauty: A Novella Retelling

The Goose Girl and The Artificial: A Novella Retelling

The Sinking: A Little Mermaid Novella Retelling

Cindrill: A Cinderella Assassin Novella Retelling

Sugarcoated: A Hansel and Gretel's Witch Novella Retelling

Blood Is Silent: A Red Riding Hood Circus Retelling

JADED: BOOK ONE OF THE JADED DUOLOGY

If the only way to stay alive was to convince your new husband not to murder you and make it look like an accident, could you do it?

At eighteen, Jade shouldn't have to be forced to marry the son of her father's enemy as part of a revenge plot for a failed rebellion. When she's thrown into the life of being the wife of the Commander's son and heir, her only hope for survival is convincing Roan Diamond to actually fall in love with her so that he doesn't kill her on his father's wishes.

While a dutiful son, Roan shouldn't have to trick his new wife into believing his family accepts her, but as the only one in a position to make the country believe Jade is part of their family, he will do what he has to before his family murders his young bride and makes it look like an accident to get back at Jade's father.

With half the country trying to protect Jade and the other half oblivious to the atrocities committed at the Commander's hand, it's a race to see who will win at a deadly game of cat and mouse.

One chooses life. One chooses death. In the midst of chaos, only one will succeed.

Now available!
Learn more about The Jaded Duology at
jadedinfo.kmrobinsonbooks.com

GOLDEN: BOOK ONE OF THE GOLDEN TRILOGY

Goldilocks wasn't naive. She was sent on a mission and Dov Baer is her new target.

When Auluria tricks the Baers into letting her into their home, they have no idea she's actually been sent by the enemy to destroy them. Intent on gathering information for her cousin to hand over to the Society seeking to destroy all of the rebel factions—including her own— she's willing to sacrifice Dov Baer to save her people... until she realizes her cousin lied to her.

Now that she's seen who Dov truly is, she has to decide between staying loyal to her only remaining family or protecting the man she's falling for. If her allegiances are discovered, either side could destroy her—assuming the Society doesn't get her first

Available now!
Learn more about The Golden Trilogy at goldeninfo.kmrobinsonbooks.com

THE SIREN WARS: BOOK ONE OF THE SIREN WARS SAGA

War has hovered around the kingdom of Scylla for generations ever since the original sirens left the mer collection generations ago after nearly drowning the human prince. Over the years, select mermaids from the royal bloodline have been trained as spies to work for the reigning kings and queens, keeping the collection safe from sirens and humans.

Celena and her partner, Merrick, work covertly for the royals—not even her twin brother knows. When they discover the sirens have broken through the barriers the mer set up to keep the sirens out, Celena and her friends must race to the old kingdom of Metten to stop them from starting a war within their borders.

When she's dragged to the surface, Celena realizes that the war above the waters is as deadly as the one below the waves—and sacrificing herself may be the only way to protect her family.

The Siren Wars have only just begun.

Available now!
Learn more about The Siren Wars Saga at sirenwarsinfo.
kmrobinsonbooks.com

All wishes require sacrifice...*are you willing to pay the price?*

Cyra spent the last seven years being trained to steal an airship in a brutal competition that leaves the victor with millions. Last year, she won.

Aladdin spent the past year fighting to get enough money to take his mother away from Horallen after his father was murdered. Now, his evil uncle Kacper wants to force him into the competition and straight to his death inside the Collection Cave.

When Aladdin discovers a genie said to have been banished a century ago, the competition becomes even deadlier, and he knows he can't trust the girl who snuck into the competition this year...but Cyra might not survive his ruthlessness either in a game where only the lion's heart can win.

All wishes require sacrifice, and someone is going to pay the price for the Stourbridge.

Available now!
Learn more about The Stealing Steam Series at
lionsandlampsinfo.kmrobinsonbooks.com

THE REVOLUTION OF JACK FROST

No one inside the snow globe knows that Morozoko Industries is controlling their weather, testing them to form a stronger race that can survive the fall out from the bombs being dropped in the outside world—all they know is that they must survive the harsh Winter that lasts a month and use the few days of Spring, Summer, and Fall to gather enough supplies to survive.

When the seasons start shifting, Genesis and Jack know something is going on. As their team begins to find technology that they don't have access to inside their snow globe of a world, it begins to look more and more like one of their own is working against them.

. . .

Genesis soon discovers Morozoko Industries, but when a foreign enemy tries to destroy their weather program to make sure their destructive life-altering bombs succeed in destroying the outside world, only one person can shut down the machine that is spinning out of control and save the lives of everyone inside the bunker—Jack.

Now available!
Learn more about The Revolution of Jack Frost at
jackfrostinfo.kmrobinsonbooks.com

THE SINKING

The sea witch wants to silence her, but not for the reason you think.

WHEN A QUIRKY OLDER WOMAN PAWNS A FANCY SEASHELL necklace at her mother's antique shop on the pier, Cara doesn't think much about the story the woman spins about the wearer turning into a mermaid.

On her way home, she accidentally drops the necklace into the ocean and is swept out to sea where she meets— a merman who volunteers to take her to his mother, the sea queen, to help her get her legs back.

· · ·

Cara soon learns that it's Quay's eighteen birthday—a day that has been a curse for his family—and is meant to be one for her too. Now she must fight to survive the sea with Quay at her side.

Fans of The Little Mermaid will love this twisted take on the beloved story.

Now available!
Learn more about The Sinking at
thesinkinginfo.kmrobinsonbooks.com

BLOOD IS SILENT

RED RIDING HOOD IS A CIRCUS AERIALIST AND THE WOLF IS ready to cage her.

Sienna has grown up working for the circus, dangling off her signature red silks every night. Her grandmother has been known to wander off to train new acts for their boss, but when Sienna tries to find her to bring her back to the show, she doesn't expect the dashing and dangerous Elijah to join her.

When they finally find Grandma Ida has been transformed deep in the heart of the woods, Sienna will stop at nothing to save her—but the wolf has her right where he wants her, and she won't be able to escape his claws.

She was told not to go into the woods alone.

Now available!

Learn more about Blood Is Silent at
bloodissilentinfo.kmrobinsonbooks.com